The Black Eclipse

By Eric Danhoff

Cover art "Mind Control" created by Rampy Vivian

I0662632

Acknowledgements

This was as much a labor of love, as it was a labor of rage and sorrow. For all that went into this novel, the list of names spans years. Significant time periods of my life that changed what this book was meant to be and how it shall be defined by those who read it. Love and thanks go to my parents Darlene and Eric, my brother Daniel, creative comrades from Chicago, Rockford and Baguio City; Annie Santiago, Carlos Zayas, Amber Glovier, Tania Rivero, Breanna Hibbs and Willie Mae Lara for all the late night discussions, emails and instant messaging about ideas and dreams of stories we always wanted to tell.

To my teacher and mentor in writing. Kellie Sorrell, my hope is that this story and those to come make you proud.

To Michael Striegl, who provided feedback at the earliest stages of the idea and a piece of his own unpublished novel. Wherever you are, endless thanks for your insight and long live the D.

To Jennifer Hervey for all the time and patience editing to turn a coal into a diamond.

A large thank you to Rampy Vivian for both his art and his blessing. Your talent is immense and its potential is without limits. Prosper.

The Black Eclipse

CHAPTER ONE

I was alive in a city of fire. The city was lost, enveloped by dark, towering flames that rose from the earth. I stood there and watched it take place. The street was, for a moment, normal. I stood in the middle, blocking traffic. Amidst the angrily passing cars were people in suits, throwing familiar hateful glances at me as they walked to work under the cloudless sky. The sun sat above the buildings of concrete and steel. The earth moved. Its plates shifted and the ground beneath my feet began to rise. The people began to scream and run away. I felt the ground expand. There were long patches of concrete that began to separate to reveal the darkness of tunnels and the smell of sewers below.

I looked toward the people running. The street had cracked, with fissures that followed those who fled, I saw the cracks overwhelm and surround them. The cracks splintered off and reconnected a few feet before me. Aching from some unknown tension and force, the concrete broke apart and then went back together, almost as if it were driven by breath, a living entity. The darkness beneath the breathing stone grew red. The ground shook. The people all around me fell to their knees but I kept my stance. I looked above and saw the sky turn black. Thunder was deafening, but I could hear the people scream with fear. The tremors and steam had reached a fever pitch.

The screams grew louder into almost shrieks of pain. I saw the reason. The burning air had melted their feet to the ground. They were trapped. I looked quickly down to my feet. A blast of steam before me and yet, they remained unscathed, and then another blast. The street had exploded. Shattered stone blasted into the sky. The largest hole in the ground opened and revealed the core of the earth.

Fire spilled out onto the street, it covered the crowds of frantic people all around me. It passed over them like rushing water. A stray flame had struck my skin, and yet, I felt no pain. The others around me did not share my fortune. It had swallowed them whole. Others who tried to escape could not outrun the flames. It followed them. It moved as if it were alive, breathing. The streets shattered like glass. It covered them, burned them until nothing was left and pulled their remains back into the pits that had collected into the pitch darkness in the center.

The cracks in the earth soon stretched out and followed the path of streets that led away from me. The fires burned through them, pulling in everything within its path until they were out of my sight. It must have covered the entire city. I began to follow the flames. I walked for what felt like hours. Every street looked the same; open holes into hell, human beings burning alive, screaming. The buildings had cracked and crumbled. The flames had cracked windows and entered. It had burned them from the inside out, and they shattered and fell to the ground before me. Pieces of the rubble and glass had cut me. I did not bleed. The stone and cement walls were lost to the fire. Those who were still alive inside the fire, looked at me in the midst of the agony, they reached out what was left of their hands, pleading for help. I could not face them. I turned away from their screams, their eyes. They were watching as I walked away from them. The screaming did not stop. It echoed in my mind, I felt the eyes upon me, their voices seemed inches away. The fires had begun to connect. From the place where I stood, following the miles I had walked. At last, the fires had all linked together. The holes had filled with the lava that covered and carried the remains of these damned and became a river of blood and flame. I walked along as the cries grew louder as the shells of their bodies floated by. I looked to the black sky. Thunder slammed the dark emptiness above me. My eyes followed the river, until I reached the center of the city.

The tower was massive. It was all that remained of the city. I turned around and saw the burning wasteland. The river of death had run through the landscape, collecting into a pool beneath the tower, the altar that it had become. It had become hell. This is meant to be punishment, their punishment. Why had I been spared this pain and suffering? What had I done to be placed among the devastation, but somehow allowed to escape their fate? The flames gathered at the base. The noise of the people, the screams of damned began to build in volume as the fire climbed up the stone giant, toward the black skies. I began to feel different as the fire overcame the tower. I saw the people within the river, their eyes and their hands, reaching, peering inside me. I closed my eyes. They were inside my mind. I then began to see things, terrible things surrounding those in the river.

I saw their sins, their mistakes. Their every judgment they had passed onto those weaker than they. I saw the businessman walking down the street as he rushed past a homeless man on the curb. He was there in the river, burning next to the man that he refused to help. I watched the mother too concerned with the night life to take care of her children. She lay in the fire with her own children. They laid there and suffered with her neglect. Each time I looked past another dying man or woman, I looked into their eyes and saw their fear, their cowardice. I began to hate them. They had done so little so save themselves or those around them. I felt no pity for them anymore. I enjoyed being in this suit, walking upon fire and being spared the spears of Hell.

I enjoyed it more and more as I realized that this was somehow my reward. I saw their children in these fires. I smiled at them as they burned. Everything in this world they gained, tainted and then turned away, for this they would dwell in this hell. It can only be theirs and theirs alone. This is not my hell. I could see every sordid scenario with each of them. Each burning face had a story to tell. Young men and women, corrupted by fate and the choices of their creators, they will pay for all they've done. It is in their destiny to be punished. This justified my hatred. I could not help but laugh at them. They chose this fate and they will pay for it.

The tower was quaking under the pressure, the pull of the

flames. It was the beck and call of Hell. Its majestic grey stone architecture began to fall away, revealing the black steel girders that made up its skeleton. The steel would never stand the fire. The bars bent and burned dark red. The remnants of the tower began to sway back and forth over the wasteland and I. The bars broke in half and the tower finally fell to the ground, with epic crashes and deafening booms, the city had finally been claimed. Hell had made its final signature here, I surveyed the surroundings, nothing had been left, it was nothing but darkness above fire, and I felt good.

There was no remorse, no regret, and no fear of what may come. This was just, and I was glad they were all in Hell for what they had done. The wasteland was endless. I walked on from the melting ruins of the tower through the old neighborhoods, places that I tucked away in my memory as a child. This was where I found my life. I spent my youngest days in the village, away from the city. There were days where my parents would take me to the city to taste my culture. Experience and education were sheltered by the strict morality of the older generation. I came to this city young to escape my family.

When my parents could not bring themselves to leave this place, I lived a life on the streets without them. The guidance, the control of other people they could not offer, I found it in these streets now destroyed. These grounds gave structure to adolescence without rules and boundaries. I found myself educated by passing faces, all of them that I remember, giving a child wisdom before disappearing into the grinding machinery of city progress and cutthroat business. I had walked past the main roads of the city and into the park. This place, where I first learned of pain. a scraped knee and my father's comfort kept me alive. His words were always meant to settle anxiety. They didn't settle anything except doubt inside his own mind. He helped me back up from off the ground.

"No wounds are made without a reason," he said.

My first memories in this park, running through the swings, laughing at the sun, so many childish things that I had loved were now reduced to ash and black steel. I had not truly looked at myself as the city burned. The crowds of people that rushed the streets were wearing rags, clothes torn by time not by fire. I looked down awaiting the vision of torn clothes and limbs covered with dirt. I saw myself as if for the first time. I wore a white suit, clean and perfect. Through the ruins of the park, I followed a path to the street where I was born. The twisted steel had made a path for me. The houses were rubble and ash. The people in the street were burning and dying before me. I saw the men, the women and children of my childhood, aged now. Torn by time and their avarice, they are now tortured with fire while I look on wrapped in this suit. I could not save them, why was I to remain unscathed? The answer dawned upon me as I walked away from their withering bodies that I chose to save myself over them. I am here because I am alive and they are not. I am here because I chose myself over all else. I couldn't save them. I didn't want to save them.

They were already dead, the moment they chose to run from their punishment. They knew the choices they made, the sins committed on this earth; to neglect, to take for granted. I had seen them my entire life. They deserved the fire. A sharp cry scorched my ears, it shook what remained of the ground and I felt my spine tremble. I tried to keep away from it. Somehow, I was drawn to the sound. Horrible screams emanating from some dark place. This was different from the screams of the others, I could feel it. I followed it. More and more the noise grew louder, as if the scream was coming from two inches away. I could not find it. The pain was searing. I stopped at this old woman rolling in the streets. I walked toward the woman, knelt down to look at her. She was naked, clothes either lost in the fire or permanently embedded into her skin. The smoke that seemed to flow off her shoulders hit my senses. Her chest covered in black, the shawl that she wore was burned into her. Her screams turned to whimpers as I approached her, I placed one hand on her back, and the whimpers stopped. Her body rolled over to reveal her face. Burned, with no hair, two thick black holes where her eyes may have resided. She opened her mouth. A tongue fell out, black and burned beyond use, her teeth cracked and brittle, falling out at the first moments of speaking.

"Bless me father, for I have sinned against man," she spoke as she took my hands, looking to me for some kind of comfort.

I could not provide any words. This woman had to deserve this, didn't she? I could not see her punishment. She had no feelings of regret, no desire to be spared. She felt pure to me. Why was she subject to this? The entire city was dying. I had never felt this purity in any of the others. Their greed, their selfish, thoughtless nature, did not reside in this cursed, old woman. My thoughts were cut short by her pleading words again.

"Please father, bless me and wash away these wounds," she said as she placed her head into my hands. There was blood from the holes in her eyes.

"I'm sorry, but I'm not a holy man, what can I do for you?" I asked.

She began to cry, and she rose off the ground. Her brittle legs gained some kind of strength and she stumbled away from me crying, she threw her hands into the air, and the cries became laughter. I looked at her and rose from my feet. She turned towards me and laughed. She pointed and screamed.

"You did this, didn't you? Don't lie to me. I know who you are. You are a devil. You are Satan."

"What are you talking about?" I asked.

"You have destroyed us! You have spared yourself the wrath of God."

She came closer to me, pointing her finger, accusingly.

"You have turned away from your own sins and brought this upon us."

She came face to face with me, touching my suit, which I had begun to loathe. This woman was burned alive, and here I stand in perfect white, what had I done? What did I deserve?

"You put this punishment upon the world around you, to protect yourself. You coward."

"I'm not a coward," I said.

"Liar!"

I felt a skeletal hand slap my face, I felt no pain. I looked at her with anger. I wanted to strike her down. Some ideal of respect had held me back. Why?

"Do you think that you are better than all of us? Better than me? Do you feel you deserve no punishment? Who are you? Who do you think you are?"

I struggled to find my name. What is my name? My name.

"My name is Paavo."

Her hand grabbed at my throat, her face becoming closer to mine, I couldn't breathe, and she began to breathe in my air. I could feel the air leaving me, I began to suffocate. I couldn't breathe. I did not want to die, in front of this woman, here, in this place. Did it matter? If all others were dead and gone, what meaning did my life take on?

"Get away from me!" I screamed.

I threw her hand off of my throat and pushed her to the ground. She laughed again, becoming louder and louder until my ears began ringing. The first pain I felt brought blood that flowed from my ears and tears from my eyes. I screamed for her to stop. Her body began to rise off of the ground. Floating there, she began to speak again.

"This is all it is, my son. All you receive for choosing yourself over all. All you receive for ignoring your sins, your mistakes, your choices."

She flew towards me with incredible speed, grabbing my neck again. I could not remove her hand. Her grip was built from a new found strength. I was lost under her control. She began to rise into the sky, taking her with me. We reached a point high over the city, underneath the black and endless abyss.

"Look at them! These are the prisoners of hope, faith and belief! Cast away all your notions of right and wrong, behold the consequence for your life. Suffering and death was inevitable. It was inescapable, this human nature."

I saw the bodies of the dying. All of them were sinners and no saints. I was no different than them. We rose higher into the darkness of the sky. The fires became nothing but red circles underneath the black ocean that we burned past. The city below me left my sight. I looked into the sky. Our rising bodies began to increase in speed.

Wind shredded past us, burning my eyes, I could not see, tears began to pour down into my hands, trying to cover the blinding pain. My body felt the crushing weight of space, pushing down upon it. I couldn't breath, my chest constricted, I shook uncontrollably. I screamed to stop, but I was helpless under the woman's grasp.

Faster and faster we climbed the darkness, she spoke again.

"Is this what you wanted? A purgatory? A place of apathy where fools reside? Of course, why else would you condemn your own kind. When you take your freedom as paradise, and rape it's simple truth. You had a choice, and you chose to save yourself."

"What are you?" I asked.

Pained words were all I could manage out of my struggling breath. Her body began to change before me, the bones burned and seething grew plain white skin deep from within itself. The skin covered her body. The new shell of white began to glow.

"I can show you things, my son. I will show you the price and the consequence. I will show you fate and destiny," she said.

Black hair grew from her head, her arms and legs. The teeth that replaced the open, bleeding mouth were sparkling white. The new eyes that were birthed from the darkness within the two empty spaces of her head, deep and green. This woman let go of my throat, and I floated in this space. The sky of black shattered open, dark clouds stormed around us, revealing white light from above. The woman before me was not the woman I had found begging on the grounds of fire and sin. She was reformed, reborn, now adorned with robes as white and perfect as the suit I found myself in. Her black hair and green eyes struck me with shocking familiarity. It was as though I had known this woman my entire life, in thoughts and dreams and other places.

"Mother? I...Mother, what's going on? What's happening to me?"

She smiled at me. It comforted me instantly. I felt my defiance crumble and contract into a ball.

"My child, you must never forget what you are. You have taken your gifts for granted. Even now, those people under you, are paying their own price, as well as yours. I am no different from you or them."

She came down from her elevated state, her hand graced my cheek, and I felt safe. The white light had now overtaken the darkness around us. I found myself between the white clouds above and the black abyss below, dark red flames that reached and pushed to touch me, dark flames that burned and purged those people to this moment, still they screamed. Mother grabbed my hand and spoke softly.

"Paavo, never forget this moment, you will learn the cost of choice."

Tears filled my eyes. I looked up to the light above us. I saw a man walking towards my mother and I. White robes matching those of my mother, his blonde hair and brown eyes scorched my fears and doubts as to why this was happening. I was frozen again.

"Father?" I asked.

"My son."

His voice was deep and booming.

"You have been spared the fire, but you will not be spared judgment".

My mother's unbreakable grip returned and I was unable to pull away from her. Her hands returned to my throat as she held me down. My father hovered above us, his white robes opened to reveal a gleaming black sword.

"Be quiet, my child," she whispered into my ears.

My father took the weapon into his hands. I floated there, between the dark and the light. Helpless, dying and facing the punishment of my actions. My suit of white was false, I should have known. The black below and the white above. Heaven and hell. My father lifted the blade, memories and images flashed through my mind, too quick to cherish, too short to remember. He raised the sword as if it was his newborn son; before he died, before he knew that his son was damned as well as he was. The sword came from heaven and fell to my neck. Then there was no pain, only darkness again.

Paavo Harker awoke to an empty bed and a dark apartment. His heart ached as a grim reminder that he was still alive. A stumbling hand reached for the lamp above his head. With a pull of the string the room was revealed in yellow light. Paavo looked around the room with tired eyes. His body and mind were awake and alert. He had trouble breathing and slept with his body positioned straight, tightly clenching the muscles in his chest and stomach. It had been this way for years.

He opened his lungs into a silent yawn. He breathed in deeply. Pain filled his chest and throat. The air rushed in. Tears filled his eyes, as he winced. Paavo's chest constricted, his stomach flattened, tightening his muscles to conserve the air. He blinked his eyes to clear away the tears. Each fell down his face and he watched them roll past his neck, outlining the collar bone, dangling for a moment. He looked down to see his tear clinging to his pale, yellow skin. There was a sharp pain, then wetness. Paavo looked to the hole in his chest; blood from the hole had begun to trickle down his abdomen. With slight movements from his thin, skeletal hands, he wiped away both the blood and tears from his neck and chest. He sighed in frustration. Exhaling was always painful for him, especially dangerous if done without careful pacing and slow breathing.

He never slept on his side to avoid sudden death on account of the condition. The children in the hospital had a name for it, 'Crimson'. He hated it, but it stuck. When it was first diagnosed to him as a child, he memorized the definition given by his doctors. A defect of the body and circulatory system in which a child is born with a hole leading straight into the heart.

"The direct contact of oxygen inhaled creates a coagulation of the blood. This process slows down breathing, movement of the limbs and joints. It tears away at the veins that carry it, and if not treated with the proper serum to create heat and oxygen blockage, the symptoms are fatal to its host."

That had been the explanation given to him, a simple reasoning that he resented as it would affect him the rest of his life. The relief came when he felt the tension in his body settle, the muscles relaxed and he could breathe that small amount of air again.

There were days as in the hospital when he saw familiar faces in the same ward as him, running carelessly, with the freedom of being a child. Playful. He would run out to join them. Seconds later, when he opened his eyes again, he saw them, looking back at him in horror. He would be on the ground choking, bleeding out, and fighting for air. The children cried watching the doctors come and resuscitate the poor boy who had wandered off without proper care. They screamed when they saw the syringe, heavy in some nurse's hand. They watched her inject it straight into his small chest. The blood that poured from the wounds was always too great for the children, yet Paavo continued to watch them work on his own body. It was a difficult idea to grasp that every breath that you take must be measured and restrained, either that, or suffer the draining coughs. There was searing pain, the documented symptoms of this strange disorder. The pain was settled only by the injection of a six inch syringe carrying a serum of different proteins and acids that create warmth in the bloodstream. The children said it was made to give you life.

The doctors used to describe the effect of taking too much air into your lungs too fast or too deeply. It set off a chain reaction of irritation of the lungs, inflammation of the chest and internal bleeding. The parents of the children looked at Paavo's condition as a mistake; that something like this couldn't happen. Other officials deemed the disorder as a medical anomaly, and it was not deemed an object of importance to the scientific community. The other hospitals had cut costs and funding that led to the downsizing of the pediatric wards. Paavo's hospital was the only one that took in children who had contracted serious diseases. Months of study were invested into Paavo, with time and effort they taught him how to live with the disorder; to run, to play, to sleep. In order to live and maintain a healthy life, the child was taught to monitor his breathing 24 hours a day. They had developed for him ways of eating, exercising and sleeping in order to appease his struggling body.

Since those years at the hospital, Paavo had programmed his morning routine upon waking into a process. The city now held different conditions then the hospital of his youth. He rose from the bed. Still feeling the air from his lungs exit the hole in his chest and out his mouth, he stumbled over to the mirror to look into his own eyes. He met his reflection with a hard gaze. He analyzed each imperfection in his face. He thought himself ugly yet he had grown used to it, a sort of affinity for it.

Black eyes and hair like black strings, pushed down and over. He brushed his hand through his hair, and it spiked upwards with every run through, sticking up as if it were a small black forest. Every day since he was diagnosed with the Crimson, he became fully aware of his own fleeting life. Death was then and now a part of him. Even as he lived and breathed, he felt that his body did not belong to him. He taunted the hole leading into his heart with his fingers, feeling the air leave his body with every breath. His face revealed slight eyes that gave away his Japanese heritage. His body was thin and frail, with ribs jutting out from his stomach. His bones were heavy and stuck through his skin. His arms were mere shells for his veins, without girth, barely noticed under a pile of small, trained muscles. He was tall and extremely lank. His hands and feet held long toes and fingers thin and unkempt with nails bitten off. The stress, the paranoia and the thought of death had worn him down so much that few could argue that he was a man of only twenty four years.

Years ago, doctors had said that many men, if treated properly and live in non- threatening conditions, die of the Crimson in their thirties. A body with the Crimson is one of weakness and frailty. He was told the body would give out quickly and not in silence. Sickness was much more of a danger to people like Paavo. Common colds that create excesses in fluids, and congestion of the throat were known to cause erratic breathing. Those people with colds took in air too quickly to combat the coughs, and it proved fatal. It was natural for them to do so, no body can function without air. A body damaged that badly pays a price in the existence of constant pain and drained energy.

Paavo looked at his body with indifference, unable to live without the shadow of death. He often asked the other children in the hospital why they should live, as only the shells that he saw himself as. The children just laughed and shrugged their shoulders. They had no answer, and they never did. When it came to questions of life and existence, Paavo looked only within himself. He never took much pride in his answers. The simple truth that he was a dying man.

From his bathroom mirror, he stepped out of the room and looked around. The apartment was dark and empty. The floors hardened wood and walls were painted black. It helped him doze off during the nights that he refused to sleep to avoid an attack. The floors were littered with dozens of white papers. Files and folders were each filled with photos. Police dossiers were scattered across the wood. He attributed it to obsession. Paavo had become deeply immersed in work as a private detective two years ago. The obsession was overwhelming.

He had dedicated himself to helping other people, ones just as weak or weaker. From then his nights consisted of study; reading books on forensic science, of candles burned down to the wick, with white wax mixing with black ash spilling over to the floor. If not reading, he spent most of his nights searching, sometimes for people, or peace or for solitude. He had been searching without pause for a long time. Paavo carefully stepped over each candle and paper with precision, moving feet swiftly between papers and files, wax and metal lanterns. Another flip of a light switch revealed the entire apartment in light. The ceiling fan began to spin a hypnotic circle of repetition that carried a thrilling effect throughout the room. The image of the city lingered outside. Towers in a shadow of black stood over the white lights that lit the streets. In the center of the room was a table carrying several candles already melted and dried.

They each held down files and photos of different cases yet unsolved.

Papers and photos were blown off the table, which until now had remained invisible in the darkness. Paavo never purchased furniture for his own apartment. Such ideas seemed to escape him often, with death following like a shadow in his mind; decorations were another trivial aspect of life. The city outside burned its white lights into Paavo's window, dying to be noticed. Perdition was there. Though the city had a real name, two old men introduced the moniker to him years ago. According to them, the city had held this name and distinction for a long time. Paavo recalled the stories from the old men on the bus he rode into town after all those years of anger, of lingering sadness and the dreams that still remained.

He came to the city to start a new life, as that was what he told himself. The truth was that Paavo had nowhere else to go. Many years had gone by and the town had formed into a city of stone and steel. The village lay only miles away, untouched and uncorrupted. It was there, where Paavo moved his grandmother. She was away from the crime and poverty of the city, where she could be safe. He remembered her asking where they were going, he smirked, showing her enough emotion to allow her to rest easy, without the knowledge of growing crime. He simply told her;

"To a safe place, Granny."

Paavo walked back into his room. Opening nearly empty drawers, he began to pull out his attire. Finding an occupation in the city was not a problem. He began working for the Police department, small menial tasks like data entry and filing. During his time off, Paavo read at a feverish pace, books from the city and station libraries about criminology and law, philosophy and literature.

There were days when he slept at the station, under his desk, in between the work and studying. Paavo spent his first two years back in the city living at the Police Station. He was fired from his position when he was caught in the middle of a sleepless night, stretching his body in the station. He remembered it vividly; five in the morning, walking through the lobby was a janitor who had seen him and reported to his superior, the commissioner, Ido. He found Paavo lying on his desk, stretching his body outward, out of breath. The janitor was holding a cross and calling for help as he stared at the blood from his chest as though he was shot or dying. Paavo fought off his attempt to use CPR, and tried to hide the nature of his disorder and what was necessary to the nearby officer. The security cameras that caught Paavo were used to terminate him. They could not take on responsibility for his "unique medical condition" they had told him, or rather, what he read in the letter left outside his door. They kept it quiet at his request.

Paavo used the small money he received for his efforts, to rent both his apartment, and another for his grandmother in the village. He made sure that she had a garden or something to take care of, to fill that void that mothers feel with no children to watch over. She feared that she had lost her creative touch. Paavo made sure that she could grow her food and her flowers. Her plants took the place of watching the spoiled children that held her lineage. Paavo could not stand to be related to them. They had no passions, no minds of their own.

Paavo threw on a black buttoned shirt. He thought of his grandmother, where she was then and now. He always fell back to the fact that of all the things that he'd done, making life peaceful for her was one that could redeem him. It was then a few months and a few unsuccessful odd jobs later, when he approached the station again, and offered his services to the department in evidence analysis and crime scene investigation, his distinct knowledge of various methods of forensic study made him a unique asset to the department. The chief inspector, Derek Long, had kept in contact with Paavo after the incident and thought him useful although in small doses, due to his eclectic personality. Long employed his services as a forensic specialist for his investigations and crime scenes. With the money he made from assisting the cops, he opened an office and began the detective service.

Paavo was usually sought out for obscure cases. He was discovered by shady characters collecting money from strays, or worried families with no money. He became accustomed to it. He became deeply involved with the concept of finding these people. It became a part of him, the search, the discovery or the inability to find them. Each case took more energy, and Paavo became less concerned with his own health as the cases piled up. The tasks performed for each of these people gave him a sense of relief and happiness when he was successful. When he was not, it pained him deeply. It hurt almost as if those people were too a part of him, and when they were found dead, he felt a connection with those he found. He was dead with them. Even worse than when he found them alive or not, was when he found nothing at all; that the person had just vanished, without a trace.

The family would have to remain of the edge of doubt and disbelief, all because he held no answers or no news of death. There was no peace of mind for them. Paavo gained small respect and attention from the city because of his strange style. Known mainly for his clothes, which were several black suits and ties he had purchased from a nearby thrift store when he first came to the city. As broke as he was, he found ways to live without much food and money. Soon, Paavo worked out of his home. The office was practically empty, with nothing but heavy blinds on the windows. There was a desk holding stacks of white paper and a typewriter to type letters and memos to the station or his clients. Paavo was always deep in his work, deeper in his work than his own life.

His lack of money, or clothes, or nice furniture should have been proof enough to those skeptical ones who didn't trust him. They labeled him as some social outcast, as a freak, that he was some strange child. Though the truth never reached those people,

Paavo never lost his humility. He thought somewhere in his heart that these people were only lashing out in the form of grief, yet that reasoning seemed to escape him as the days grew into months and years. The humility always left an impression upon his clients. He made them feel secure somehow by saying nothing. They felt the sincerity. He asked only the important questions, never taking notes as those years of reading and study had developed an incredible memorization skill within him. He would tell them that he would do only what he could; to search for what is missing, with everything in him. He never promised to find anyone anymore, because it hurt too much to fail. Paavo's practices and methods were laughed at by other officers, yet the agency survived, much to the contempt of some members of the Police. A cold wind shook the windows hard. A storm began to manifest outside.

Paavo threw on the jacket he usually reserved for Wednesdays. Fixing his collar and straightening his tie, he glanced again at the mirror. He was a vision in black. Nothing offsetting except his own pale face, hands and the white inlays of his pockets. Looking at himself, Paavo saw an emptiness that could not be defined. There were days when he could have felt good about what he had done in his life up to now; the success of solving a crime, the feeling of completion bringing someone to justice. In his own mind it was never enough for him. He put his head down, closing his eyes quickly. He felt something shake within him. He emptied his mind before any other thoughts could cloud his focus. It was time for work, Paavo mapped out the schedule for the day in his mind, just like every other day.

"Check the office, screen calls," he thought.

Paavo looked at the mirror once more, playing with the thought in his mind about when he was going to see a doctor about the condition of his body. He hesitated about going, putting it off for days into weeks and then into months and even years, until it simply faded from his mind. After all that time, he stayed in a city that battled nearly constant cold temperatures and the harshest winter. His body was battered. Some days Paavo felt he was going to shatter upon going out into the snow. The visit was inevitable. Paavo knew that he had to go, two years of this punishment and something would have to give internally. There was a slight silence. He would go this morning, today. Paavo looked at his own reflection and spoke with a bit of sarcasm.

"Maybe tomorrow," he said.

Paavo stepped outside, clicked the light near the door, the apartment bathed in darkness and silent once more.

CHAPTER TWO

The revolver shook within Derek Long's holster as the car sped past the heavy grey industrial buildings made brown with the early morning streetlights. His foot tapped the floor of the car nervously. He looked to the ground. The cruiser burned through slight traffic. Its siren was tearing the dull morning silence to shreds with blaring noise. Derek passed a glance to the outside; a blurring of lights, dozens of grey shapes. He felt a sickness within as he tried to look at every passing object. His eyes were going too fast for his own good. He closed them quickly, overwhelmed by the speed of everything around him. He felt for his badge and analyzed it to ignore the small talk and chatter of the other three Policemen in the other cars. Wind hit the car with a terrible thud and a sweeping noise of air, barely audible over the siren. The other officers jumped at both the noise and the smacking of air against the glass.

"Some rough wind tonight, huh?" asked his driver.

Long didn't answer, he continued staring at his badge. Though the voices spoke loud enough not to be ignored, he tried.

"The winter is starting, pretty soon we'll be covered in snow," said an officer over the radio.

"How long do you think it will take before it gets here?" asked another.

"No clue...probably a few hours."

The badge in Long's hand was a faded gold with rust around its edges from age and wear. He found himself in a state of nothingness, not thinking of anything in particular, just aware and alive speeding toward a hostage situation somewhere in the lower east side of the city. The five men were armed and holding a young girl. Demands were ten thousand, just enough to get them a car and plane tickets out of the city. It was a shame to Long to think about the reason why young men kill. Perhaps it's the same reason that an old man kills; maybe they too were struggling to stay alive.

Still, he looked at the badge, clearing his thoughts. The badge repeated the same word to Long over and over every time he looked at it. His thoughts rang out clear, as if he were speaking with his men. They're laughing, rested and oblivious. They could die tonight, especially with that kind of carelessness. They could be killed, and if they did, he would be responsible. As the acting commissioner, Long had been leading these men and women into these moments of danger for over two years now. His job, as he saw it, was to bring some notion of justice, of law and order as a desperate reminder to a city growing too quickly for its own good. Somehow, the law was still in control. The former commissioner, Ido, had stepped down due to his involvement in a corruption trial.

Long would never accept the title given to him as a way to sweep the smear of dirty politics under the rug as opposed to being for his years of service in the force. He never saw himself as a leader. Personally, he thought the pressure was too great. Before he disappeared, Ido told the men that he would be back in six months, only to find out that the man had skipped the trial altogether, heading overseas to escape prosecution. Their alliances changed. Grizzled veterans respected him, the young ones followed him. A weight too great for his shoulders he had always thought, yet they pushed it onto him, asking that he take control of the force because he was a good and honest man. Long felt a deep resentment to those helpless people who put him in charge. Naturally, at a younger age, he was proud to take on the challenge and responsibility. Yet those years of regret and shame watching the city degenerate into the sea of darkness that it was had worn a hole into his pride.

He placed the badge back into his pocket, and took out the revolver from his holster. He checked the barrels. Each carried a massive silver bullet that gleamed with the reflection of passing city lights. He thought of the other officers in the car, still talking and laughing. They were without care or self-awareness. He wanted to go it alone. He would tell the men to stand guard, call for backup, and not to follow him. The hostage situation was going to be difficult. Long recalled the first description; five men heavily armed holding a young woman, sixteen, on the top floor in an apartment building. He knew he did not want another dead cop on his conscience or his reputation. He recalled these same suspects, brought in on drug charges for a bad deal by the docks nearly a month ago. They were released due to a lack of evidence.

He remembered watching them, as the one who brought them in those weeks ago. They were out of their minds. The deal on the docks was full of holes, a lot of unexplained things going on. The man on the inside was wired with a small recording device that stopped working halfway through the night. Electronic equipment died in and around the surrounding five blocks. It was considered a power outage. Analysts could not determine the cause of their insanity. There were no traces of illegal substance within the bloodstream. A part of him didn't believe it but he felt in his heart that any and all choices are made by you. It was just a matter of having the angel or the demon in your heart. Heaven or Hell. Light or dark. It was all a matter of choice.

Long believed that every man was actually two, it was all a matter of which one you accepted. That ideal allowed him to keep his sanity and peace of mind in a city of crime and injustice. He remembered watching those suspects on the docks. They tortured a bum they caught hanging around by the docks. They did it two feet away from him. His men couldn't blow their cover. There was no choice but to remain silent. The last remaining minutes of the recording played out with a noise that could induce madness upon listening. With guilty eyes, their man on the inside watched them cut the bum to pieces. The tape ended with them laughing maniacally. He had seen the demon within their eyes and inside their voices. It hurt so much to feel helpless, but he felt different on this night.

Something told him that he had to do this on his own. Anyone else involved could be a mistake. He made the choice. He was going in alone tonight. The wind blew hard as the car sped around a corner, barely missing a streetlight and turning into the parking lot across the street from the apartment building. It was large and grey, blue stones along the top and down the sides of the building, leading straight into the foundation. The only way in was through a white screen door. He stepped out first to access; the wind was blowing harder than ever, pushing Long to the right as he tried to balance himself. The three other officers were already disoriented when they stepped out of their cars. Long checked his watch. The first real snowfall of winter had begun. The snow had crept into air, blending with the wind, creating a rough hail that banged across the windows of the surrounding cars and buildings. The noise had picked up into a rhythmic storm. Long felt the shards of ice and snow cut his face. Small winces of pain rolled onto his stoic expression. The officers were blinded.

Long saw this as the perfect opportunity to get into the building. He looked at the building, one hand covering his eyes and nose to create a field of vision. He took note of the fire escape on the fifth floor, it conveniently led straight up to the top floor as well as the roof of the building. Ideas began to form. He stuck out his hand to the officers, who were already walking towards the street, stumbling with hands over their faces.

"Hold on boys, go ahead and start taking a look around, I'll stay here and get on the horn," Long said.

"What are you talking about? In this weather?" they asked.

"A look around?"

"How can we take a look when we can't even see anything out here?"

"A little reconnaissance, try to be back in ten minutes," said Long.

The men were quiet, no doubt preparing themselves. They soon shook their heads.

"Watch the streets, make sure none of them try to bail...got it?"

One of the men signaled. Long pulled the collar of his black trench coat over to protect his ears, already red with potential frostbite. He walked across the street, nonchalantly into the building. The white door leading into the place was electronically locked, Long walked to his left and discovered an alleyway that led into the adjacent street. There was a side door, half way opened, and there was a light from the opening. A surly, fat man was standing to the left side. He introduced himself as the hotel owner. Long figured a few questions with him would not hurt. The men upstairs were clearly not in their right state of mind, he told him. They spoke in low voices and moved sluggish, probably drunk. The owner was just happy to get them off the road. Hours later, there were gunshots and screams from the top floor. He thanked the fat man for his time and returned to the cold of the outside. There was a familiar blinking light inside the car. He reached into the open window and turned the knob to raise the volume.

"Sir, we found them."

It was one of the young officers.

"The men are on the top floor, the room to the corner, opposite the street," he said.

More noise came from the device. Gunshots, screams from the trapped woman. The officer shouted in fear.

"Shit! We need backup now!"

Long spoke in a slow voice, trying to calm the young man.

"Where are you now?" he asked.

"We're pinned down in the hallway, there's got to be another way around them. Do what you can. We'll be here, trying to hold them off."

The aging cop dropped the phone and walked toward the door in the alleyway. He entered and shut the door quietly, he figured he was in someone's apartment as he walked up the dark staircase and flipped on a light switch to reveal a grey hallway dividing into a broom closet and another room. His hands began to shake with extreme excitement.

A turn around the corner revealed a laundry room, smothered in white paint and failing drywall. Long followed the staircase out of the laundry room and into the main hallway of the building. The hall was silent, with only the sounds of wind and snow outside. He took steps out into the open, checking corridors for a possible ambush. He relaxed himself and took deep breaths. The surroundings were looked over. Each entry to the apartments around him had the same uniform colors. A few doors were streaked with dirt and what looked to be footprints. The grey walls held horribly slopped on paint which dripped onto the sides of the blue staircase leading to the upper floors.

He walked up five levels of stairs slowly, still thinking about using that fire escape to reach the top. Walking to the end of the hall, he noticed a bathroom to his right and entered to collect his thoughts. Long could never agree that his ideas were too reckless. He was very critical of himself and he made it a habit of forcing himself into moments where snap decisions need to be made. This morning was no different. Those boys upstairs wouldn't hesitate to kill the girl. They had to be stopped. It was unavoidable. He finished and walked to the sink to wash his hands. There he met his reflection. He was an aging Japanese man; greying roots at the base of jet black hair living in the depths of middle to old age. He looked at his own squinting eyes and the browning wrinkles that cracked across his yellow face, pale with time. Forty three years, those words spoken silently to himself. He took a breath in to feel his stomach take in the air and release it. There was a quiet cough and he laughed at himself.

The storm began to manifest as Long stepped out onto the fire escape, the wind and hail were increasing in speed and size, he winced as the shards cut into his face with cold and sharp pains. He had adapted to the warmth of the inside of the building. His face and body were unprepared for the cold again. He climbed up the black metal steps slowly. His eyes were blind to the snowfall. He closed them to avoid the cold, narrowing them into focus and following the spiral of yellow lights within the windows of the other apartments. His movements began to pick up speed, pushing his body a little too quickly, each floor climbing higher and higher. He counted the number of levels.

Each breath felt shorter and shorter and Long felt his muscles tense. He inhaled cold air. Feeling the sudden drop in temperature, he fell to the metal steps. Long rested against the metal railing of the fire escape, mere inches from a free fall of thirty feet back to the cold earth. The snow had frozen his eyelids and made them immobile. His trench coat was heavy with water, it's brown shade darkening. Both the black office shirt and faded grey work pants were wet and damp from the snow that had fallen. Long's ears were burning, yet he still heard the sirens, screeching noises of tires and the cackle of officers, ready to storm the building.

"The fools," he thought.

"They'll kill her if they try to raid the place."

Long struggled to rise to his feet, taking slow breaths. The only sounds in Long's ear were the high wind, beating him with bursts of force. His heart was beating intensely. The streams of blood felt like gunshots, loud and thunderous. He had to make a move. Long stopped at the twelfth floor, he barely opened his eyes to see that he was almost two inches away from the window, as one of the men stared through it. Long looked at an angle which concealed himself from the other adjacent window. He could see three of the five men, all masked but one.

The one looking out the window, he knew the face. They had laughed at the homeless man, at all the blood. They laughed in the face of his officer, becoming sick to the sight of what they had been doing. Two of the men left the room, leaving only the window gazer alone. Long thought of the girl, bloody and lifeless. The laughter and anger rose from within him. The anger was bright and alive and burning. The opportunity was there, waiting to be taken. Long moved without noise, climbing onto the ledge connecting to the roof of the building. He didn't feel anymore pain or fatigue, he was running on adrenaline. Pure instinct.

His eyes were again blinded by the rushing snow, yet Long concentrated on the hostage inside. It was too much for him to think those thoughts, but it gave him strength and fury. Long's hands began to shake. He grabbed an iron bar close by, and found a spot directly above the window. The shadow of the man remained at the window, Long took hold of the bar with both hands, swinging it downward fast and silent, shattering the window as well as the face of the young thug. Long peered down to see into the room. The man's face was destroyed, a trail of blood and teeth lay before the window. The lifeless body was covered in red and glass. Long moved quickly and grabbed the man, pulling him out into the cold air, leaving his body on the roof for later. Back in the room, there was shock and fear in the voices below.

"What the hell? Who...Who's there?"

Long heard the nervous creaking of footsteps, an approaching shadow. Another man stuck his head out of the window to see what had happened. Long waited only three feet above him, silent in burning anticipation. The man looked up, and saw an iron bar and nothing ever again. Long smashed the eyes of the thug, weighing the man down with his own body. He looked into the room to see someone grabbing for his gun. Long pulled his revolver quicker than the other and fired a shot. The bullet ripped through the man's skull and the body fell to the ground. Long quickly climbed inside. Hearing the sounds of the Police marching up the stairs to raid the apartment, he walked straight into the next room. The remaining three were already downstairs, locked in a firefight. The girl was out in the hallway with them. He heard her screaming for help.

He heard noise from one of the men in the room. His head moved to the window. The young man stood with his hand on the hair on the young woman, and he snickered. He moved his gun in a circle, and she followed his motions, helplessly. Her face winced in pain as she walked across the floor. They had made her walk across the floor through broken glass, it had to be. The path went from one side of the room to another, back and forth and back again to the corner. They had trapped themselves between two opposing forces, yet they had the upper hand in such close quarters with a hostage in their grasp. Long backed to the wall, and had decided to hide behind the overturned table. The room was a mess; chairs broken, the walls torn bare, lamps on the floor leaving shards of glass everywhere. The spots of red looked like tiny circles across the floor leading to the space in front of Long. He saw the pair of socks and shoes in the corner with a puddle of blood there.

He realized that it was the blood of the woman. Long pictured it in his mind. The anger returned yet his hands were relaxed again. He pushed the table into the corner, giving him a view of the surrounding room and its exit points. The men would come back in, and he would be there, waiting for them. He closed his eyes and waited, the gunshots continued. The storm cried harder than ever, everything moved too fast. Too blurry were his eyes, the fear returned, the anger solidified into a heavy stone in his hands. He couldn't breathe, the voices in his mind became louder and louder.

"You'll get her killed. You'll get her killed. You'll get killed. You'll kill her. You kill."

He opened his eyes. The men ran back into the room, with

the girl dragging behind, her feet bleeding onto the carpet. One of the men grabbed her and pulled her over to the table near the corner. One shot fired, the man flew backwards onto the floor, all red and nothing moving. His hand released the woman, as she fell to the ground unable to carry herself. The other men looked at the fallen man first, enough of a distraction for Long to pull the girl behind the table, he covered her with his body. Guns blazed towards the old man, he buried the woman's head under his coat, and they lay flat on the floor, bullets breaking through wood, screaming past his head. Another man approached the table, his gun empty. He fumbled to reload.

Long put his revolver to the hole closest to his eyes. He pulled the trigger twice. Bullets pierced the legs of both men, and the first man fell to the ground, still reloading his gun. The other on the ground was trying to regain his footing. Both were shaking in fear. He was playing with them now. Long pulled the trigger again. A bullet went through the face of the fallen thug. The man fell lifeless. The old man looked to see the last man raise his gun as he limped towards him. He jumped back under the table as gunshots grazed his head. A hard kick to the table sent it across the floor sliding towards the man. He jumped over the table, even with his leg shot. Long fired, it hit him in midair as he jumped the table. He fell to the floor, dying. The old man finally got to his feet after a few minutes. Knees buckled once he was upright. He walked over to the man. His body twitched and contorted in pain. Long could think of no words of comfort for him, not that he deserved them as it was. His face was different from the others, so much younger.

All was quiet again, the storm raged on outside, and Derek watched another man die in front of him. The woman removed the trench coat and moved towards the corner of the room. She looked innocently at Long. She was wearing a white dress. For a moment, his heart rose from unknown depths to see her. Angelic, she was. A few seconds passed before blood could be seen pouring from her legs and to the floor. The image was replaced with reality. Cuts and lacerations on her legs and feet laid a foundation of deep scars in her arms not fully healed. The eyes that were swollen and purple, her heavenly aura destroyed in an instant. She was an addict. He spoke softly but stern.

"Downstairs, they will take care of you," he said.

"Thank you." The woman spoke mumbled words with tears running down her eyes.

"Don't," he said.

The woman was taken out. Long still looked on at the body and at the open eyes of the young man. His reflection was there. Fear. For Derek, a choice was a choice, whatever you chose was you. The question was whether you had the angel or the devil in your heart. He had lived with the devil in his heart for years.

CHAPTER THREE

The office was dark. The lamplight had burned out a long time ago. Paavo made his way towards the door. The key and lock were both rusted. A bit of force was needed to push it open. The wood cracked with old age as it revealed the room. He noticed splinters within the edges of open space inside the shell of the door. It was heavy, the noise it made when closing echoed throughout the abandoned hall. This place was a mess, falling apart as the floorboards struggled to maintain the weight placed with each step. It was decided many days ago that this place was no longer safe to inhabit. Without money or proper resources, it would have to do for now.

Paavo went to great lengths to avoid any danger and set up safety precautions for his time in the office. Loose nails were hammered down and covered with cotton pieces and bubble wrap. Black paint was slathered over any opening to distract the wandering eye from the little hidden pieces of iron. He wasn't going to let a little thing like the risks of gangrene stop him from conducting his business. The nails held little droplets of infection, which he avoided with careful movements over the failing boards. The black paint had faded over time, it left streaks of darkness between the wood. A lone window was opened to let some light in, enough to replace the burned out lamp.

There were several rushes of cold air that shook his body. He felt a chill run deep into his bones. Fearing a coughing fit, he closed it once he found the rag and a new bulb. The rag was oily and flaunted numerous burn marks. Lamps were hard to come by these days. Instead of spending precious money on a new one, Paavo found a way to fashion one out of a few wires and an old fire lantern. He replaced the light with furious speed and moved it over to the desk to test out the makeshift lamp. He continued to work in the dark. There was a silence in the room as he moved without hesitation. Over time, Paavo had trained his eyes to settle in pitch black conditions. Reading a book was out of the question, but he was working on it. The plug sparked when contact was made with the old outlet. Paavo moved his eyes towards the center as the lantern began to light up. New fire was born. A small sense of victory now as he put away his things and waited.

Soon enough, there was a familiar blending of noise. The doorbell and the ring of the elevator. A man stepped out from the double doors with a look of nervousness. The detective agency had established a reputation, not only for being in a tough part of town, but also in the back corners of the highest floor of an empty hotel. Anyone with common sense would try to avoid this place, unless they were in real trouble or on the run from someone. This was a place to hide. The location allowed him to filter out those who really needed help from those who would waste precious time.

"The door is open," said Paavo.

He waved his hand back in his direction as Paavo headed back inside the office to wait. The man moved carefully around the holes in the floor, each step made a loud crackling sound which only increased his nerves. The hallway down towards the office was just as derelict. Complete with sheets of plastic wrap that covered the other open doors, signs of unfinished renovation. The man looked in each one, nothing but a window and holes in the floor, some which could take you down ten stories. Paavo had moved around the desk and took a seat on an old leather chair. His gun was ready underneath the desk drawer. It was pointed towards the doorway, parts of the desk had been drilled out to leave space for clear shots on all sides.

"I am working on getting the place fixed up," Paavo deadpanned.

"I couldn't tell," the man laughed. He seemed to lighten up after the dangerous crawl.

"How can I help you, sir?" Paavo asked.

"You can call me Lau. Yeah, that's pretty much all it said in the phone book, Paavo Harker, detective agency. Pretty cut and dry,"

"It's to the point," said Paavo.

"I figured there would be some fancy name for it."

"Why is that?"

"All the detectives have some kind of clever name for their office," said Lau.

"Sorry to disappoint,"

Lau waved his hand to move on.

"What can I do for you?"

"Some people say you're the best in the city," said Lau.

"I'm not. They only say that because I work cheap."

"But you have a reputation, whether you like it or not. That's what makes you one of the best, you will take jobs others wouldn't dare touch, help people others would never put their necks out for."

"I'm listening," said Paavo.

"There's a guy I'm looking for. He's a thief, a damn good one. My bank account was hacked a month ago. They took off with a shitload of money from my savings. Not completely dried out, but enough to warrant help outside of the cops."

"They couldn't find him?" asked Paavo.

"No proof of who he is, no traces," said Lau

"But you found out something they didn't."

Lau turned towards the window as Paavo took a drink of tea.

"That's right. Turns out he's a Mob lackey, and sweeping folks like myself is just a side job," said Lau.

"How much did he take?"

"Three hundred grand."

"A hell of a lot," said Paavo.

Lau shrugged it off, staring into the snow.

"I get by. My business just reached its second wind, the economy is always hard during the winter, but I've been lucky."

"Not so lucky if you've got someone snooping around your income," said Paavo.

"The price of success is paranoia. Eyes behind your head become a necessary mutation."

"What kind of business do you have?" asked Paavo.

"I sell medical equipment to the local hospitals, a middle man for some of the big manufacturing companies. It's not much, but it keeps the bills paid and the wife happy."

"Let me know if you need a receptionist. I'm always looking for a new alibi," said Paavo.

Lau left him with some good clues, enough information to get a lead on the Mob lackey. A piece of paper with three names was left on the table, along with over two thousand dollars in marked bills. Paavo shook his hand and saw him to the hidden elevator, the safe exit, inside his office.

"You're a strange bastard," said Lau.

"Thank you, I'll keep you posted."

Seven was the alias of the thief. Johnny B's was the restaurant he frequented. Paavo kept his distance in watching the front door. The rooftop from across the street was easy to access, but the cold made it hard enough just moving around. He wrapped himself in thick blankets from the car, followed by a heavy green tarp. Men in long coats and expensive suits exited their cars and headed inside. He took a few notes on a small notepad. Words were scribbled in messy, black ink.

The words read like a dossier, making tabs on each gangster type that stepped out into the cold. Paavo's office computer didn't pull up many reports on Seven. People around town would have to know more than the cops had on file. The third name of the paper was what could prove trouble. Jimmy the Recluse was written with a line through it. Supposedly, one of the Mob's shining stars in recent years. Jimmy's been on the lamb for almost a year after a sting operation. He earned the nickname by renting a penthouse and never stepping outside. All this time spent holed up, he was still able to make a name for himself by getting jobs done through faceless helpers. They were reliable, but expendable hoods. Jimmy had a method behind such madness. His likeness was plastered everywhere, in hopes of someone getting nervous and calling in with a sighting. No one called. No one could find him in a year. Those penthouses were raided, they found nothing. He had slipped by the cops on five separate occasions. A true ghost. Some had said that Jimmy died a long time ago, and his legend was getting by through careful planning by a group of confidants and some word of mouth. It might be true. Paavo had never seen the man either.

A black limousine pulled up to the restaurant. Paavo lowered his binoculars and headed down the staircase on the fire escape, towards the street. A sharp dressed man stepped out with a smile on his face. The bartender inside came out to greet him. They exchanged pleasantries as Paavo crossed the street, walking in stumbled steps.

"Gino! Good to see you."

"Anthony, a pleasure."

"You never call me. My wife, she worries."

"Strange times. I'm just getting back to the normal everyday."

They spoke in code, for good reason. Anyone could be wearing a wire. The men who worked as a driver for any of the made men were followed home themselves, a practice put forward by Jimmy. A lot of good men were killed due to distrust.

"The meeting is inside, the family's here," said Gino.

"Good to know, this weather is murder on my sinuses, tell everyone to head down to the basement, you can watch the game."

Paavo moved quickly towards the men, he made sure he ran into them and fell to his knees, he slurred his words.

"Sorry, man. This street's slip, slippery..."

"Hey! Watch it you damn bum!" yelled Anthony.

"What are you, drunk or something?"

Paavo reached up for a hand.

"I'm trying to get home, man," he said.

The man in a suit raised his hands and pushed him off with a disgusted look on his face.

"This is what you deal with in this city everyday, Anthony? Jesus Christ, you gotta get these pieces of garbage off the streets!"

Paavo fell to the ground, weakened. He shook his head when he spoke.

"Thanks for your time," he said.

The bartender kicked him in the chest.

"Get the hell out of here, you little shit!"

He rolled over to his side and stumbled to his feet again.

"Come on! We got business here."

He used the tail end of the limo to get to his feet. They began to advance on him.

"I'm going, gone."

Paavo shuffled off around the corner away from their laughter. When they stepped inside, a remote was pulled from his jacket pocket and turned on. The directional microphone slipped inside Gino's pocket. It would trace his words, and his location. Paavo winced as he opened his coat to see the blood, a result of the kick. The wingtip on the bartender had found its way into his lungs. Paavo closed his eyes for a moment, he took several deep breaths. A cramp inside his chest gripped him with pain. The slow breathing allowed his body to settle, the tension slowly left him, his chest raised and lowered in a quiet rhythm.

His heart quivered with each calm movement, it struggled to slow down. Several minutes of nerves passed, he rested easy for a moment. Towards the end of the curb, Paavo angled himself over the side and spit out a gob of thick blood and headed back to the car.

Johnny B's was a gangster hangout for the past twenty years. There was a great deal of old Italian tradition and history inside that place. The bosses were no longer seen out in the open. The captains were assembled and placed in charge of the day to day operations. Each of the three bosses took their top earners in the streets, the ones that they trusted, and put them in expensive suits and diamond jewelry. Word was put out on the new system. The rest of the bottom feeders and mid level guys reported to them now, all money and info channeled through a captain and back to their respective bosses. The territories of control had been set in place many years ago after wars of words and bullets.

Jimmy the Recluse had burned his way to the near top of the food chain as the highest earner of the lower end territory, which belonged to the Capotellis. They made the most money by selling out the old traditions of the families and doing business with the Japanese. They needed someone to take the reins long after they were gone. Jimmy forced himself on them. He became the only captain in the territory, with the promise of getting the job done, whatever was asked. His intensity proved necessary when dealing with outsiders trying to make their move on the family. Dealers and con men who came straight from the prisons on the other side of the ocean, trying to get their feet back onto solid ground in the city they left years ago.

Things had changed since their time. New blood ran through the streets, unafraid to not only disrespect the old guard, but to kill without question. They weren't going to make their name off of us, they told him. Jimmy made sure his impact was felt, anyone trying to move in or make an impression was handed swift violence from his men, sometimes from Jimmy himself, before he went under the radar. Their turf sat alongside the coast of Perdition. They controlled the ports, the harbors. Anyone looking to trade or pick up a shipment had to do business with the Capotellis, which meant they had to make friends with Jimmy. Inside, faded pictures of each crime family lined the walls, each one surrounded with a polished black frame. Hardwood floors echoed the steps of the captains, who stopped for a moment to prepare for the meeting.

The atmosphere of Johnny's was that of a quiet evening, candlelight and weathered white walls provided a background. Mothers close to the family brought their children here to have dinner. They played old records and turned the lights down for ambiance. When the place was near empty, they told stories from their own upbringing, and marveled in disbelief at the follies of the new generation. The jukebox at the end of the room had been there for over thirty five years. Sometimes, it worked. The PA system inside would be turned off and the old machine would play an LP before making the same crackling noise. It was considered a trademark of Johnny B's. In the center of the room, an antique chandelier hung from the ceiling. Artificial candles circled the intricate design, each holding its own dying red light.

An old jade bottle was pulled from the alcove of crossing white wood pieces, along with several fine glasses. The captains took their drink of wine and contemplated what the man could possibly be thinking to bring them all together and arrange a meeting like this.

"This is crazy. Does anyone know what he wants? Why the hell are we here?" one of them asked.

"I got a message on my phone about discussing something spur of the moment, big cash," said Anthony.

"That's all well and good, but we're all captains here. Tell me, when did we start taking orders from him?"

"Cause he's the golden boy. The families respect him, more than us."

"How does he get more respect by being a killer?"

"You say you're better?"

"No one here is clean. But what he does brings shame to us," admitted Anthony.

"It's not about how he looks. It's about the money he brings in. And he's heartless. No wife or kids to watch out for. Just himself."

"Heartless or not, Jimmy takes care of the family, all of us."

Some of the earners were downstairs, hooking up a laptop to the old monitor they used for watching the boxing matches. Once they were ready, the bartender signaled them to head down into the basement. Since the man would not step outside unless absolutely necessary, his meetings with earners and captain alike took place via satellite, broadcast from wherever he was, to the designated spot. Someplace quiet, away from areas heavy with population. He liked using the older tech when broadcasting, it was harder to track. Many of the meetings had their fair share of hackers, whether working for the Police or otherwise. Tricks were put into place to avoid finding out his location. If caught, they would find themselves handing over their information to the Recluse, and they were dealt with as quickly as anyone else who crossed him.

The men inside had begun their meeting, nothing but trash talk for the first few minutes. There really was a collective inside, part of him thought of calling the cops, but that would not get him any closer to Seven. He watched the snowplow struggle on the city street as he listened, until the noise was cut down by a louder voice: Jimmy the Recluse.

"Gentlemen, welcome," he said. His voice sounded different than the others, it was processed.

"For obvious reasons, I couldn't join you at Johnny's today, but we got important business to discuss."

He was talking to them from somewhere else, maybe a video feed from a television somewhere. That feed could be traced.

"Yeah, Jimmy always has us in the dark. But when he comes out, there's a big payoff," said Gino.

"That's right. That is why you are here. A payoff is indeed in the works. You are all invited to a piece of it, that is, if you can help get this operation off the ground," said Jimmy.

The men laughed it off.

"Why the hell do you need us?" asked Anthony.

"Because I need firepower, and as you all know, my men usually don't last the weekend." There was even more laughter between them.

"I need guns, with skilled hands to wield them. I know you boys just recently got your hands on some high priced gear, with a little intel from yours truly. Consider this me, asking for something in return."

"Alright, we're interested. What have you got in mind?" asked Vincent.

"We're hitting the largest bank in the city, in two hours," he said.

There was loud laughter.

"The Outlook?" the men laughed even louder.

"Jimmy! You're crazy. How the hell are you gonna do that?" Gino finally asked.

"That place is like a damn fortress," he said.

"It sounds like you boys are missing some balls." Jimmy was unimpressed by their reactions.

"I thought you would all like a little adventure in your lives. All this high living is worth nothing without risk. How can you deserve luxury if you don't earn it every now and then? This is your chance."

"Pretty funny coming from a guy who can't even step out of his cubby hole to get his own hands dirty, wherever that is," said one of the captains.

Jimmy grew silent, the men inside became nervous now. His temper was short, and killing a man for lesser insults was almost expected now. One of them decided to open their mouths after twenty seconds of dead silence.

"Even if we wanted to help you, two hours is almost no time to get ready. What could we do in that window?" the same man asked.

Jimmy did not respond. Paavo looked at the remote. There was a sense of tension in the basement. Inside, the captain who spoke the insult looked away from the television. His eyes were pointed down towards the floors. Jimmy the Recluse was staring directly at him from the faded glass. Another minute passed before he turned away from him to address the rest of the group.

"I understand your concern, but what if I told you that I have a guy on the inside already?"

The men were listening.

"My guy opens the vault and you boys move in and grab the cash," said Jimmy.

"There's going to be an open manhole that leads you out through the train tunnels, out towards the river."

"What about the cops?"

"My disposable men, as you say, will be there to draw their fire. All you need to do is grab the cash, and my guy on the inside, take him with. He's valuable."

"What's your guy's name?"

"Seven." said Jimmy.

The captains knew who he was.

"Getting a little famous, isn't he?" asked Anthony.

"We've heard a lot of good things, like that armored car job."

"Seven's been freelance for some time now, but is going places, this will make or break him, whether or not he opens the vault, bring him with you. He's either getting a promotion, or a bullet," said Jimmy.

Anthony shook his head in disbelief.

"Always life and death with you, huh?" he asked.

"You're goddamn right. Do any of us have time to waste? Maybe some of us. Most of you just sit around, get fat and line your wallets."

"What are you about, Jimmy?" asked another voice.

"Money is fine, but a little anarchy is always good," he said.

Paavo stepped out of the car and headed towards the restaurant. The driver in the black limo had his head down, buried in the newspaper. A rock on the street found its way into his hand. The window smashed with a loud sound. The voices began to stir from the remote. Men had begun to head upstairs. Paavo ducked into the back alley, a small detonator was aimed high. Annoyed voices and questions reached the top floor, just enough time to blow the sticky bomb beneath the back tires. He had placed it just before they were ready to jump on him. Paavo looked down towards the side exit from the basement to the alley, at least one of them would head this way. Positioned behind the nearby garbage cans, he waited. Anthony raced out from the exit and into the street to survey the damage.

"What the hell is this?"

Paavo hopped over the rail and made his way into the basement. The basement was dark with dim lights. A television in the back still held Jimmy's distracted face. He lowered the volume of the remote in order to avoid getting the attention of the man onscreen.

"Hey, what happened? What did you do?"

The driver outside was shocked, he had no clue what happened. Several phone calls were made for new tires. They made the poor man raise the limo and remove the busted wheels. The sticky bomb was small, barely noticeable against the matching silver of the back bumper. He hadn't used one in ages. The fact that it still worked was a welcome surprise. Paavo covered his head with an old hood from the sweatshirt underneath the suit jacket. The television was hooked up to a computer. It would only take a moment to get the upload address. He moved with the shadows towards the desk. Later on, he could cross reference it with any terminals used in the last six hours. Paavo produced a drive and inserted it into the side of the laptop. A few keystrokes started the trace program. The program was at forty five percent. Paavo looked at his watch. Thirty seconds. A man upstairs was on the phone, yelling in Italian. He could not make out the words outside of the profanity. It was getting louder. Mindful of the noise, his hand slipped inside his pocket and lowered the volume to nothing. It was too late, he was noticed. Jimmy finally got a glimpse of a man in black.

"Who are you supposed to be?"

Paavo was silent. He turned the television off. The program

finished just as the men were returning to the inside of the restaurant. The drive was placed back into his pocket. Paavo headed for the door, his right hand turned the television back on, and Jimmy's words of warning could be heard from afar as he hit the door. His face, blazed in anger, flashed back on the screen.

"You son of a bitch! I'll kill you!"

Paavo moved quickly to the car, still running. No one in their right mind would steal this broken down thing, even in the middle of summer. The car stalled for a moment before jumping forward with a hard push of the pedal. He joined the oncoming traffic, always busy in the early morning. The men from Johnny B's could be seen just getting outside, in search of him.

"Damn scavengers!"

"You gotta get some tighter security, Anthony."

The drive back to the office was halted by a meeting a couple of blocks down. Lau was pleased with the results. The café was nearly empty, outside of the usual sobering poet or failed writer sitting in the back with groups of cups, shaking off the effects of too much caffeine. The walls were painted a dark brown. It had the feeling of an old eatery from the 1930's. A white ceiling fan made crooked circles, trying to hang onto a loose nail. Paavo looked up nervously and moved over a seat or two to avoid it, just in case it decided to fall. Lau did the same a few minutes later. He showed no interest in the whereabouts of the Recluse.

"That's your own suicide mission, I only want Seven," said Lau.

"There's a chance he could be in the same place."

"Not possible, he wouldn't keep him close, not if he's ready to kill him that quickly."

"Should we head to the bank, then?" asked Paavo.

"I will be there. Let me know when you see him."

"Should I lure him outside?"

"No, better to grab him when the job is in progress. Are you going to go after Jimmy?" asked Lau.

"I'll think about it. See you in two hours."

It was enough time to do both, he decided. The drive back to the apartment was always hell until he reached the highway. The café was close enough to an off ramp to cut some precious minutes off from the trip. His elevator got stuck midway through its trek up to the top floor. The computer was hidden underneath the desk. It was a large piece of equipment. Somewhat of a rare find as well, which is why it had been hidden away, too valuable to replace. The whiskey and tea was of no concern, but the terminal was. It had been pieced together from other, more expensive computers, along with parts from old typewriters, keepsakes of Paavo's. After stumbling with the numerous cords, the machine lit the dark room with shades of blue and white. He decided to leave the lamp off. The drive was inserted into the side of the terminal.

The trace program was opened and put to the side. A map of the city was brought up and maximized to take over the whole screen. Paavo turned on the remote and let it run into the open port on the side of the monitor. This would provide a sample for the program to follow the source of audio to a specific location. Gino's loud mouth would make a map of any hideout in the city. It felt good to use the machine again, it sounded like an old typewriter still. Each key smacked the metal piece inside aimlessly with no paper to press ink onto. A mansion at the edges of town held another meeting and a game of poker for a few of the Mob's captains. They discussed the plan. Two of them were out, too dangerous. Gino was in. He said he would provide the guns Jimmy wanted.

"I'll do it. What the worst that could happen?" asked Gino.

"The guns could lead them back to you." said Vincent.

"Jimmy won't let that happen, the guns I'm using I bought from him."

"Not a good idea to use something given to you as an olive branch out in the open."

"He's all about living dangerously. What's the setup?" asked Gino.

"Don't know yet. He said to expect a call."

The trace software took the information and ran for a minute or two, before finding the location of the broadcast. It was midtown, two blocks from the bank Jimmy had targeted. This was huge, he thought, the location of Jimmy the Recluse. With a single press, a map of the street was replicated onto a sheet of paper, yellow with age and crusted edges. The directions were scribbled into his notepad and stuffed into his jacket pocket. On a whim, he decided to get some information on Lau. Nothing came up, not the business he mentioned, or anything with the name he provided. There was one man who shared a resemblance.

Paavo's computer was rare not only for its strange build made from new and old computers, but the modem, which allowed direct access to Police databases. Criminals could be researched without worry of leaving a footprint in their access history. The man was named Junpei Kotaro, arrested over three years ago for suspicion of armed robbery, no convictions.

It seemed the alias had been around for a long time considering the shelf life of most criminals in this city, there were robberies of armored trucks dating back almost two or three years ago, an intricate number sharing their namesake painted onto the side. He made notes and stepped out into the outside world. The car sputtered along as he drove back into the city. Endless cars battered the highway. He wondered why they hurried to get in front of him, only to slow down to a crawl. Time passed as each stop and go moment allowed him to watch the falling snow flood the city in shadows of white and grey. Skyscrapers hovered over the packed street like old giants, made of stone. The car sputtered along until his destination had been reached, he parked alongside the street opposite the bank. He walked towards the safe house.

Dead Square was the nickname given to the empty side of Perdition. There were too many cars, too many people driving in the middle of the street, businessmen and teenagers with no concern for traffic laws. It was impossible to walk without fear of getting hit. There was only one street that you took from one side of the square to the other, everything else curved around the Outlook bank and whipped your car back out into the side streets and towards the labyrinth of downtown. 23rd street was battered with snow and the scars of heavy traffic day in and day out. The potholes were wide and deep, many swerved to avoid tire damage. Broken concrete and cement revealed hidden edges, pointed like knives toward weary travelers. At the end of the corner sat The Great Hall, a place of worship that had existed since the origins of the city.

The architects of Perdition were smart enough to spread out its places of interest. They found a way to separate the most important centers of commerce and business to all sides of the city, leaving a derelict institution of religion at its center. Manufacturing was located more uptown, places like the Kirilov Building and other socially abandoned areas like the factory district, which sold huge military weapons and defense contracts. Dead Square held the most important bank. It was the keeper of all finances. The Outlook was constructed in the origins of Perdition. It was one of its oldest structures not owned by the Capotellis. Re-designed every five years, soon brick and cement were shoved over the layers of wood and nails. It was synonymous with dangerous traffic and a high cost of living.

No one could afford the price for one of the townhouses down here. Good living in Perdition seemed to coincide with wealth and favors. Everything had a uniform look, many of the adjoining buildings were painted the same colors, had the same adornments. Each building looked the same, every failing business and high priced apartment connected at the wrist. The workers in Dead Square had to migrate down here just as well as anyone. A nice business suit could cover so many secrets. No one here had anything to worry about, the grind of daily work, the commute back and forth, so many people bouncing off each other. There were quiet waves of frustration which lay beneath the professional dress and restless upkeep. Paavo felt it when he walked these streets along with them. The people of the city were waiting for something to change.

There was a phone booth down the block which provided a good cover. The snow began to pick up. He stepped inside and picked the phone off of the hook. Jobs like this usually require pay phones, since they can't be traced to a direct number. By the time they get there, you will be gone. He placed a directional microphone on the base of the phone. He loved these tiny machines, but he noticed he was running out. More would need to be made soon. He searched his pocket of any loose change. Nothing on either side. Paavo stopped to notice a lone quarter sitting on the table holding the phone. Someone was planning to use it. a call was going to be made to the apartment, maybe to keep tabs on the bank, or the status of the cops. This meant he was being watched. He decided to dial Lau's phone, he picked up after two rings.

"It's time to meet, I'm outside the bank. Your friend is holed up two blocks away," said Paavo.

"Really? Are you gonna do anything about that?"

"Maybe. If you want to get your man, you better come down then."

"Good. You work fast, Harker."

"How did you find out about Seven?" asked Paavo.

"I did some digging around. He always leaves a calling card.

A number painted in red and black."

"You found this where?"

"It was programmed into my computer. When I turned it on, I was greeted with the number and a message."

"What did it say?" asked Paavo.

"It said to prepare for the harvest. It was on one of my trucks as well," said Lau.

"Jimmy spoke to some of the captains about a joint effort on the bank, this won't be easy. He mentioned killing Seven if any mistakes are made."

"We'll make sure there aren't any."

"Why are you so worried about him?" asked Paavo.

"No reason for worry, plenty for getting back what's mine."

"Why not let the gangster kill him? The less blood on your hands, the better," said Paavo.

"Let's just say that the bastard is going to be coming with me. That's all there is to it."

"I think you're lying to me."

Lau was silent.

"What makes you say that?" he asked.

"Because you would have caught him yourself with all your resources. You would not have hired me to find him, but to kill him for you. The fact that you want him alone and away from Mob captains tells me that you want him alive and safe."

"Do you give all your clients the third degree like this?" asked Lau.

"Answer the question."

"If I had known you were going to play good cop, I would

have paid someone else."

"What is he to you? Family?" asked Paavo.

Lau was quiet for a few moments. There was hesitation in his voice.

"Damn it, Harker."

"What is it? What's really going on here?"

"He's not just someone who stole from me, he's my brother."

Paavo's eye reached a window of Jimmy's penthouse, there was a man looking out with a camera, its lens stretched out a good ten inches. He wasn't spotted, but like others on the street, he was being watched. The phone would be swept for any wires.

"Seven is just a nickname we had for him since he was a kid, along with his six brothers. We were named after the seven archangels. Our parents died young, never had anybody around to teach any of us right from wrong."

"Don't worry about trying to justify," said Paavo.

"We survived on each other's backs. I'm not saying that I'm totally innocent, but I'm no saint either."

Paavo looked out into the busy streets of Dead Square. Angry faces in their overpriced cars, struggling to get to their next aimless destination.

"No one is."

"He got caught up with Jimmy's men. I found out too late."

Lau was silent for a moment.

"You have to help me get him out of there," he said.

"Couldn't you give him a job in your line of work?" asked Paavo.

"He wouldn't take it. These are the signs of teenage rebellion; spitting on the coat and tie, the refusal of the desk job.

He's got his own mind, his own growing up to do. All you need to do is help me get him out of there. I'm no cop. I don't care about the Capotellis or Jimmy the Recluse. I just don't want my only family getting killed."

"Fine. We'll get him out. Get down here as soon as you can, we're running out of time."

Paavo left the microphone there and stepped out of the booth. He made his way into a nearby coffee shop and waited for one of his men to sweep it. The waitress inside asked him what he wanted to order, he excused himself, saying he was trying to warm up for a moment. Her face changed and she asked him to warm up away from her tables. Paavo nodded his head and asked for a glass of warm water. He didn't have money for anything else.

CHAPTER FOUR

A man in a suit made his way to the booth and looked underneath the phone, in the corners and inside the phonebook. The alleyway on the side of Jimmy's building had a large iron fire escape. The bottom level was too high to reach from the ground. Paavo moved towards the end of the alley and ducked around a corner and waited for the man to step out. Paavo held his breath.

"Get out of here! Go chew on some rats or somethin'!" The man screamed out as he grabbed a phone of his own and proceeded to dial.

"Jimmy, yeah, it was nothing, some homeless guy tried to make a call and he came back here to peek out of the trash," he said.

He swept snow off his expensive suit. His eyes followed the homeless man's run through snow with breath baited. The man soon turned around and headed back into the penthouse.

Paavo made his way back to the car. There was no way into the building. He would have to lure him out. There was pain in his heart. Running too fast, he thought, too quick, can't move like this, too reckless. He felt his chest clench up. Teeth gritted with every heartbeat, his breath slowed down to calm the blood. An hour remained before the bank job. The car was nearly out of gas but Paavo camped out inside with the blanket on the roof across Johnny B's.

He made careful movements to avoid further injury. He felt the usual warmth and wetness from his wound. Bleeding outward now, he laid back to rest, the windows were fogged enough to block anyone from looking in. The remote was turned back on and left on the dashboard. The directional microphone was usually good for a week if pocketed somewhere safe. It could still be squashed by someone's weight, or ruined if left in the wash. Otherwise, it would sit there tucked away and record every word a person said, until its battery died. The man could have found the microphone, but like others, they look for wires or earpieces. Paavo designed it to look like a piece of fuzz. No one could tell the difference.

Another thirty minutes passed with no sign of activity. It was going to be close. Paavo took a rag and wiped the condensation off the windows. The remote began to emit static. Lau suddenly appeared and stepped into the coffee shop. Static was a side effect of dual mics in the same area. Gino was waiting in the booth as the phone rang.

"Yeah, it's me."

"We're ready to begin," Jimmy's voice was calm and collected.

"Where are your boys?"

Both mics recorded their words. Paavo reached for the remote and lowered the volume on one of them.

"On the way, where are yours?"

"Here with me, the guns too."

"Good to hear," said Jimmy.

"How should we proceed?" asked Gino.

"At three o'clock, your boys are going to hold up the tellers." Gino looked down at the phone.

"What about your guy?"

"He's going to give you the signal, that's your spot to get the money. Hold down the front while they make the move. When they are done, you grab Seven and get out of there."

"What does he look like?"

"Brown hair, glasses. You'll notice him," said Jimmy.

Paavo stepped out of the car and headed toward Lau in the coffee shop. He flagged him down.

"It's time to go."

Lau nodded and followed him out towards the bank. They walked around the corner and made their way towards the next street. The stoplight took a few minutes to arrive at red. Some cars ignored it and barreled their way through. Paavo moved slower than usual, Lau looked back at him. He wasn't able to hide the pained look on his face.

"Are you alright?"

"Yes, I'm fine," said Paavo.

"Did you get shot?"

People heading for the bank had swarmed around them, busy on their way. The noise from the street crowded their voices. No one noticed Paavo sporting drops of blood onto the snow covered concrete.

"An old wound, hard to stay closed sometimes." Paavo moved ahead. Lau followed him, trying to avoid the drops.

"Don't worry about me, focus on your brother."

Lau nodded, refocusing.

"Outlook is one of the more prominent places in the city for key finances. It's going to be crawling with security," he said.

"I'm curious as to how they're going to pull this off," said Paavo.

"Right, did they say how many were hitting the bank?"

"No idea how many. There's going to be two teams we have to contend with."

"Are you armed?" asked Lau.

"Not really."

"You're a detective! How can you not have any guns?!"

"Guns aren't going to get him out of the bank. We have to be smart about this."

"We're going to get killed," said Lau.

"No, we're not. I know you have some weapons of your own."

Lau stopped him.

"What are you talking about?"

"Your name isn't even Lau," said Paavo.

"How the hell did you..."

"I told you not to worry. No crisis of conscience for me. I always find out who I am working with, whether they tell me or not. Let's go, Junpei."

Lau stood there in disbelief for a minute, he watched Paavo shuffle towards the bank, barely holding together. People were beginning to notice, they moved him as if he had the plague.

"Hey, stop! We can't go in there with you looking like shit."

"You're right, you head in. I'll be right behind you."

Paavo sat down on the ground and took a moment to rest.

"What am I supposed to do?"

"Tell Seven to get the hell out of there before they start."

"Alright, I'm going."

Lau took a few steps before turning back towards Paavo.

"Harker..."

Paavo pulled a piece of torn blanket.

"What now?" he asked.

"I'm not a criminal. Just someone who doesn't want their kid brother to fall down the same path."

"You've got fifteen minutes to make sure that it doesn't happen."

Junpei nodded before running into the bank. Paavo wrapped the piece of blanket around his chest and knotted it. Then and there, he had decided to see the doctor. This could not go on any longer. All the pain had to stop. Whatever it would take to stay alive, he would do what needed to be done. There were voices coming from the static remote, he pulled it from his pocket and raised the volume, there were two men talking from inside the phone booth. One of them placed a quarter inside and began to dial. The other loaded a gun.

"What is this for?"

"An electromagnetic pulse, once everyone's in the dark, the boys on the roof will move in from the top floor."

Paavo looked up to see a group of men readied at the edge. Junpei stepped inside the bank with nervous energy. The guards stopped him for a routine check. He looked around for Seven. The place was beautiful; marble and tiles made the bank look more akin to a Roman palace than a place to stand in line to cash a check. The architecture was carefully crafted. There were only two or three exits, all ground floor.

Seven was standing nervously in front of three steel vaults. His suit was too tight. Streaks of red surrounded his neck. There was sweat that somehow managed to noticeably stain a black business suit. He looked out of place immediately. Junpei yelled his name. He tried to look away.

"We've got to go."

"Jun, what are you doing here?! You picked the worst time to talk about this!"

"I had to find you! We have to get the hell out of here!"

Paavo listened to the remote. A truck began to make its way down the sidewalk, towards the bank. The phone rang three times before being picked up. Paavo headed inside before the first team stepped out. A young woman answered politely.

"Welcome to Outlook bank, my name is Julie. Would you like to inquire on your balance?"

A loud screech of noise was emitted before the line was cut. Lights turned off immediately. The street became dark. Cars stopped dead in the middle of the road. Paavo's static remote shorted out in his hand, shocking him with a serious jolt of current. The pulse had shut down the entire block. All of Dead Square was frozen in place. Paavo got to his feet and looked up to see the men on the roof repel down to the second floor. They were suited in blue with masks. They moved down the front of the building in seconds. Security readied for an attack and shoved everyone in line past the checkpoint. Paavo made his way up to the second floor to see people running in circles trying to escape.

The vault was open with no signs of the two brothers. Glass shattered behind him as the squad of men landed from the window. Their guns were locked on the bank workers. Paavo moved behind cubicles towards the downstairs exit, Jimmy's men stormed the floor. A stiff strike to the back of Paavo's head sent him to the floor.

"Where do you think you're going?"

A gun was pointed in the back of his head and a heavy hand dragged him back into light. The men had been too fast, he could not escape in time. The squad brought everyone into plain sight in the center of the room.

"Stay here, folks. We'll be out of your way in a moment or two. Thanks for your time."

One of the men stood near the window, he seemed to be distant from the group, watching them. The leader, he thought to himself. Blue suits took turns circling with their assault rifles, and tossing each other bags to fill with cash.

"Thirty seconds!"

Paavo remembered the plan was to draw the fire of the Police. The men would grab the cash and protect Seven from gunfire. They were taking money and stashing it in the corner near the marble staircase. Sure enough, the other team had arrived on the floor. One of them was the captain from Johnny B's. He remembered his voice; the one who insulted Jimmy.

"Where's the money?" he asked.

The leader of the squad spoke up finally.

"Some of the bags over there are ready to go."

Paavo looked around. He eyed some of the possible exits. There was no way he would get the jump on Junpei stuck here. The men in blue continued to load bags of cash from the vault. The bank workers were frozen stiff. They sat with their heads down, away from the men in blue. The captain was visibly nervous. Paavo looked up at him. His hands were shaking. Why was he here? Each man readied a bag over their shoulder and reloaded their weapons. The blue suits looked to their squad leader, he moved through the crowd of workers.

"No hostages. We keep moving. All you fine, upstanding citizens will be on your way in a few minutes."

A room behind the vault could be seen from Paavo's vantage point. That's it. That's where they went. Through the room and down through the sewers. The captain's team moved down the stairs, the nervous man was stopped.

"Not you."

The man turned around. His team stopped at the middle of the staircase. Some of the blue suits had approached with guns drawn. The leader waved his hand toward them.

"You guys move on, we need to talk with him."

The captain's men were unsure of what to do.

"Vincent?"

"So that's your name."

The leader moved to his side and spoke under his breath, just enough for him to hear, and no one else. Paavo watched them intently.

"Our leader has a policy for short tongues. He cuts them off and stores them in a jar."

"What do you want from me?" asked Vincent.

"We don't require apologies on our team. An insult to a man who has done so much for this city is like slapping one of our children."

"Jesus, I didn't mean anything by it. No disrespect to you or anyone. Jimmy is my friend, why would I insult him?"

"Why indeed?"

"Come on, what is this? We're running out of time. The cops will be here soon, we have to go!"

"Just for the record, you are not, nor were you ever Jimmy's friend. He has no time for people like you. Scum of the city, taking the traditions and reputation of the Capotelli crime family and dragging them down."

"Now I'm scum? What the hell is wrong with you people? What are you going to do? Kill me right here in the bank?"

A single gunshot echoed through the building. Some of the people on the floor were shocked. A few of them squealed at the noise, there was a collective shake in their bodies. Some of them had looked on as he was killed. Paavo sat in silence. All was quiet as Vincent fell to the floor. His team raised their guns.

"Vincent!"

They aimed for the leader's head. There was no reaction from him, only a smile on his face, unfazed.

"You sons of bitches!"

The rest of the crew stormed the top of the staircase, guns locked and loaded and pointed in their direction.

"Are you sure you boys want to do this?"

They were surrounded by every member of the blue suits. They had the high ground, no choice but for them to proceed.

"Take your money and go. Don't go looking for Seven. Follow the path down the sewers toward the dock, two left turns and right down an old corridor. It will lead you out to the harbor. There will be a boat for you."

Vincent's men were still. They slowly lowered their guns and began to take the stairs. The blue suits waited for them to disappear before leaving through the room behind the vault. Paavo slowly got to his feet and moved over the prone body of Vincent. Police were on the way. The sirens filled the background. This was the price for anyone who crossed Jimmy the Recluse. All were dealt with the same way. In his pocket held the piece of paper with the safe house directions scribbled in faded pencil. Paavo tucked it away inside the breast pocket of Vincent's black suit, now covered in running crimson.

The room behind the vault led to a security door, locked electronically. With no power, it had to be left open, which allowed safe passage into the lower level and down into the sewer through the service tunnel. The Mob used the tunnel for shipping money using some of the trains beneath the streets. Jimmy's men were ahead. Paavo stayed out of sight, trailing them until they found Seven. From his pocket, the remote echoed the noise from the last directional microphone. Volume was low to avoid alerting the men. Their voices could be heard, going over the score. A hail of gunfire echoed through the dark tunnel. There was silence, followed by footsteps.

There were familiar voices; Junpei Kotaro and a young man stood over the bodies. They quickly removed their guns and began to switch the cash from heavy bags into three large cases. Both of them moved with precision, they began to take off in a matter of minutes with the money. The tunnels moved directly into the storm drain, the temperature was unreal. Heat coated his body as he moved through the entryway. He had lucked out that the drain was the only way down into the train tunnel. The city left portholes open to stave off overheating of the pipes. The darkness and heat carried him onward. Beads of sweat dripped from his chest and neck, some found their way into his wound.

Paavo felt a sharp sting as they mixed with his blood and open heart and the taste of sweat on his tongue was thick. A train was oncoming, its lights approached with speed. Paavo quickly looked for an opening to squeeze into. There was a spot, beneath the girders that ran down the miles and miles of tunnel. He found a way in and waited for the train to go by, the sound was deafening. He watched the sparks and the flashing lights from underneath. How many of these people already know about the bank robbery? How many of these people really care?

The plan for escape was to follow the tunnel until the dock. Paavo found an open manhole, light beamed down from the sky. Falling snow entered the tunnel before melting into moisture from the heat. He climbed out and onto the street. Only blocks away from Dead Square and the Police, who had taken over the scene. Paavo took a breath and watched the lights of the squad cars, people had begun to crowd around to look on. An ambulance sat in front of the Outlook, a covered body was loaded into the back, the body of Vincent. Paavo moved down the street, towards the safe house to see a line of Police cars, commotion inside. The bodyguard for Jimmy the Recluse was pulled out into the open by two officers.

"Arrested on suspicion of murder and robbery of Outlook bank."

Paavo turned his head to hear Junpei's voice. It was coming from the remote. From the rooftop, the detective looked so small. He lit a cigarette and took a drag.

"It seems you found your brother."

"Yeah, we lost contact in the middle of our operation. Jimmy is a hard man to spy on. Too many handlers, the only real way to rip off the Mob is to get inside."

"Your brother's not Seven. You are."

Lau laughed and raised his arms into the air, as if being held at gunpoint.

"Guilty as charged. You're not a bad detective, Harker."

"Why hire me if you knew where he was?"

"I didn't. I only knew who he was running with. No idea which bank, no idea when. That's where you came in."

"Guys with masks crashing through the front window from the roof don't seem like the usual routine for a captain."

"Neither does the EMP, those men weren't expendable, that team came from someone else."

"Any idea who?" asked Paavo.

"No clue, maybe you can find out that one, as well."

"I wasn't expecting to hit me in the back of the head, either," Paavo placed his hand behind his head to cover the spot.

"Yeah, I saw that," said Lau.

"Were you hoping that I got killed?"

"I was, actually. The identity of Seven must be kept secret. Jimmy thought that he found a powerful ally. This was to be the proving ground."

"It's nice to know you work alone," said Paavo.

"You'll be alright though. Especially once you see the sedan across the street from you, the door's unlocked, open the trunk."

Paavo moved to the other side of the street carefully.

"Don't worry. It's not a bomb or anything," said Lau. The trunk opened to a stash of blankets, a spare tire, odds and ends.

"Look underneath."

Paavo lifted the blanket to see an envelope, packed tightly with money.

"The rest for a job well done."

Inside was more than the other half. It was double the amount promised to him in the beginning of the deal.

"Are you trying to bribe me to keep me quiet?" asked Paavo.

"If you went to the cops, my brother would have shot you."

He looked up to the roof of the next building, the younger Kotaro waved his hand gleefully, rifle in hand. Paavo waved back.

"He's been watching you ever since you stepped out onto the street."

"Is every one of Seven's jobs like this?" asked Paavo.

"No, this was the first. A little risky for my tastes, but for good reason. I am building a dynasty, a family business."

"I thought that he was too young for this, you wanted him to choose his own path?"

"You did so well. Don't disappoint me now, Harker. All part of the sob story."

Seven pointed out towards the people watching the cops. They were covered in snow, standing in place and shivering.

"Do you see them out there? Wasting their time? This is how the world works. People stop and stare at the drama around them. They never get the big picture. The storm goes on with or without you watching."

"I've never stolen from anyone," said Paavo.

"The Mob's not a bad place to start."

"I'm not like you."

"You take what you can get. Nobody should care about anything but their own problems. We all have to take care of ourselves. Spread the wealth while you still have the chance to. We will all die alone. Make your money and spend it all before the end. You can't take it with you."

Paavo looked down at the money.

"Take it or leave it, either way, enjoy yourself, Harker."

Seven turned around from his unknown location and began to walk down the street.

"See you around."

He was gone. The audio from the remote only replaying echoed footsteps. The young man disappeared from the rooftop and Paavo was alone again. A bitter wind blew across the street as he pocketed the envelope and buttoned his suit jacket. The sounds of a car approached him as he passed the corner.

A black limousine pulled up and stopped at the end of the street. Inside was Jimmy, who had ducked the cops at the last moment. Paavo looked at him. A glass of wine in hand, red silhouettes appeared as his face was illuminated. The driver looked back at the man staring deep into the glass. The red liquid kept spinning in circles.

"That was too close." The driver answered back with optimism.

"Hey, we made it. Giovanni put up the distraction we needed to get you out. That's all that matters."

Jimmy was quiet.

"It makes you wonder who tipped them off," said the driver.

"We'll find them. There's always something left behind, always a paper trail that leads you where you need to go."

"I have faith in you."

"A part of me feels regret for killing Vincent today."

"He disrespected you, boss. You told us all when you got the gig that those who don't follow know what's coming to them."

"But he was one of my own men, a fellow captain."

"Are you worried about your safety?"

"I crossed a line. One of the other captains may retaliate. We may have to go into real hiding, for a long time."

Jimmy looked out towards the street, he met eyes with Paavo. The car turned down the street. Power seemed to have been restored to the district. The lights lit his pathway down the street. Paavo walked beneath them, his shadow moved across the snow covered sidewalk, and snow littered the street as an endless dust of diamonds and light.

Should I take the money? He asked himself the question for hours. How easy would it have been to drop it to the ground, to hand it over to the Police, only blocks away. Seven had tested him by doing this, giving him more money than he agreed to. Paavo damned the thief for making him choose between the normal routine or dirty money from the largest bank in Perdition. Further easy living? Or perhaps not eating an actual cooked meal for a few days? He reached his hand into an envelope and counted the money in the middle of the open street. Three thousand dollars in total, he took half and placed it back in his pocket.

The envelope grew heavy in his hand after only a few blocks. Near the end of the street, was his car, still parked in the same spot. The snow plows had buried him in. He was stuck between a large minivan and an almost obnoxiously sized pickup. Paavo reached for his keys and opened the trunk to look for a shovel. He might have had one stored in here for the winter, anyone who didn't was fooling themselves into thinking travel within the city was going to be easy. Paavo took several deep breaths before carving a path. The snow was wet and thick, its color turned from white to shades of dark greys and browns with the mixture of mud. On the curb ahead were some beggars asking for change. They approached him.

"Hey man. How you doin'?"

"You got some money for an old veteran?"

Paavo ignored them and continued to dig himself out. The snow had to be lifted and tossed away in huge chunks.

"Hey, I'm asking for some money, you got any? I haven't eaten in days, man."

He stopped and looked at the beggars. He took a moment to breathe, and then tossed them the envelope, full of money.

"What the hell is this?"

Paavo went back to shoveling his car out.

"Look inside," he said. Both men opened the envelope and were overwhelmed by the amount of money. At first, they shouted in joyous voices, thanking him.

"What the hell?"

"It's yours, use it well."

Paavo waved at them before tossing the shovel back into the trunk and going towards the door to start the car. The two men stopped him, asking for more.

"I don't have any more money."

When he said those words, they laughed and asked him anyway. The same excuses he heard moments ago were tossed away for more extravagant stories to earn his attention. They began to pull on his shirt, his jacket. He felt their fingers reach into his pockets.

Paavo twitched and moved his body to avoid them grabbing the rest, including whatever little money of his own he had stored inside.

"Where you think you're going, rich man? What about my friends? You going to help all of us?"

Others from the alleyway had come around the car. They surrounded him with their hands outstretched. Paavo moved his hands nervously, unsure of how to protect himself. There were men and women, all asking for money. Some of them had smiles on their faces, they were laughing. Paavo finally pushed through the people. He looked down to watch their hands. He began to have visions of one of them stabbing him. Some of them were trying to shove their hands into his pockets to take whatever was inside. Those in front of the door tried to put their weight on it. Paavo shoved them to the ground and went for the driver's seat.

A hard fist connected with his jaw, he felt his knees buckle. The street was dark. A man in shadow threw a punch that split his eyebrow. Paavo fell to the ground. His body made quick contact with the asphalt and snow. He could faintly hear the muffled laughter of thieves. The hands covered each of his pockets. They took out his wallet and searched it. There were no credit cards, no cash, just an ID. The leather piece was dropped onto the ground and kicked out towards the middle of the street.

"There's nothing in here, what kind of shit is this?"

"Just toss it, man."

"Looks like you don't need this." His vision, still blurred from the attack, could see the shadows hovering above him, outlines of faces and figures.

"You got some nice clothes, man."

"Let us borrow some for a minute." His toes were cold. His shoes were gone, taken and tossed into a bag. They began to reach for his coat when a car horn had driven them off. Paavo fell in and out of consciousness for a few moments. His eyes opened at last to a gathering crowd. A dizzy spell came over him, a rush of blood to the head made him feel sick. There were hands, fingers that were poking and prodding at his chest and face, trying to wake him up. There were old men and women, staring down at him. Their black clothes gave them the far off appearance of a funeral procession. Snow hit his face, causing a flash of energy to jump through his veins. He sat up and moved to the curb of the street. The crowd moved back in surprise.

Desperation filled his hands, he swiped them forward. Trying to gain his bearings, he moved his hands out towards the darkness and damaged vision. They looked at him as though he had been trying to steal the air and keep it for his own. Questions interrupted the wind, he ignored them. Hands were outstretched to help him get back onto his feet. He pushed them back and began to remove around to the car door. The crowd stood in place like dolls. His skin was pale and freezing, Paavo moved with no natural rhythms, the mind was coated with fatigue, which bled down to the body. Almost half-alive.

"Are you alright? Those boys did a number on you, didn't they?"

A deep shiver shot through his body. He then realized that he stood barefoot in the dead of winter. One of the men in the crowd placed his arm around him, as though they were friends.

"Say, do you have some money we can borrow?"

Paavo pushed the man away in disgust. "Times are tough, you understand."

The street was soaked in dirt and melted snow. It took a minute to find the wallet. It was placed safely within his pocket. The man did not let up.

"Hey, where are you going?"

He threw himself inside, locking both doors. They knocked on his windows. He could hear some of them trying to open the doors to keep inside. He started the car and began to pull out onto the street. There were at least thirteen people hounding him. All this for trying to be generous. He felt embarrassed. What the hell had just happened? How desperate were these people? Why the hell didn't I just keep all that money?

The people did not move for him. He saw their eyes through the windshield. Angry, bitter eyes. Some of them spit onto the glass. A well placed elbow cracked the rear passenger window. He kept his foot on the gas and shoved his way out onto the busy street. Other cars had stopped and sounded their horns. He wanted so badly to just get out of there. The small crowd dispersed as drivers had begun to go around the crowd, causing noisy near collisions. They pushed and shoved, angry and wanting. Paavo looked at them, trying to understand why this was happening? Why couldn't they just take the money? They didn't even need to thank him. He pushed forward and down the street, silence soon took over the atmosphere, his anger subsided in time. The car had enough gas to take him where he needed. He thought about it long and hard at the next red light. Tomorrow morning, he would make that turn, not for the office, but towards the hospital.

CHAPTER FIVE

The room in the doctor's office was cold and white, a stark contrast to his preferred surroundings. A gleaming fluorescent light above revealed his pale frailty to the man in the white coat and eye glasses behind him. Paavo took a deep breath, he looked down to his spare shoes as he did so, feeling the hole in his chest expand and contract. He hated doing this, he felt like a child again. A hard wind blasted the windows. The winter had begun with a furious storm. Paavo began to think how the cold air would raise hell within his lungs. The doctor took notes with a fast hand, scribbling jumbles of words, what had to be observations.

"What took you so long to come to a physician?"

"I just figured that it was time," said Paavo.

He looked down at his name tag, Wiles, J. This doctor was young, he thought. Almost too young. A part of him had hoped an older doctor would have been here to check over his wounds. He wouldn't understand my condition. He'll just prescribe some half-ass medication to regulate blood flow. Some blood thinners, perhaps, it'll make me sleep for days, I'll turn into a damned zombie and get no work done.

"Can I see it?"

"How many times do I have to show you?" asked Paavo.

"I have to ask. How can I treat you if I can't even see what I'm treating?"

Paavo's heart was open to the doctor. The man's jaw dropped again. He was taken aback by the sight of a man's insides sticking out.

"Can you take a deep breath for me?"

He struggled but Paavo obliged.

"I cannot believe this."

The young man resembled a living, breathing autopsy subject. James Wiles had not seen a person's body in this fashion, despite his experience in the operating room. The hole in Paavo's chest opened to reveal parts of skeleton and muscle. When he exhaled, the covered heart quivered slightly, and a stream of blood began to leave from the side of a damaged vein and run down his ribs.

"It's beautiful," said Wiles.

Paavo began to regret coming here, by doing so, he may have exposed himself to a new curious medical community that would have no trouble subjecting him to many rigorous tests, experimental treatments and pills in order to fully understand this bizarre medical occurrence. He spoke again.

"Your condition is bizarre, and for lack of a better word, amazing."

He didn't like his tone, it sounded more curious than concerned.

"Thank you," said Paavo.

Doctor Wiles stared intently at the clipboard, holding the results.

"Is my life-threatening condition interesting to you?" Paavo asked.

"I'm sorry. I apologize, I didn't mean to offend but what I've come across is quite intriguing."

The storm had begun to pound against the windows. It was a deep thud against the glass. The sound bothered him, as if the pounding almost seemed to match his own irregular heartbeat. Paavo knew what questions would come next, and he got them out of the way as quickly as possible.

"Would you be interested in coming in for more tests?" asked Wiles.

"No."

"But this could be considered somewhat of a medical breakthrough."

"No."

"I understand your concern, Mr. Harker, but this could help you."

"I just said no..."

They were both silent. Wiles looked at Paavo with disappointment. He tried not to let it show through, but Paavo found it instantly. Some part of him enjoyed the doctor's frustration. He wanted to drag it out some more.

"I don't understand. Why did you come here if you did not want help?" asked Wiles.

"You don't have to try and save my life."

"That's kind of what I do for a living."

"I'm very busy. My work is very important and I don't have time to be your guinea pig, or a test dummy for future generations," said Paavo.

"It won't be that way."

"Just tell me what I need to know," said Paavo.

"I will, but there is so much more we can do to help."

"Give me a diagnosis."

"These tests will help you find ways to prolong your life," said Wiles.

"Suppose I don't have much of a life either way."

"What makes you say that?"

"I've already been chewed up and spit out by the health board and the rest of the community of this city," said Paavo.

"How could they ignore this?"

"They ignored it fifteen years ago, when I was labeled an unofficial medical anomaly, and shoved out into the street."

"There have been major improvements in heart and blood care since that time. Things are different now. No one here is going to turn you away from this place."

"They could have helped me in the beginning but it's too late to start now. My body is in a bad way. No starter kit is going to patch up this wound. I just need a diagnosis, please."

Wiles sighed. He fixed his glasses and looked down at his notes.

"Well, to be honest, it is amazing that you have survived this far without a proper treatment."

"But there is something else, isn't there?" asked Paavo.

"Your body is deteriorating at an alarming rate. The entry point in your chest has opened almost organically and is past the point of closing off. Edges around the wound show previous treatment, it shows me that those who treated you last used Liquid Skin."

"Sounds familiar."

"It's a kind of adhesive, a bandage system for large cuts, cutting off blood flow. It was pretty versatile, even useful for amputations. Since it's water based, it is a purely temporary means of closing the wound."

The doctor's words brought up memories of children covered in the substance.

"Skin isn't used anymore, in light of new advancements. But it's obvious from the boundaries of your wound that it's been growing larger as time goes on. As your body grows in development, so does the hole. The body reacts to protect itself. The lack of Liquid

Skin caused your body to develop a sort of new coating of cells over your organs inside. It allows me to reach in and touch that piece of your heart if I wanted to, and you, somehow you are not dead. What this means, is that your heart and your bloodstream are almost in direct contact with the oxygen around us."

Paavo put his head down, away from the white light, and closed his eyes.

"And?" he asked.

"Your blood has been beginning to coagulate from the introduction of this film that protects your insides. That explains your bleeding after taking deep breaths or coughing. The coating is your blood, slowly becoming hard, like a glass. Your body is slowing down."

Paavo looked towards the corner of the floor. He wanted to tell him to get to the point.

"The blood is hardening, flexibility will become physically taxing. Your ability to conserve breath and compress bodily functions and blood flow is unique, like nothing I've seen before." Wiles said.

He found himself staring at Paavo, in awe. His eyes closed again.

"It's difficult to say if you will continue to live this way for an extended period of life. The simple fact is that you are dying. Your body is beginning its slow collapse into itself."

Paavo opened his eyes, pointed them toward the doctor.

"How much time do I have left?" he asked.

The doctor's eyes met with his.

"The longest I can say, is nine months...maybe less," said Wiles.

"Nine months?"

"I'm sorry to tell you this, but it's the inevitable outcome of this disorder."

"How did you come up with nine months?" asked Paavo.

"Based on the age of the subject, hardness of blood, and the width and depth of the wound. Also, an average I calculated with others who have experienced the same affliction."

"You've heard of this before?"

"I have."

"How is that possible?" asked Paavo.

"I've been studying the Crimson for years, reading and searching for some kind of evidence to prove that it wasn't just theory. Trying to find what remaining journals and articles they are."

"I thought they burned all the records."

"Most of them are gone, but some of the stuff you can still find, lost somewhere online. This is the stuff of legend. There's never been a disease or condition that they've hidden away instead of exposing to the world."

"And what did they tell you?"

"They being 'the medical community or board of directors', you mean?"

Wiles used air quotes for those words. Paavo looked at him in disgust for a brief moment.

"The elder doctors considered people with the Crimson Disorder lost causes. There was talk of paranoia due to the fact that no one had a logical explanation for the condition."

"Lost causes? That should give you a reason why I haven't stepped foot into a hospital," said Paavo.

"With no knowledge of its origins, people had no clue for a treatment. Some were even worried about the spread of infection within other patients."

"You mean they were afraid of getting it themselves."

"I've never agreed with their ethics. As jaded as they may be, they were trying to protect others in the hospital," said Wiles.

"By kicking us out on our asses, they were trying to protect people."

"Some of the patients were really sick. They had no idea what they were doing at that time."

"How much reason is required to turn away fifteen half dead children?" asked Paavo.

"I won't try and defend them, Mr. Harker. The body is meant to fade and wither. The elders gave up trying to discover the secrets of this disorder. It's too bad that there are not more survivors of it here today."

Paavo looked away from him and turned to the window cutting them off from the blinding snow on the outside.

"Where they failed, we shall succeed though." Wiles said. He moved around the room, full of new energy, almost excited.

"How so?"

"I'm going to prescribe a treatment to you to prolong the coagulation of your blood."

Paavo raised an eyebrow.

"What kind of treatment?" he asked.

"It's going to be an injection," said Wiles.

Paavo immediately refused.

"I won't take it."

"And you have every right to say no, sir. Then again, I can always place you under hospital care immediately and indefinitely," said Wiles.

Paavo was getting hot now, the doctor had backed him into a corner, he would no doubt be tracked down by men in white coats if, in fact, he attempted to leave.

"Blackmail doesn't suit you. It doesn't mesh with your enthusiasm for saving lives." Wiles smiled at him.

"Whatever it takes to save one."

"You're a prick," spat Paavo.

"Are you saying that you're not worth the risk?"

"I've been asking myself that question."

Paavo had exposed himself to the public, and the doctor now saw him as a commodity to help his situation and clout in the hospital ranks. If he didn't play ball now, he would be studied and exploited again one way or another. They had his information, they would find him, and there was no choice. He looked up at the doctor. He knew he had to take it.

"I'll take it. But I'm not staying here, understand?"

"With this treatment, you'll be able to carry on your regular workload, although at a slower pace, and you'll be able to go home tonight." What kind of work do you do, anyway?"

Paavo looked away from the doctor as he spoke.

"I alphabetize insurance forms in a small basement office."

The doctor nodded.

"Nice, if possible, I would stay out inside until this storm passes." Wiles said.

But he was dying either way, maybe this treatment would help, he thought. Wiles produced a syringe and a bottle. The syringe was massive. It's edge, almost five inches in length.

"Look, it seems as though you have taken great lengths to hide this from your peers, maybe even your family."

Paavo said nothing.

"I will not try to blackmail you or track you down. This is all for you, I don't want to see any man die slowly like this. Whatever I can do to help, I will," said Wiles.

"You don't have to try and save me," said Paavo.

"I'm not. It's come to a point where we may not be able to, but it's worth a shot. I'm trying to make your life just a little longer. That way, you can enjoy some of it. Take 5 milligrams of blood, and inject it into the bottle. I need a sample from your heart preferably every twelve hours."

"Why?" asked Paavo.

"We need to learn your heart, study your blood. If a serum can be designed to treat this, the idea is to capture different stages of your body's daily process."

"What good will that do?"

"The effect should allow increased blood flow which could cause sudden fatigue and drowsiness that can be cured by long hours of sleep."

"Sleep is not an option right now," said Paavo.

"It's not much, but it will help you in this winter storm, the cold air will be fatal without some kind of treatment, even with your techniques, you will be very vulnerable."

The doctor breathed an air of optimism. He was silent a moment, Paavo then spoke up.

"I've always been vulnerable," he said.

"I apologize. I will leave you alone."

He nodded in thanks. The doctor looked towards his watch.

"Come back in a day or two. Take care of yourself Mr. Harker."

Wiles left the room, leaving behind a white towel and a small black case. He had closed the door, revealing a mirror, in which Paavo saw himself, different from this morning. That feeling of fleeting life was apparent more than ever. Nine months to live, he thought to himself as he opened the case, it held a syringe and a small clear bottle.

Paavo looked at the syringe and the bottle lying on the table. What he had said was true. The skeptics within the medical associations did neglect children like him, and many had died waiting in the wings. When they did take over, the old serum they gave the children was only experimental. Some were paralyzed, and some put into a coma. Paavo could not stand it. He left the hospital before the merger was complete.

The city officials were just another part of the corruption. The deaths of the children he grew up with were explained to the public in half truths. The parents of the dying children were paid off to keep quiet about the sickness and the hospital. Reporters attributed their untimely death due to complications in dealing with their respective disorders and to be just a part of the process. Wiles had confirmed to Paavo that this new serum he was to take now was only a refined form of the coma-inducing drug the children were given.

"The proper form of treatment regulated by medical associations...a serum designed to heat the blood, to create a system of flow in the bloodstream..."

Paavo would take the drug and fall into long hours of sleep and numbness. He felt the hole in his chest. It was now more than just a scar or novelty. It was his bane. Part of him wanted to leave and forget, get back to the quiet isolation of the apartment. The deadline was real. The clock was still ticking. Paavo grabbed the bottle and placed the syringe into the top, puncturing through the cap. He pulled the shot away from the bottle, pushing out the air and found himself staring at it. He looked at the mirror.

"You are going to die..."

Paavo pressed the needle through the hole in his chest. A deep pain cut into him. The bottle was filled with the necessary blood. When finished, he dropped the syringe. His hands caught the bed before his body could collapse. The crimson ran down his chest and to the floor. He was a dying man. Paavo struggled to rise.

He wiped the blood from his chest with the towel left behind by Wiles. The blood on the floor remained; a pool three inches in diameter and length, drying into colors of dark red and black. Paavo wanted to piss off the doctor for doing this to him. It was petty but he found it amusing to leave a piece of him; to leave behind some blood as a parting thank you gift. He put his black suit back on. His limbs began to tense up. He felt the muscles clench as he placed an arm through each sleeve of his shirt and jacket. He remembered Wiles said there would be severe fatigue in the body. Driving in the midst of a winter storm could prove fatal.

Having to take a nap every twelve hours will do serious damage to his plans. Paavo started to think how irrelevant safety and self-preservation have become. Would it matter if he drove in this weather? Would it matter if he walked home in this cold storm? Did it matter that he was still alive? Fully dressed, Paavo walked to the window and observed the storm that thrashed the city streets outside. The wind was blowing hard as ever. The morning had changed. The fleeting life that he held onto with silent dignity was gone. Everything would now have to be altered to slow down his death, which approached with every step and breath taken. He wondered if this was the right thing to do. Paavo didn't deceive Wiles or himself when he said it was time to find out. He walked past Wiles without saying a word, leaving the good doctor with a memento.

"You are going to die." He said quietly under his breath as he moved towards the door.

Minutes later, Paavo stepped out and walked through the hallways of the hospital. He tried to erase the room from his mind. The blinding white lights made him squint to see in front of him. The staring eyes of the patients, the cold floor, the sterile smells, were all overwhelming. He felt a deep sickness in his stomach as he walked through the hall with nervous footsteps quick and uneven in pace. He began to perspire. Sweat dripped from his forehead. His thoughts began to taunt him.

"You are going to die. Your blood will harden like stone, and your lungs will be filled with it, it will drown you, you will choke inside your own body, within your own blood."

Paavo walked faster, trying to outrun his own awkwardness. His words followed him like his own footsteps.

"The blood will freeze in your veins, your limbs will move slower and slower until they are unable to move."

Paavo laughed at this perverse way of dealing with his own fear. He imagined rolling on a white floor in agony; his stone blood pouring out. The vision was disturbing and yet, it felt alright to picture a violent death.

"Your heart will explode and you will be dead."

He felt a pain in his heart as he walked by the other patients. Paavo quickly ducked out of the hospital entrance and into the furious storm. The people left in the lobby stared at him with strange interest. Paavo took their glances for contempt. He looked up as snow blinded his eyes. He quickly made for the car. The air was cold, and the wind relentless. He held his breath until he reached the car. The muscles in his legs tensed from the fatigue.

The sample had drained him. Paavo rushed toward the car and stepped through piles of snow. He felt it enter his shoes and the legs of his pants, filling him with a harsh cold. He opened the car door and threw himself in. He released his breath and felt his lungs tear open. He clenched his fists. He contracted his stomach. The muscles tensed with pain and pressure. With slow expanding breaths, the pain subsided, the muscles relaxed, and he was alive again.

Long found himself in the heart of the city, breathing hard in the storm. He swallowed spit and surveyed the crime scene. The snow poured down as cars moved slowly in the surrounding black. The pool of blood before him stained the snow and concrete a deep scarlet. Someone was killed here, there's enough red to conclude that, yet there was no body. Snow fell upon the scarlet pool, mixing in spots of white with the dark red. The image was beautiful. It seemed as if the storm was covering the blood, hiding it away. There were no trails, no sign of dragging a body, no evidence of attack. There were no footsteps in the snow, yet the blood was fresh, like it took place minutes ago.

"Hey, it's the killer."

"Any idea what happened here, inspector?" The words came from two rookie officers.

Long didn't turn around to address either of them.

"No, this is something I've never seen before."

"What do you think it could be?" one of them asked.

"Don't know. I'll have to get a specialist here to get a look at this. Before you go, though...What did you call me?"

The first officer looked nervous. The other one just smiled.

"The killer. Everyone's talking about what you did the day before, that hotel shootout. Some of the boys down at the station said it was you were like a one man army," he said.

The first one spoke under his breath.

"Enough, man."

"They said it was a goddamn bloodbath." Long looked to the skies. His heart burned with guilt.

"I had to help. Those boys were pinned down," he said.

The officers had begun to bicker. His smile did not leave him. The other did not want to cause a commotion. They slowly moved away from the inspector, until he stopped the first one again.

"Do you think I'm a killer?" asked Long.

The kid was silent for a moment.

"I'm in no place to say."

"It's a yes or no question."

"We watched you from a distance. It was like a work of art."

"Don't look at it like that. We do what we have to do to survive. There's no glamour. Either we succeed or we fail," said Long.

"Yeah...I guess so. But no one is going to blame you. This city is hell, sir. Kill or be killed. No shame in that, either."

The officer moved away to leave the old cop alone, staring into skyless space.

"Sir? Are you alright?" asked another voice.

"I'm fine." Long said. He turned around to see no one next to him. The storm roared with black winds again.

Paavo opened the door leading into his office. The building was falling apart. Asbestos crumbled to the floors creating a fine mist. The place was all ancient green paint, wood warped and metal corroded. The place was sold to Paavo for three hundred dollars. The roof had collapsed three years ago which killed three people in the building. The remainder of the clients had left the building, leaving Paavo to tend to it. He set up his office and left the building in its state of ruin.

He replaced the roof and with instructions online. It had been kept alive through countless numbers of small payments to the landlord to keep from turning the place into another overnight gas station. The office was a mess; each corner held its own tapestry of cobwebs. The floors and windows shared the clouds of dust and dirt between them. Paavo felt a sense of foolish pride in ownership of that dirty little space, despite its flaws. He turned on the light switch near the door, the old lantern contained a light bulb that awakened in dim yellow, painting the room with dirt filtered light. He opened the heavy blinds over the windows. The storm could be seen through the slits.

The city was covered in white. The sun had ascended over the towers, giving light behind the clouds. The sky had evolved from the darkness into a blend of grey and blue. Paavo turned away from the window to his desk; a large piece of wood sitting in the middle of the office. Scratches and scrapes were etched all over its brown surfaces, covered only by the phone and answering machine sitting silently upon it. The machine's light turned red every other second. It displayed a number "2" flashing alongside the light. Paavo pressed the play button and walked over to the bookcase. The machine clicked several times before speaking in a mechanized voice.

"You have two messages. Message one. Wednesday. Seven. Thirty. A.M."

"Hey there, stranger, it's Derek."

Paavo's eyes widened when he heard Long's voice.

"I don't mean to interrupt your morning brooding but we've got something for you to look at."

"Bastard." Paavo said.

"Come down to the city as soon as you can, I'll be here for about two hours before I head back to the station. It could be time you came out of hiding, friend. Take care."

The machine made several clicking noises. Long was a friend to him long after his stretching incident at the station. Paavo's ways were strange but useful; an asset during the most complicated of cases. Paavo had always been the first one that Derek called on to investigate crime scenes, collecting evidence, analysis, anything that Long needed. In return, Paavo was given a sort of immunity, allowed to conduct his P.I. business without interference from some of the force, who had taunted Paavo ever since he met them. A few of them would never let Paavo work freely without harassment. Long defended him from the older officers. Regardless of his attitude, Paavo had always been grateful. He had decided to see Long at the crime scene. The fatigue set in a little more. Nothing has changed, keep going, he spoke to himself. The machine began again, first with clicking noises, and then it's slow, dissected voice.

"Message Two. Four. Twenty. Two. A.M." "Hello? If this is the detective can you please pick up?"

The voice was shaken and nervous. She was full of fear.

"I need help. Please I can't talk right now."

There was a wave of sorrow that seemed to pour through the machine. Paavo's mind cleared. There was heavy breathing between each pause.

"I didn't know what else to do. I decided to contact you because my daughter is missing. Please help me."

There was the sound of tears and weeping. There was familiarity. He quickly removed those thoughts of fatigue. He had a new purpose.

"My address is..."

The old woman left her information.

"The name is Aki. Please."

The machine clicked again. There was a sound of a tape rewinding. Beeps.

"You have no new messages."

The light turned off and Paavo held his breath again to face the threat of the cold. Directions to the crime scene were easy to come by. He followed the colors that stuck out from the early morning grey. The radio was covered in a slick static. The noise slipped in and out interrupting commercials and the rushed words from the newscaster who came in not without interference from the telephone wires and passing gadgetry. Every street picked up the scrambled signals from another's phone. He caught bits and pieces from nearly every other station in reach.

"Another victim of a fatal stabbing was reported last night..."

"Mysterious figures in white have been spotted on city rooftops for the past few days..."

"Strange activity reported in the financial district. Several messages were found written into the crawl of the daily stocks..."

"This, along with several shutdowns of the grid's power supply, leaving groups of major buildings without lights or power, lend weight to the theory of hackers attacking our fair city..."

There was always talk of death in the media. That was its obsession, its way of keeping an audience captivated and always watching.

"Gas prices are at an all time high, with this weather expected to continue for another two weeks, the endless winter is proving to be another test for the people of this city..."

He soon reached for the volume knob. Paavo had felt the desperation of the people first hand. The beauty of the landscape had become more mechanized. Prosperity soon turns into an obsession for the best and the shiniest things. The most expensive clothes, cars and other forms of greed had taken over the people and the media.

Two years ago, Paavo had only wanted things to improve. The city had not improved. People became accustomed to chasing a sense of success. Where were they now but in a high priced metropolis, too expensive to live in? There was nowhere else to go to meet their staggering demands. Paavo and Long met at the end of the street. It was a silent corner amidst the scramble of flashing lights and sirens. It had been more than two years since Paavo had disappeared. The reports at the station called it a discharge, but he knew that he'd been fired. The phone call hadn't changed his mind about helping the cops again, but Long needed him.

There was an exchange of serious eyes between them. For Long, nothing had changed.

"It's been a long time. You look like hell."

"I can't say that I disagree with you," said Paavo.

A loud laugh was uttered from the inspector, followed by violent coughs from Paavo.

"Let me show you around," said Long.

Paavo was led to the crime scene. After an hour, the picture had remained the same. A deep pool of blood beneath the corner street light. The fallen snow had found its way into the pool, forming shapes of pink and white. Paavo surveyed the area and began to question.

"No footprints?" he asked.

"None. Even when we arrived, there were no prints or signs of movement in and around the street," said Long.

"Unless you think someone driving in a car randomly spilled a bunch of blood in the middle of the sidewalk."

"I was thinking more like a helicopter or small biplane," said Paavo.

"Could be a gang of some kind." Paavo's eyes widened as he

spoke.

"A group of angry test pilots? Maybe some drugged up fiends who take to their used compact and traverse through the night to splatter blood across dark streets?" Paavo suggested.

"I thought you said it was a helicopter?" Long laughed before lighting a cigarette.

"I think they need a menacing name of some kind," said Paavo.

"Don't be a dick. I guess you don't know what to make of it?"

"Have you taken a sample of the blood for testing?" asked Paavo.

"There's someone looking it over at the lab now," said Long.

"Mind if I take some of my own?"

"Be my guest," said Long.

Paavo moved towards the blood. He reached for his flask in the breast pocket of his trench coat. He opened it and tasted the remnants of what was inside. Black tea. It chilled his throat as it slid down. Paavo felt familiar ice in his chest. It soothed him for a second before returning to the bitter cold.

"Drunk ass," said Long.

Paavo looked back at Long with emotionless eyes.

"Jealous? It's a shame that you can't drink on the job and all."

"Who said I wasn't?" asked Long.

Paavo slid the flask across the edge of the pool a few times. Its silver finish shined underneath the artificial light. He made sure to get everything inside clean and none of the sample on the outside of the flask. After a few swipes, he closed the cap over the top, placed it back inside his breast pocket.

"Nicely done. Why don't you come to the lab with us?" asked Long.

"Do I have to?"

"We can take my car," the old man waved him along.

CHAPTER SIX

Long showed him to the car. It took time to warm the seats. Paavo watched the forensic crew clean up the site through windows wet with melting ice and snow.

"How's your family?" asked Long.

Paavo eyes rolled to the side.

"The same," he deadpanned.

"How so?" Paavo turned to face him.

"Still there, in the village."

"And the garden?" asked Long.

"It's not much, but it's something to keep her away from this."

"Even in this storm?"

"It doesn't snow in the village, it just gets cold. The garden wilts and fades and she brings it back to life," said Paavo.

"Is her sight getting any better?" asked Long.

"She's been blind for years."

Paavo's eyes kept on the outside. The scanner filed the car with noise; irritable chatter, numbers and codes, reports of downed power lines and outages. Paavo stayed quiet, focused on his heartbeat. He slowed his breath and counted the beats. The pattern was still irregular. He closed his eyes and drowned out all sounds. Paavo contracted the muscles in his chest and stomach. He felt the beats of his heart line up for a few seconds. He was interrupted by the revving of the car's engine.

Long signaled that it was time to go. The cleanup crew was finished. All that remained was the falling snow. The cruisers followed each other then spread out on different routes. Paavo watched the streets blur past the window. Long move quickly down several side streets to speed towards the station. The old man began to speak, his delivery was almost robotic as he focused on the road, speeding through and around early morning traffic.

"We should be there in a few minutes."

Paavo looked at him irritably.

"Why did you ask me to come down here?" he asked.

"This was as bizarre as things get around here. I figured you could help us," said Long.

There seemed to be an air of hesitation with his words.

"I thought maybe you needed the work or something."

"You're lying," said Paavo.

"Look, it's been a long time."

"Did you miss me, sir?" asked Paavo.

"Yes, you little bastard. Listen, things are getting hectic. We could use a hand in some cases, odd jobs here and there. You do need work, don't you?" Long asked.

"No, actually. I might be working on something."

"Really? You haven't had a steady job since when?" asked Long.

"It doesn't matter. I get around either way."

"So, someone actually called you?"

Long asked as he turned sharply at the red light. Several cars stopped suddenly as they barely made the turn. There was a blast of loud horns. Paavo kept quiet about the job at Outlook bank. The cops were all over it. No one needed to know his involvement with the theft, willing or not.

"How long have you been working on this one?"

"I just found out this morning," said Paavo.

Long was dumbfounded as he returned to the view of the road.

"This morning? You get a phone call and you haven't even replied?"

"No. We haven't met face to face yet." Long looked quickly again.

"Not exactly work, then."

"She doesn't have a cell," said Paavo.

"Call was from a pay phone."

"You could tell?" asked Long.

"There was hard wind in the background. She took breaths between her words. She was feeling the cold."

"Which could mean little to no money to be offered."

"It's a job, regardless."

"Still sounds a little bizarre to me. What's the score?" asked Long.

Paavo furrowed his brow.

"I don't know, actually."

"You really do have a talent for attracting the mysterious."

Paavo nodded silently to himself.

"Make sure this isn't some kind of sick joke. Watch yourself."

"I always do," said Paavo.

There was a short silence before Long spoke again.

"You know, the wife is making dinner tonight. You should come over. She asks about you all the time."

"Consider it done."

An invitation to dinner caught him off guard. He hadn't expected this. It was a welcome change to be around good people. The car sped swiftly around the station and into the underground parking garage. Long made several turns around stone pillars. The lights were dim and coated the area in a yellow shade. The old man found a nice spot in the shadows and parked in a spot between two squad cars. Paavo was impressed. For an old man, he could still drive like a madman. They left the car and walked quickly inside. The lobby was quiet and cold. The people were barely awake. He remembered the highlights; the routine shuffle of feet, voices across hollow hallways, shattered reflections in the shiny floor tiles, blinding fluorescent light. Long led him through waves of people, cluttered desks, past the department boardroom to the forensics lab.

The lab was cut off with panes of glass, rows of computers and measuring devices. The windows were covered with white shutters rolled up, letting angled trails of light into the room. Paavo stood alone in the corner before he was led to the inspection table. A wiry fellow introduced as Kenta Yamagishi was busy entering information on the terminal next to the sample taken from the crime scene.

"Inspector, you grace us with your presence," he said.

"This is Paavo Harker, a detective, one of the best." said Long, pointing in his direction.

"One of the best? Seriously?" asked Paavo.

Yamagishi was not deterred. He moved with strange body language. He slid around a table and quickly bowed towards the detective.

"Greetings, Mr. Harker. Feel free to look around."

Long grabbed the notes taken by hand from the side of the desk. He read it closely while asking questions.

"Well, what have you got?" he asked.

"I analyzed the blood taken from the crime scene."

The back of the room was coated in an orange light. There was something on the windows.

"You found who it belongs to?" asked Long.

"No, there was something laced," said Yamagishi.

The orange glow was created by film negatives placed over the window. Behind the desk, two young women shot up with black leggings, wrinkled white coats and gleaming smiles.

"Hi there!" said one.

Paavo stepped back slowly. He looked at their name tags. Kuriyama was a lanky creature, with thick, black glasses to match her eyes and hair.

"Hello, detective!" said another.

Motoko was shorter than Kuriyama; medium build with even thicker glasses, a shade of brown through her hair. They stood smiling and waving at Paavo. He looked at them with a raised eyebrow, put his hands out and slowly moved back towards Yamagishi and the inspector.

"What was it?" asked Long.

"Ammonia and lots of it," said Kuriyama.

The old man was disappointed.

"How much was there?" he asked.

"Enough to render the blood useless. The program has been coming across a lot of errors these days. I may need to stab it a few times, and leave it in a pool of ruined motor oil on a street in the middle of winter, eh?" asked Yamagishi.

He looked to Paavo for a smile, but saw him slowly backing away from his assistants like they were diseased. He returned to the screen, sighing.

"Anyway, it had to have taken place about less than two hours ago."

"How do you know that?" asked Long.

"The blood was still warm when we found it, even in the snowstorm." Yamagishi said. He fixed his glasses.

"Our analysis has several different methods of determining conditions and scenarios." The tech was irritated by the system delay.

"Using measures of viscosity, fluidity and comparing it with samples provided by a living body."

Long looked puzzled.

"What the hell does that mean?" he asked.

"It tells you the age of the blood, changes to its physical properties; telling you when the crime took place. It's called lividity," said Paavo.

"But what does that have to do with the actual crime?" asked Long.

"It means that this person was attacked and bled out onto the street. Someone had to have heard a noise and reported it right away," said Paavo.

He looked towards Yamagishi to make sure he was correct.

"This happened almost instantaneously, whoever it was, found a way to remove any traces of their activity. No prints of any kind. And there may be something else in this blood affecting its properties, but the chemical is making it difficult to test."

Yamagishi nodded in agreement. Long was impressed.

"The belief in the survival of the dead brought about the practice of offering food, spilling blood at the grave, as acts of piety or worship of one's ancestors. In case, you needed a possible motive," said Yamagishi.

"I suppose we'd better get to work on this," said Long.

The old man took Paavo out of the lab and into the lobby as the tired technicians took to their stations to begin cross referencing the name with official city records. It wouldn't take long to find them. Hopefully when they do, they'll be alive. Long's face changed as he turned the corner to an empty hallway.

"Jesus, did you see all that blood?" he asked.

"I know," said Paavo. His eyes lowered.

"Do you think they could be alive?" asked Long.

"I don't know. There could be a chance. But we know nothing else."

"What're you going to do with the sample you took?"

"Nothing as interesting as you've got in that lab," said Paavo.

"The people or the methods?"

"Both."

"They're good people, a little strange, kind of like you," said Long. Paavo rolled his eyes and muttered to himself out loud.

"When can I turn in my application?" he asked.

They stopped at the front door of the lobby near the parking lot.

"Don't play with me, I might just hire you," said Long.

Paavo moved closer to the inspector, lowering his voice.

"What happened to Ido?" he asked.

Long looked around. "Ido is in prison now, thirty five years for perjury and sale of illegal weapons. I've been in control of the station since then," he said.

"How does that kind of power feel? I imagine you've squandered all influence and reputation in hopes of control of the city as well," said Paavo.

"Not a chance in hell, especially with the lab rats back there now working full time. They may look a little mousy, but they're talented."

"Where did they come from?" asked Paavo.

"They were university students, here on an internship from overseas. At the same time, pictures had surfaced showing Ido meeting with the patriarchs of the Capotelli crime family."

"Why would Ido become involved with the Mob?"

"The rise in crime made him believe that heavier guns, more expensive hardware were the answers. Apparently, they had been in talks for longer than we thought. Ido handed over Police secrets for a lesser price on his guns," said Long.

"Seems more idealistic than criminal."

"The problem is that we knew about it, but did nothing. His heart was in the right place. None of the old veterans disagreed with the state of the city. We always lacked the right kind of money and representation to do our jobs properly."

"Don't make excuses for poor leadership," said Paavo.

Long changed the subject.

"Do you remember John Masonori? He was the federal agent brought in for one of the last cold cases you helped us with," he said.

"Vaguely."

"He had come to us in private, stating that Ido was under investigation. He wanted us to work for him in collecting some evidence for his case, part of the deal being that we would have to volunteer to assist him find evidence against our boss. I remember him saying that our loyalty would not put us in jail, but would put us out of a job. It killed us to agree to sell out our own boss, but we had mouths to feed as well."

"Corruption begets corruption," said Paavo.

"The lab rats were the first to agree to assist in the investigation. They found the paper trail, which led all the way up to the Chief of Police, and the case wrapped up in a matter of days."

"That must have been what weakened the Capotellis."

"So much that they resigned to leave their power in the hands of a younger individual. In one of the photos, there is a kid in a tight fitting business suit. It's rumored to be the only picture of the youth who grew up to become Jimmy the Recluse."

Paavo knew what he looked like now.

"Masonori was awarded all kinds of medals, pomp and circumstance. The city officials asked him to stay on as the Chief of Police and he agreed."

"You work for the guy who put your boss in jail?" asked Paavo.

Long nodded.

"The lab rats were given positions here as forensic scientists. Masonori asked me to be acting commissioner, until someone more qualified came along," he said.

"That's insane, who else would there be?" Paavo asked.

"No one since the veterans took cuts in pay, demotions in rank to avoid putting Ido behind bars."

"You're an officer, not a bureaucrat," said Paavo.

"I know. Kyoko and I have been saving up for plane tickets and a little vacation home, out of this city. As much as I love it, the darkness is all around this place. The devil lives in the hearts of many here, and we deserve peace in our twilight years."

A tired, defeated look came over the inspector. Paavo looked to the ground.

"Are you taking me back to my car?" he asked.

"Yes. I assume you're going to the woman? Take care, will you?"

"Always."

"Dinner tonight?"

"Yes."

They parted ways, Long hobbled slowly back into the crowd of suit and ties and Police. Paavo stopped him.

"Hey, old man."

"What is it?"

"You've seen this before, haven't you?" asked Paavo.

"What do you mean?"

"I'm talking about a pool of blood left in the middle of the street, with no record or ID on who it came from? Is that why you called me back? Because people are starting to disappear again? Just like they did last time?"

"You still haven't gotten past that, have you? Still searching for them?" asked Long.

A sense of tension entered the air. Paavo looked down toward his hands which slowly became clenched fists.

"I never stopped. Unlike you."

"I can't believe you never let that go," said Long.

"That kind of blemish on your department's record isn't something you should brush off. Maybe that's why no one here respects the police. You forgot about those people. I never did."

"But you never found them, did you?" asked Long.

"The search is ongoing," said Paavo.

"A group of people go missing in one day, and you've been

looking for them for, what is it, two years now?"

"There were close to fifty people reported missing in a single day. No blood, or prints, or witnesses. They vanished into thin air."

"I remember, but what can we do about it?"

"We keep looking," said Paavo.

He turned around and stepped out into the parking lot. His face reflected off the glass in the revolving door. He felt a strange stab at his heart. He was unsure of what he wanted to do. He thought of the message from the office. The last names were the same. It haunted him. The woman was pleading for help. He did not want to go. He felt like dying then. It had been too long since Paavo had taken a case. A few months of obscurity and the interest in his service had dwindled until he found himself without work, without money or food. Paavo's mind raced. He moved quickly through the streets lost in thought. Now there was a reason to step outside besides the counting of the death clock.

The decision was made. He would go. The car made straining mechanical noises as it struggled to start in the intense cold. He let his breath out slowly, his chest heaving. Some sick bile was caught in his throat, and he coughed a little. He could not restrain it in time, he felt a familiar burning and tasted blood. Grey now was the sky as Paavo drove to the address provided by this Aki woman. The heat of the car had calmed his nerves, and brought his body back to a subdued state. The blood in his mouth had traveled up from his lungs, there was more than he expected, his mouth filled quickly with it. He kept it inside for as long as he could. He played with it, rolling his tongue around in the red muck. He grimaced at the taste of iron, stale in his mouth. He had found the address. The car had stopped a few feet from the front door of the house. Paavo had to gather himself, to focus his breathing, or the blood would continue to flow from the internal wound. He held in his fill of breath with his nostrils. He opened the car door and walked towards the door. It was a small, run-down building.

He remembers living in a place like this. A home was still a sanctuary, regardless of the conditions. There were no signs of anyone home; some of the windows were broken, covered in plastic tarp and taped to the wall. He could see through the tarp into the living room. Paavo spit the blood onto the snow-covered grass, turning it a bright red. He knocked on the door. There was some stirring inside. Paavo waited there courteously, yet his throat and chest were burning from breathing in the cold air. It was murder for him, but he held it. There was a second knock. He had to close his eyes to fight back tears from the pain. Finally, the door opened slightly.

"Who is it?"

"Paavo Harker. Are you Miss Aki?" he asked.

"What?" she asked with sudden fear.

"You left a message asking for help,"

She looked nervous to speak.

"About your missing daughter?" asked Paavo.

"Please come in, I'm sorry."

She opened the door. She was an old woman. A blue blanket covered her pajamas and pink flip-flops. Although he was angry, it was internal, waiting in the cold left him in pain. His anger left quickly when he made eye contact with the old woman. She looked at his face. He put his head down.

"May I take off my coat?"

"Of course," she rattled.

They stepped into the front room. The lamps were turned off, the grey from outside filling the room with a murky darkness. She smiled.

"Sorry...no lights."

Paavo nodded.

"It's ok," he said.

He saw the deep sorrow in her eyes. Miss Aki kept a courteous air, as if nothing had happened at all. She hid her sadness, her fear. She hid them well. He kept his head down mostly as she slowly ambled through the front room, toys and papers look like they were tossed all over the place. He placed his coat under his arm and followed her into the kitchen. It was a mess; dirty glasses and plates covered the surrounding tables, bits of spilled food and drink were spotted on the floor. She must have been like this for weeks, he thought to himself. There was a pot on the stove, steaming. She turned to him.

"I was making tea when you came, would you like some?"

"Yes, please."

She turned toward the sink and searched through the stacks of wet cups and dishes, after a few seconds, she held up a clean cup. Paavo pointed towards one of the chairs.

"May I sit?" he asked.

The chair creaked as he sat down. She tipped the pot and poured the tea into the cup. She added some sugar and milk while telling Paavo the story of the tea and its origin.

"My mother made it this way. I liked the taste. I make it the same way for my daughter."

She handed the concoction to him. He tasted it. The sugar was too much, too sweet for him. He closed his eyes to simulate a good reaction to the taste. He smiled briefly.

"It's very good," he said as he placed the cup down, taking up the pen and notes from the pocket in his suit jacket.

The old woman's smile disappeared slowly.

"Tell me about your daughter."

Her head looked to the floor. She fought back tears as she spoke.

"She's small; black hair and eyes, thirteen years old. She's a good girl, you know, when you meet her you'll like her. Her name's Naoko."

Paavo put his pen to the notebook.

"It's such a pretty name don't you think?" she asked.

"Yes, it is. How long has she been gone?"

"Five days? She was playing with her dolls in the next room before running out to join her friends in the snow. I was making breakfast. She never came back," her hand covered her eyes, there were small sobs.

"What was she wearing?" Paavo asked.

"A white dress. I made it for her. It has the ripples in the sides. She had a flower in her hair, picked it from ones in the park. In the summer, you know, we put it in the freezer and left it there." She smiled a little bit.

"Naoko took it out and put it in her hair, it looked so pretty. It looked just like it did in the summer."

Paavo took a drink of the tea. He swirled it around, used to the taste now. There was so much he could say. He wanted to tell her that he would find her. A promise would do much to help. But he refused to lie, refused to set someone up for disappointment. He felt alone. There was a pressure building in the back of his neck, and it was difficult to breathe.

"She didn't have any shoes in the house. I can't imagine her walking on the ground outside now for five days," said Miss Aki.

Paavo felt a wave of fatigue come over him. It was sudden, his eyes closed and opened again slowly. He tried to keep his eyes open, to appear awake to Miss Aki. It had to be blood loss. The effect had begun, but he couldn't leave yet. He needed to see Long. He needed more information, she had not given much, but enough to start an investigation. He slowly drank the last of the tea.

"Do you have any idea where she might have gone?" he asked.

"No...We would go to the nearby park every day in the summer...but it's too cold to go there now. Church is too far a walk." she said.

"Do you think anyone could've taken her?"

"I don't know. We don't know any bad people. No one gives us any trouble. We don't have anything that someone would want to steal. She's just a little girl. Do you think someone kidnapped her?" her voice trembled with new fear.

"I don't think so, I'm just asking questions," he said.

The room was a deep grey. He needed to see the room where she was taken.

"Can you show me the room?" he asked.

"Yes...it's here."

She took him to the room and opened the door. It was a child's bedroom, the sheets and cover lay on the floor. The grey and cold wind outside poured into the room from the open window. She flipped a light switch and the bulb above their heads blinked on. It was an old bulb, with little energy inside, the room was barely lit. Paavo kneeled down to look at the mattress. Miss Aki saw his face, hidden in the shadow of the room as he looked over the bed.

He noticed something about the mattress itself. He realized that someone else had been there. There was a small cup on the nightstand. He looked up to see her face. She looked afraid for a moment.

"Did you ever call the cops?"

"I did. They came and took pictures, said they would fill out a report and would notify me if they found anything."

"That was five days ago?"

"Yes, please tell me. What is it? Do you see something they may have missed? You will help us, won't you? Please tell me you will help us. Please help me find my daughter."

The old woman began to cry. She moved towards Paavo and buried her head into his chest. He stood still. Part of him wanted to tell her about the search now being conducted, about the massive and bizarre pool of blood in the middle of a busy street with no visible footprints. All he could do was hold the old woman in his arms, wrapped deep in a black sorrow. Paavo asked for more tea. He drank it faster than before, trying to warm his heart for the outside cold that seemed to be creeping in through the makeshift windows. Miss Aki sat closer to Paavo and he struggled to make a brief sad smile. He hoped that news of the search and the crime scene wouldn't reach her, at least until he found out enough information to add to whatever Long's people find.

He thanked Miss Aki for the tea, and stepped out quickly into the cold, holding his breath. Looking back, the old woman was standing in the dark wind and snow. A sort of bewilderment came over him, so weak compared to an old woman who's just lost her daughter. Stumbling to the car and struggling with the keys, Paavo tossed himself into the car while fighting off fatigue from the shot and vicious chest pains. He began to cough wildly as the steam left his body. He let the cool air into his lungs and he tasted blood as he started the engine and began to drive back to the office for his supplies. Still more work to be done. At least there was dinner to look forward to.

The snow continued to fall as Long stared at the city streets. His window fogged with moisture and white. He saw visions of the men from the hotel. He remembered their faces, moments from the final gunshots that finished them. He felt tremendous guilt. It had to be done, he thought. The girl would have died, I would have died. There was a knock at the door, He did not answer. Chief Masonori stepped into the room. His suit was a mix of grey stripes against dark blue. A damp trench coat and hat folded at his side.

"Derek? How are you?"

"Falling apart, as usual," said Long.

As the acting Commissioner, he had the responsibility, and the accountability of everyone underneath him. Their mistakes were his own.

"Rough day so far, wouldn't you agree?" asked Masonori.

"How do you figure?" Masonori stepped to the same window.

"A bank robbery, a hotel shootout, at least one hundred cars backed up along Dead Square, four blocks of office buildings downed due to a power outage and a pool of blood on a quiet street corner, all in a matter of a few days. I would say that ranks as one of the strangest goddamn weeks we've had in some time."

Long had forgotten about the report regarding the attack on the Outlook bank. It sat buried beneath piles of photos and files.

"I'll let you take a moment to gather yourself." Masonori said. He pulled the second chair, a loud scraping of wood across tile, and sat down with elbows on the table.

"Because you are going to explain why all this happened today, one step at a time." Long buried his fingers into his eyes, clearing the crust and dirt away.

"Now is not the time for an apology, sir."

"That's where you're wrong. Now is the time to get on your knees and thank me for not committing you to a damned padded cell.

Now is the time to thank me for keeping your dirty work under wraps, again, because there were more deaths again today, Derek."

The inspector turned away from his commanding officer.

"You promised that you were going to scale back, let the boys do their jobs, and sit from a position of leadership."

"How many innocents were hurt in that shootout?" asked Long.

"At what cost?"

"You haven't answered the question."

"I don't have to answer it. You killed people today," said Masonori.

"The woman is safe now, because of me."

"Do you realize that some of the cadets have begun to refer to you as a cold blooded killer? You're So unaware of what is happening underneath your nose. Why aren't you paying any attention, Derek? Wrapped up in your own feelings of guilt? Why do this to yourself?" asked Masonori.

"Those kids can say what they like. They will have their time. Let them live to fight another day," said Long.

"Learn to let them go, make their own decisions. You cannot protect everyone and yourself at the same time."

Long took a moment to think of the cadets, sneering behind his back, laughing at him.

"It's gotten to some of the officers as well. Your own men, expressing discomfort working with you and your erratic behavior," said Masonori.

"I'll scale back. Take it easy for a while."

"There's too much shit going on, Derek. There've been reports about rival gangs battling in the middle of busy streets, opening fire on populated city blocks. All these things going on, you've done nothing. What happened down at the docks?"

"I've had my men check the ships up and down. No signs of drugs being dealt, they were careful, very discreet. There's going to be a report with the shipping manifest included," said Long.

"What else did they bring in on that ship? There has to be some kind of clue."

"There was food, paint and textiles," said Long.

Masonori was puzzled.

"Have there been any orders that stuck out from the rest? Who was it from?" he asked.

Long was embarrassed to answer.

"We made sure to question everyone onboard the ship, there was no strange activity. The canisters were full of all kinds of paint, for an art project based in town," he said.

"First the missing weapons shipment, then this," said Masonori.

"Our computers have been downed. Something is messing with our terminals. There's been issues with electrical systems downtown as well. There's been reports of trouble with their computers missing or changed files, some even vandalized. What about this missing shipment?" asked Long.

"Three days ago, weapons ordinance 13 reported a lot of guns taken from their armory. Whoever took them was able to sign in with a company login, taking the weapons right before they were scanned into the system. Every operation run down there is automated. No robot arms are stealing weapons. There had to be a team of some kind, who could get in there and slip out undetected with those weapons."

"Is that why you've been out of the city? Chasing missing

guns for the government? Perhaps you're losing sight of your civic duty," said Long.

"Don't be an asshole. Those guns were handled by Kirilov. They're the reason this city still stands in the economy we have now. My ties in the bureau have kept me in close contact with those in charge of the investigation."

"A few unmarked guns were found at the Outlook job. The Mob is in dire need of that hardware. There have been rumors of a possible mutiny on Jimmy the Recluse."

"That fantasy has been in your head for two years, Derek. No one is going to cross him, not for you, not even for me. If those guns are loose in the city that means more trouble for your men. That includes street gangs, bounty hunters, and anyone with deep pockets looking to light fires."

Long knew what he meant, hunters were increasing in numbers over the years.

"Part of me wonders if this hacker isn't messing with the systems all over the country, not just here."

All these facts, these problems began to enter his mind at once, his head moved to the side, as if falling into a restless R.E.M.

"Are you even listening to me? A goddamn computer hacker could be messing with our entire infrastructure!"

Masonori slammed his fist on the table. Long reacted slowly to the noise.

"Explain this pool of blood to me, now."

Long turned his eyes towards the floor of the room.

"Just blood. No footprints, no fingerprints, no signs of struggle. No witnesses."

Masonori shook his head in disbelief.

"Just like the others, how many does that make it now?" he

asked.

Long took a moment to count.

"This would be forty nine," he said.

"Damn near fifty people missing, in a little over that many days." Long swallowed hard, he felt his hands begin to shake. His part of the world seemed to be falling away from him.

"Who else knows how many are missing?" the Chief asked.

"Just my men, no media outlets. The families have been in close contact with us. No reporters."

"Good, keep it that way. Put your best men on the gangs and the hackers of the city."

Long refused.

"What about those people?" he asked.

"What can we do? You have no evidence, no leads on what happened to them? Do you even have a positive ID on who they all are?"

"There's an updated dossier on each."

"Hand it off to someone private, low end. No one can know about this. There would be mass panic if people heard about these abductions, or that maybe they themselves could be abducted," said Masonori.

"Maybe they could be. We have no idea."

Masonori took a breath. He got to his feet and began to pace around the room.

"I'm asking you to handle this job quietly."

He stepped in, mere inches away from Long's face. His shadow covering the light of the room, drenching him in shade.

"All you've done is take out your frustrations on the men you're supposed to be apprehending."

Long returned the tense glare.

"Don't judge me. I've done that enough myself," he said.

"You bring them in. Don't punish them or yourself," said Masonori.

"I'm a murderer."

"Don't say that. Be a leader to them. Help get this shit solved. This is your last chance. If you can't handle it, then I'll find someone who can. Do what you have to do. In the meantime, you will be enrolled in therapy and a psychiatric evaluation. No questions, understand?"

Long did not speak. He thought of Kyoko.

"Derek!"

The scream had echoed through the halls of the floor. After more than a minute, he agreed.

Masonori left the office with the door wide open. The old man was alone again. A voice from across the office called out.

"Sir?" asked another voice.

"What is it? What do you need?"

When Long finally turned to see who it was, there was no one there, a passing cadet asked him who he was talking to. There was a moment of silence as Long drew his head back towards the window, he gave him a few quiet words.

"I was talking to no one..."

The door of Paavo's office flew open as he walked towards the desk. He moved to each of the closets surrounding the room. Bags and cases were tossed viciously to the floor. It was still daylight outside. The storm clouds swirled around the white light making the sky revolve through shades of dark blue and grey. The snow continued to attack the city. The streets were buried in ice and white. With quick swipes, Paavo cleared the desk and began to toss up the cases from the closet. He opened each one by flipping the metal clasps. Without looking up, he switched on the light above his head. The old dusty light came alive, coating the room in a yellow shade and making the dark walls and floors green.

He removed the contents of each case, dropped the bags to the floor and gave each one an individual space on the table. There were metal contraptions, each with small wires and scopes and small detachable pieces that littered the desk. Paavo feverishly worked on assembling the leftover pieces to their respective machines. These were his own inventions, his studies in forensics along with limited access to Police equipment led to the creation of these machines.

There were four, each with simple methods of analysis and cross- referencing. He had been experimenting with them for years now. Unable to afford the official equipment used by the Police and their team, he needed some kind of independent devices for his own practices. Their appearance was often ridiculed but the success rate was never debated. Paavo laid his evidence out on the table: a sample of the blood pool beneath the streetlight, along with photographs of the crime scene.

Paavo placed a small cup on the table. It belonged to Naoko. He pocketed it while Miss Aki showed him the apartment. Prints of her fingers and lips still stained the cup, which smelled of sweet tea. Each piece of evidence was placed beneath the devices. Colored lights began to blink and Paavo took notes as the machines worked away with noises of plastic and metal colliding. The blood from the sample was lifted and raised by a small platform, revolved under different lenses and scopes until the colored lights changed the blood from a deep red to a bright green and finally set down.

To the right, the cup was lifted and twirled by a robot arm and sprayed with a clear substance. The fingerprints and lip marks were turned the bright green of the blood sample. Paavo continued to take notes and turned his attention to the middle two machines. Photographs were turned and rotated beneath flashing light. On the side of one of the machines, a series of negatives were produced and dropped onto the table. Paavo lifted each of the negatives and held them to the light. The colors of the scene were inverted. The snow was painted as a deep black.

The pool of blood itself was now a brilliant white. Ammonia laced inside the crimson appeared as well. The pool was surrounded by a slightly larger border of black. Splashing from an open bottle, maybe? They were in a hurry to cover their tracks. A lighter shade of black traveled across the concrete and stopped at the pool of blood. Each photograph held the same pair of black footprints. The last group of photos showed another set of prints; a path made of drips and lines. The body must have been dragged off somewhere, he thought. The last photograph he took was of the street further down. The path of white had followed the street down and turned the corner into the nearby alleyway.

Paavo collected the negatives and pocketed them. The ammonia was poured out into the street to cover the smell and identity of the victim. Finding out the type would be easy enough. The bottle could have been left around the area in the garbage or somewhere in the street. Perhaps those hands used to pour the liquid were in enough of a hurry to leave a trace. He felt himself fade into sleep and stopped his face hitting the table.

The sample taken had done its damage and he needed to rest before nodding off again. Before he left, he took out a compartment of the far right machine; the spraying device that coated the cup of tea. The car stalled on the way onto the highway. It was going to be a long drive back to the apartment. He tried to cloud his mind with thoughts of the case to keep awake. The lights above the lanes of traffic moved with speed. His vision began to blur. Each streetlight blazed a trail of dazzling fire. The radio was unresponsive, too much static and white noise. He found it impossible to concentrate on the sounds.

Why would Long not own up to those missing people from two years ago, after all this time? What was the point of trying to deny the mistakes of the past? The cases were nothing but a wild goose chase, dismissed by the Police. Paavo took time to help in the search. Those families had put their trust in him. When his efforts proved to be futile, they turned on him. Paavo was hated and criticized. Some of the worst words were former clients dissatisfied with his efforts, wanting answers that would never come. They hated him for not solving their problems, and in turn, Paavo had begun to hate the city. He could hear their words, still in the back of his mind.

"What the hell have you done? After all this time, you found nothing?"

"We could have taken this to the Police! Instead, we've been sitting around, wasting our damn time with you."

"You're just as worthless as the cops...You people make me sick."

That last man spit in his face. That was the day he went into exile. To find those missing fifty people, he gave up everything to find them. In two years, he had not found anyone.

Paavo made it there after a few false starts. The snow was devastating now. His eyes watered trying to see forward. His body was slowing down. He turned his key. Another nod off into sleep and bright flashes of white woke him from deep darkness. There was sensation inside his fingers. He turned the knob and ignored the voice calling him off in the distance. He slammed the door and fell to the floor. Paavo climbed towards the bedroom and slowly found the mattress and collapsed.

CHAPTER SEVEN

I am alive in a broken eternity. The battlefield lay open to me. I am a small child caught within a war of blood and hostility. Ill will and malice coats my heart. No real reason to feel this way. My body moves without control, pure weakness. My limbs are slow to react, as if using them for the very first time. There is no city to be saved, or sights to remember. This is a new and unfamiliar land. Shades of cut skin and scars scatter across my neck. The angels from fables and stories and religions of old are here with me, and they weep at my sides. My eyes open not to fire, but to sorrow and light. A suit of black covered my body. The sleeves are tight enough to make it uncomfortable to move my arms. I feel hands pulling at my clothes. Battered women lay all around me. There are wings severed from their bodies. Wounded hands reach up for help. Some wings move on their own, attempting to fly, as if still attached to their host. They pull at me to stand again. I am motionless. Their bodies are losing energy. A faint sound of a body's collapse filled my ears.

There is no background; no clouds or palace of marble and gold, only a blinding spotlight behind me that reveals the horror in the distance and beyond. There are thousands of them. Fallen to the earth are the bodies of countless angels. Shredded feathers fall into collecting pools of crimson blood. The messengers of the divine word, found here broken and destroyed before me now. Their bodies are covered in tattered shawls of white. Some of them hide their bruises and cuts, others stare directly into me. There are sounds of explosions now, along with the faint smell of gunpowder—I looked to the sky for answers.

Millions more fall down from on high. They are overpowered. Bodies tailspin out of control. Wings are pulled back by the strong wind, soon torn from their backs by the extreme force. They fall to the ground. Their frames were so fragile against the white light which held me upright. Beautiful creatures collide with the earth. Their faces full of fear and surprise. I watch them shatter into pieces, just like normal human beings. The fall is quick and severe. It made me uncomfortable, hard to watch. I did not turn away. What was it that was supposed to have made them stronger? What made them so different from us?

In dreams and books I would imagine the elite warriors of heaven. The explosions grow louder in volume and the screams begin again. Every one of them hits the bottom. Strange silence fills the area as each descends to a violent and final fall. At my feet, the women emit sounds of intense pain. They could feel the impact of each of their own, they are linked. They are more than brothers and sisters; joined by their souls, combined by some kind of unwavering faith. I move through the piles of limbs and broken shells. The white below my feet begin to melt and change shape. The liquid wraps around the bodies. It travels a path downstream where it pours into a center and bleeds outward a walkway of steel beams and rods. Elements and powders from the earth and dirt mix with water out of thin air and fill the empty spaces as blood within veins. I step out of the liquid and onto the structure as it begins to rise up and over the dying fleet. The pathway is lifted high by a large foundation of rock, high off into the unknown.

I found myself towering over a sea of divine light. Over the railing revealed an ascending mountain of hardened stone. The streams of moving liquid consumes the angels, all their blood and severed wings meld together in some strange alchemy. Everything is drowned, and absorbed into a massive river of dead. Colors change from red and white to mixtures of dark blues and purples. The angels' bodies are torn into pieces by unknown waves of anger and power. Shadows of grey and black swarm in and out of the river. It splashes onto the shores of the rising rocks. Blood and bone, feather and flame smash together into new shapes and colors. Corpses tumble and squeeze into one mass. Sick hues of green and brown erupt from the storm within the water.

The mountain ascends towards the sky. The death waters below rise and grow into a sea of life. Figures move and awaken inside the liquid, their forms blur by the bubbling waters. My eyes search the mountain for a way down, there were too many jagged rocks and other natural dangers. I stand my ground along the stone walkway. Its steel beams remind me of human designs. The heat rises from the sea of dead, now brewing into an ocean. It spreads its reach far out into the distance. Beneath the mass of rock, a furious mixing of angel flesh and earth seethes. Into the sky shoots a sphere of light, the force is enough to knock me backwards and almost over the edge. My hands scramble for a corner to hang on. The rocks are sharp, blood runs across my wrists. The rolling water smashes against the bottom of the mountain. I feel fear for the first time. The sounds of scraping skin and knuckles make me sick.

It's blinding, the light. Within it, bolts of lightning, travelling back and forth, gaining intensity and speed. I contemplate dropping to the ocean below. The surroundings are barren. No other land to swim to, I was trapped here. With the sphere growing in size, I climb up once again, towards the top. It was more difficult to fight back up the mountain then it was to slide off the edges. The cracks of lightning are deafening. I dreaded facing the growing light above my head. My suit of black is now shades of brown and red. There were rips in the seams, torn holes in the shoulders and legs from the ascent. I found myself face to face again with this massive ball of light and death.

An enormous bolt strikes the ocean. It creates a gust of wind blowing dust and debris into my eyes. The waters turn black and spin into a vortex. It becomes a portal, swirling with intense fervor. I approach the edge of the mountain to peer into this massive darkness. The portal changes colors, from black to blood red and then to a bright green. It morphs several times before spewing tiny specks of dust into the awaiting ocean. The particles grow once they settle into water. They shake and explode into smaller particles.

Soon the entire area around me is infested with creatures. There is no way off this island now. Who could tell what these things were made of? Are these the creations of angels? The millions of specks blend together, much like the fallen angels had done. Dust melds into dust and becomes solid. Skin sprouts fins, appendages and eyes. One of the creature's throats splits open in several areas and it opens its mouth to inhale the waters.

Creatures appear from this fury of black and purple. They move slowly at first, then with speed and expertise in the water. In time, the creatures take over the ocean; some travel far off into the distance. Others found themselves dying in a matter of moments, from the blistering heat of the sphere or from the cold of the ocean. I step around the edges of the mountain to watch them. Some devour each other, I was horrified by this. Others had found a way to enter each other and they occupy spaces inside themselves. My fascination grows with the creatures. Others had found a way out of the water and to the shore of the mountain, where they shiver and bounce across the rocks. Water is the key to survival. Once on land, they die within a matter of seconds. Some perform a strange ritual, a dance of some kind. From this dance, smaller ones, made of different colors are born. They are green, these offspring. One of them struggles to swim. My eyes follow him, overcome by the current. I felt sorrow. It would not survive this environment.

It begins to shake and convulse against the shoreline. The creature stands upright and walks out of the water, where it stood with lungs full of air. Many of the creatures follow its lead. The sphere of light fires another bolt of energy into the portal. Plumes of fire shoot back into the sky, producing overwhelming heat. The fire moves around the ocean and stacks itself high. More pours from the center of the vortex, until it builds itself a wall of glowing flame.

The walking creatures form smaller ones, similar to the black ocean. Their colors are stricken with fire orange and red. Fires surrounding the mountain dissipate into the ocean and from the ashes come other mountains. Immense stones and structures rose from the waters. There was now water and land for the creatures to inhabit. They traverse across the lands, running with feverish excitement. The colors blend together as each of them find partners to carry across the unknown landscape. There is a noise behind me. I turn around to see the first creature to grow legs, which found a way to climb the mountain.

It's skin is stained by the sun. It moves towards me with fear, until it stands next to me overlooking the ocean and empty lands. The sphere fires another bolt of life into the black waters below. I looked down towards the creature. It shakes in fever. It falls over the edge and towards certain death. Somehow, it never reaches the ground. The creature had grown wings of its own and skated up into the atmosphere. A bolt of lightning strikes the sky and rips open the endless white to create blue skies for the creature to fly across. I am overcome. What is happening to this place? Where am I? A voice came into my mind, it spoke soft words.

"You are where you belong,"

I turned around to see no one. I was still alone in this place.

"Is someone here with me?" I ask.

"Yes."

"Please, show me where you are," I plead.

The sphere of light moves towards me. It shrinks in size, enough for it to stand with me on this peak. The sphere loses its shape for a moment and then from the pool of light, a woman rises to her feet, her hand reaches towards me.

"We are always here with you," she says.

"What is this place? What were those creatures?"

"There are so many questions to ask, never enough time to explain everything."

"What can you tell me?" I ask.

"What you see around you is how life is made."

"Those angels were killed. They fell to the ground and broke like glass. Is this heaven or earth?"

"This is the space between. Everything is born from our labor, our sacrifice. All things are created off the backs of angels," she says.

"You are one of them?"

"I am something more, a collector of souls and a planter of seeds."

"Am I?" I ask.

"You are far from it, my son."

"This is how life is made?"

"Do you not see it? Creatures that crawl from the deep, primordial soup find their way to traverse the land, the sky. Look out towards the growing world around you," she says.

The red lands turn to startling yellow and brown. The creatures from the ocean begin to build. They make buildings and houses. Rain falls from the dark blue sky above our heads to coat the grounds in green grass and plant life. Their movements speed up, as if put on fast forward to cover for large amounts of passing time. Soon massive skyscrapers rise from the miniscule towns, life was now domesticated and modern. I had seen the evolution of man from its origins, to present time, all created from the flesh and bones of fallen angels.

Planted seeds from bloody war created water, land and air. The woman speaks again, her arms outstretched.

"I know what you are thinking. The cycle restarts at the end of every civilization. From the ashes of man's avarice, comes new life, new worlds to behold."

"Thank you for showing me this. I cannot help but feel that this is all for nothing, when do they fall? When will they poison their society from the inside out?" I ask.

"What causes this war to end life and start anew?"

"Greed, the lust for power, the need for safety and security, foolishness created this war. You see in your own time. This is what will happen," she says.

"My own time? Meaning that this hasn't happened yet?"

"Not yet. Soon, war will ravage your lands and from it, new life will be born and take your place."

"Is this some kind of battle between heaven and hell?"

"Something like that, try not to think of it as heaven and hell only. We are all children of one in the end."

"You are talking about God," I say.

"I am talking about the father. We share the same one. We are part of the same family."

"Why am I here?" I ask.

"You're about to be reborn."

"Reborn as what?"

"All children must find their way, from the bottom to the top. From drifting through the world, you will find your wisdom," she says.

"Drifting..."

"Your own salvation will be waiting for you here."

The woman moved her hand, removing the clothes from my body. I kneeled before her, naked atop this mountain, standing over the modern world.

"Rise."

I stand and gaze over the world. My skin is clean. No wounds on my chest, any blood or pain inside the heart. Below me, the world revolts, turning on itself. There is panic in the streets. Pollution coats the skies, the waters fill with forgotten trash and their miniature dead. I see wings spread from my shoulders. Sharp feathers cut out in a beautiful display. The woman marvels at my body. I hear familiar noises, the sounds of war over this city. It catches fire.

"This is where you belong," she assures me.

"I don't know where that place could be."

"You belong here, in this city of fire."

"Why?" I ask.

"This is what you made. This is your burning paradise," she says.

Her hands caress my gentle wings. With a sudden swipe, she rips them from my back. I fall to the ground in agony. The wings are tossed away like toys. Her face changes. The woman gives me a look of contempt. She moves towards me and plants a kiss on my head.

"Such a weak one. Your judgment begins now."

A man steps out from some hidden shadow of the mountain. His wings are bright and burning with flame. The sky turns black as the city burns like dreams before.

"Fall to your destiny, my son," he says.

His foot is swift and powerful, enough to knock me from the edge. I fall. The city of fire is rapidly approaching. My eyes open to see the river of flame, the crumbling of buildings, and the crushing of guilty souls. Life had been created, only to be broken apart in war and fire. Angels sacrifice themselves in the rebirth of mankind, only to see humans follow the same pattern, to suffer the burning city, again and again is life now.

For both you and I. For everyone around us.

Hours had passed. Paavo was back at the former crime scene. He produced the negative that most revealed the path and walked to the exact spot of the attack. He took out the spray device. His finger struggled to find the correct grip for the trigger in the cold. He pressed it down and a small amount of liquid hit the sidewalk. A small piece of the ground was illuminated in yellow. His eyes went back and forth between the street and the negative. A longer spray further down the sidewalk outlined the path made in the photograph.

Paavo walked to the alleyway and stopped where the negative ended. He looked up to see the alley. He held out the spray and let out a long stream at the pathway ahead. Streaks of yellow followed down the pathway and into the shadows. He inhaled a small amount of air. The cold burned his chest and he emitted a small cough. Paavo walked slowly into the shadows. The alleyway was filled with trash. Broken gates led to derelict houses with each group of steps. As he walked by, a rabid dog barked behind a chain link fence. Paavo smirked and continued forward through the dark passage. The end of the alley split off into backstreets that splintered into the main roads. Cars sped by splashing water and sweeping up noise all around. The wind began to pick up. He raised his coat to breathe safely despite the storm. His hands began to hurt from the wind but continued laying down the spray underneath his jacket sleeve. The trail of yellow was getting more difficult to follow as snow began to fall more aggressively.

He looked back to see the trail behind him dissipate beneath the harsh weather. He began to memorize his footsteps and the surrounding buildings. The trail doubled back out onto main streets. Paavo passed a mission and the nearby church before it led him to a group of dumpsters. The cold was starting to penetrate his thin jacket and he thought of getting back to the car. Harsh winds blinded him.

The garbage inside the dumpsters was near frozen. Ice had

built up from the falling water from the edge of the rooftops. Etches of pain stretched across Paavo's face as he used his gun to break through the sheets of frost. Shards of blue cut him as fingers moved around; picking out objects, looking for a plastic bottle of some kind. Nothing in the first container, but he went through the others, in search of the ammonia. His hands bled from the cuts. Paavo used leftover gauze to wrap them and continue the search. Near the middle of the third can, a plastic bottle was lodged beneath two heavy bags of trash. He pulled it from the container and held it up. The label was in English. Everything else in the trash was printed in kanji. Paavo wrapped the bottle in gauze and headed back towards the car. He inched forward, trying to find his way back out onto the main street. Paavo felt his eyes close.

He had fallen asleep again, resting on the wall of some building he couldn't identify. He looked around to see people scrambling to some kind of shelter. Paavo was alone on the street. It was impossible to keep his eyes open. His body was going to shut down. The storm forced him to stumble around trying to find a place to rest. He found the church from before and pushed the doors open. Paavo quietly fell into one of the pews.

The church was immaculate; finished wood formed structures sat high above the floor, stained glass created colored messes of the red and white carpets. A priest spoke loudly over the booming winds to several faceless bodies. His echoes rattled the hollow walls. Paavo watched him speak but did not listen. He had his fill of organized religion during his childhood. Before the sermon ended, Paavo collected himself and rose to his feet. He walked down the aisle at the end towards the front of the church. There was a door behind the altar that led to an office. He quietly walked into the room. Papers and files were neatly organized. Religious pictures, crosses and trinkets were placed around the walls. Paavo stepped silently across the red carpet to the desk. Gordon Wen, read the name. He had never heard of him. The drawers were searched carefully to find nothing out of the ordinary. Footsteps echoed from the outside. Paavo stood up and sat down at the chair. The priest from the altar stepped in the office.

"Young man, what are you doing here?"

"My apologies, father, I have questions to ask you, if you have time."

"Of course," the priest smiled. He sat at his desk and placed his hands at the table.

"You may ask your questions."

"A little girl disappeared five days ago, Naoko Aki."

Paavo produced the picture of the girl.

"I don't know the name, are you police?"

"Private investigator," said Paavo.

"Who hired you?"

"Her mother, of course," said Paavo. Wen nodded.

"I can understand her worry and why she would do all she can to find her child," he said.

"How well do you know your visitors?"

"Some of them arrive every Sunday to the shelter for sermons. We would provide food and drink for the less fortunate."

"You speak often?" Paavo inquired.

"Men and women come to me for prayer and forgiveness at any hour. Times are trying these days, people do all they can to survive."

"When was the last time you saw little girls playing in the alleys?"

"Days ago, about the same time as you told me. Children are just as welcome. The children of the neighborhood never miss a sermon."

"Will more be here this Sunday?" asked Paavo.

"I can only hope. This mother's heart is crushed and she needs God's love and protection now more than ever. I hope that she does come."

"Can I see the shelter?" "It is closed during these hours. We are housing some needy souls. Some are sleeping, so we will have to be quiet," said Wen.

"Of course. After you, Father."

The priest smiled as he grabbed his coat. Wen nodded and stepped out of the office and exited the side door down the hallway. Paavo followed.

"The storm is strong this year. I feel as though God is testing us. Testing our spirits," said Wen.

They stepped back out into the cold. Paavo held in the last of the warm air from the church. He strained his chest as the priest led him down the same alleyway where he became lost. Following Wen, he looked around and made sure there were no traces of the lines he followed from the device. Wen produced a set of keys and pulled one to open the large steel doors near the dumpsters he dug through. The doors opened creaking and scraping against the ground.

"This way, my son."

Paavo followed him into the shelter. Beds and blankets were laid across the floor alongside trays of food and candles burnt down to their last embers. People shuffled into their makeshift beds for rest.

"Why don't they sleep in the church?" Paavo asked.

"It's warmer than this place."

"The city would not allow such a thing anymore. Men in suits came and ordered me to find another place to put them. It violated some kind of building code, I how men with families and money and houses can tell me where people with nothing should be placed, as if they weren't really people, treating them like they were objects, in the way."

"Making those wealthy churchgoers feel uncomfortable," said Paavo.

"Perhaps, but we offer a place for any and all here."

"Any and all? Even drug addicts? Like the ones down the alle?"

"We offer a place for those who want help, not for those lost and in no place to reach for salvation," said Wen.

"Don't you think they need your salvation the most?"

"You say that as if you don't need it yourself."

"I don't." Paavo spat back.

"You're too young to say such things. Do not lose your salvation in light of the dark around us."

"I lost it a long time ago, father, I have seen enough to know that your salvation is in short supply, and there are certain requirements."

"It pains me to see you this way, young man, to speak these words of denial. You are always welcome in this place," said Wen.

"I won't be coming here again, you've been helpful."

"Take care. I know you will find your way, I believe it."

"Don't waste your time. Believe that someone will find the girl."

"I know the way out," said Paavo. As he stepped away, the priest spoke one final time.

"Don't lose your salvation."

Paavo saw someone in the dark watching him leave. Their

hand held a glass filled with red liquid. They reared back and began to drink and shake with exhilaration. Red dripped from the sides of their mouth. Paavo stepped out into the cold again, haunted. He took in a small taste of the air and he coughed roughly. He quickly brought part of his coat over his mouth and exhaled. The dealers were back on the corner. Paavo watched them from a distance. They sold off something wrapped in paper. Paavo turned towards the alleyway and began to walk from the corner. The dealers passed Paavo and exchanged hard looks.

"Want to get high kid?"

"Yeah...Come feel the holy spirit!"

The last one laughed hard, trying to frighten Paavo who stared through him with dead eyes. Their white teeth were the only things visible in the dark of the alley. Paavo checked his watch. Dinner with Long was approaching. He followed the street around the corner to find his car. As he got in, he saw who bought from the dealers; a group of men and women. They looked like a family. Their tattered clothes were dirty and ripped, worse than those in the shelter. Paavo wondered if they were kicked out by Wen. They opened the paper and put pieces of something in their mouths. The family salivated. They made grunting noises, full of satisfaction. They were ravenous. Was it food?

One of the boys was young. They reached for the food and the other men and women pulled away slowly. They threw him a small piece that landed on the curb. The boy's sadness resonated with Paavo. The others licked their lips and fingers. They shuffled away, leaving the child alone. He was trying to decide between dirty food and going hungry. Paavo stepped out of the car and approached him. They backed away in fear.

Paavo put one of his hands into his pocket. He produced a twenty dollar bill and gestured for the boy to take it. He snatched it away from him and ran away. Paavo looked down to the curb and saw the food. It was a dark red piece of meat. Paavo used the paper they were given and wrapped it up. He walked back to the car and remembered he had just given them his last twenty. Losing that money was more than alright. He made his way to that warm, home-cooked dinner.

Long sat in darkness. The familiar faces of the station were beginning to clear out for the evening. A sense of loss seeped into his clothes, into his blood. He wanted for things to be easier. Crime was still as high as it was with a corrupt official in charge of the force. With the capture of several Mob captains, he was moving up the chain towards the Capotellis. The Recluse was his main target. Everything was moving along without worry, and then those random people began disappearing. They vanished leaving no trails, only these pools of blood like a taunting puzzle, impossible to solve. It drove him nearly insane to be so helpless. The blood was tainted on every occasion. The longer it took to find those people, the more doubt was cast towards Long's reputation. Was he the hero cop that everyone thought he was? He never put any stock into their opinions. His daughter and wife were the only ones of importance. The job would never overtake them. The angel and the devil had been in constant argument inside him. They pushed and pulled him in different directions.

His heart had closed up. So much anger with nowhere to place his rage. What could be done but push forward? Masonori wanted answers, what made them so difficult to find? The families were asked to keep quiet as their cases were swept under the rug and taken over by federal agents while whoever was behind it escaped without justice. Long got to his feet and went to the lab with Yamagishi and the others. The rats were working on some leads. The blood work was put to the side once logged into the database. He watched them work. What could he do to help lighten the workload?

"Sir, we didn't notice you there," said Yamagishi.

"What can we do for you?"

"Just tell me what you found. Be honest," said Long.

Yamagishi nodded his head.

"You wanted us to look into the hacked messages and lights going on across town. We've looked over the reports."

"Thank you for doing this. Tell me what we got," said Long.

"The messages are in binary code. It seems like whoever is uploading the message is searching. That's all they indicate, nothing else but "harvest leads us to the one.""

"Who is the one?"

"No idea. But there is a signature, written into the code."

"A signature?" asked Long.

Yamagishi fixed his eye glasses again, excited.

"Yes, like a calling card. Whoever is doing this is leaving clues. There has got to be something else that can point us in the right direction. It seems that they want to be found."

"What kind of trace? Maybe we can find them," asked Long.

"It's difficult to explain. Let me show you an example." Kuriyama said as she moved towards her computer. Long followed behind.

"We found footage from the skyline choppers who were filming the incidents, both nights they occurred. Watch this."

She increased the speed of the film to show a night's hours in a matter of seconds.

"What are you doing? You're going too fast," said Long.

"Trust me. I found a pattern," she said.

"What kind of pattern?"

"A small character in the alphabet appears between the

binary, the lights trace it out," said Kuriyama.

A word in kanji was traced out by lighted windows.

"When comparing the patterns from both nights, back to back, it forms the word 'snow'. Does that mean anything to you?"

"Do you know of any hackers with that name?" asked Long.

"There is one," Yamagishi said.

"What do you know about them?" the old man asked.

"Next to nothing. Their identity is unknown. There's a number of communities that work together in breaking security code. The only reason this message appears would be because they allowed it to."

"I can put some people on it. But what about the other message? If this person's putting themselves out there, the question is why? Who are they trying to find?" asked Long.

"No idea," said Kuriyama.

"Maybe they want someone in particular to find them."

CHAPTER EIGHT

Paavo found himself staring into space. Two messages sat unchecked in the dark office. It was Wiles. He spoke in a breathless voice.

"Mr. Harker, I was unsure of how to contact you. I thought you left a number with the receptionist, it turns out we don't have you on file. I looked in the phone book and, hopefully this is the right number."

There was a bit of silence, papers could be heard shuffling in the background.

"My home is a bit uptown, I can meet you either here or at the hospital, but it's imperative that you meet with me about your condition. Please call me at my cell number..."

The message ended abruptly. The machine began its usual clicking before playing the next one.

"Damnit! The message thing cut me off. Ha! Okay, please contact me as soon as you get these. Thanks."

Paavo looked around for the office phone. The plugs still fit into the old outlet, not without a few sparks. In a few moments, the dial tone could be heard buzzing from the other end; he dialed the doctor's number.

"Mr. Harker?" asked Wiles.

"What do you want?"

"Where are you? Are you busy? Can we meet?"

"Yes, we can. But I have personal business to attend to, this cannot take long," grumbled Paavo.

"It will be brief, but very important. Where can we meet?"

"The hospital will be fine."

"Very good. I will be waiting for you outside," said Wiles,

gleefully.

The drive back towards the hospital was more hectic than last. City lights kept him distracted. Wiles stood shivering near the front entrance. His brown coat was covered in snow. He welcomed Paavo inside and took him back towards the office. The hospital lights were dimmed as the night took over. People moved with less urgency. Wiles kept silent during the elevator trip and took turns swiping away at leftover snow in his hair and on his shoulders.

"Don't you have a cell phone?" Wiles asked.

"You should get one."

Back in the office, the doctor produced a black case along with dozens of sheets, folded, yellow paper.

"I've spent all day trying to find a way to begin treatment on your condition."

"Don't you have other patients to worry about?" asked Paavo.

"Not really anything important, a few pregnant mothers, flu victims. Who cares about them, really? They can take care of themselves."

Paavo looked at him strangely.

"I'm kidding! This is a medical breakthrough," said Wiles.

"What have you got?"

"A temporary serum, designed to slow down the course of flow and create warmth within the bloodstream."

"What will that do?" asked Paavo.

Wiles continued to search through his papers.

"You mentioned before that with working your muscles and lungs, the body can suppress the pain."

He grabbed one of the papers and showed Paavo a crude

drawing of a body and its circular system, starting with the heart.

"Here, take a look. Direct contact with oxygen hardens your blood. This blood runs into the heart, causing that pain and tension which you designed a system of moving and breathing to safeguard from." Paavo nodded his head, beginning to understand.

"Now, if we introduce an antibody which will keep the blood heated, direct oxygen would not create such a drastic change in temperature to perhaps break down the hardened coating from Liquid Skin. You would be able to maintain normal physical activity, without resting or taking breaks in your day to relax your body."

"You said it was a temporary serum?" asked Paavo.

Wiles reached into the black case, he placed a bottle, filled with golden liquid, onto the table in front of them.

"A heating agent, it raises the temperature of your blood to offset the contact of oxygen, thereby stopping the attacks," he said.

"How would I take it?"

"The agent would be injected, directly into the heart." Paavo backed away from him.

"What? Are you insane? You're going to get me killed!" he shouted.

Paavo felt a stab at his heart. He took a deep breath and calmed himself.

"I'm trying to stay alive, remember?"

"This isn't going to be easy, Mr. Harker. To be honest, this is extremely experimental and I'm kind of risking my job in trying to help you, the way you wanted to be helped," said Wiles.

"Experimental, meaning I could die from this?"

"Possibly, which is why I want to try a small dose tonight, if possible. We have to see the effects of the serum, to see if any changes need to be made for the dosage," assured Wiles.

Paavo looked towards the bottle and remembered the liquid they gave him as a child. He wondered if it was the same.

"How much?"

Wiles produced a syringe.

"Let's fill it to the halfway point," he said. Paavo shook his head in disbelief.

"Are you sure this going to work?"

"The sample of blood you gave me provided a lot of necessary information. How your blood changes from the moment it pumps out from your heart is a very delicate process. This is why the serum needs to be attempted. One theory is that the heating agent would not only keep the blood warm, but perhaps over time, cauterize your wound, making solid skin like scar tissue."

"You mean it would heal the wound? Cover it up?" asked Paavo.

"Maybe, and then you could live a normal life." Paavo hesitated.

"What do I need to do?"

"Just take the shot, fill the syringe to the halfway point and inject it straight into your heart."

Paavo's eyes traced the point of the needle.

"You need to take injections in intervals of every six hours. For now, take half the dose now and the other half in three. You need to get home as soon as you can. Rest your body to become accustomed to the serum. Record anything strange or uncomfortable and get back to me."

Paavo committed it to memory.

"I will leave you to it. Don't worry about the light. Take the case with you as well," said Wiles.

The doctor collected his things and walked out of the room. Paavo took the necessary amount and tapped the edge. The liquid was warm. He could feel it through the glass. Several minutes passed as he stared into the hole in his chest. The mirror at the end of the room was asking for him. He stepped towards his reflection once again. His body was frail. The wound was staring back at him. Paavo aimed the shot towards his heart. The syringe stabbed through muscle and flesh. The blood poured out as he pressed the plunger down and let the warmth flow through his body. A towel was left on the door knob for him to clean up. The effects were immediate. Paavo felt drowsy and fell to his knees. The towel ran red.

Paavo struggled to keep his eyes open. A beautiful sleep called him. He focused on the sounds of wind outside and cleaned the room. Wiles was gone. Paavo took the case and used the patient exit back out into the city street. Dinner was waiting. Snow crunched and cracked beneath his feet. Something was different about the cold now. His body felt a bitterness rising with each step.

"Why am I fooling myself? Could this treatment really work? You are going to die and you know it...You cannot stop it."

It didn't make sense to him that this doctor would try so hard to cure him. What was in this medicine? He thought of taking it back to the apartment to test. Was he slowly becoming a pet project?

The kitchen was filled with steam and smoke. A woman well into her middle age stood over the stove adding ingredients to her meal. Long stood in the corner, in awe of his wife. They had been together for twenty two years. She had a quiet beauty and a certain humility that set her apart from every other woman. Long saw that from the beginning. She was the woman to hold onto.

"Why am I making more dinner again?" asked Kyoko.

"Someone's coming over tonight, supposedly."

"Who?" she asked.

"You'll see, my dear." The snow collected outside their window. The storm was never far.

"They say this winter will be the most difficult in a long time," Kyoko spoke over the crackle of the pan.

Long turned from the window to face her again.

"It gets worse every year, I don't know if this city can take another winter like this," he said.

"It will get worse, and we will have to endure, but that's alright."

"I suppose. You always seem to make everything sound so easy, I could never do that."

"Once you recognize the difficulty of the task, the task loses its danger. It's about action, not emotion or worry," said Kyoko.

Long placed a light kiss on the back of her neck. She smiled slightly.

"Of all the cities in the world, in this region, we had to be born in old Perdition, with its endless winters," he said.

"This is a great city, but where should we escape to?" she asked.

"How about a small island?"

Kyoko leaped into the air with the excitement of a small child.

"Sunny skies, tropical drinks, and no more snow."

"It's a date," he said.

"We should talk about the hotel," Kyoko muttered.

Long's face lowered from a smile into a grimace.

"It was horrible. Thank God the girl was still alive," he said.

"Did you kill any of those men?" she asked.

"Why do you always ask me that?"

"Because I need to know," she said.

"I did, I had to. I had no choice," he admitted.

"There is always a choice. How many of them did you kill?"

There was a brief moment of hesitation. She repeated the question, and he answered. "All of them."

She slammed a pan on the counter.

"How long are you going to keep doing this?" asked Kyoko.

"It was either them or me, or the girl."

"I realize that, but what does this do to you? How can you continue to put yourself in these situations?"

"I don't know...I don't want anyone to get hurt. The younger ones are so green. I know they're adults. They've had the training, the same as all of us...but they're dumb. I have to protect them," Long trailed off.

"You should go back into counseling," she said.

"I've already been summoned for it next week. But I'm not going."

"Why not?"

"There's nothing wrong with me. Next time, the young ones will go in with me," said Long.

"You could just let them do their job and stay out of the line of fire."

"We both know I cannot do that," said Long.

"You're not the same person I met, not the same person I married. You're changing into something I don't understand."

"I still love you," said Long.

There was a knock at the door. Paavo coughed loudly. Kyoko left her husband hanging. She opened the door and gasped.

"Paavo!" she screamed.

"Good evening," he said. Kyoko looked back at Long, who was smiling. The tense corners of her mouth relaxed and she laughed slightly, tears wetting her eyes. She squeezed her husband tight and whispered in his ear.

"You're a bastard, we'll talk about this later."

Paavo looked around the doorway. Kyoko quickly turned around laughing hysterically.

"Paavo, you are a welcome surprise," she said.

"It's been a long time. Good to see you as well."

"Please come in, eat with us, you look skinnier than ever."

"Thank you. I brought beer for the old man."

"What the hell?" Long barked, laughing.

"Come in from the cold, Paavo, please sit," said Kyoko.

Long's house changed decorations every six months. Kyoko would grow tired of the curtains and the colors of the wall every couple of months. She would roll up her sleeves and change everything. The last time Paavo was there, the house was painted red and yellow. He could only imagine how time this house was changed. Kyoko went back into the kitchen as Long showed him the house. The house and the rooms inside weren't large but always comfortable. The living room was a stark green with black borders that traveled across the corners.

"Looks inviting, as always," said Paavo.

"Easy for you to say, you don't live with her." They laughed.

"I heard that!" Kyoko yelled over crashing dishes.

"Where are the old plates?" Paavo asked

"They're upstairs. I usually bring them out for the holidays."

"Just in time, I suppose."

"You're always invited to dinner, Paavo," said Long.

"There's something for you to see, later on." Paavo whispered.

"Second dinner is ready!" Kyoko exclaimed.

She bounced around the kitchen like a schoolgirl to place plates and silverware across the table. The kitchen table was covered in red tablecloth. The walls were colored a sunny yellow with small designs stenciled in that stretched across each side of the walls and ceiling. The storm outside was drowned out now by the sounds of happiness and good memories.

"Please sit and enjoy!" she said.

Paavo sat down and began to salivate in anticipation of Kyoko's dinner. She took Long to the side and smacked him in the chest.

"Why didn't you tell me he was coming?" she asked.

"It was a surprise."

"What? You think I wouldn't let him in? What's wrong with you? Has he changed at all?"

"He's not the way he was when he left us, that's for sure."

"I'm so happy he's okay," sighed Kyoko.

"So am I. Now come on, you have to enjoy your own dinner as well." Kyoko sat down as Long began to serve dinner to them.

"I love the way the house looks, Kyoko."

"Thank you very much, Paavo. But now you talk about yourself."

"What would you like to know?" he asked.

"Where have you been? What have you been up to?"

Paavo took a minute to collect himself as he produced a fork and took a piece of his dinner. He raised the fork to his mouth. The food was delicious. Kyoko was always adept at making all kinds of food. Tonight was Italian; meat and sauce, garlic and green peppers, Paavo thought of the dangers to his heart, but it tasted too good to worry about it.

"I bounced around from place to place for a while, but now I have an apartment on the edge of town. It's a nice little place on the overview."

"You'll have to let me see it," said Kyoko. Long sat down at last, ready to gorge on the food prepared.

"No, you wouldn't like it. Pretty empty, not much there but papers for work and music, things like that."

"What kind of work do you do?" she asked.

"Two years ago I officially became a P.I."

"I'm so proud of you, Paavo. Are you going to work with Derek?"

"I am now, actually," he said while shoveling food into his mouth.

"Yes, my dear, I called Paavo in for one of the newer cases we've got. I just tried his old number and got lucky, I guess."

Kyoko placed a kiss on the young man's cheek.

"Well, I'm glad you did. It's been too long. So, tell me Paavo...What do you do in your spare time? Are you going to school?"

"No, but I have been studying."

"What do you study?" she asked.

"Forensics, blood work, anatomy."

"That sounds too complicated for someone not in school."

"Yes, but I love it." Paavo assured her.

"Think about taking some classes in the future," she looked at Long and moved in closer.

"Do you have a girlfriend?" she poked at his side, eliciting a smirk.

"No, I've never had one," he deadpanned. Kyoko's jaw dropped.

"We have got to get you one! How could you never have a girlfriend? You're so cute!"

Both Paavo and Long raised their eyebrows.

"Sorry to disappoint you," said Paavo.

"You better be, I'll get you a girlfriend before the end of the year, I guarantee it!"

"Okay, thank you."

"No problem, See honey? I take care of everything!"

"Yes, you do, that's one area I am lost in," said Long. Paavo nodded in agreement.

They talked for hours. Paavo was stuffed with Italian food. They drank wine and told stories. All was well within the house. He felt well for a bit before a pain in his chest began. It must have been from the food and drink. He smiled slightly to hide it as Kyoko went on about domestic life and good times. Midnight came. Kyoko excused herself for a moment to get ready for bed. Long told her that they had business to discuss.

"Paavo, you must come back soon, I have more food for you to eat," she said.

"Thank you very much. I'll be back as many times as I'm

allowed."

"I'm looking forward to it," she kissed Paavo on the forehead and waved goodnight as she traveled back into the hallway towards the bedroom. Long pulled the beer from the cooler.

"Let's talk shall we?" he asked.

Into the basement they went. The stairway was down the hall to the left. The steps creaked and buckled under their weight with age. The basement was covered in cobwebs and old furniture from Kyoko's exploits. Long took a towel and wiped off the dirt and dust from the counter top. Paavo had forgotten about the bar that Long once had downstairs. Buddies were invited over and the beer was consumed like water every Friday night. Paavo was never able to come down to the bar. Kyoko held him upstairs. He was still underage back then.

Long invited Paavo to sit at one of the stools; red leather, beaten down with wear and tear. The neon lights still worked after a few crackles of electricity from the outlet. Long smiled as the light filled the basement with artificial light. Paavo looked around, humbled to be allowed in the place where he always wanted to be when he was younger.

"Never thought you would let me down here."

"You're a man now; at least I hope you are," said Long.

"So it seems," Paavo looked to the floor.

"It seems like it would benefit us if we work together on our cases."

"Sounds good. There were matches of traces of DNA I obtained a few hours ago; faint matches with the blank pool of blood still warm beneath a streetlight found this morning."

"Even with the ammonia? Where was this?" asked Long.

"Miles away from the woman's house."

"If you have more, please share. The lab rats can work with another sample of the blood."

"What did you have to show me?" asked Paavo.

"I did some looking around for that little girl. Some eyewitness reports of the girl going to school, playing with friends outside the neighborhood church. Were you able to find anything with your blood?"

"The blood I took from your crime scene came back unknown. There were footsteps through the pool that I followed to a church," said Paavo.

"How did you pick up on these footsteps?" asked Long.

Paavo produced the photographs of the street processed and printed through the machines. He placed them on the table. Long studied each one. The street corner was reduced to white outlines and layers of shadow.

"What is this?" Long pointed to the white puddle that seemed to smear the photo.

"Those are traces of your blood."

"I must say, in case this whole detective thing doesn't work out. You've a bright future in the realm of photography."

"Look at the next one. There are traces that follow down the street and into the alleyway," said Paavo.

Long followed the trail. It was barely noticeable, but there.

"How did you find that?" he asked.

"The machine is designed to break down the environment in the photo, piece by piece. It comes from the editing equipment used to analyze videos of ghost or UFO sightings."

"How did you do that?"

"The vector searches for forgery, anything pasted onto the

original video. I reversed the scope so it inverts the film. If you paste something on top of that, you look for anything that matches up. The software can use existing samples to tag something reproduced on film; traces of substances that hit the ground," said Paavo.

Long raised his can of beer into the air to toast.

"Well done."

"Thank you, sir," Paavo raised his as well. Their cans clinked together.

"Another one of these pools was reported today." said Long.

"How does the second pool look?"

"The same as the first; fresh blood out in the middle of the street. The rats were working on them both, trying to make a connection," said Long.

"What did you find?" Paavo asked.

"There was more than ammonia laced in that blood. There is something else in the mixture they can't identify. Not sure what to make of this. We don't know what kind of tactic this is yet."

"Is it possible they were attacked and drained?" Paavo asked.

"That makes the most sense," sighed Long.

"You think they are already dead."

"Is that wrong?"

"There's always a chance that their bodies are buried in the snow, hidden away somewhere," said Paavo.

"You always say these things. You walk around with your head down. Me against the world, then you tell me to have hope," Long spat.

"Don't think like they're dead. I talked to the little girl's mother, there's always a chance of finding her."

"How did the footprints follow into the church?"

"I used the spray. It created a trail that led to a church and shelter down the alleyway."

"The spray? You mean that piece of metal you used to have with you all the time?"

"What's wrong with that?" asked Paavo.

"That's unreliable. You can't use something you invented to find forensic evidence."

Paavo smirked and took another drink of the beer. "You have praise for the photographs, but you have doubts about the spray?"

"It's just a science project that you try to flaunt around."

"Maybe so, but there are drug dealers around that church. I saw them," said Paavo.

"Did you approach them?"

"They were selling this," Paavo produced the wrap of paper, and placed it on the bar.

Long unwrapped the paper, it revealed a piece of dark red meat.

"What the hell is this?" he asked.

"I don't know what to tell you. It's ground beef, but I think they put something else in it."

"What did your device tell you?" asked Long sarcastically.

"Don't be a dick. I brought it to you first."

"You want us to analyze it?"

"Yes, I'll take a small piece with me and we'll see what we can find," said Paavo.

His eyes traced the edges of the paper as the can was raised to his lips. The taste of cold beer was a sweet escape. The sting of the liquid was bitter. He ran his tongue across his teeth to remove the taste from lingering there.

"Why would dealers sell food to people on the streets?"

"Maybe there's something in the food to make them keep coming back," Paavo shrugged.

"Did you ask anyone in the church about it?" asked Long.

"The priest was shady but it seems like anyone without a place to stay is put in the shelter around the back,"

"You always say priests are shady."

"They're not?" asked Paavo.

"Some aren't. You think the dealers had something to do with the missing girl?"

"I saw people fighting over the meat, it's got to be looked into."

"Why didn't you do more?" asked Long.

"I'm not a cop? I'm a little more cautious now, that's all."

"Don't tell me you're getting soft on me, young one. I'll have the lab take a look at this food and we'll run it with the blood," said Long. Paavo took a swig of beer and flexed his stomach, trying to keep the alcohol down.

"What can I do to help?" asked Long.

"Help me look for the girl. I started with the church, the shelter. I'll try the school and neighbors. Can you check witness reports from the day she was reported missing?"

Long stood up from his chair with his beer in hand.

"You know, I remember the days when you slept upstairs. She misses that time in our life. You made this house so lively, even though you barely said a word."

"I didn't know that," said Paavo.

"She talks about you all the time. When you left, there were no notes or messages. You disappeared without a trace, like a ghost.

Kyoko was so heartbroken by that, you have no idea. It's as if you were her child."

"Is that why you never had kids of your own after that?" Paavo asked.

"It is. After you left...After Simona passed away, there was too much sadness. To try and replace that void with another life, it would be foolish."

"I wouldn't say that," said Paavo.

"Have you ever felt a part of you die? This is what we felt and still do. We walk around half alive, half filled. There are days when we wake up to the falling snow and yearn for that missing piece. This city will always be trapped in snow. It's beauty is deceiving. Staring at the same thing for a lifetime can drive you insane. I supposed it's time for us to leave this place?" he asked.

"Maybe it is," said Paavo.

"I'm glad you came over, thank you for letting her see you again."

"It's the least I can do. Can I see the bedroom?" asked Paavo.

"Of course."

Paavo produced a pair of gloves and ripped a small piece of the food and paper to fold around it. The house was quiet. Kyoko had just fallen asleep. Both made careful steps to the second floor. Paavo felt the creaking beneath his feet. He checked the time and made a note of when to leave. There were four doors down the hall. Paavo picked at the small holes of chipped acrylics.

"She'll settle on something later this week, I hear," said Long. Paavo smirked as he approached the door and opened it to a dark bedroom. He fumbled for the light switch. His hands traveled down the side of the wall and back up again until he found it.

"You never changed it," said Paavo.

"I haven't been in this room since you left." Paavo stared into the bedroom that belonged to their daughter. It was where he slept when he ran out of money for his apartment. Long never went into detail about her passing. Some drunken fool, out of control was all it took to remove the old man's smile.

Paavo remembered the carpet that he used to scrub until his hands were raw trying to hide the bloodstains that hit the floor. The barren closet where Simona would hang her clothes was now only an empty white room. A collection of swords hung there now, tucked behind a loose board. Paavo knocked on each panel, looking for the right one. If he remembered correctly, the piece would fall to the right. A square of white moved slightly as he knocked along the back wall. Those were the same ones Long used to train him. He grabbed a katana and tossed it to the old man.

"For old times," said Paavo as he moved towards the window. He dropped the sheath on the floor.

"I wish I had met your daughter."

Paavo held his breath and turned back swinging the blade. Long brought his up in time to meet with his own. The edge of the sword missed Long's neck by mere inches.

"So do I," he said.

They circled each other. Long moved his blade into position and stabbed forward, Paavo ducked to the side and scraped the sword across his mentor's. The blades were sharp. They made a noise like thousands of razors. He wondered if Long still sharpened them on the grey block.

"She probably would have thought I was weird, and she would have played nice for you," he said.

Long seemed impressed the young man could still keep up. He remembered what I had taught him, he said to himself, not so lost after all.

"You are weird, but in a good way," said Long.

Both moved in sync with their weapons, Paavo dropped one arm to his side and swiped with his right hand, Long turned and parried at just the right time, their blades clashed once again in perfect time.

"But she would have ignored me outside these walls, I bet." Long began to remember the hours it took to perfect this routine. The young boy would get angry and toss his sword to the floor. He looked down for a split second to see the same gouge in the ground where Paavo lost his temper.

"Maybe not," said Long.

Swords met yet again and both men smiled. When Paavo finally learned the routine, he moved around the room with grace and blinding speed. It almost hurt the boy sometimes, but Long felt good knowing that he had passed on some knowledge. Perhaps he was skilled for battle and nothing else. They stopped and lowered their swords.

"Good."

"Thanks to you, Senpai. Thanks for letting me come in here."

"Don't mention it," said Long.

"It might be time for you to change this room, paint it a new color. I'll paint it black, just for you." Paavo closed his eyes and stumbled in his footing.

"I guess we're skipping the rest of the beer?" asked Long.

"Yeah, I've got to go, call me with what you find, yeah?"

"Sure thing. Don't disappear on me now," said Long.

Paavo said his goodbyes and stumbled off to his car. It was slow to start and slow to warm up, but Paavo drove home quickly, passing cars left and right as the pain in his chest increased. The doctor had lied to him, didn't he? He said that the shot would take effect and that it would cause sudden sleep. He never said it would stop the pain. Paavo did the math in his head. He had gone past the deadline for the next shot by a few hours. The pain grew in intensity. He cursed the doctor, his body, and the traffic as he dodged car after car, barreling through snow and storm. Paavo became angry. He hit the steering wheel.

The last thing he wanted was to develop a dependency on whatever drugs they gave him. He would find a way around it and then wean himself off. But what if this serum actually worked? Would he be able to live longer? Would it close the wound? Maybe life was attainable through this pain. He nodded off again and opened his eyes quick enough to see blinding headlights. He swerved quickly and missed a speeding car.

He slapped himself, trying to stay awake and darted through streets to the driveway. Paavo got out of the car and ran up to the stairs to get into the apartment. His limbs swerved in and around as he tried to climb the steps into his place. Paavo fumbled with his keys and held them close to his face. He unlocked the door and fell to the floor. He crawled slowly to the bathroom. It felt like an hour had passed before he reached it. The black bag rested on the sink. Paavo used the toilet to hold himself up before he yanked the bag down. The syringe fell out of its case and the bottle of serum rolled towards him. He caught the bottle and fingered the shot out of its plastic case. He took a dose with the syringe and rolled to his back. The pain was beyond intense. His hands began to shake while the syringe hovered over his chest. He thought of good things; drinking beer in the bar with Long, the people on the street eating the red food with ravenous mouths, Kyoko's cooking and good stories, having friends, a place to go. Sanctuary. He thought of his mother and father. Paavo shoved the syringe deep into his heart. His head and neck shot up in shock. He pressed the plunger down and felt the warm liquid enter his body. He faded, wondering if it was sleep or death. He closed his eyes as the room became quiet again.

CHAPTER NINE

Paavo awoke in the bathroom with his face sore from pressing on the tile. There was a trail of drool that connected his mouth to the floor. The window still blocked snow and hard wind. He felt a sharp pain in his chest and looked down to see the syringe still in his heart. Paavo wrapped his fingers around the tube and pulled it out slowly. He opened his eyes and saw the bleeding. The wound was gaping, engorged with blood. Over the course of the night it had hardened and cracked. Dark fluid leaked out. He took a handful of toilet paper and swept it beneath the faucet water to clean his chest. Paavo thought of placing a bandage over his heart but decided not to. The removal process would be too damaging. He buttoned his shirt and saw the round spot of blood over his heart.

His first day under the new medicine was a success. Paavo needed to find a way to work around the treatment. The doctor informed him that they would have to replenish the serum. Paavo checked the remaining amount. He still had a week to go before meeting the doctor again. Paavo sat down at the table in the center room and turned on his machines.

The machines spun in circles and flashed lights around the bottle of ammonia. The devices uploaded findings to the terminal across the room. Paavo wrote out new routines feverishly. The sample had finished, its results for matching fingerprints printed out onto a small sheet of paper. Paavo wondered if he should make the apartment his new base of operations. He doubted clients would be able to make the trip out to see him. He would still have to drive but all work could be done from here. No need for extra travel and risking more pain.

There were five possible matches for prints. His eyes followed the lines of the paper to the wires leading to the terminal. Paavo took a seat in front of the main screen and began to search for more information. The terminal took up the entire desk. It's structure of mix and match CPUs and processors made it resemble a monster. There were two monitors, two keyboards and a series of towers he could attach and remove for the right access to Police files and other programs for analyzing photos and film. Each tower had its own safeguards to keep anyone from finding out where the information was leaked. Paavo needed to find a way to get into databases without creating a paper trail.

The manufacturer of the ammonia bottle was based in America. The label was decorated with colored squares. The company had been one of main importers of goods and products into the city. He scribbled notes onto his pad of paper before quickly bending down to reattach another one of the towers below the desk. In a few minutes, he was able to go into inventory lists for the harbor. He checked for any recent shipments of the product into the city through the docks. There was a series of ships that had come in; each one listed the brand of ammonia and other similar imports, drain cleaner and lead based paints.

Three of the five possible matches for prints were dead. The two men listed as alive in Perdition were Daniel Jupiter and Lyoto Shirigami. The database was scarce on information about each man. Jupiter was a guard for Allied Arrows, a major security company. He had been hired by a large temp agency for those looking for easy work. Shirigami was a machinist in the industrial district. A phone call interrupted the silence of the room. Paavo answered it after four rings.

"Who is it?" A lilting voice stumbled into his ears.

"You know who this is, cousin. Don't try to hang up this time."

Paavo grimaced upon hearing the voice. He took a small breath and gritted his teeth.

"What do you want, Kazuhiko?"

The young prince laughed at the question.

"Grandmother turns eighty one this year. We are worried about her."

"She is doing well," said Paavo.

"We have tried to contact her with no luck, are you sure?"

"You won't find her in the phonebook. You might have to get off your ass and look for her if you want to establish an actual relationship."

"No position to lecture me, cousin. You should heed your own advice when it comes to associating with real people, maybe get yourself a woman and integrate into society," said Kaz.

"She is in good enough shape to not need your help, or your presence in the village."

Kazuhiko was one of many blood relatives who made him sick to his stomach. His mother's side of the family was one of great wealth and reputation. Family was the link that he could never hide from. Two years in exile, lost in dead end cases and slowly drowning in time was not enough to keep the family from searching for the missing piece of the savings.

"What happens after she's gone, Paavo? Are you going to take the savings for yourself? Maybe use it to fund a little adventure into that pathetic little pipe dream of yours? You wanted to be a detective right?" asked Kaz.

"The money is not for you. It's what kept her bills paid and that place going all these years. I made it this far on my own."

"Which isn't much of anything, you can barely support yourself." Paavo's anger began to boil over, his voice rose.

"You've lived comfortably your whole life. Are you that desperate for an old woman's money?" he asked.

"We should ask you the same question. The elders of the

family are all gone, except for her. We carry the legacy now. She needs to be protected."

"Protected? Or put away?" asked Paavo.

"You want the money, and you want her away from me. Why else give a shit about her until now? You've always been a coward."

"And you're a half-breed who didn't deserve the good life you were given...The life that your parents fucked up for you and themselves."

"The next time you speak of my parents, will be the last day that you walk with two legs," said Paavo.

"Do not threaten me, cousin. It's too easy to get the law involved with our little situation."

Paavo was seething. Grandmother didn't deserve to be taken away from her home. The family had squandered its money, and now they were going after the last one left from the old generation. He didn't have the finances to take them to court or fight for her. His heart began to sink at the slow realization that they were not going to stop until they got her.

"Are you there still...Family?" Kazuhiko's voice was taunting.

"You won't take her from this place," said Paavo.

"We can take her whenever we want. Remember that she is the one who needs help. You are too blind to see it, or perhaps too dependent on the precious little human contact you have left."

"Stay away for her, never call this number again."

The prince laughed again.

"You really are a ghost. Barely alive, haunting an old woman close to death. You'll be hearing from us soon."

Paavo listened to the empty drone of the phone line for several minutes before he got into his car and drove into the city.

The storm was raging on. The snow was pounding. Swirling white covered streets and buildings. His car swerved at hard turns. People bundled up with hats and heavy coats scrambled to get inside. Paavo decided to park and walk the rest of the way. He stepped out of the car and let out slow, controlled breaths. Steam poured from his mouth as he placed his hands deep into his pockets. A shortcut through the park would lead to Naoko's neighborhood. He moved down the stone steps, away from busy streets. The noise seemed to fade towards the bottom of the walkway. The park was split between a bike path around a small lake and a playground with a mass of iron shapes to climb on, separated by an old courtyard in the middle.

The lake was covered with a sheet of solid frost with a small sign warning those in the park to not step onto the ice. Paavo followed the bike path. Large trees loomed over the area. Snow was captured on their branches. They looked as giants watching over the park, protecting the children that played.

A group of kids ran past, laughing. They circled around him, chasing each other. Each was covered in snow. Paavo stopped for a moment to let them continue the game. They poked at him. One threw a large snowball that hit his chest, inches away from the covered wound. He felt no pain. They waved goodbye as he moved further down the walkway only to turn around and toss a flurry of snowballs at them. They screamed and ran away playfully. All roads seemed to lead back to the courtyard, further away than the shortcut. He decided to take a look.

Dead grass and withered leaves decorated the ground. The courtyard was small but one could view the entire park and surrounding city blocks from there. Paavo moved past a few rows of benches and tables to get a better view. The tables were immaculate, carved and perfectly shaped in stone. The sky above burned with a mixture of sunshine and grey that filled the area with a dark light.

Paavo stood silent until a figure walked across the courtyard, covered in a blanket and shawl. Their face was wrapped in a scarf, which made it impossible to tell if they were man or woman. The figure took a seat at one of the stone tables and produced a small wooden case from somewhere. Paavo stared as the figure removed the leather strap and unhooked the clasps on each side of the case. They opened up a piece of painted wood that was folded into four squares, connected by golden hinges. The wood was laid out onto the stone table. The paint was patterned into squares, an equal number made black and white. It was a chess board.

"Do you play?"

The voice was rough, it was hard to tell what was beneath those clothes, and Paavo was taken back by the question. It took a few moments to reply.

"I do," said Paavo.

It had been a long time since Paavo had played a chess game. The figure moved an arm towards the table, hands still hidden.

"You are welcome to join me."

"The weather calls for an indoor game, don't you think?"

The figure scoffed.

"Nonsense," they said.

Paavo was unsure of what to say next.

"Are you afraid to lose to me?"

"Not exactly."

The figure turned back towards the board, pulled a black bag from the inside of the case and held it upside down. Chess pieces fell onto the board.

"What's your name, son?"

"Paavo."

With movements of his hand, the figure separated the pieces

by color. White on their side, black on Paavo's.

"Interesting name. Do you know what it means?"

"No. Do you?" Paavo asked.

"Of course, but I'm not going to tell you what your father should have long ago." Paavo paused at the mention of his father.

"Did I strike a nerve? Hahaha. It means humble."

Paavo bowed his head towards the old one.

"How would you know?"

"What you just did, bowing to an elder, a sign of respect."

"I was raised alright."

"That remains to be seen. It also means small. Maybe you lack confidence, eh? Maybe you lack heart."

"Do I look like a coward?" Paavo asked.

"Not yet."

"And what is your name?"

"If you beat me, I will tell you." The old one said as they continued to assemble the pieces on the board.

"Don't you have something better to do with your time?"

Paavo scoffed at the idea.

"Seeing as how I'm going to die soon, I suppose I do."

The old one did not react to the revelation.

"How is it such a young man is already facing death?"

"It's a rare heart condition. I was born with it."

"The world feeds on the energy of the sun, just as the city feeds on tragedy."

The pieces on the white side were complete.

"For a dying man, you seem to be taking it well enough."

"What choice do I have but to push forward?" asked Paavo.

"You have no choice in the matter. Life goes on until it ends. At least you have a set time. Think about how some feel; walking down the street, content with their small lives, until they're struck down with no warning, no time to sit and think about what they've done."

The old one laughed. Paavo said nothing.

"You don't smile that much do you?"

"It takes a lot."

"Sarcasm suits you. As well as it could a dying man."

"I suppose my name doesn't matter in the end," Paavo suddenly did not feel like leaving. He continued the conversation.

"Our actions and words all have a purpose," he said.

"Names do not determine character. Instinct and emotion dictates that, not the choices that we make." The old one said.

They seemed more wise than crazy.

"People these days give their children such silly names. They think that giving the young ones names of royalty, of honor, of dignity, that will bestow them such character."

"I think I was lucky enough to avoid such bad taste," said Paavo.

"You did. So many born into this world, tainted with corrupt and ignorant thoughts before they even have a chance to defend themselves. They think elaborate names demand a sort of respect. They don't. Respect and honor must always be earned."

"Every youth has a period of defiance. They feel it necessary to spit in the face of authority. I can relate to that," Paavo said.

"Unfortunately, some men never moved past those days. I wouldn't know, I don't think past first impressions, anyway."

"Do you judge people based on the things they say and do? Or the way they look? Clothes they wear? By what label they were given as they were born?" asked the old one.

"I don't judge people."

"That's a lie; all creatures of this world were born with judgment."

"I don't judge innocent people," Paavo explained.

"Not yet. But don't feel bad, everyone does. It's a part of all of us. Your time will come."

The old one finished assembly. Small armies were set up on each side. The white pieces were made from a beautiful ivory. The black pieces were smooth, without fingerprints, as if they were untouched.

"I have outlived the importance of a name. I have survived and seen enough to last lifetimes, there is no need to define myself. I am what you see before you. Simple."

"So what am I supposed to call you?" asked Paavo.

"You aren't supposed to call me anything. I just am." Paavo's eyes moved towards his watch, it felt like he had been talking for hours. For a moment, he felt like staying. He felt like sitting down and playing a game of chess.

"Why did you come here?"

"Passing through."

"I've never seen you here before."

"I was gone for some time." Paavo said. The scenery seemed to change around him. The grey sky had darkened slightly. The trees all around grew long and brought shadows. White clouds moved with the passing of the sun. For a moment, the old one had no shadow.

"You're searching for answers. The answer to every question

can be found inside this game here. I'm an old ghost with no one to talk to. You're different from the others. They lacked respect. You'll always be welcome here."

"I do need answers, but I have somewhere to be," said Paavo.

"If your path takes you back here, we should play a game."

"Another time."

The old one turned towards Paavo, still unable to see his face inside the deep darkness.

"Good. I will be here when you are ready."

Paavo walked down the path, away from the courtyard. The old one moved one piece and raised their arm. Paavo felt a severe chill run down his spine as he moved towards the end of the park. He took another look back at the old one, expecting him to vanish. They never did, the hooded figure remained stationary, playing the game, moving piece after piece at a snail's pace. Paavo thought about the children. He could never have been able to play with them when he was their age.

The sight of blood pouring from the chest and the mouth of another would have scarred them. Maybe they weren't that innocent after all. Would they have taunted me as a child? He asked himself over and over again. The old one had said he would soon judge everyone. He tried not to think about it as he walked. Paavo asked himself if he would return to the courtyard to play a game.

He made it to Naoko's neighborhood. The storefronts didn't really know anything. The neighbors weren't as responsive and mostly shut their doors in his face. Those who chose to speak provided no information. Paavo tried his best to look presentable and professional. Nothing worked. He went to Naoko's school, still hoping to find some kind of lead. Her teacher was empathetic to the situation. She spoke well of Naoko, but said the girl was taunted and troubled. He tried to tiptoe around the Akis' personal business, but their poverty was well-known.

He could still see spots of dry blood on his clothes. He tried his best to hide them by rushing into the bathroom to wash away the dried blood. The water from the sink was hot, which burned his pale hands a deep red. Paavo decided to take a look at the shelter, which meant testing the blood found at the crime scene.

The machines would analyze traces of DNA, and reproduce them in liquid form to contrast using special black and white photographs. The tracking liquid could work as a spray. Paavo used it to see where they took the possible body by showing footsteps akin to black light analysis. Back at the office, Paavo divided the meat into two and placed both beneath colored lights and scopes. He fed the machines photographs of the church, shelter and alleyway.

The photos came out the other side, littered with colored pathways of yellow and black. The machines replenished the spray with yellow and black liquid once they were finished. Paavo looked over each of the photographs. Trails and footprints followed alongside each other into the church, across the alleyway and into the shelter. Both pieces of meat were dotted with the same substance. Paavo sprayed a small amount of liquid onto the outside of the paper that held the meat. If the colors matched, then it would signify the prints in the photos belonged to the dealers. The paper was soon dotted with yellow and green. In an hour or so, the office was cleared out. Paavo collected his bags and dropped them in the trunk of his car.

The machinist's apartment was abandoned with a key taped on the door, according to the owner. He lived there for many years with no complaints. He was a quiet man. Lyoto paid his last bill and had moved out overnight. He left no signs that he was leaving, just the key on the door and an empty room. Paavo had asked for a chance to look around. The curtains were opened wide, letting light into the room. Plain white paint coated the walls. There was no substance to the apartment. Paavo wondered how a man in his fifties was able to get all the furniture out without making a sound. Paavo moved through the rooms, searching for signs of anything strange. The owner had said that he did not inspect the entire apartment. He was going to finish that up tomorrow morning.

The bedroom had a closet, boarded up. It didn't take much to pull them apart. The door swung open to an empty space. Paavo looked down to see a pool of blood. The smell was strong. He bent down to take a sample with the device. A green light and alert had sounded. It was a match. The blood was tainted with the same ammonia. Paavo left the room and notified the owner to call the Police. The snow outside died down for a moment. He decided to wait for them to arrive, and then head to Lyoto's job. The other tenants were left to gossip.

"What are the Police doing here?"

"Do you think he was killed?"

"We didn't hear anything last night or the night before."

"Maybe he lost his job and he killed himself..."

"Why the hell would you say something like that?"

"I'm just saying..."

"Who asked you anyway?"

"Why do you even care? He's just an old man. None of us gave a shit about him."

"Still, it's sad."

"Yeah, well...Life goes on."

Paavo shook his head as they shuffled by. To them, he was just another missing body and it wasn't their problem. He left in disgust, wondering what the hell he was doing all this work for. On the way to the factory, he made a call.

"What is it?"

"Wendell, it's me."

Paavo still owed him money for the office.

"How are ya?"

"I'm alright, I wanted to tell you that I'm done with the office."

"All of a sudden? I can't let you go like that, kid. I need cash.

"I have to go underground for some time, whatever you need. When do you need it?"

"A.S.A.P. You know the deal, kid."

"Of course."

"You're a good kid. You got something up on the others out there. You got manners. That's what separates you. You're gonna turn into something successful. You're gonna go real far, get me my money and you take care, alright?"

"No question. You take care as well."

"If you ever need anything, call me, yeah?"

"I will."

The money from the bank job would have done wonders for him. There was the village. He could take some from there. He felt a pain in his stomach about using money meant for grandmother, it didn't belong to him. No choice for now. He would return the money once he got paid. Lyoto was a worker in the industrial district. Researching the buildings, only two were still in operation during the winter. Each year, the factories would shut down and send everyone home for a couple of weeks. The place would be abandoned which gave him a chance to take a look around. Paavo needed something that Lyoto had been in contact with; anything that had traces of the substances he'd been finding.

Heavy snow and rain continued to mask the city in white and grey shadows. The factory sat at the end of the street like an old relic. It was a sleeping giant of stone and brick. There were glass eyes that dotted its body and horns of a devil that spewed smoke from the furnace engine beneath the concrete. Paavo needed to get in and out with no sign of breaking and entering. There were no maintenance doors or fire escapes. He stopped over a manhole. There had to be a storm drain, a place for the water to be cleaned and redistributed into the bathrooms and sinks inside. He lifted the cover to a pitch black drop down.

Paavo slipped on a pair of old gloves and made his way down. He left the cover off to allow light in. Flakes of snow danced down into the shadows with him. The light from above had dwindled into nothing but a halo of distant grey. Paavo stepped into a deep pool of melted snow water. He was up to his waist in freezing cold liquid. From the street above, he moved east. The cold water began to numb him after only a minute of wading into the darkness.

His heartbeat increased in speed as he rushed forward in hopes of finding the storm drain. Rats moved through the collected garbage, searching for food. Paavo kept his hands to his sides not wanting to be bitten. The end of the hallway revealed a dimly lit bulb above a sealed door. His gloves gripped onto the wheel but did not move. Paavo wedged himself against the wall and turned. Nothing moved. He switched off on placing his weight on each arm, pushing and pulling the wheel until it began to dislodge. The rust and chipped paint has cut deep into his hands. Sounds of squeaking iron echoed through the sewer until the door was open enough for him to push through the water and close the door behind him.

The drain area held a high ladder; another climb to reach the sub basement. Once inside, there was a freight elevator that took Paavo to the main floor. Several staircases curved up to the offices that branched out and over the production area. The employee lockers were stacked three by eight and stretched for the entire length of the floor. Faded green paint revealed older shades of red and brown. The place had been there for many years though the machines were brand new. The walls barely held together with patches of missing brick and cement crumbled onto the floor. Each row of lockers was arranged by last name. Lyoto's was broken open; the padlock removed, the door open for anyone to take what was inside.

There was nothing inside but a photograph attached to a piece of paper folded and placed underneath the broken padlock. The film depicted a black and white mountain range that stretched across the land. In the foreground stood a group of hooded figures with faces covered by a white cloth draped over each of their bodies. He grabbed the paper and opened it. There was nothing but a single phrase, written in a thick red ink.

"La Récolte."

He took the paper and pocketed it. From his jacket, Paavo produced a small brush and a special mixture of powder to scan for fingerprints. He quickly dusted the padlock and locker. No prints were left. He next produced a vial of PH solution with a form of Paraffin. Paavo emptied it out onto the floor. The clear liquid turned bright pink; traces of dirt and acids from the machinery, as well as grease and water from the boots of workers.

The trail of pink had turned into a dark red; a sign of foreign substances. Paavo dropped in a small pill of dissolving wax with a pit of tiny magnets. The pill mixed with the solution. Paavo watched it swirl in random circles. The pill began to follow the path of liquid. He stepped behind the magnets as they marked the trail. The trail marked footsteps that entered through a side door. The path stopped at the entrance to the maintenance area. The door was unlocked.

Inside the office was an open window. A small pile of snow had begun to build on the floor. Who had done this, if not Lyoto? Paavo collected his things and left the factory through the open window. Some of the solution slipped from his hands and hit the note left in the locker. It reacted with the ink, showing two separate agents in the mixture; more blood and ammonia.

The Police station was nearly empty. The white snow mixed with bright sun outside, casting the rooms in a dim yellow. A strong gust of wind bashed into the windows. Long stretched out in the back of the lab. The rats studied the piece of meat found by Paavo. Motoko worked beneath the microscope. Kuriyama shined her glasses in the corner. She had been there since four in the morning.

"There's some unique red coloring here. The whole thing is doused with it," said Motoko.

"What is it? Blood?"

"Some of it, yes. Traces of the same ammonia are here in the food. No results from our tests."

The old cop furrowed his brow.

"That's all you have?" Kuriyama put her glasses back on.

"We can't find anything wrong with it. It's just food," she said.

"A problem still unknown after 24 hours? I'm disappointed. This is a first for you nerds," said Long.

Motoko lifted her head from the scope.

"We've been trying to figure it out. There are some trace elements of saliva," she said.

"Whose saliva? Whoever is dealing this crap is going out of their way to hide any traces of who they are," asked Long.

"The saliva comes up with more possible matches in the database. The ammonia or the unknown could be causing interference."

"You mentioned fingerprints as well?" He nodded.

"Probably from whoever ate from the meat? Prints might be

from the dealers. We need ID's on anyone who's touched it."

"New substance smells good. It's sugar based, with several DRIs," said Motoko.

"What's that?" he asked.

"DRI means Dopamine reuptake inhibitor," said Kuriyama.

"Keep going," said Long. Yamagishi fixed his glasses to his face as he dug deeper down into the view of the microscope.

"It's a drug used to treat ADD and Narcolepsy. It blocks the flow of Dopamine to the presynaptic neurons in the body, causing an overflow of synaptic transmission," he said.

"How long are you going to keep using big words without an explanation?" asked Long.

"Think of an electrical current that flows through the nervous system. The current flows through neurons, which make up the impulses. Impulses provoke each cell, causing movement in the human body."

"So, it stops people from moving?" asked Long.

"Quite the contrary, it opens the gates of neurotransmission. It becomes an overload of the senses, a feeling of extreme euphoria. Like an animal tranquilizer, DRIs are notorious for their high abuse potential and liability to cause cravings, addiction, and dependence." The inspector shook his head in disbelief.

"What the hell," he said.

"Forms of DRI include drugs like cocaine and ecstasy. Each one acts as an agent, releasing this current throughout the body," said Kuriyama.

"What kind of DRI is this, then?" asked Long.

"We aren't sure yet, there's a tainted mixture inside this meat. We aren't able to trace it. It must have been strong enough to mask that this meat has gone bad. Really bad," said Yamagishi.

Long threw his hands up.

"So what next?" he asked. Kuriyama smiled and shrugged.

"We have to keep looking."

"Oh, you will. Reference it with everything you've got, that means anything in store, industrial, any and everything in this city. What are some side effects of this medicine?" asked Long.

The lab rats looked at each other.

"Possible reactions to an overabundance of DRI can lead to serious psychological and physiological problems," said Yamagishi.

"Give me some examples," said Long.

"Besides an increase in energy, rapid talking and hyperactivity, there's also an increase in aggression, rage, tachycardia," said Motoko.

"Then we start looking for cases anywhere in the city," said Long. The rats lowered their heads and resumed their work. Long stepped out of the lab at a loss for words. What kind of people would sell drugs inside rotting meat to the homeless? he thought.

"If you're hungry enough, you will eat anything," said Motoko. She handed him an envelope.

"What's this?" Long asked.

"The names of the dealers. You forgot to grab it." Long took the envelope. He decided to call Paavo. There was no answer but decided to leave a message.

"Hey kid, how you doing? I've got some information on your piece of meat; give me a call when you get the chance."

Long turned around and saw Masonori stepping out from the snow. He cleaned off his black suit jacket and threaded fingers through his hair.

"Good morning," said Long.

"We need to talk, get your ass inside."

The phone rang. It was Paavo.

"What is it?"

"Busy morning, kid?"

Paavo scrambled for a piece of paper.

"Something like that, I have something for you," he said.

"What's that?" asked Long.

"My address."

"Oh, really? My wife cooks you dinner and you're coming out of your shell now?"

"It appears so," said Paavo.

The machines buzzed in the background.

"What's that noise?"

"A lead."

"Good, we've got something you might be interested in," said Long.

Paavo's eyebrows rose.

"Tell me," he said.

"That piece of meat you found was tainted. Dealers sold meat covered with all kinds of shit to those people you saw last night."

"It doesn't smell like it," said Paavo.

"I know, lab rats found something in there, some kind of medicine. We got traces of saliva and prints that we're going to cross with our records. They're still finding things in this shit," said Long.

"Strange."

"Saliva's got to be from the people who bought the meat. You said they tore into it pretty quickly, right? But this medicine is something we have to look deeper into."

"I'm going back to the church. I have to follow those dealers, see where they get that meat from," said Paavo.

"I've got their names right here."

"They work quick. What are the names?"

"Len Kimura, Ota Shimizu."

"This is good for now. Let me know if you find them," said Paavo.

"You're looking for them?"

"Am I supposed to ask you for your permission?" asked Paavo.

"I'm a little worried about you running around in a snowstorm with a bunch of crazy assholes," said Long.

"I'll be fine. The priest didn't know her but the ammonia in the blood left on the street corner came from a bottle made in America. Maybe a shipment came in through the docks? I found some prints."

"Any matches?" asked Long.

"Two; A man named Jupiter and a machinist named Shirigami. The second one was an old man who disappeared. His apartment was empty, a pool of blood in the closet. Someone took him. There were traces of foreign substances at his job, as well."

"What do you need from me?" asked Long.

"A way to contact your rats," said Paavo.

"I'll have more evidence by the end of the night."

"What shelter were you talking about before?"

"There's a homeless shelter behind the church near your crime scene," said Paavo.

"I've never heard about a shelter over there."

"Neither did I. But there are groups of students and teachers that go there every Sunday," said Paavo.

"Do you think that place is dirty?" asked Long.

"I don't know. But I've got to get going."

"What do you think they put in the medicine to make them want to eat this shit?"

Paavo thought of the factory.

"It might not be the medicine. Maybe something else inside there that they want besides that," he said.

Long questioned him.

"Like what?"

He began to walk towards Masonori's office.

"Designer drug?" asked Paavo.

Long took a hard look at the city behind him before it disappeared behind a wall of snow and wind.

"God, I can't even imagine..."

CHAPTER TEN

Paavo headed towards the church and shelter again. He took his time, knowing what was to come. It had been years since he'd done any stakeouts. The countryside was so beautiful in winter. For every calm image and moment, he was reminded of the pain.

When they first met, Long asked him how he was handling school and work full time and how he liked the city. The young man told him that it was like hell. The dry, morbid sense of humor was something Long like he needed. The boy never really laughed. He just lowered his eyes, nervous to react. Long didn't mind. The kid just lost his parents, he thought. It'll take time to learn how to get on with life. Wounds like that never heal properly. He was used to the sadness. A kid on the street, damaged by addict parents was nothing new. Who knew how many others were like him? Long hated to think of the kid as another statistic.

"I need to ask you a few questions. In private," said Masonori.

The man was only a few years older than Long, though his frame was much larger. He brought up a folder, sealed off with rubber bands to keep the contents from falling out.

"Take a seat, Derek. We have much to talk about."

The Chief dropped the folder onto the table. Long took a seat. This form of conversation made him uneasy. It took a great deal of energy to not expect the worst.

"What's in the folder?" asked Long.

"These are photos from the security cameras at the Outlook. We found some images from the day of the robbery that were a bit striking."

"There was an EMP blast used during the robbery, where did you get these shots from if all the cameras were down?"

"Backup generator," said Masonori.

"We spoke with the security in the building. It takes a set amount of minutes for it to reset. These men knew the bank inside and out. They knew how much time they had."

"I'm not sure where this is going, John."

Masonori opened the folder and dropped the first photograph in front of him. The shot was taken from the live feed of the Outlook security footage; a group of men holding guns and gathering the workers in a circle on the floor. The second was a shot of the leader speaking in the center.

"Is there anything I'm supposed to find here?" asked Long.

Masonori looked at him with contempt.

"Keep going," he said.

Long pulled out the last shot; the gunshot fired into the skull of the leader. A figure in blue held his gun high as workers on the floor grimaced and screamed in horror. In the bottom corner sat a thin figure in black. His expression was blank. His face was familiar. It was Paavo. What the hell was he doing there during the robbery?

"Do you see it?" Long tried to hide his emotions.

"What is it?"

"The kid in black, sitting in the corner."

"What about him?" asked Long.

"He's an accomplice. We have several eyewitnesses placing him there, with one of them."

"And the kid wasn't there when we arrived, which means he escaped. Maybe he was in the wrong place, wrong time. He got spooked and left as soon as there was an opening?" asked Long.

"The outside cameras caught him walking with a man identified as Junpei Kotaro. The men took the money and went down in a hail of gunfire in a tunnel beneath the subway. Junpei Kotaro is suspected to be Seven, profiting off robbing his own business partners, even himself."

Long was surprised.

"The infamous thief, eh? What was he doing interrupting a bank score?" he asked.

"We don't know, that's your job. The real question is why the kid was escorting him into the place? Was he a part of it? Get Seven inside to get the drop on the other groups? Only half of the money was recovered. Some of it is still out there. Maybe your detective friend can help us? Do you think the kid's got it stashed somewhere?" asked Masonori.

"Someone like Seven can't be stupid enough to steal from a bank covered with cameras."

"What's his name? The kid..."

Long bit his tongue. Masonori nodded, getting what he wanted.

"Paavo Harker? What does he do now? Detective, right?"

"He's a P.I. He used to work at the station two years ago," said Long.

"That's what some of your boys say. He's got a bit of a reputation down here, doesn't he?"

"He created a lot of tech that we use now for crime scene study, forensic sprays, recording equipment, the works."

"I'd like to meet him," said Masonori.

"If you can get him to stand still, you might."

"If we showed them these photos, what do you think he would say about them? What was this kid doing there?"

Long threw his hands up.

"I have no idea," he said.

"The man who was killed in the picture was Vincent Celino. He was a captain for the Celino crime family; one of the three we're investigating, along with the Capotellis," said Masonori.

"Maybe the kid was looking for Jimmy the Recluse."

"He didn't find him. Instead, we've got a major player in organized crime gunned down by a group of masked men, who got taken out themselves. Something's happening between the families. Maybe a coup."

"Our men found Jimmy's bodyguard, he wouldn't talk. He said that he was considered already dead if he was caught, no good to us. He would rather be put in prison to protect his own wife and kids from the Recluse," said Long.

"I want to talk to the kid in this picture. Bring him in for questioning. If you don't get to him, we will."

The Chief left the room, leaving the folder on the desk. Long stared into the photo. Paavo's face showed no emotion as a murder unfolded before him. He took a moment to pray for the kid.

Paavo's chest burned. He held his hand over the wound. Having to take the serum and be out of commission would ruin the stakeout. Paavo stepped out into the alley; a stark contrast of black and white with hard rusted metal and wet concrete blanketed in snow.

His sneakers left a path of long footprints that he went back and mixed up with his feet, not leaving a trace of his presence. He scouted the area, looking for the dealers. Paavo checked his watch. He still had about nine hours until the next shot.

He took several long breaths and studied the photographs. He reached for his cell phone. It's screen lit up with a press of the power button, revealing a crack across its face. He dialed a number and hit send.

"Hello?"

"Good afternoon, father," said Paavo.

"I have a few more questions for you, concerning the missing girl."

"Of course."

"Have you ever had any convicted felons in your employ? Two men were picked up for dealing, two men who I saw working at your church." Wen was quiet for a moment.

"Who were they?" he asked.

"Kimura and Shimizu," said Paavo.

"Both of them were troubled at best." His reaction seemed almost apathetic.

"I had hoped my program would give them a chance to start a new path without the shackles of drug addiction."

"They asked for you, not family or friends," said Paavo.

"They are lost. I failed to steer them in the right direction. But I don't see what this has to do with the missing girl you are looking for."

"It just seems strange that you would use people with checkered pasts for your hired help."

"What do you think would be best?" asked Wen.

"I don't know, it's not up to me," said Paavo.

"The choice to give them a chance to clean up their act was mine."

"Will you help them?" asked Paavo.

"In time, they must repent for what they've done. Everyone must atone for their past."

"Even you?"

"Of course. Your burdens are mine as well to carry," said Wen.

"There are so many others who need the money and work who sit in your seats, add to the collection plate and listen to you talk." Paavo spat.

"I don't think you like me very much, do you?"

"You believe in something I turned away from a long time ago."

"What made you do such a thing?" asked Wen.

"The reality of my situation. I'm dying. Religion can't help me forget."

"But it can bring you peace," said Wen.

"I should go, thank you for your time."

The phone call ended before Wen could say anything else. The priest lowered the phone and moved off towards the darkness of the office. Paavo waited in shadows of his own. The doorbell rang at Miss Aki's apartment. Paavo waited for her.

"Hello?"

"This is Paavo."

"Oh yes!"

The old woman's voice seemed to leap out of the phone, there was a brief silence.

"Please tell me you have found her."

"Not yet, I need to ask you some questions."

"Please, Mr. Harker. You have to find her. You must help me. Whatever you need, just name it," she said.

"I just need to ask some questions about the church and

Father Wen."

Miss Aki's face changed when thinking of the priest.

"You know of Father Wen? Such a good man."

She calmed down as she spoke.

"What is there to really say? He was a saint, so helpful for Naoko and I."

"Very good. Did you ever stay at the shelter?" he asked.

"Yes, there was a time when we stayed there after the factory closed and money ran out."

"What did you do at the factory?"

"I packaged toys to be sent off to big department stores. The church was always a big part of the neighborhood," she said.

"Sounds like fun."

"A job is never fun," Miss Aki laughed.

"Tell me about the shelter," said Paavo.

"It was cold. We had small cots to sleep on, lots of blankets. There was some food, but there were so many people, you know."

"How long did you stay there?" asked Paavo.

"A few weeks. Father Wen helped everyone," she said.

"Were there a lot of children there?" he asked.

"Many families, actually. We all became close," said Miss Aki.

"Do you think Naoko ran away to the shelter, maybe?" he asked.

"No, there is no shelter behind the church anymore." Paavo stopped for a second.

"What do you mean?" he asked.

"The shelter was closed down," she said.

"Why would they do that?"

"A lot of people were put out by them abandoning the shelter. I think it has to do with Father Wen's death."

Paavo nodded and then stopped.

"Father Wen's death?"

"Yes, he died fifteen years ago; it was so tragic." Paavo hesitated.

"How did he die?" he asked.

"It was a stroke, it was a painful time for him. He lost his voice at times and began to limp, and then one day, he was gone."

Miss Aki's voice began to cut up, she had begun to sob.

"He laughed and played with the children. Days later, he disappeared and we never saw him again."

"I am sorry," he said.

"Tell me about the last time you and Naoko were at the shelter."

"It was so cold. We cleaned up and bundled our coats tight. I had to walk slowly, you know, Naoko was still in my belly." Miss Aki laughed a little.

"I could picture her waddling down the road with the other children, like little penguins."

Paavo wanted to fake a laugh, but stayed silent.

"The shelter was cold, they were always working on the building, making it so we could have a place to pray and get some good food."

"What did they have to eat?" he asked.

"They made us stew, noodles whatever they could get. They took care of us. I'm so grateful that place was there."

"Did Gordon have any children, any family to follow in his footsteps?" he asked.

"Not that I know of, no," she said.

"That church, do you still remember the address?" Miss Aki rattled off the numbers.

"Thank you for your help and patience. I'm doing everything possible to find her," he said.

"You're welcome, Mr. Paavo, please find my daughter, thank you so much for helping me." Miss Aki began to sob again.

Paavo's voice lowered.

"Of course, I'll be in touch."

Paavo looked up into the white sky as the snow fell around him swirling with wind and freezing drops of rain. The shadows of a man huddled on the corner showed through blinding white. It was one of the dealers from the night before, cramped together over a makeshift fire. Paavo inhaled in and out with each step. He readied his gun in the breast pocket of the blazer.

The man turned to see Paavo approaching at a glacial pace. He ignored the thin black shape moving towards him. Paavo raised a hand towards him.

"Hey, you on the job?" he asked.

The man turned and faced him, he smiled. He recognized him from the night before and sized him up. Paavo's sneakers were wet with snow and ice.

"Depends."

A struggle in the storm would do no good. Paavo moved his head to the side to avoid some of the cold.

"I've heard good things about the church, that you provide a good service for the people," he said.

"Yeah, it's not free."

"I've got cash," Paavo assured him.

"That does just fine. What you need?"

"I was looking for the Holy Spirit."

"Oh, yeah? That's kind of a specialty order. Things need to be established before we get it."

Paavo's head turned slightly.

"Like what?"

"I don't hold any of that; it's given to me," they said.

Paavo felt the cold wind and snow burn his eyelids. He thought of the dead priest. Who were these people? Paavo lowered his head and took a breath under his jacket, he let out a hoarse cough.

"How long would it take?"

"Come back in two hours, I'll have what you need..."

"How much do you need?" asked Paavo.

"Two hundred. This spot, two hours."

Paavo said as he stuck his thumb up. The man looked at him strangely then turned down the corner. Paavo slowly walked back to the car as the storm gained strength. He opened his door as snow spilled onto his seat. The heat was cranked all the way up. Paavo put his hands over the vents and cursed the vehicle. He worked his limbs, trying to get the blood flowing again. The shipyard late shift was easy to cooperate with. He asked them over the phone if they would let him take a look at some on the manifests for recent shipments. They agreed and gave him a time to come down. Meeting with Wendell would kill enough time. Paavo placed a call to 911 to drop an anonymous tip.

Long received word that two men were apprehended outside the church. The café was open, but empty. There were a few people passing by, covered in coats and scarves quietly braving the harsh weather. The lights inside flickered and dimmed. Long sipped on black coffee and moved his lips across his teeth to take the bitter taste away.

Thoughts of Paavo making moves without him began to take the place of strong drink. An officer dropped the report off on his table. Long and the man exchanged nods. Shimizu and Kimura were found at a drug spot. Both claimed to know nothing of the red meat or a man with long hair. Long returned to his coffee and glanced at the cars moving slowly over snow and ice. The young man had been through enough to know how to take care of himself but the hole in his heart never healed. It remained after all this time, still bleeding on. What did this mean for the boy?

An old man moved slowly through his apartment, slippers hit the tiles of the kitchen floor. His hands clutched a bowl of noodles. The bowl sent lines of steam out into the air. Wendell prepared for his meal. He rested the bowl down and shook his hand a few times, still feeling the warmth exiting his food. There was a knock at the door. He grumbled and moved towards the door.

"Yeah, yeah...Hold on, damn you."

Wendell unlocked his door and opened it. A black sleeve covered an arm outstretched. The pale hand inside held a wad of cash. He smiled immediately.

"You little shit. I didn't think you'd make it up here that fast!" He swiped the money from Paavo's hand.

"Come on in...I've got food."

The rest of Paavo emerged from around the corner, and smirked.

"Kid, you look like all kinds of hell, come on now."

"I'll be alright." Paavo said.

"You look like you need some tea."

"No, really, I'll be fine. I need some sleep...which I'll get this evening." Wendell smiled.

"Too much time with the ladies, I see..."

"No time for women, and besides. No money for women now, thanks to you."

"Ahhh! Yes, indeed! No money makes leads to no women! Now what will you do?"

"Get to work, I suppose..." Paavo shrugged.

"You'd best get your ass a job! Snow or not! You need a job, you need money, and then everything else falls into place. Wendell looked up and down at Paavo; his face was a pale white, those black clothes finely tailored before were dirty and damp.

"You really ought to sit and eat with me. I've got room for one more."

Paavo sat down at the table. He folded his hands and bounced his legs in place. Wendell disappeared for a minute to return with a spare bowl and chopsticks. He dropped it on the table in front of Paavo.

"Hang on."

Paavo kept his hands on the bowl as Wendell poured the remains of the pot into the bowl. Noodles and broth splashed out onto the table. Paavo used to eat there every week. He smelled the shrimp for the first time in ages. His mouth watered, and a rush of warmth hit his chest. Wendell sat down and brought his food to his face. He always watched Paavo when he ate. It was so bizarre to him. Sure enough, Paavo began his eating ritual, and Wendell looked on like a small child.

Paavo collected a portion of noodles with his sticks, rolled them and placed it into his mouth. Paavo placed his hand over his heart as the muscles beneath his wound began to contract. Wendell quickly got up to pour some hot tea. He was about to hand off the cup before realizing he forgot Paavo's favorite ingredients. He dropped a lemon slice and some sugar inside the drink and swirled it around with a spoon before placing it at the table.

"Thank you," said Paavo.

His hand stayed over his heart as he felt the moisture come from underneath the shirt. Wendell had known about Paavo's condition ever since they met. He told the young man war stories about old girlfriends. Wendell could see the wet spots on Paavo's shirt. Heavy laughter made him bleed out. Wendell was shocked when he saw it for the first time.

Long stepped back into the lab. The rats were hard at work. The clicking of computer keys filled the air. He waited impatiently for them to present their findings. Yamagishi was first. He stepped away from his computer and pulled Long over to the side.

"The men caught today? We found a list of their known accomplices. One of them was at the hotel shootout and another by the name of Clayton Jones," he said.

"If they're linked together with that deal at the docks, then those drugs are what we've been chasing all this time, and it's already hit the streets. We still don't know who's supplying it or where it comes from," said Long.

"I wonder if Paavo's found anything new," said Yamagishi.

"Yeah, thank you, keep up the good work." Long spoke up for them all to hear.

"All of you. Great work."

Yamagishi nodded and went back to his desk with the others. The furious clicking continued as they each exchanged smiles.

Paavo had finished his meal and gotten up to leave.

"You young people are always on the move. It's good to see you eating healthy again," said Wendell.

Paavo smirked and shook his hand.

"Take care, sir."

"Stay alive, young man."

Paavo took a bow and left the apartment. The footsteps echoed throughout the building. He checked his watch; there was still too much time until midnight. A sharp pain hit him. He grunted loudly in frustration and slowed his pace. All he could do was breathe in and hurt until he reached the bottom. He leaned against the wall and found the paper with the number to the shipyard. The workers spoke in gruff voices.

"Hey, you're the detective right?"

"I am. Did you find anything?"

"Not really, there was only one ship that came through from overseas. It sticks out like a sore thumb, man. We don't get a lot of shit from the other side, you know?"

Paavo coughed slightly.

"The other side?" he asked. Laughter burst through the receiver.

"The faraway place, man. The other half of the world."

"Fair enough. The cops were down there watching a deal take place. That ship had something hidden. Did they search it?" asked Paavo.

"It's barren. We took a look inside, nothing. It must have been emptied out days ago."

"What was on the manifest?" asked Paavo.

"There was a package near the bottom of the deck with a note." Paavo took a breath and felt the blood flowing underneath his throat.

"What did the note say?" he asked.

"It was some French shit. There was paint on the boat, a whole container of it. Somebody came and picked it up, saying that it was part of the load. He signed off for it and everything."

"You have his signature?" asked Paavo.

"Of course, nothing gets out of here without a record of it."

The man took off. Paavo waited patiently, feeling the blood inside his body. He felt sick as a silent river travelled through his veins. The man returned with a name; Daniel Jupiter. The workers remembered a man, calm and collected, walking up to them with a suitcase.

"Very chill guy. He came in really polite, and had a nice suit. He claimed the package, signed the book and left in a matter of minutes."

Paavo thanked them and hung up. He stopped at the bottom of the steps, sat down in the middle of the floor and crossed his legs. He slowed his breathing, flexed the muscles in his stomach and arms. Paavo pushed the air out of his body. He felt a sharp pain in his heart. Blood welled up inside his wound. Paavo concentrated. This was his ritual; a way to cope with the pain and the wound for all these years. He placed his hand over his chest, and felt the warm air leave his body.

Minutes later, Paavo slowly removed his hand from his chest. The fabric of the shirt peeled slowly off his skin and left an imprint of blackened red on his shirt. A warm spot that hovered over his heart; it would tide him over for a while. He stepped out into the cold. The snow began to subside, the outline of buildings and streets became visible for the first time in hours.

CHAPTER ELEVEN

The scanner was a fury of static and voices. Paavo swirled a glass of warm tea in circles. The apartment was a mess of equipment brought over from the office. He listened for more information regarding the church. The terminal sat idle on a page listing every man within a hundred miles with the name Gordon Wen. He found him; the priest who had died fifteen years ago. Who was this man staring back at him?

This Gordon Wen had a certificate of death, as well. Paavo inhaled the last of his tea and took a screenshot of the priest. Perhaps he felt some deep connection with the city. Why keep the same name? How had no one from the original shelter come to find him? What was he hiding from? Paavo had shuffled through the graveyard where he was supposedly laid to rest. The cemetery was empty and the cold snow unrelenting. He was unable to locate the grave. With no money to have the body exhumed, he thought maybe someone had taken the priest's information and placed it over their own. The newspaper archives had a record of his death. For hours, he stared baffled at Wen's obituary, no mention of family or friends. The scanner began to buzz with mention of the shelter. Long had enough evidence to build a case, it seemed.

"What did you find?"

"Just some bums, hanging around. They looked like zombies, just walking up and down the street. Whoever was here, they cleaned up shop and skipped town pretty quickly. They sure left one hell of a mess here."

"How many people were down there?"

"At least twenty. We're taking them to the hospital. Dead eyes, man. No expressions on their faces, just moving around with their hands towards the sky...They were asking for God."

Paavo turned off the scanner and walked towards the

window. They had escaped the cops before they could get shut down. Once the dealers got picked up, the whole team moved. Paavo got to his feet to get dressed. His black button shirt lay flattened. Once in hand, he put it to his nose to see if it was good for another day. The shirt smelled of blood and sweat.

One more day, he said to himself, putting it on and buttoning to the very top. The nearest window gave him a glimpse of the city that was always alive and pushing forward. He wondered why those people pushed forward. Family? Children? Maybe it was for a lover. His eyes followed the concrete lines and lights that hung over the highway.

Paavo had never been with a woman. It made him sick to be so nervous around what he considered to be regular people.

Women with bright eyes and bubbling personalities covered the city. It was sometimes hard to walk the streets without losing composure. Those he had feelings for had never known. Paavo resigned to his safe silence and moved away to watch them live oblivious from a distance; hoping they see him without all the weird gestures and cracks in voice and share the same quiet. Some nights, he would dream of opening his arms and letting a woman place her hands on the hole in his chest. There would be blood, but it would not matter.

He moved away from the window and back to the terminal. Paavo brought up a map of the city. The screen lit up with bright green lines; railways, subways, sewer systems. The foreign substance found at Lyoto's plant was processed salt. Was someone onto the investigation? He had to be careful. The next thing to do was find Daniel Jupiter. The sound of the office phone startled him. Who was calling?

"Paavo, this is Derek." Long sounded tired.

"We need you to come down here," he said.

"Right now?"

"Yeah, there's a woman here who has been asking for you."

"Me?" asked Paavo.

"Found her outside the abandoned shelter. Can't be living there. Dressed too nice for that place."

"I didn't meet any woman at the church. How does she know my name?" asked Paavo.

"She doesn't. She keeps asking for a man in black from the papers. That must be you."

The Police databanks kept an inventory of crimes committed and solved. He searched for similar occurrences, focused on homeless shelters opened and closed in the same period. Only one name came up; Salvation. Religious organization; no names listed for owners or benefactors. The Salvation company was backed by local supporters, all anonymous.

Paavo looked around the room.

"Should I leave now?" he asked.

"Don't bother. I have some men coming to pick you up."

There were no names for its figureheads or its financial backing. Paavo matched their addresses with the most recent shutdowns in the downtown area. They needed someplace far off from the cops and the center of the city. There was a big gap between closed businesses and the reach of support from the members of Salvation.

"You're sending cops to my apartment?"

"Is that a problem?" asked Long.

"Yeah, it is. Why the hell do you want cops from the city having access to my address?"

There was a chuckle on the other side of the phone.

"Why are you so paranoid?" asked Long.

Back on the map, there was a space of five miles tucked away in a quiet corner of the city that even had a salt processing plant in the area. Paavo wrote down the names of the streets and programmed the scanner according to the cops assigned to them.

"Do you plan on breaking the law any time soon?" asked Long.

"I might be. Have your databanks been edited or changed recently?"

"They don't care where you live, kid. Why would I know that?"

"It's for research. Tell them to meet me on the end of the street. I don't want them to know where I live."

"Fine, have it your way. I'll tell them to pick you up where you decide. Feel better?" asked Long.

"Lots."

Paavo hung up the phone and readied himself. Notes left from the conversation with Miss Aki were scattered on the table. Near that plant was the church where Gordon Wen had died, according to the old woman. The cops were there only ten minutes later. They drove into the city with their sirens on and cars moved for them. Paavo was envious of their influence. Some of the officers tried to start a conversation. Paavo waved them off with a hand. He was more focused on the woman.

"Hey man, this girl is pretty cute."

"You're a lucky man if you're really the one she wants to see."

The men took turns bitching about the snow. Paavo ignored them and watched the skyline in darkness. The station was covered in white.

"You look familiar, man. Did you ever work at the station?"

"No," said Paavo. The other officer spoke out, starting to recognize him.

"Yeah, you're that weird detective aren't you? The one in the phone book, I've heard about you, man. You wore black all the time. You got fired from the station cause you were sleeping there."

The driver began to laugh.

"Jesus Christ! Were you broke or something?"

"Somehow, he hurt himself and the janitor found him. He was bleeding all over the damn place."

Paavo's eyes remained on the floor of the car.

Inside the parking area, the car wedged itself between packed spaces near the staircase. Paavo followed the men in through the service door and downstairs towards the interrogation rooms. The concrete corridors stretched far off into the distance. Yellow lines were faded as the old paint had cracked and smeared from the endless footsteps over time. Long met them at the halfway point.

"Welcome."

"Has the woman said anything?" asked Paavo.

"Not at all. She refuses to speak to any of us."

"Do you want me to talk to her?"

"Go right ahead, if the ride here wasn't too much for you," said Long. Paavo looked at him cross. The old man laughed out loud and gave him a playful shove. He was motionless. The cops smiled. They gave off an air of camaraderie. Long waved them off and waited until his men turned the corner to speak.

"The detective in black," he laughed.

"It sounds better than it looks," said Paavo.

"Yeah, you're right about that."

"Thank you, sir," Paavo muttered.

"Come on, I'll introduce you," said Long.

He led Paavo down the pathway into a hall of several rooms. The lights in each were off all except for one. Glass separated them from seeing others. Paavo looked nervously into the interrogation room. The woman was beautiful. She stared at the edge of the table. Her blue dress covered her from neck to her knees. It was simple. Elegant. Paavo's eyes traced the curves of her body.

A cigarette lay on the cusp of a clear ashtray. It was still burning, untouched. Long pressed a button to unlock the door that startled him. They looked at each other for a while before he stepped into the room. She didn't notice him. Her skin was colored a pale olive, smooth and unscarred. His steps were silent, stopping every few seconds to look at her again. Her shadow curved around the floor beneath the light. He waved his hand to signal the woman. After a moment, she turned towards him and stared with a look of familiarity. Paavo moved awkwardly towards the second chair across from her. He sat down quietly and introduced himself.

"Good evening." Her voice was nervous and sweet.

"Hello."

"What is your name?" The woman turned towards the glass.

"This is the detective, right?" she asked at her reflection.

Paavo was taken aback.

"Who are you?"

"My name is Lia Jones. I remember you from the church." Paavo raised his eyebrow.

"How do you remember me?"

"I help out feeding the people in the shelter. I usually work nights with my brother, Clayton. I came in on my day off and I saw you there, standing in the back of the room."

"How long have you worked there?" he asked.

"A few months ago, we were assigned to the place for community service, but I came down for my shift and the place is gone." Her voice changed, it became filled with sadness.

Paavo looked to the ground as her sobs grew.

"There's a bunch of cops around and they are looking for my brother."

"Why are they looking for him? Wasn't he working at the shelter?" he asked.

Lia turned towards the cigarette in the ashtray. She placed it in her hands and took a small drag. The smoke was too much for her, she coughed it out in a matter of seconds. Paavo looked at her with a sense of longing, unavoidable.

"Do you smoke?" she asked in between loud coughs.

"No. But I have been told it helps during times like this," he said. Her eyes moved around, unsure of where to stare next, embarrassed. He gave her a moment to collect herself.

"Where is he now?" he asked.

"You have to understand, my brother would do anything to keep us safe. He lost his job a year ago, we had no money. He's been selling drugs in and around the neighborhood. He's so protective of me. It wasn't supposed to be this way. He didn't want to deal with criminals, but he thought it was the easiest way to make quick cash," she said.

"Sometimes it is. We always have the choice of following a certain path. It's up to us to decide which one is worth the trouble."

"He thought being a drug dealer would help us, it's only come to tear us apart as family."

"Did you work with Kimura and Shimizu as well?" Paavo asked.

"They came in and worked with us, sometimes. Clayton didn't like them, didn't trust them." Paavo sat back in his chair.

"They were picked up, too," he said.

"They got into fights a lot. He threatened them just for looking at me."

"Do you think he may have escaped?" he asked. Lia put down the cigarette.

"Probably hiding, I don't know how though, he's huge," she said.

"Oh yeah? How huge?" Paavo asked, curious.

She began to widen her eyes.

"He's massive, like a giant. I don't know where he got it from. We practically come from a family of dwarves. You have to help me find him."

"Do you think we can arrange a meeting?" Paavo asked.

"He's disappeared. He won't answer any of my messages. What's going on?"

"Calm down, go with the Police, they can help you find your brother."

"I don't want to. You don't know my brother, he gets out of control, and he may hurt them...I," she began sobbing.

A few officers had brought in Lia and were in the process of moving here to the station for further questioning when she began to ask for a man in black. Paavo looked around for something to offer her. He finally settled on a tissue from the box at the end of the room. He fumbled over to the other side and stuck out his hand for her to take it.

"Oh, thank you." she said.

Lia reached for the tissue. Her hands seemed to latch onto his for a brief moment. Paavo looked down towards their hands together. They met eyes.

"If your brother is dealing, convince him to turn himself in."

"He won't," said Lia.

Paavo moved the chair around to the edge of the table and moved close to Lia.

"He will if you ask him to. You're the one he cares about, right? Tell him that we are bringing you in, Clayton will come out of hiding."

"Do you think that will work?"

"It has to," he said.

"Will you take him to jail?" she asked.

"Not yet. We just want to talk, like we're doing right now."

"But they will, eventually, right?"

"We need to ask him some questions about the shelter."

"Did they tell you what was going on?" She asked.

"The only thing I know is that the men who run the shelter may be involved with the dealing of drugs around the area."

She shook her head in disbelief.

"That can't be true. Can it?"

"We are going to find out," said Paavo.

The cops set up a phone with a tracer to allow Lia to call Clayton. Keeping him on the line for more than a minute would be enough to find out where he was. Long and Paavo stood back in the shadows and watched them set up. Lia sat in the center of the room as her legs twitched with nervous energy. Paavo tried to keep his eyes focused towards the tracer. He wanted to see how it was done.

A small microphone was placed on the receiver that attached

to a battery. Paavo recognized the design for the directional microphone, it was his own. Memories of running around the station with the designs in hand came to mind. He remembered looking for Long, to show him what could change the work of undercover officers for the better. The inspector was impressed with his work. Ultimately, his superiors vetoed the directional microphone, saying that it was not cost effective to their operations at this time. Their design had been altered in order to avoid taking directly from the patent that Paavo had put in place soon after. That move angered a lot of people in the station. He took a little satisfaction in that.

"Does this look familiar to you, kid?"

He looked up to see one of the older cops.

"Yeah, we make good use out of your shit these days!" The laugh stung his sides.

"Come on, boy, have you got nothing to say? I remember how you used to run around these same halls, full of piss and vinegar. The inspector watched over you like a hawk. No choice. Look at you. He was a fuckup. Are you still a fuckup, kid? Did you grow out of that shit? The only reason we don't drag your ass into one of these cells is because of your foster father."

"That's enough," said Long.

The battery was new. The wires would transmit the source of power for the mic. Paavo's designs involved making a tiny battery to slip inside each individual mic, as opposed to hooking one up to a main power source, one at a time. This meant that someone had to find a way to pocket a battery, wires and a microphone. The logic behind carrying more suspicious items as opposed to something that could be confused for a piece of fuzz didn't carry through.

Paavo was unable to keep eyes away from Lia. Her legs were a distraction. He kept turning back towards their shape and texture. Their color was a silken white. Her hands were smooth. Coming into contact with them caused all kinds of unknown pain in his body. She kept turning her head to meet eyes with him. Paavo was unable to look, so he slipped out.

"Kid, where are you going?" Long followed him out of the room.

"Did they check her belongings down there? asked Paavo.

"What do you mean?"

"She was working at the shelter. Did she have any food with her?" Long was intrigued.

"Do you mean food that her and her brother cooked up before heading down?"

"Exactly," said Paavo.

The evidence lockers were not too far away, Lia's personal effects were there when she was picked up in front of the empty shelter. There were two duffel bags. Each was filled with food and drink, followed by pieces of red meat, wrapped in carefully folded paper.

Long was the first to pull one out from a duffel bag.

"One of the rats should still be awake tonight." he said.

All in all, twenty three different pieces of the red meat were packed away inside the bags. They were carefully hidden among other meat for subterfuge. The page wrapped around each piece was a selection from the bible, namely Genesis.

"My breath shall not abide in man forever, since he too is flesh. Let the days allowed him be one hundred and twenty years," said Long.

"It's true, you know."

"What's that?"

"That man cannot be trusted. Take a look around at all the

things we've done wrong. The greatest chance any creature was ever given. We squandered it. Oceans are filled with trash and children in our major city are walking through snow with no shoes to eat rotten food," said Paavo.

"Every place has a dark side. It's time you find some peace with your own darkness."

Thoughts of the dead men from the hotel hit Long again. Paavo had noticed. He looked at the old man with dead eyes, no emotion.

"Maybe you should take your own advice."

"Come on, let's get back." Paavo followed Long into the room to watch Lia make her phone call. After several attempts, along with a few frantic messages, Clayton finally answered back.

"What the hell are you doing calling like this?"

Lia was shocked that he had answered. Maybe a part of her was hoping that he wouldn't, he thought. She lowered her eyes.

"Clay, the cops are looking for you."

"Don't you think I know that? I'm trying to stay away from you so that I don't use you to get to me. The shelter was already raided."

"They already got to me, Clay. I'm sorry...I..."

"What the hell were you doing?!"

A vicious pounding noise struck out from the other line.

"I told you where to go in case this happened! What are we going to do now?" The bad noise made Lia flinch. She was afraid of him.

"Clay, they want you to come in. There's a detective who says you can get a reduced sentence if you talk to them at your own will."

"I'm not going in there with those stinking pigs. They can go to hell!" One of the men watched the tracer, he waited for the signal.

"Now I have to get you out, Lia. Where are you?" The officer gave the thumbs up for the trace to complete. Others took to their cruisers.

"I...I..."

"This is a clean line, isn't it? You could be traced right now."

"I don't know...I..."

"Damnit..."

Yamagishi walked into the room with tired eyes. Long took him outside towards the evidence room to have a look at their findings. Paavo stayed in place and watched Lia, motionless until she was taken to the interrogation room.

Paavo then spent the next hour with Yamagishi, who spread the pieces of meat out over a white table. The lab was quiet and dark.

"I received your message about the ammonia. Very insightful. We were able to find out if any was shipped into the city. And there was. There was one ship in particular. A package was picked up by a man named Daniel Jupiter. Another peculiar part of the puzzle was when we came across the page in the database, there was an anomaly, very hard to pick up on."

"I'm listening," said Paavo.

"The IP address for the Police database is approximately 38 numbers long, separated into groups of twos and threes by a period. Any archive listing Daniel Jupiter has 37," said Yamagishi.

"What do you think that means?"

"The page was manufactured and slipped into the database. Since the name was missing from most of our records until fifteen years ago, it is doubtful that the grown man who picked up the package in question was just a teenager. The fake IP seems almost too easy. As if they wanted you to pick up on it. This may be some kind of trap for you. We recommend extreme caution when attempting to locate this man."

Each piece of meat was coated in different colors, shades of red and orange. Several rotating lights flashed as they hovered over each piece, studying the substances. The results were the same ingredients as before; rotted meat weeks old. The ammonia was strong in each sample. Each one was coated in a preservative to keep it fresh, used as smelling salt. When applied to red or dark meat, a sharp, sweet smell emanates from the flesh.

"More of the same. Thanks for bringing this to us. It took time to break down the meat at a cellular level to find the right traces not tainted by chemicals," said Yamagishi.

He invited Paavo to sample the odor; a mixture of candy and chloroform, way too strong. The next part of the puzzle was a dopamine inhibitor, the clear substance that had been found earlier.

"What is it?" asked Paavo.

"Medicinal. A painkiller created to induce heavy sleep without worry of lowering heart rate or blood pressure."

"Experimental?"

"Not at all. In use by most stores now, small doses of course. Not only in animal hospitals, but commonly used in everyday local drug stores. But completely "street legal" as they say," Yamagishi said as he used his fingers to quote the air.

"The substance is known for its sensory effects. The smell is overwhelming. There's also Ketamine, a drug used to cloud the mind and place its subject into a state of hallucination. The official name for it is dissociative amnesia, creating the zombie effect they mentioned to you, what they saw outside of the shelter," said Yamagishi.

Paavo stepped towards the sample taken from one of the

pieces. He inhaled a strong breath and nearly collapsed. Yamagishi tried to catch him to no avail. Paavo caught himself on the table and found balance. He signaled to him everything was okay. The lab worker fixed his glasses and returned to the computer screen, staring away from him. A person starving for food would eat this and turn into a damn maniac.

"More than likely, it is a form of ritual. There's a strong religious undercurrent." Yamagishi spoke as his face stayed glued to the computer.

"There are even smaller amounts of other drugs here as well; painkillers, cocaine. Both are mixed in deep, but we have visible amounts. The smaller drugs inside the meat are not enough to cause an overdose or blackout of any kind."

Paavo watched the analysis on the computer screen.

"The mixture of a strong sedative increases the reaction. We have novocaine for your mind; it numbs them so the drugs inside are felt at the maximum. Not only dangerous, but growing in popularity."

"What do you mean?" asked Paavo.

"This mixture is a form of designer drug, something growing in popularity in other cities. It's getting a serious reputation among those in the music industry, only identified by the letter 'T'."

"Any information about long term effects? Brain damage?"

"Good question. I'll look into possible detox methods and forward them to hospital officials, we will have to study their brain activity and motor functions to know for sure. God knows they have their hands full right now with them as it is," said Yamagishi.

Paavo walked down the stairs and headed towards the interrogation rooms again. Every piece of meat was coated with store bought medicine and lined with the drugs they intended to sell. They had found a way to ship their stock through safe means, even if it meant impersonating a dead priest. He still needed proof. Clayton could provide it. He wanted to know more about the priest; why he decided to take a dead man's identity. A part of him wondered, if Daniel Jupiter was slipped into the database, what stopped them from doing the same for the priest? Long had stopped him before reaching Lia's holding cell.

"Paavo, they caught him. It took seven guys to bring him down."

"Seven? How did they take him down?"

"A hell of a lot of mace and everyone jumping on him at once with a stun gun," said Long. Paavo seemed impressed.

"A very dangerous man. Some of the men were thrown around like dolls, a few broken arms, broken ribs. One of my men lost an eye. They're on the way now."

Paavo interrupted him.

"It's drugs in the meat. They coated each piece with a preserve and a sedative, laced it with their stock. It's all store bought."

"Jesus..."

"They had to have been selling it to those in the shelter," said Paavo.

"Damn, we've got to stop this." Paavo turned towards Lia's cell and began to walk. He motioned Long to come with him.

"I have an idea."

"What have you got in mind?" asked Long.

"When he comes in, put him in a room and the girl and myself."

"Why?"

"We need to get information out of him, the right way. You

won't be able to intimidate him if he's bigger than the entire squad. We need to just talk to him. Offer him something to make him speak up," said Paavo.

"I'll think of something."

"Where did they pick him up?"

"Midtown."

"We need to know where they are going to set up next."

"As soon as we can fit the bastard through the doors, we'll put him in a room. You'd better go and get ready," said Long.

Both men reached the outside of Lia's cell. She sat at the end of the makeshift bed, facing the window.

Paavo tapped lightly on the glass.

"He's coming in. We're going to talk to him," he said.

Lia smiled for a moment. She seemed to realize the circumstance surrounding the meeting and moved back towards the window in regret.

"I swear to you, I didn't know what was in those bags. I thought it was just food for the people at the shelter," she pleaded.

"I believe you."

"I'm not a drug dealer. You have to help me stop this. Don't let them take me to jail."

Paavo moved away from the glass and found himself a yellow chair with tin legs. It was shaky under his weight, likely from the girth of overweight cops tired from the graveyard shift. Paavo checked the time. A dose of the serum would be needed soon. He checked his jacket pocket for the syringe, filled with golden liquid. Fingers ran across the glass, still warm.

Lights went out and returned seconds later. He sat forward and buried his head into his palms with eyes closed. There was a brief moment of sleep before loud voices barreled into the area, to announce the arrival of Clayton to a room with his sister. Paavo saw seven men holding extended chains that lead into the shadows of the outside. Clayton stepped into full light. The man was indeed a giant; seven feet tall, with arms and legs like trees.

CHAPTER TWELVE

Clayton wore torn green carpenter's pants and a thermal brown shirt. His hands were linked by three pairs of handcuffs, along with larger versions attached around his elbows and knees. With control of the joints, the men could maneuver him the way they wanted. Paavo took a moment to collect himself then made for Lia's room. There was just enough time to place a mic into the empty coffee cup on the table.

Long came into the room. He had been watching the whole time.

"Are you alright?"

"I'm fine...Just nervous," said Paavo.

Long laughed, he followed with a pat on the back.

"You saw him, huh? The bastard is huge. I doubt even you will be able to get anything out of him. Even with the "brute force" I know you are capable of."

"Maybe I can make him angry enough to lose his cool and say the wrong thing."

"Don't get killed," said Long.

Paavo handed him the remote.

"Take this. Hit record," he said.

"For what?" asked Long.

"Evidence."

Paavo turned around to look at Lia. She was staring at him. He turned back towards the entrance of the room and asked Long to step out. As soon as the inspector left, he pulled up a chair, away from the girl but facing the door. The men lead Clayton inside. It took a few minutes for him to fit through. He was led in one arm at a time. Paavo thanked the men and asked them to take off the restraints.

The officers refused. Clayton kept his eyes closed. The light bothered his eyes. Deep red circles surrounded each, the results of three empty cans of mace. Tears poured from his eyes by reflex.

"Do you want to get killed?" asked one of the officers.

He kept his gaze towards the giant.

"Maybe I do," said Paavo. Long interrupted through the static of the old intercom.

"My associate is assisting us with this case. Keep your guns on Jones. I will send someone in to remove the restraints."

A cop came in with a series of keys and began to remove the carefully placed handcuffs. Clayton's eyes finally opened, he focused them on Paavo. He felt a shock flow through his body, as if he were staring into the eyes of a monster. Clayton spoke.

"Lia, you've disappointed me."

His voice was low, hard to understand.

"Why are we here right now?" he asked.

"Clay, I am so sorry this happened."

"Don't talk right now." The officer with the keys collected the leg chains and dropped them into the corner. Each of the seven men aimed their pistols at Clayton's head and heart. Paavo looked at the officers.

"Keep your guns on him, one move and you take him down for good," said Paavo.

"Tough talk, kid. I like you already."

Once his arm chains were removed, the officer began with his wrists. Clayton moved his limbs, stretching them out. He looked as though he was preparing to run a marathon.

"How old are you? Sixteen? Seventeen?" asked Clayton.

"Twenty four."

"You should probably get some facial hair if you want people to take you seriously."

"I'll keep that in mind. Let me ask some questions about you first."

The cops with guns in hand stepped back to allow him room to sit down. He moved casually to the chair and table. Clayton moved onto the chair. He readied his arms and hands to catch himself if it should break. It steadied after a moment. Once it did, he turned towards Paavo.

"Don't say my name again. I'll kill you."

"If you say so," said Paavo.

Lia moved her hand out towards the giant. He looked back towards the cops, their guns were focused and waiting.

"Are we really going to talk like this? I feel nervous."

"Is that what it's going to take to get you to tell us what the deal is behind the shelter?" asked Paavo.

"It depends on how you ask the questions."

Paavo nodded towards the glass, the men lowered their guns and moved out of the room. Clayton turned his head slightly, watching the door until they all left and sealed the door behind them. His head curved around towards Paavo. A jagged smile stretched across his face.

"Go ahead and ask your questions." said Clayton.

"What were you selling to the homeless people in the shelter?"

"I wasn't selling anything. My sister and I give out food to the needy, and we help out cleaning the church."

"Then why were you arrested?" asked Paavo.

"I don't know. You're the detective. Figure it out. I'm sure that's what they barely pay you for."

"They don't pay me."

"Sounds like a shit job, then." Lia stepped into the exchange.

"Clay, tell them the truth. It doesn't help to lie. Don't even look at him. Look into my eyes and tell what was going on down there."

"Nothing happened down there. Don't make me say it, especially in front of these bastards."

"Were you dealing drugs in the food?" asked Lia. The giant hesitated.

"Tell me!" Lia's shouting was cut off by several gasps of air as she wept openly into her hands.

"We're going to jail because of this! At least tell me why we have to go to prison," she said.

"I didn't know what was in the food at first. All we did was pick up what was on the list. We brought it to them and they did the rest. They paid us at the end of the week. The drugs were our own to sell or keep. It was payment for our help. But all they wanted was what was on the list."

"Who are they?" asked Paavo.

"The priest and his helpers, they were running the place. We followed orders. They didn't treat us bad. They always had smiles on their faces."

"The priest, what is his name?"

"I don't know him too well, but he was pretty clever. I watched him from far away. He was smart enough to take the old man's name and face, that way no one could trace him," said Clayton.

"How did he take his name and face?"

"With computers, they were able to change names around, to make it seem like they were dead, and that their real names never existed. He even paid us to move the body and mark the grave with someone else's name."

Long stood behind the glass. His grips tightened on the recorder.

"Can you tell us where the body is?" asked Paavo.

"I don't remember."

"Do you know what those drugs are doing to those people out there?"

"It's not my problem. She is my only problem. She's the only one I have to worry about," said Clayton.

"These guys were nothing but small time thugs trying to make something of themselves then, eh?"

"Yeah, real losers they are. Look how far they got this time."

"What does that make you then?" asked Paavo.

"It's not a good idea to talk down to me, little shit. I could crush you with my bare hands, and they wouldn't get here fast enough."

Paavo looked away from the giant. Long placed his hands on the glass and waited for a signal to get him and the girl out of there.

"When did you find out what was in the meat?"

"A few weeks ago, they were doing a deal by the docks..."

Some of the men listening with Long began to whisper amongst themselves. Long was starting to connect the dots in his own head. The men from the hotel were working for them. They wanted more of what was fed to those people in the shelter.

"Boring talk with men in suits and ties for hours. It was a waste of time. There wasn't even anything worth buying in that ship," said Clayton.

"What was in it?"

"They poached a small carrier off the coast a week from then, so the food was already spoiled."

"How much did they pay for the contents of the ship?" asked Paavo.

"Too much money for that worthless crap. They handed us some boxes that smelled awful then told us to load them into the truck and take them back. I remember picking maggots off of my clothes."

"How many men ran the operation?"

"About ten. Some of them were cut off by the father. They began to like the meat too much. They became like the bums in the seats."

"The priest started to become paranoid and cut ties with your men little by little?" asked Paavo.

"More than paranoid, and they weren't my men. We were all just looking to get our hands on some money, something to tuck away."

Lia turned her back to Clayton.

"Some of them homeless went along, you know," he said.

"How many are left? How many are with the priest now?" Paavo pressed on.

"No one left but him, the others will find a new place to work, but everything belongs to him and him alone now," said Clayton.

"Where are they?"

"The father is kind of crazy, you know. The meat had an effect on all of us. It changed us. When he started out, he was just a speed freak who wanted to make some quick cash, but then he started having all these ideas about life and death. He started doing all this research. The origins of man, the war of heaven, anything he could get his hands on. He really wrote those sermons and he practiced them in front of a mirror at all hours of the day. We left him alone and got our work done."

"This is all so crazy!" Lia slammed her hands on the table.

"Why didn't you tell me? I was there working with people, trying to help them," she said.

"You would have gotten in the way if you were doing anything else," said Clayton.

"I cared about those people, and you were poisoning them," said Lia.

The giant lowered his eyelids. He was tired now. His body leaned over to the side, as if he was fighting off sleep.

"I'm tired of hearing you talk, little sister. I've been awake for days. I need some rest."

"A few more questions before you go." Paavo leaned in closer to speak, he grabbed the coffee cup containing the microphone that was near the end of the table.

"What did the meat taste like?" he asked.

"It was weird. I knew it was bad. We all saw where it came from. Something about it made you keep eating and eating. It was hard to stop. The men from the docks soon returned with another ship. We took it with no money down, anything for another taste of the meat."

Clayton closed his eyes at last. Paavo looked at Lia and then at the glass towards Long before trying to wake him. There was a tense silence in the room.

"Clayton?"

The giant opened his eyes suddenly. He let out a violent scream which shook the walls. It knocked Paavo back into his chair. Lia was frightened immediately. Massive hands grabbed the table and lifted it high into the air. The girl fell to the floor.

Paavo went to the ground to cover her from the impact. The hands launched the table towards the entrance of the room. Long signaled the men to attack. The officers reached the door and began to open it when the impact of the table pushed them to the floor. It had lodged itself between the doorway. They were trapped inside with the giant. Clayton turned towards them, screaming.

"Where is it?! I want more!"

"Get that door open, now!" Long shouted orders at his men. Paavo could not speak.

Lia screamed back at him.

"What do you want? Don't do this!"

"I want the taste! I want the meat."

"We'll get some. Open the door," said Lia.

"Don't deny me."

"Paavo! Do something!" Lia screamed.

"Just a small taste, please?" the giant asked.

His hands were like bricks. Paavo felt the first one nearly take his head off. It was a backhanded slap which knocked him back to the ground. His ears popped from the impact. Paavo was disoriented. He saw the hands move towards the girl. The giant wrapped them tight around her neck and began to squeeze. He was strangling her, talking the entire time.

"Sister, give me some meat. I need to taste it one more time. Just one more time."

Lia was in a state of shock.

"Damaged goods. You were always weak," said Clayton.

Paavo looked towards the door. Men were kicking frantically to knock the door ajar. They were almost through. He threw himself at the giant, tearing at his eyes and wrapping his arms around his neck, trying to pull him off the girl. Clayton tossed him away like a small child. Paavo hit the wall and fell to the floor. The wound in his chest began to throb. He felt the blood begin to flow to the outside. Long stepped back into the control room to see what was going on. Lia did not resist the hands of her brother.

She felt the air leave her body. Her hands dropped down to the floor. Paavo ran towards the giant and tackled him at his knees. He fell to the floor and lost grip of the girl. He found himself punching downwards with reckless motions. Clayton's face did not show any pain. There was a dead look in his eyes. Paavo continued to thrash down. The giant raised up, lifting up and carrying him in one quick movement. Paavo was thrown hard against the glass. Long jumped back from the crack in the glass.

Paavo landed punches across the jaw of the large man pushing him through the glass. His knees buckled again, enough time to grab the bent chair and slam it across the face of the giant. No effect now. His strength was too much. Hands clasped around Paavo's neck. He felt air leave his body in no time. He was so weak, so pathetic. The last thing he saw was the giant's eyes, no intent or purpose. He was staring into the eyes of a machine. Lia ran towards him. He let go of Paavo and slapped her down with one hand. She hit the floor. Her beautiful skin collided with concrete. There was nothing he could do. He was helpless. She screamed in pain.

The table was broken down by a group of officers. They rushed into the room, guns drawn. Long watched from a distance. He told them to advance. They approached the giant with caution. Paavo's hands began to twitch. The lack of oxygen went to his brain. The old man yelled out to them. The men rushed Clayton, only to be thrown backwards to the wall. There was a sense of panic in the room now, overwhelming. The giant had managed to hold off three men while maintaining a tight grip upon the throat of Paavo.

A loud gunshot burned through the arm of the giant. It was Long, holding his revolver. Paavo dropped to the floor, his body limp and struggling for air. Blood streamed down the side of the giant. He gained new fury at the sight of the flowing red. Long looked at the psychopath with indifference. He was without fear and ready for the attack. The cops had pushed the table through the doorway. The officers were ready to move at his command, but he was in the front of the line and waiting. Clayton let out a deafening scream and charged at him. Long waited for the right moment. The giant's hands were inches away from his neck before he fired the shot. It was point blank.

The bullet entered his head, exploding through the other side. Jones staggered. Another shot was fired from the magnum, and the giant's head erupted in blood. The body flew back and hit the floor. The officers moved into the room as Long stood absolutely still. He inhaled the smoke from the chamber. The giant's body twitched from muscle memory. Men in uniform moved around Long, trying to avoid touching him.

Paavo and Lia were helped to their feet and taken to the infirmary. The nurse was an older woman with messy red hair. She was soft spoken and patient. Paavo was watching the girl, a line of blue skin stretched across her neckline. He was waiting for her to speak. She didn't. They did not meet eyes like before. He refused to take off his shirt when asked.

"I'd rather not."

"But sir, I need to check for lacerations from the glass." she said.

"I'm fine. Worry about her, instead."

"Thank you for what you did." Lia faced the wall as she spoke.

"Don't mention it."

"My brother was a madman. He always used to hit me. Sometimes, he would say it to toughen me up, to make me a stronger person."

"You must be stronger now," said Paavo.

"The problem is, he never stopped. Maybe I am damaged."

"We're both damaged, then," Paavo whospered.

Lia turned towards him at last. They shared a brief smile while the woman finished her work. She finally moved to his side and whispered into his ear.

"Can you take me home?" The air from her breath heated his blood.

"I can't," he said. There was paperwork to sign, to show they were not seriously injured, good enough to go home tonight. Lia spoke quiet words before she walked away from him, finding her own way out into the snow. She told him where she would be.

"Next time, less stressful circumstances?" she asked.

He felt something being slipped into his pocket then, a piece of paper, a number and an address, along with her name was written. Paavo left the room and met with Long to discuss. They both seemed distant.

"Are you alright, young man? That was a lot of weird shit that happened all at once."

"All that matters is that we find the priest. Once we know who he is, we can start searching for his people," said Paavo.

"The deal at the docks, I knew about it. One of our men was in there with a wire. The buyers were out of their minds."

"Did they mention a package? A man came by the docks to pick up a box left behind by these dealers. The ship is still in the impound. The man who made the pickup was named Daniel Jupiter."

Long thought about the name.

"Never heard of him, certainly not on our list of guys," he said.

"Your helpers in the lab were a big help in trying to find out more about him. That person might not even exist."

"What do you mean?" asked Long.

"The database entry was a fake. There's someone wanting us to follow the name, it was meant to be a clue for us."

"I don't like this. Hackers are leaving us clues for our investigations? What makes you think they are part of it?"

"Maybe they are watchers, looking at everything going wrong with the city, trying to point us in the right direction," said Paavo. Long was not convinced. Paavo continued on.

"What about the others after the drop-off?"

"They took a hostage at a hotel. It turned into a damned shootout." Paavo looked at his mentor differently.

"What happened?"

"They got her out of there. No signs of reason from the captors. They had guns and were blasting the hell out of that place trying to get out."

Long was lying to him, the images of the young men, shot dead were still fresh in his mind. He could not forget them. He changed the subject.

"That was a nice trick with the microphone."

"Make sure you commit it somewhere," said Paavo.

"Are you sure you don't want to go to the hospital to get

looked at?"

"No, I'm good. Are you okay?"

Long was quiet for a moment.

"Yeah, just a little shaken up."

"What about the girl?" asked Paavo.

"She seems okay, almost relieved that her brother is dead."

"Is she under arrest?"

"For possession? No. She said she had no idea. Clayton's words corroborate with hers. The lie detector test will prove whether or not she's lying. But that can wait for now."

"I should get going..."

The inspector grabbed at his arm.

"What is it?" asked Paavo. Long took a moment to collect himself.

"What were you doing at the Outlook during the robbery?"

Paavo looked to the ground.

"How did you know I was there?"

"They have you on camera. My boss has been asking for you. I want you to keep helping with the case, but you're wanted for questioning. They want me to bring you in on suspicion to aiding grand theft."

"I didn't steal any money," said Paavo. Long drew closer, lowering his voice in volume, not in intensity.

"What the hell were you thinking? I'm risking my job having you down here right now."

"Some of your boys already gave me a hard time about being in the same room with them, you saw it yourself. You had to break them up like kids in a classroom. Spare me the lecture."

"Tell me what happened." Long demanded.

"Seven came to me as a client. I didn't find out until later on. He was using me to find his brother. They took the score and tried to give me half."

"Shit...Did you take it?"

"No. I tried to give it away. For that, I was jumped by a group of homeless people, they mugged me for it. I thought I was going to die that night," said Paavo.

"Jesus, kid. That was a huge mistake. We can't be seen with each other in public, not as long as Masonori has his eyes and ears out in the open, looking for you."

"What do you want me to do?"

"Keep in contact, away from cell phones, in case they try to listen in on my conversations. The men I brought here today have promised not to start any shit, who's to say what they'll do or say tomorrow morning, after this disaster," said Long.

"If he wants to bring me in, let him try to catch me. I don't give a shit what your boss believes. I still have a job to do."

Paavo slammed his fist into the concrete wall.

"She's probably dead anyway, right? Let me stay out of jail long enough to see the dead body."

His foot shot out, kicking the wooden chair across the hallway. Long stared at him for a moment.

"What's wrong with you?"

"Can you tell me why we're putting ourselves through this? Old feelings of wanting to spit in the face of the Police are beginning to reappear," Paavo said. He clenched his fists.

"Calm down. Get home, keep working on the case. Whatever you find may help us catch whoever is abducting these people."

"We start with the priest. Find out who he's working for," said Paavo.

"Do what you do, stay in the shadows."

They shook hands. Paavo stepped away from the Inspector and walked alone down the hallway to the outside parking lot. Long watched him leave and stood lost in thought for some time. He remembered the eyes of the giant. They were crazed. He felt as if someone was grabbing for his hand, he turned to see no one there.

Cold air shocked his body once outside. Paavo saw the approaching car, two officers in front with Lia in the backseat. He watched her being taken away and wondered why she gave him the piece of paper. This feeling was strange and brand new to him. How could someone feel an attraction during a time of personal crisis? She had been questioned and threatened with jail time, as well as strangled and beaten by her own brother. Despite this, she had wanted to see him again. Another car had pulled up, he hadn't realized. The image of Lia staring into his eyes, the warm air from her mouth leaving a moist spot on his skin, for a few moments he thought of something other than death. A car horn woke him from the trance and he approached the driver side door, two unassuming Policemen sat in front, the window rolled down slowly.

"Drop me off at the restaurant two blocks off the highway." The location was far away enough from the apartment.

"Why?"

Paavo raised his eyebrows at the question.

"I need some pancakes."

They had smirks on their faces. He wondered for a moment what could be so funny.

"You took a beating back there, kid. Are you going to be alright?"

The passenger door opened and he was able to squeeze inside

the back. Paavo still held the piece of paper in his hand. He squeezed it tightly, his voice still deadpan to mask his excitement.

"Better than alright."

The car took off and followed the familiar path from the station back over the highway. His mind moved alongside the wheels of the vehicle. The mind needed to be clear for the facts, images of the woman should be tucked away for now, he said to himself. What did he know now? The priest was not a dead man. He was now a victim of identity theft by some of the more intelligent drug addicts of the city. Long revealed more information about this deal at the docks. I'm surprised he didn't tell me about it earlier, he thought. A possible location was found, the question was now if they would return to the place where Wen's life ended. He was that much closer to finding Naoko. Preparation was needed, as well as another dose of the serum. The cops dropped him off in front of the restaurant. Two blocks was not so bad of a walk to the apartment. Paavo pulled the lapels of his jacket together to hide his chest from the bitter air. He walked alone towards the distant signal of traffic lights. Perhaps he would not have to walk such streets without a companion.

The door to the apartment opened to pitch black. Paavo found himself staring off into nothing against the lone kitchen light. The piece of paper was still in his hands. The number found its way into the keypad of the phone. It rang twice before she answered.

"I was waiting for you to call me." Her voice was calm. She spoke low and relaxed.

"We just saw each other two hours ago."

"Two hours is too much time," she said. Paavo felt strange, as if he was calling a phone sex line.

"I'm not used to this sort of thing."

Lia began to laugh.

"Do you mean talking to a woman?" she asked.

"Yes."

"I wonder what other things you could be skilled in."

Paavo began to sweat. Lia continued.

"You should come over sometime. I need someone to talk to in this place. With Clayton gone, I am all alone here."

"Alone is what I know about. It's not so bad when you get used to it," said Paavo.

"I feel like this is all too much, too fast. But I want to know you. You looked at me like no other person has before. It made me feel protected, even when I was being choked to death."

"I will be here for you. Things are busy for me sometimes. Send me a message when you like."

He began to envision the bedroom. Dark lit candles covered the room in a golden hue. There were shadows dancing across the walls from a burning fire in the middle of the room. A woman lay in bed, covered in nothing but blankets, rolling in circles. A hypnotic crawl, he could almost taste the air of sweat and sweet skin.

"I will," she whispered.

"I should go." Lia stopped him.

"Do you have to go right now? Can we talk just a little longer?"

Paavo looked at the clock. Another dose of the serum was needed. Late night conversation was not part of the schedule.

"The midnight hours are not good for me," he said.

He struggled for an excuse to leave early. There was a dull pain inside his chest. The wound was calling for the serum.

"I need lots of sleep. I have a condition. It requires a lot of medicine and sleep. I can barely get any work done as it is."

There was a soft moan through the receiver.

"Keep talking to me...Please."

Paavo began to look around the room.

"What are you doing?"

"Listening to you."

"Why?" he asked.

"The sound of your voice, it drives me crazy. Why won't you stay on the phone with me?"

Was she really serious? Now? Of all times?

"There's a time and a place for that."

"Stay with me, Paavo. I am almost there." Her breathing became heavier.

The apartment was covered in shadow. He stood in silence listening to her breath. Unsure of how to proceed, he stayed quiet and let her finish. Paavo may have been inexperienced in terms of contact, but as a young man, he had done plenty of research on the human body and the mechanics of sexual activity. He could imagine what she was doing; the path her hand would travel across smooth skin, down to her lips and further inside. There was something fascinating about how a person's body takes over. How quickly the mind moves from thought to action, the rapid movement of the body. It was something he wanted to experience with another.

"Just give me one more minute." Paavo began to feel his heartbeat rise, it became heavy.

"Why are you doing this?" he asked.

"Because I need it." He looked up to the ceiling. They were both alone. Voices of reason were outshined by voices of desire. What was stopping him?

"It feels so good...You should be here with me."

Paavo sat in the corner of the room, his legs crossed.

"Yes. I should."

"I'm so wet right now. You should be here, inside me."

He was silent. The apartment was deathly quiet, he made his way to the bedroom and laid down, staring into the ceiling. The images in his head were moving in rapid succession. He tried to picture how she looked, moving her body with jagged movements, writhing over the phone.

"Can you hear me?"

"Yes, I can," he said.

"Do you want me?"

"I do." The woman gasped for air.

"Will you stay here with me?" she asked.

They talked for hours. Time seemed to move in half time. Paavo watched the shadows of the room move along with the passing lights of cars on the highway. The clock went off, signaling the next dose of the treatment. He refused to hang up the phone. She was a beautiful woman, begging for him to speak. How could I refuse? He asked himself. The conversation went on through decadent turns. Lia led the charge. Her words twisted and whirled around his head like a dark predator. Seductive and calm, he could not help but stay in place, barely breathing, listening to her moan uncontrollably. It went on for hours. Paavo was enamored with the woman.

There had to be some way for this moment to continue, he thought. Some way to keep it at arm's length, to pull at a moment's notice and experience it time and time again. For every part of him that wanted to die, there was another that screamed I want to live. Death had followed him close. There had to be a way to experience every facet of life before the end. He had to feel a woman now, before his shadow grew full and he was claimed by this sickness.

It felt as though she was almost next to him. She described the bedroom, the last door at the end of a seedy hotel where she and her brother had stayed. It would be so easy to leave now. He wanted to, but she made him stay where he was. Her words were hard to ignore, the voice travelled through him like electric current.

"Say it again. Please," she said.

"I want you."

Paavo closed his eyes for a moment. The noises had stopped. Lia had left the line. The dial tone woke him from his lucid state. The phone had gone dead. He opened his eyes to check if she had ended the call. She did. The phone fell from his hands to the side of the bed. Shadows danced a black waltz within the room, against the wall. He watched them glide from the fingertips of the open curtains with grace. Could this really be happening right now? What kind of woman was this? Was this a smart move? Attempting a relationship for the first time? Paavo reserved himself. What are you talking about? What makes you think you can handle this woman? There was so much happening at once. It was overwhelming.

"You will need to play it cool," he spoke calming words.

"Keep them asking questions, and only give them half the story."

He checked the time, another shot, another dose of the serum. Paavo closed his eyes for a moment and began to imagine the warmth of the liquid, rushing through his body. He could picture the golden medicine flowing through his veins like running water within the pipe work of a broken labyrinth.

Unseen sensations continued to manifest, the fingertips of a woman, brushing the back of his neck and chest. They would open his shirt, and run across his pale skin like raindrops. He opened his eyes to view his own body. The light from the living room was still showing into the darkness, a beacon in the middle of a sea of darkness. His hands reached up into the air, he could see them against the light. Each finger was thin, frail. Paavo studied each hand, they were wrinkled, aged, calloused. Who would let him run these dead hands across their own body, he thought. Every day that had passed since meeting Wiles, he felt himself turning into an old man, the serum slowly carrying him into a shriveled existence, no energy and endless sleep.

There were times like this where he could not tell the difference between dream and reality. Perhaps the treatment was a way for him to die slow and without warning. So close to death, with so much left to do, and you are thinking about a woman. The black case sat in the bathroom, waiting for him to rise and began another draining dose. Paavo closed his eyes again, and another dream had begun, selfishly and without care. Hard winds hit the window, the storm ongoing with fury. The clock continued to count down towards the unknown.

CHAPTER THIRTEEN

The darkness covers me completely. There are no lights or figures. Nothing here but a deep black, inescapable. It feels like sleep. Something strange about it. My heart moves at a steady pace for the first time in ages. There is a feeling of relaxation, of peace. It feels wrong. Something is amiss in the serenity. There has to be. There is no vision or movement, only a numbness. No way to move. I am frozen in this state; drifting in and out of sleep, cold but calm. My true body is replaced by water. There is complete dark; no feeling, a sense of hopelessness.

The body floats weightless in deep space; blindly moving towards some unknown destination. Beyond the horizon, rays of distant light fade into vision. It doesn't hurt to watch. Rays came on slow, in dim colors. My eyes settle into the foreground. The lines shift and take shape to form a skyline, far away from me. More light above and I looked up to see a black moon. Its shadow is a blazing streak of blue fire. I see now. My hands move across still darkness. There's something holding me up, keeping me afloat. Water is cold and endless. No land in any direction. I am stranded. Alone. Within the sky are tiny spots of white. They catch my eye and never leave. Miniature stars burn away in a far off place. Each one holds its own shape and luster. I want to touch them; to reach up and feel them sear my hand. I want to feel pain for once, something. Anything would be better than this void. Still, weightless and lost, unable to move. The tide moves in waves of pitch black. The body is no longer mine. It belongs to the deep darkness now. A feeling of fear asks where could it take me? Where is there to go in this place? I follow the tide. It takes me further into nothingness. My only beacons are the burning black moon and the rising sky.

Something touches me and my heart stops. A hand keeps me still. The figure holds me in place to avoid being swept away. I look up, nowhere else to stare, nothing but black and the approaching madness slowly making its presence felt. I mouth words, to thank them. No sounds. My lips are wet, a taste of water. A soft kiss cuts off my struggle for words. Overwhelmed now, I am unprepared for this chance meeting. Kisses are soft and sweet upon my eyes and lips. Skin is sleek. Feminine. I struggle to move with no success. There are a few twitches, small reactions. She doesn't mind. Her lips move with skill and grace over me.

She digs her hands deep into the ocean of black and produces a hand, mine. Fingers poke and prod my limbs. New sensations move across the waters, beginning to feel once more. The hand brushes across her face. The skin was moist. Lips rubbed against my fingers, caressing her contours. The kisses come with playful bites from her teeth. The body shivers as my heartbeat gains intensity. Fingers travel over my own face; they trace the outlines and find their way into my mouth. I taste her at last.

Sweet skin and dark flesh hover over me. The true body returns to me, through her. I am awake now in the darkness, brought back to life by an unknown woman. She feels for my second hand, carries both to her face. We kissed for what felt like days. Endless and eternal, I want it to be. In time, the body will be mine. At last alive and in love. Our lips tear away for brief moments. There is just enough space to explore the surfaces of our skin. Her lips and tongue find their way to the edges of my ears and neck. Waves of warmth shoot through me. I pull her close to taste the skin of my mysterious savior. Lips travel down the neck, over the shoulders. Her hands clench me tightly.

Our bodies are perfect and strong. The water moves for us now. The black moon burns in silence over our fluid movement. My mouth is drawing back to her lips for breath. For precious air, I find solace within her. The blue fire etches streaks into space, and we have shadows at last. Her face is visible. She was beautiful. Her eyes shine like black diamonds inside a sea of their own. My hands move her black hair to the side, to admire this vision. She smiles and stares deeply into me. I am frozen now, afraid of what to do next. She takes my hands and brings them back underneath the cold waters. I feel her body. My eyes fall to the sea, fighting off sleep. She never looks away, always staring into me. Smiling, striking.

The stars come closer to us; no longer distant flashes of white, but bright flames of white and silver fire. Each one swarms us and fills our passion with color and vision. Her body is extraordinary. My hands move gently. She gives herself up to me. I open my mouth to make a sound. I say my first words in who knows how long.

"I love you." She returned with words, a voice strong and lilting.

"I love you, too. Who are you?" I ask.

"I am yours." I felt release, my shoulders lowered, tension gone.

"What is your name?"

"You may call me what you wish," she says.

"But I wish to know your name, who you are." She smiled once again.

"I am an angel. We do not have names of our own."

"An angel?"

Another deep kiss stifled my words. I fought off more sleep. I wanted to know more.

"Where did you come from?" I ask.

"From the afterlife, my love. Another place, far from here. I am here for you."

"No heaven?"

"A place not unlike your definition of paradise," she says.

"Where did I come from?"

"You came from the darkness you see all around you. Reborn in light under this black moon, this abyss."

"Will you leave me?"

"Never. We are here forever, my love. I will not leave your side."

"You will stay with me?" I ask.

"Yes." Something in my eyes, not water, but a tear.

"Where will we go?"

"Nowhere, as this is where we belong." The stars burned brightly around us.

"For how long?"

"We are here forever."

"I want to leave this place," I say.

"Kiss me," she pleads.

"Can we go?"

"Soon, you will not want to leave. Kiss me," she says. Moving towards me, I hold her in place. Waiting for her to react, she does not. She is still and silent. Her smile never wavers. It feels real. This is a place where I can stay. Where we can stay.

"Kiss me," she says. I move closer to her. The eyes of the angel lower, her face comes closer. I stop her just before and she struggles slightly.

"Please, kiss me," she aches. Our lips meet again. We are breathless. The angel opens her mouth.

"Take me."

I felt her legs wrap around my body beneath cold waters. The tide moved and rushed and pushed us along. The waves surrounded us and pulsated to a perfect rhythm. She followed with movements of her body. With each wave, she took me inside her. The body lost *control and moved alongside the rhythms of the ocean. The black moon above changed shape.*

"Do you see?" she asks.

"This world moves for us."

"What is happening?" I ask. It grows heavy with fire of purple and blue.

"We are alive."

The moon emits beams of energy. Colors flash across a dark sky. Electricity moves throughout the water. Our bodies melt into one. The angel takes me into her arms with a desperate embrace. Her full body is in view now; wings of black flowed outward, releasing feathers into the sea. She is a creature from dreams, beyond beauty. A legend interpreted over time by cultures and peoples thousands of years ago, until now. She is mine. Amidst this electrical storm, we make love in darkness and in burning light. The sky is visible, clouds move in rapid succession. Stars glow in a heavy neon rain. We cradle inside the fever of the storm with a silent promise to stay, and protect. I fall into sleep with visions blurred of purple skies cracking with lightning. The black sea returns us to our point of origin. We both fall with arms locked. My siren burns bright even in dark waters. My desolation angel sleeps at my side at the end of time.

There was a faint clicking in the darkness. It was familiar, alarming. It was the loading of a gun.

"Now...you have me."

Lia stood over Paavo's prone body, aiming a revolver at his heart. She stepped out into the faint light coming in from the outside. He dropped the phone onto the bed and began to raise his hands into the air.

"Calm down. I've got enough of a drop on you where you wouldn't be able to get the gun off of me anyway."

She bowed toward him in a curtsy.

"As you were, love," she said. Paavo looked at her, dumbfounded.

"What are you doing here?" She pointed towards the window. The lock had been broken. How long had she been waiting in the dark?

"I'm delivering a message."

"How did you find me?" he asked.

"The cops were very knowledgeable on the subject of you. It's funny how you think that asking them to drop you off somewhere else would throw them off your trail. You were never off the grid. No one gave a shit about you until now, really."

Paavo became filled with anger. His heart began to pound, and it pained him. His fists clenched together as he thought of a way to get the gun off of her.

"Your whereabouts were easy to come by. It was days ago when their men tailed you from the church. They wanted you dead right then and there, but I said no," said Lia.

"Change of heart?"

"I like you. So they had to die."

"Why the phone call?" Paavo asked.

"To distract you; the lonely, desperate type. I figured that a beautiful woman, showing an interest along with just enough damage to her psyche, would draw you in. I didn't even need to be talking much. You prattled on long enough before passing out. Some drugs you're on."

Paavo shook his head. This was all happening too fast.

"Think about it. Do you really think someone like me would be with a freak like you? What kind of apartment is this? You don't have any furniture," Lia laughed.

He couldn't stand to look at her. He turned his head down to the foot of the bed.

"What's wrong? You don't want to look at the pretty girl anymore? That's okay. You can turn around completely."

She pulled the trigger back, he complied.

"Now...lie down on your back," said Lia.

The sight of her appearing upside down was disorienting. Lia got down to her knees and began to slink towards the bed. He could see her approaching, the gun still aimed towards his face. Her smile stretched far across, crimson red lips opened to white teeth and ruby tongue. The barrel became closer until it came into contact with his eye.

"My assignment was a simple one. Find out how Seven and his brother made out with the money from the Outlook bank job."

Paavo remembered them, and their parting thank you gift.

"They were easy to contend with. I found my way into their safe house with the promise of enjoying my body, much like how I did here with you. The young one did not put up a fight. His hands tensed as I tightened the noose." Paavo felt his heart, well with anger.

"The infamous Seven had begged me to spare him," she laughed. It was a different, darker laugh.

"The Recluse paid me well enough before forcing me to stay in his pocket. Nothing was going to keep me from finding out about his accomplice, or anything else he asked," said Lia.

He could picture it in his mind, begging to be spared.

"There were tears when I showed him his brother. This is what happens when you play games with the wrong people. He tasted the steel just like this."

She moved the barrel into his mouth.

"He tasted the bullet as well. The gunshot that preceded his words were nothing but spit in the face of the dead."

She was heartless. There was no remorse in her words.

"The accomplice, who walked away with something belonging to my bosses," she said.

"What did he do to you?" Paavo asked. Her gun pushed against his face.

"Don't ask questions...Where is the money, Paavo?"

"I don't have it," he said.

She laughed again, quietly.

"I don't believe you, dear."

He looked towards the open window.

"The money was left for me in an unmarked car, in an envelope. Some bums had raided the car, taken it," said Paavo.

Lia's smile left her.

"I checked your account, nothing there. You live in squalor for one reason. Not for appearances, but because you are a poor piece of shit."

"How long did it take you to find me?" he asked.

"I've watched you from day one. With your little camera, taking pictures of the church. It was so easy to slip in and watch you from a distance, your little detective work."

She paused for a moment.

"But in doing so, you made a huge mistake. Whatever you were looking for affected me as well. My brother is dead, and you are going to find out why."

"You want my help?" he asked.

"My only family is dead, and you are going to tell me the

reason why he did what he did. Why he attacked me, I want to know what they did to him, whatever is in what they fed him."

Lia moved her head over Paavo's.

"You're going to find out and avenge him for me. I'm still held to them by a contract. Once they have what they are looking for, they too will pay a price for taking him away from me."

"You don't have to hold me at gunpoint to ask for that," said Paavo.

She placed a small kiss upon his forehead.

"If you have the drugs, give them to me. They know who you are and they're watching your every move, because of me," said Lia.

"The drugs?"

She moved the gun from his eye and positioned it over his cheek, at a moment's notice, she took his face off with a pull of the trigger.

"Do not play dumb, what else could have driven him mad like that?"

The people in the hospital, he thought.

"Where are the drugs? They want it, whatever you don't have; you're going to get for me."

"They..." Paavo stopped himself.

"The old cop, he's a friend of yours? They know him as well. You say a single word, and he dies, his wife dies," she said.

Lia began to unbutton his shirt with her second hand.

"Maybe I could make an exception to taste you before I eventually pull this trigger and claim you as one of my own."

Once the buttons had been loosened, she pulled one half of the shirt away and began to caress his chest and stomach.

"Such a fine creature," Lia whispered.

Paavo was seething with rage. Her tongue flicked out of her mouth and moved quickly across her lips before she lowered her head and ran it across his own. He showed his teeth and moved his neck to avoid the contact. She continued to run her tongue across whatever came into contact with it. He felt a slick wetness on his neck.

"It's a shame to kill you."

"Are you working for them?" he asked.

"I work for no one."

"Then tell me who they are."

"You don't get to tell me what to do, Paavo. The gun is still aimed in your direction."

She moved her hand to the other side of his chest. The other half of the shirt was moved and the hole into his heart could be seen in full light. Her eyes opened in surprise at the wound. Staring at the heart, she could see it move, pumping blood in and out. Her fingers travelled the outside of the hole, tracing the lines and scars on the surrounding skin. She was in awe.

"Such a strange heart you have."

"Don't touch it," Paavo pleaded.

Her fingers caressed the heart itself. Paavo winced in pain as she dug her nails into the muscle. She watched the blood run down her hand with a sick smile. He gritted his teeth, waiting for a moment to attack her.

"You're right. We're both damaged in our own ways," she said.

Paavo threw his hand forward and snatched the gun away from Lia. Her eyes widened into a rage. She shoved her hand down into the wound. Paavo screamed and turned his body to avoid the pain. He was able to aim the gun at her, she pounced on him. They fell to the floor and wrestled each other to gain control of the weapon. Lia was strong and ruthless. Her hands clawed and scratched at his eyes, his chest. He avoided as much as he could, using his weight to hold her arms down to the floor.

She flailed her body wildly to become free. For a moment, she stopped to look at him. He stopped as well. Their eyes met the same way as in the Police Station. She was enamored. Without warning, she kissed his lips. There was such passion in the movement. Paavo was caught off guard, his hand still remained pinning her down. The gun was still out of reach for her. She did not want it. She was there for this. He threw her to the other side of the room.

She hit the wall with force. Her shape had left a dent in the wall. Paavo stood up with the gun now aimed to the heart of the woman, who got to her feet smiling once again. He stared into her with ravenous eyes, fearful, ready to fire a shot without warning. He had never killed someone before.

"You're not weak, but you are afraid."

He said nothing.

"Have you ever killed anyone before?" Lia asked.

"Would you like to find out?" Paavo asked.

Lia motioned to the gun.

"Kill me."

"Get the hell out of here," he said. The woman turned her back and opened the window to leave the apartment. She turned her head towards him to speak.

"You have proven yourself to me, but they are still watching you. Avenge my brother, or the old cop dies. You have 24 hours."

She disappeared into snow and darkness. Paavo lowered the gun and barricaded the window. His thoughts were racing, how did she get into the apartment? Who was watching me? He ran his tongue across his lips, he could still taste her. Images of her scratching at his heart entered his mind and he began to hate the woman once again. It was true what she had said, that he had never taken a life. He was not about to begin tonight. He sighed a breath of relief as he went into the bathroom, eyeing the black case. He cleaned the wounds carefully, a piece of cotton dotted with Hydrogen Peroxide.

White spots materialized on his skin, his heart. He prepared another dose of the serum and ran the last words of Lia through his mind. 24 hours. Avenge my brother or the old cop dies. The syringe was filled with golden liquid. It was true that he was afraid of killing a man, or woman. There was hesitation now; if he missed and happened to die, here and now, Long would be in danger. He took his time, aimed the needle at the middle and inserted it deep into his heart. The towel was left on the floor, still dirty with old blood, dried to a dark brown. His knees buckled. The body became wrapped in warmth and he fell to the cold tiles of the bathroom, blacking out to visions of Lia Jones; wrapped in shadow and begging for his blood.

CHAPTER FOURTEEN

The sun rose high over the clouds producing pounding snow. Patches of light began to glow behind the endless grey that stretched across the skyline of Perdition. The view of the city from the train was magnificent. Steam settled high over the city streets below. The monorail moved quickly over a labyrinth of white and concrete, the snowfall rained into the open air like confetti. A woman rested against the cold steel of the pole, transfixed upon the passing of snow covered train tracks. She leaned into the side of the train car. Pinned to the window was her bag, letting her back straighten out.

Nyalla Rice had always been awestruck by the visuals of the city. The apartment left behind this morning was cold and unclean. Work had become less of a welcome necessity and more of a death trap. She was able to support herself but there was a longing, a desire to make great change. The business casual dress attire of the Kirilov building gave her enough leeway to wear the clothes she wanted. Her coat of wool rested plainly across upright shoulders. That day, she wore a flowing dress of tattered patterns. Red, orange and yellow hovered over the grime of wet footprints and melting snow on the floor of the train car. That's the way things were in this city, it seemed. Things were just comfortable enough, not more or less, nothing to make your question your place.

She stared intently into the center of the window. It sat like a massive television, feeding you the view of Perdition's busy downtown commute. Her right hand reached for an itch on the back of her neck, she took a moment to scratch it with a careful finger. Dark brown hair jumped out in curls never falling below her shoulders, large earrings of gold hung from her ears. Each piece of jewelry left a circle of shadow over the curves and straight lines of her neck. Her skin was a rich mix of brown and olive. Half African and half French, black eyes sat between white spheres like floating diamonds. She would make her co-workers laugh at the bar by being the only girl who could dance them under the table with the influence of rum and whiskey.

Black heels lifted her five inches off of the ground. The train car turned the familiar corner, making a stop at 7th street, just two more blocks before her stop. 9th and Carry. The street name was weird to her. It was easy to remember. With a sudden stop, the car halted. Machinated voices greeted the passengers, both doors in front and back opened to let in those others waiting, covered in snow. The trains in Perdition were multilingual, addressing its riders in several native tongues, no barriers for language in a place like this. There were several screens in the corner of each car, playing the breaking news of the morning. Women and men in business suits stepped into the train, shaking off the snow and wetness before finding a chair to occupy.

The quiet of the trip was ruined by the chatter of people on their respective cell phones. There were panels that stretched across the length of the car, displaying the next stop between maps plastered on each wall. She stared into the passing letters. The lights of red were static and pixelated. The layouts of the stops were ripped and torn from the walls. Small pieces of graffiti could be seen at the bottoms of the train car.

"The Underground is watching you."

Anything above waist level was cleaned off by the automated system, a series of arms, complete with scrubbers and high powered water spray that came from the inset of the car. It kept vandalism to a low. Nyalla stared at the crawl until the cab began to move again. The next stop was approaching. She readied herself for the exit. There were men in the back who had been watching her. She met eyes with them once, young men with leather jackets and heavy boots, before turning towards the sparks of the tracks. Their hair was spiked and cut into bizarre shapes, they were hoodlums. Eyes looked her up and down, as if she was meat. There were bad vibes about them. She always stayed at the front of the car during the commute. There were too many people around for them to try anything now. She wasn't sure if they were looking at her because she was black, or because she was a woman.

9th and Carry was announced and the train made its stop. With careful steps, she made her way onto the floor and through the revolving doors into the train station. The lights inside were blinking on and off, a cause of the heavy snow and wind. It coated the area in a brief darkness, as quick as her footsteps, she could see in front of her again. The lower staircase led down to the street, she took it and braced herself for the hard winds. Her eyes kept on the Kirilov building, only a block away. It was massive, a tower that sat over the rest of the city. On a day like today, she was happy to be gainfully employed by a company with enough money to keep its building heated. Golden doors opened automatically to lead incoming people to the main lobby. The receptionist greeted her with a smile.

"Good morning, Nyalla." She sighed and returned the gesture.

"Good morning, Grace."

"Lovely weather, isn't it?"

She reached down for her ID. It was needed to gain access to the elevator to the top set of floors. Out of three hundred, her station was on 119.

"You could say that." Grace reached under the desk, producing a small card reader. She placed it on the table and waited for Nyalla to insert the ID.

"How are the kids?" asked Nyalla.

"Fine, driving me crazy as always." She placed the card into the reader. With a few beeps and clicks, the light on its side turned from red to green. She was cleared for entry.

"Are you coming out with us tonight? Only eight dollars for

shots," offered Grace.

"That sounds like a bargain, but I'm going to Parker's. There was an ad in the paper about the old band backing up Sadie Reed a few nights ago. It's going to be a great time," said Nyalla.

As she placed the ID back into her bag, Grace thought about her plans for the evening.

"Do you mean like a rock band or something?"

She lowered her eyes at the fact that she had to explain.

"No, it's a jazz club."

"Oh, sexy!" Grace's voice squeaked.

"Indeed," said Nyalla. She rolled her eyes at the comment.

"Have fun, won't you?"

"I will. See you around, Grace."

The elevator at the end of the hall had opened. The card reader sent a signal to call for the lift. The lower levels were for the restaurants, the coffee shops and food court. The place was a giant commercial; advertisements, bright colors, loud noises beckoning for your dollar and attention. Standing in the middle gave you a sinus headache. She stepped through the crowds of people gathering in the lobby, making her way into the elevator. It was tight quarters at the start of the day, too many people standing around, like obstacles. She found a spot near the back wall and waited for the doors to close. The other riders of the lift squirmed as she squeezed by them. She exhaled slowly, calming her nerves. Any business that wanted to make it in the city needed a small piece staked out in this building. The food in the courts was too expensive and tasted like plastic in some cases.

The elevator ride was cause enough for madness. The train ride took twenty minutes. Getting from the lobby to the 119th floor took almost forty, every day. There was a sort of controlled frenzy with people stepping off the car, getting a moment to breathe in, only for twice as many to get on. She had worked there for more than a year and had settled in on the best possible routine for getting to where she needed in time. Floor 119 was like most of the others on the 100 block; thousands of cubicles and desks. She came through the elevator and walked in a hurried pace towards the entrance. The echo of her footsteps rang out, filling the room like a pendulum going back and forth. Checking her watch with the time displayed above, she had made it by six minutes. Glass doors opened to the work area.

Computers were set up, fingers were already in a frenzy of steady typing, busy work. This was her life now; accounts payable for the Kirilov building, one of the most well known weapons manufacturers in the world. Her desk was cleaned and organized. She sat down and pulled up her table, holding the keyboard and mouse. Every cubicle was a uniform brown. The carpets were grey with tiny flashes of red, white and blue. The walls of each divider were off-white with a piece of framed glass over each section.

She looked to her sides, waiting for the arrival of William. He shared the divider with her, both desks in each section were separated by a small table. The opposite side of her section was cluttered and swimming in papers and half assembled action figures. He labeled himself as an Otaku, and decorated his area with Japanese Anime; replicas of robots and Samurai. They sat in intense poses, waiting for battle. Where was he? She asked herself. Soon, her stout supervisor had approached in his tight fitting suit of blue.

"Good morning, Ms. Rice," said Charles.

He wanted her, and did not keep it private. She tried not to think about it when he spoke to her. There were moments everyday when she wanted to punch him in the face. She imagined him tripping and falling down a flight of stairs, it was difficult to contain her laughter sometimes. He would turn his head when passing her desk.

"Hello, Charles," she spoke calmly, not making eye contact.

"Where is Hiraga? Too busy to come to work?" he asked.

Looking over to the empty chair, she replied.

"I have no idea."

"When he gets here, tell him to see me in my office," he winked before leaving.

She forced a smile and began work, periodically staring at the empty chair, wondering when or if he would arrive.

Paavo warmed his hands. The car created steam and metallic noise within the stirring of snow and wind. He watched men in suits handing off food to the children, men and women from the shelter. Another one scratched off the list written in faded pencil. The weather was always brutal. Winter would come quickly and with harsh precision, rage with blinding snow and ice and leave in only a few weeks time. They were wearing ragged clothes, their faces were dirty and unwashed, and their shoes carried holes that collected snow with each step.

There were children there as well. Paavo watched them as they hurried through the snow, shuffling feet and breathing hard, just to grab the food held with arms outstretched. It was hard to not look away but he was waiting for the priest, the supposed Father Wen, to come out of hiding. The clock was ticking, with only half of the day remaining. This had to be the place. The number of shelters in the city was low. The map from the night before pointed towards this region as untouched by the mark of Awaiting Salvation. He was waiting to see him among his people, walking and talking with those seeking guidance. Paavo knew that he wouldn't take such time to carry out his facade, he would have to bide his time and corner him alone. He would have to confront him about the little girl, the dealers in and around the neighborhood, the strange operation taking place amidst these holy conditions.

There were no services today at the church. Wen never appeared and he had no reason to be here today. Paavo checked the time. He was waiting for the call from Long. People were stumbling around the church, in the same place the priest had stood when he died, fifteen years ago. They were looking for the priest, waiting for another taste of the meat. The man with long hair came back to that same spot two hours later, a package in his hand. He found nothing but a cop car, his name was mentioned with the others like Jones, the package was filled with blood red meat, the pages that wrapped it were ripped from an old bible.

The shelter was shut down, it's inhabitants turned into dead eyed, lifeless bodies. The giant was one of the men dealing drugs through the guise of being an assistant, a hired hand. The effect of the meat drove him insane. Paavo listened to the scanner; news of people attacking storefronts early in the morning. He paid close attention to the details. Some of them were identified as those released from the hospital the night before after being looked at. They all had the same symptoms as Clayton; ravenous eyes, they tore the place apart with their bare hands, asking for meat.

He knew that Long would get his team to look at the food, and find out if there was something else behind it. As strange as the situation seemed, he had faith in the old man still to stumble upon the truth. Paavo opened his phone to view a missed call. It was from an unknown number, it happened thirty minutes ago. No message was left. Perhaps they were watching him. He wanted to thank him for risking his job to keep him on the case. The robbery was out of control, bizarre. He dialed the number to set up a meeting. Long told him that the meat was covered in different medicines, psychotics melded with ammonia that blocked them from tracing the unknown blood. The substances were dotted with cocaine and painkillers. A form of designer drug like he had mentioned at the station, they would do more tests on the meat. Not only that, but the people brought into the hospital had suffered psychotic breaks of their own, not unlike Clayton in the interrogation room last night. He agreed and drove down to the station. He went inside to see Long waiting with a cigarette in hand.

"Drugs in their system?" Paavo asked out loud.

"Yeah. You were right about the designer drug. It's something that's been growing all over major cities, some call it Temptation, and there's been a lot of clamoring for it."

"Because it keeps them in some kind of a trance?"

"Depending on the region, they put a whole stash of drugs in the meat. The shelter you were staking out must have some kind of crooked operation going on. No one else is stuffing this shit into rotting meat. You remember what Jones said. They had plenty of stock to sell. When their feelers on the street were picked up, they took off and shoved out the rest of their merchandise in the last batch of food," said Long.

"Too much of it must have driven them over the edge."

"It must have been in exchange for this or maybe for both the drugs and some real food." Long sighed.

"A bunch of savages," said Paavo.

"There were others who followed, we have to find them. We need to wait for the priest to return home."

"Are you talking about the one the giant mentioned?" asked Paavo.

"He's the one we need."

"They must be packing up shop, we've been digging around, trying to find whoever's selling this stuff out there, there's been talk of them leaving town. But why would they leave town if they've got a successful operation?" asked Long.

"Maybe they're trying to quit while ahead," Paavo shrugged.

"That's insane. You said you saw them selling it to people?"

"They're probably feeding it to the children in the shelter as well..."

"You can't be serious." Long said.

"I have no reason to doubt the idea. Especially when you consider that the priest died and the man I spoke to is a fake."

Long's head shot up from the corner.

"What?"

"Fifteen years ago, the priest in charge of this church and shelter died, that's when Miss Aki stopped going," said Paavo.

"Seriously? That is what Clayton was talking about?" Long asked. Paavo looked away from him.

"The missing person? Her daughter?"

"Yeah, I found nothing. She said she was only thirteen years old. But Naoko must be older, just like the people I saw on the street. What did you find out? Anything?" asked Paavo.

"I had some of the boys ask around, we found some family members, and they didn't know she was missing. Miss Aki hasn't seen her sister in years, and they live less than ten miles away from each other. Some people look down on the poor, even if it's their own family," said Long.

"The last time the little girl was seen was playing with some of the kids from the shelter, almost a week ago. You said that she was reported missing a few days before we met up? It points to that place. Prints lead up to the closed down shelter. I took a look around the place in the company of the priest. He refuses to bail out his own helpers. The ones who could provide proof of what he's been doing are too crazy to talk. I'm going back there tonight."

"You'll have some backup if something goes wrong," said

Long. Paavo refused.

"No. Let me go in there first, I'll let you know if I find something."

"You seem to think that we're back where we were two years ago. It's my decision to let you go in there or not." Long warned.

"You don't trust me?" Paavo asked.

"Why now?"

"I'm worried about you," said Long.

"Don't. I'll only be a few minutes, then if I find something, you can take over."

"It's best if you weren't involved directly with the investigation. You're not exactly appreciated by the station," said Long.

"They should have forgotten about me."

"Someone will notice you and mention something upstairs about it."

"Are you on a fine line, sir?" Paavo asked as he smirked slightly.

"Let's just say that in the minds of the higher ups. Your presence in high-profile cases wouldn't help anyone."

"I suppose then it would be better if I slipped in and out unnoticed with no evidence in hand?" Paavo sighed.

"Consider it done. I'm staking out the church as we speak."

"Have you seen the priest since yesterday?" asked Long.

"No. He knows I'm looking for him, especially after his men were rounded up." Long scratched at his chin.

"Maybe he's already gone." Paavo shrugged.

"Either way, after nine when everyone shuffles from the

church back into the shelter for the night, I'll head in and check it out."

Paavo turned around and was stopped by Long.

"There's something I have to say to you."

"What is it?" asked Paavo.

"I know that you are busy with your own case, finding the missing girl for the old woman, it was strange that my case led you to the same spot."

Long had never spoken like this. He was dancing around the subject.

"They were connected. You found a pool of blood. Do you remember how I told you there were a few more pools of blood appearing around the city somewhere?" asked Long.

"Yeah, a couple."

"The rats have been hard at work identifying each victim. There's no apparent connection with any of them, it's like they were picked at random. Someone is attacking these people, I believe it but I cannot find anything new. Nothing but these damn pools of blood all around town."

"All around the city?" asked Paavo.

"It's been hard for me to keep this quiet. This case is growing into something big, Paavo. Bigger than I may be able to handle."

"Why would you need to keep this quiet? I haven't heard anything on the scanner." Paavo asked.

"You still have that thing?"

"Yes, but how many people are missing overall?"

"The news would have a field day with this." Long was avoiding the question.

"How many of them are there?" Paavo asked again.

"It would induce a panic in the city. People would be afraid to step outside their homes." He was talking as Paavo continued to ask.

"Sensei, how many more?"

"Fifty reported so far." Long admitted. Paavo was shocked. The inspector moved his head to confirm.

"Every single one of them left behind a pool of blood in the middle of a snowy street."

"Why didn't you tell me sooner?" Paavo asked.

"I've got good men on the case, but it's becoming overwhelming. We can't keep up with the volume. The men are starting to worry, that maybe they will join those missing."

"Fifty people turning up missing in almost a week, just like last time?"

"This is bizarre. I'm not sure how to handle this," said Long.

"What can I do to help?" Long refused.

"I don't want to ask you, I know you are swamped with this Naoko Aki. You want to find her for the old woman."

"Just tell me what you need. I'll do whatever I can," said Paavo. Long was hesitant.

"Things are moving really quickly, I don't want you to get caught up and make a mistake."

"I could say the same for you."

"Things have taken a turn for the worse since the Outlook was robbed a few days ago, it was a real mess, you know?" Long pressed.

Paavo looked away towards the window.

"Really?"

"Yeah, it was. A rumor saying that it was Mob related, even.

I've been working on that, plus this case that dropped out of the damned sky."

"Let me help you, then," said Paavo.

Long opened the case on his side and produced a stack of dossiers.

"This is a list of the missing," he said. Paavo opened the folder and went through the names and faces.

"This has to be under the radar, no one can know about these people. Their families are asking so many questions. The media will get involved soon. All of them vanishing in thin air will cause a storm much worse than this damn snow," said Long.

"I will keep this quiet for you, sir."

"I'm counting on you. You're one of only two others who know about the scope of this thing."

Paavo was beginning to doubt the old man's judgment. He was the acting Commissioner, why keep this sort of thing quiet? Was he trying to avoid an incident? Did he have a theory about mass abduction?

"How long are you in charge of the department?"

"The commissioner retired two years ago. I've been given a trial run. This will destroy my career if we don't do it right."

"So all this time I've been gone; you've been running the show?" asked Paavo.

Long began to laugh to himself.

"It's not exactly the promotion I had in mind, it's been hell trying to keep the place moving, I'm starting to think that is too much for me to handle. Too broken down to be in charge now. Better off shouting orders from the sidelines."

"That sounds like a man in charge to me." Paavo said as he walked away from the table, the folder in hand.

"Hey, where are you going?" asked Long.

"I'm going to get some sleep, get ready for tonight."

"Good luck, hopefully we don't run into each other."

"We won't," said Paavo. They shook hands.

"See you soon." Long said.

Paavo placed his hands deep in the pockets of the suit jacket. The hospital was crowded and the workers were not in the mood for someone poking around, asking questions.

"Everyone! Move to the side! We've got more coming in!"

Paavo stepped to the side to allow the stretchers to enter the building. There were people in the waiting rooms, coughing. They struggled to catch their breath from the cold outside. They looked at him strangely as he moved past the waiting lines. He asked to speak to the most awake and aware of the patients. The receptionist was a stout woman wearing blinding white. She ignored him for more than a few minutes.

"I was wondering if I could speak to one the people admitted last night; the ones that were outside the shelter."

"We're really busy right now. Who are you?" She asked.

"I'm a detective. I just wanted to talk to one of them for a few minutes. No cops, no difficult questions, I just want to ask if they saw someone the night before. I'm looking for a young girl who disappeared days ago. She was seen in and around the shelter where they were found."

"What's your name?"

"Paavo Harker."

"Let me put you on the file. Not a lot of visitors for any of the strays picked up from last night," she said.

"Strays?" he asked.

"Well, yes. When we ran their records, they had no recent addresses, no immediate families."

"They were all in a state of shock, any of them who are awake now and wouldn't mind speaking to me would be a great help."

The woman's face lightened up a little.

"I'll badge you in," she said.

There was a loud buzzer which signaled entry into the next area.

"Thanks." He walked into the next room and heard laughing from the woman who let him in and her girlfriends working the desk.

"Did you smell him? Jesus Christ!"

"Who the hell was that guy?"

After a series of questions to random people in hallways, he had found the rooms where they held the "strays" as the woman had said. A nurse was standing to the side. He emptied a bedpan and caught Paavo's eye. He started with the nurse. When asked who was awake, he was pointed towards an older man in the middle of the room. Paavo approached lightly.

"Hello?" he asked. The man stared into his eyes with no emotion, no reaction. He was dead inside.

"Can I ask you some questions about the church?"

"Meat. I need meat," said the man.

"Do you remember a little girl standing outside the shelter with you?" asked Paavo.

"I need to taste it again, I want it. Please help me."

"Can you tell me about the meat, then?" The man's eyes changed, there was desire.

"Do you have some? I'm hungry. I'm really, really hungry."

"I don't have any. Can you tell me about the priest?" asked Paavo.

"The father knows where it is; you have to find the father." The man spoke the words again, and again, and again.

Paavo left the hospital. He walked through the piles of snow plowed to the sides of the street to clear a way for the main path. His sneakers wet and freezing, he shivered walking towards the car. The car door was hard to open. He heard the crackle of ice as it flew open with the sharp motion of his arm. He put his key in and turned it. The engine started better than the day before. Soon, hot air filled the space and Paavo watched the moisture fade from his windows. It revealed the city slowly, the snow beginning to die down for the evening. He looked up to see the sky now a bleak grey of clouds, a mix of beauty and dreary darkness.

The streets were hard to navigate. The car slid forward at every stoplight. A nervous pit in his stomach began to take form. Paavo took breaths in, slowing his pace. The bags from the trunk were dropped off at the apartment. The ride back into the city was worse. Expressways were packed with cars and lights and noise. The trip to and from took up too much time. Paavo still enjoyed the arrival of the night from his window. Seeing the dark grey move into deep shades of velvet blue calmed him; seeing the sky change instantaneously, without warning. Paavo watched the slow transition as he moved bumper to bumper in loud, stressful traffic.

Grey skies filled slowly with light blues like running water. As minutes passed, the rays of white and blue darkened and bloomed as a garden of colors. Dots of white light began to appear on the steel spires hovering over the street. They reached all the way back into the city. As the skies grew darker, the lights remained the same, further separating him from the comfortable darkness that surrounded. The city lights were visible from the car; bright white lights that dotted the blue and purple skies now reflecting onto the snow below. The colors were amazing to see.

Kyoko sat down to read from her book; the latest purchase from the old bookstore a few blocks away. Her shirt was covered in blue stains. Spots of white paint dotted her pants. The quiet was good for them both. Even when Derek was there, no sounds echoed through the house; no yelling, just peaceful calm. It had always troubled her that the quiet of the room left her husband nothing to talk about but the advancing spectre of trouble that followed his work. The pages were difficult to read. The story was not entertaining at all. She put it down and began to walk through the rooms of the house. The pressure to succeed was placed on his shoulders not only by the Chief, but also himself. Without any real warning, he was given a job and expected to make miracles happen for the city at large. As much as he did for them, the first group of people began to disappear. Then, something within him changed, a weight took shape in his mind.

Each room felt like a museum. Dead air was stuffed into corners. It made it harder to breathe, sometimes. The guilt he felt began from those above him, imposed with greater weight at every wrong turn, every dead end in the case. What was the reason for their disappearances? There were times when some were taken day after day, other times the next abduction was months later. It was at all times random. As if God himself were plucking people from city streets with a hand in the sky with no rhyme or reason. There were no leads, no clues, and no support. Everyone was speechless, but any blame and responsibility went solely towards Derek. The longer the case dragged on, the more withdrawn he became. The silence of the house was then covered with grief. From the kitchen, she moved into the dining area. The wood table stained a dark cherry red.

When Kino died, Derek did not speak for days. The visions of his murder haunted him ever since. Kyoko did what her mother told her to do when she was a young child. Stay strong for the man, be stronger than he is. There were times when he came home to his wife, only to collapse into her arms. There were no tears, only the breaking of a facade he had built up for all eyes outside of this house. The energy left his body the moment he stepped back inside. She felt the words leave her mouth every time.

"What will you do when I am gone, love?" Her memories were stopped short by a knock at the door. Kyoko stopped and turned towards the clock. Who was this?

"Hello?" She stopped at the keyhole. No one standing in the light.

Kyoko opened the door to nothing but a view of a busy street, smothered in snow. There was no one there.

Parker's was a laid back jazz club in the lower downtown area of Perdition. Amid the snowfall, few clubs stayed open and Parker's was one of them. Nyalla walked the street alone. Fog and flurries set the background against the shadows of the towers. The sky above was a mixture of purple and brown. Black clouds covered much of the scenery. It sat between two tenement buildings and a barber shop. Outside, the place could have been mistaken for an old thrift shop. The sounds of busy cars and furious trains drowned out the crunching of snow beneath her feet. With the work week almost over, this was a tradition of sorts for her; a way to relax.

Two familiar faces stood outside, braving the cold to have a smoke. They exchanged waves as she headed inside. The designs of the room were based on the Cotton Club, as if you walked away from the modern day into the carefree nightlife of the 1920's. It was one of the last few clubs in the city where the music was played on records, old 45s that still worked despite the wear and tear.

The air smelled different inside. The nightclubs on the other side of town were loud, overwhelming. Children barely old enough to get in where struggling to move without falling down in a drunken stupor blocked your path. Nyalla had chosen this place as her getaway from the beginning. Velvet red leather and wood, mahogany table tops with black cloth covered everything. The lights were dimmed so low that it was difficult to see in front of you sometimes. Some of the tables still had candle holders, upon request. One could have dinner and a drink with friends or lover under candlelight.

Nyalla took a seat at the bar for a moment. The bartender was a sweet, older gentleman who walked up to her with a smile revealing a gap between his two front teeth, his hands busy wiping down a glass dripping with water.

"Good evening, gorgeous. We've missed you."

"Sonny, I was here last week," she laughed.

"That's way too long to be without you here, some of the old timers wanted to have a dance with you again."

She smiled, her red lips opened to gleaming white teeth.

"That was a one time deal. Tell them to behave and it may happen one more time."

"Alright. What'll you have?" asked Sonny.

"I'll have a whiskey on the rocks."

"Well, damn. That kind of day, huh?"

"You could say that."

"Coming right up, sweetie," said Sonny.

The drink was bitter, but went down smooth. She felt her chest warm, as if she had stumbled over a heated oven. Small sensations began to travel through her body, down to her fingers.

"You got your ticket, honey?"

"I do." She reached into her purse and pulled it out.

"Slow house, tonight?" she asked.

"Once she starts going, that will change." Sonny said as he took the ticket with a smile.

"You're the only one who pays for the show, thank you so much."

"It's my pleasure. Someone has to," said Nyalla.

"You won't be forgotten. Enjoy the show."

The band had finished setting up. Sadie Reed would begin her first set of the night. Nyalla ordered another drink and took a seat at one of the tables in the back corner of the room. Sadie was a regular for a select few of the bars in town. She had been singing standards for decades. Her voice was always strong. Nyalla had researched her work; a nearly forty year career. The voice had peaked into a rough howl which Nyalla had fallen in love with since that first night at Parker's.

Two weeks after she had settled into the city, co-workers dragged her out of the apartment and to this place to unwind. The setup was always the same; simple trumpet, drums, bass and guitar. There was one microphone, standing in the middle of the elevated stage, a single spotlight hovered over. Across the way, there was a strange man at the bar. His suit was dark red, a rose threaded into his lapel. A crimson bow tie stuck out from the black button shirt. After a minute or two talking with Sonny, they caught eyes and he sauntered his way over to her table.

"Hello, darling. How are you this evening?" In his hand, a strong Singapore Sling mixed with extra grenadine filled the glass.

"Good. Yourself?" She spoke in between sips of her own drink.

"Very well. I have a few questions for you, if you have time." He took a seat next to her.

"I suppose I could have some," she said. The man in red smiled. The vermillion shade of his drink had covered his teeth in the same colors.

"That is what I like to hear. This town is certainly going to hell. A pretty, young thing like you needs all the protection in the world." She saw the lines behind his shirt, shoulders straps for holsters. He held his hand out.

"The name's Valentine," he said.

"Bounty hunter?" She asked. He grimaced at the mention of his occupation.

"Are you a friend of Sonny's?" she asked.

"Absolutely," said Valentine.

"No, you're not." She cut him off.

"No hassle from me, just a couple of questions about where they are, what they might know," he said. She looked at him, eyes narrowed.

"You certainly don't have a lot to go on, do you?" The red smile returned.

"That, my dear, is where you come in," he said. She placed her drink down on the table.

"Go ahead," she said.

"William Hiraga is your co-worker, correct?"

"Are you looking for him?" she asked.

"Not exactly," said Valentine.

"Then what are you looking for?"

"A lot of missing guns."

"What would he have to do with it?" she asked.

"You both work for the largest weapons manufacturer in the

world. We all buy our guns from you, despite the channels they're sold in."

"And you think that he stole them?"

"I think he knows who did, and he's hiding out." He said. She stayed quiet. It would explain William's disappearing acts as of late.

"What makes you think that he knows something?"

"I've done some asking around. There've been people looking for him, just like me," said Valentine. Another drink and a feeling of warmth covered her body.

"You've told me nothing new, and I'm not convinced. Try again some other time," said Nyalla. Valentine nodded his head.

"That's okay. I understand if you are looking out for your friend, but your silence now may bring regret later." He dropped the rose into his empty glass before stepping away, disappearing behind the crowd of bodies.

"We'll be in touch," he said.

She checked her watch, wondering what had happened to Hiraga today. He had promised to meet her tonight to finally see Miss Reed on what could be her last run in the club circuit. The woman was in her sixties, yet the voice still had fire, passion. The band members sauntered onstage wearing matching smoking jackets, not much younger than Sadie herself. Blue silk shimmered beneath the house lights. A young waitress approached the table and lit the candle on her table, providing just enough brightness to see the outlines of her fingers. Nyalla raised her glass, saluting the woman. A side door opened up and the record player was shut off. The people inside Parker's went silent, unsure of what was happening. An old woman stepped out onto the floor and climbed the stairs towards the stage. There were some bursts of laughter from some of the patrons. Sadie Reed wore a golden shawl, draped over a dark blue dress and shoes to match. With the ensemble onstage, they looked like a sort of Egyptian lounge lizard cover band, all blue and gold and shining. She stepped to the microphone, and spoke with the voice of a pixie.

"Good evening, ladies and gentlemen. My name is Sadie Reed, and we are your entertainment for the night. Sit back, have some drinks, take a trip with us back to the good old days...Where your darkness went hand in hand with your love, where your bad days coincided with your best love making, where time...loses meaning."

Nyalla took a sip from her drink and moved in her seat. The lights went out, leaving only the spotlight. Her hand gripped the microphone as the band exploded into the first note. A loud crash of brass and drums shocked the crowd. The people were physically moved.

"The shadow of your smile...when you are gone..."

The band entered into the song with grace and technique, as though the first blast was to get the attention of the audience. It had worked. The place was dead silent, all eyes on the old woman who stood perfectly still. Her voice delicately danced across the piano lines. Her vibrato was clean. The bass lines were thick. The players had been doing this for just as long. Nyalla sat back in awe of the beauty and the skill. You could imagine riding in a train car, watching the city lights pass by. The music drew you in, like a siren song. You could let go of all negative energy, and wrap yourself in the sounds. They comforted you, caressed you in the midnight hours. This is what drew her back to this place, time and time again. A high pitched voice interrupted her swoon, she opened her eyes.

"Hey, love." She turned to see Hiraga. He was smiling madly.

"Well, hello there," she said. He took a seat next to her. He was wearing a hooded sweatshirt, torn jeans and combat boots.

"You know, William, there is a dress code here." He laughed it off.

"They know me here, just like you." She offered him her drink, he declined.

"This is the old woman you told me about?"

"One and the same, Will."

Both stopped and listened to the music. The song was short, over in less than a minute.

"Impressive, Nyalla. I'm glad you invited me."

"I have very good taste," she said.

"That's true." William took a small sip of her drink. His eyes closed, his mouth curled as he struggled to keep the alcohol down.

"What happened at work today?" she asked.

"Research, I got caught up with research."

"You're endangering yourself, Will. I don't want to see you get walked out."

"Let it happen if it must. There are much more important things happening in the world outside of the Kirilov."

"There was another report of hackers toying with computer systems in the news today..." William soon became defensive.

"Are you going to pin everything they report in the news on my journeymen friends and I?!" he asked.

"People at work are talking. Last week, Charles found empty spray cans in your desk drawer. Are you part of some kind of gang or something?"

"Not a gang, but just good friends. You can trust me when I say that I am not doing anything crazy on days when I am missing from work."

"Is this what you call having a crisis of conscience?" she

asked.

"We work for a weapons company. Whether we do payroll or data entry. We are part of a much larger machine, one that deals death to other countries for a profit."

"The people we work for are trying to make money. They're not tyrants, trying to take over the world or anything," said Nyalla.

"There's something else going on underneath the concrete. All those executives, they're hiding a secret. I may have stumbled into something that may tear the entire company down."

"What are you talking about?" she asked. His voice lowered below the loud vibe of the bar, he brought his head in close, only she could hear his words.

"Do you remember weeks ago when we started getting those reports of missing weapons from the ordinance? Whole shipments of weapons had turned up missing, even though the serial numbers for each checked out before hitting the ground and the warehouse?"

Nyalla took a drink.

"There was talk of an inside job. They nabbed a few of the dock workers on suspicion. That was the last I'd heard of it. Do you think there's a conspiracy behind that as well?" he asked.

She began to laugh at him. William's face remained unchanged. She realized it took, this may have been different.

"I've spent a lot of time digging around. I think I know what happened to the weapons."

"What's that?" she asked.

"They were stolen by our own C.E.O, Alexander Caine."

"...That's crazy."

"Have you met him yet? You have been working there how long and you haven't seen him face to face?" Nyalla was quiet for a moment.

"No, I haven't met him," she said. William looked at her with regret.

"You will eventually. He is a strange man. You won't doubt me after you've spoken to him," he said.

"What's so strange about him?"

"He's an oddball. Information about him and his family is pretty scarce, especially online."

"That doesn't make him odd, he's a private man from a very wealthy family."

"Have you ever seen his office?" he asked.

She shook her head. It was peculiar that these things did not enter her mind until now. It had been almost a year. How had she never seen her boss? He had never even introduced himself through a video for new employees like most corporations.

"It's crazy in there. Lots of pictures and art splattered all over the walls. It's the most art house corporate office I've ever seen."

"What's wrong with lots of art? You like art too, just as much as I do, right?" she asked.

"Yes, but this is different. I'm not trying to bring up commonalities in an ill-fated attempt to seduce you." Nyalla laughed and took another deep drink from the glass.

"This is occult art. Things that I know about that other people in that position would not be caught dead having in their office," he said.

"I don't know what to say."

"Hopefully, you never have to go in there. I'm a pagan and I felt uncomfortable there."

"What does all this have to do with him being the one harboring the weapons?" asked Nyalla.

From his pocket, he produced a piece of paper. His handwriting was nearly illegible. Rips and tears coated the edges of the sheet.

"It simply means that the guy cannot be out of the running as a suspect. Look at this. Every time a new shipment of hardware comes in from overseas or shipped out domestically, there are scanners that search for every piece of hardware on that ship. The data is collected and sent to us, and our job is basically to catalogue it, right?"

Nyalla agreed.

"The scanners check each piece three times. In the directory list, the shipping unit and the gun itself. Tiny barcodes are embedded in the black paint, usually around the handle or trigger."

"You told me about how those barcodes read the DNA of soldiers' fingerprints as well," she said. Will threw his hand up.

"Nevermind about that. The point is, that any discrepancy with the serial numbers, and the line is shut down until they find it. These streets are bad enough without some punk kids getting their hands on an assault rifle."

The folds of the paper opened to a maze of notes, letters and lines.

"The ordinance reported at least one hundred guns missing. The serial numbers checked out for each spot, except for the barcodes. Somehow, these weapons were mass produced blank, without identification and shipping to or from the city."

"Mercenaries and bounty hunters are not uncommon now. People with the means prefer guns for hire over the Police."

"But Caine is ultimately the one who signs off on the release of those weapons. He had to have known these weapons were made blank. The ships were never stopped and searched. The assembly line certainly didn't explode when they came across these phantom guns," said William.

"So, you think he's selling them off?" asked Nyalla.

"He may even be keeping them for himself. Who knows what kind of army the guy could amass with all the resources he has."

"Why would he keep those guns? Isn't it a possibility that they were sold off?"

"Do you think I would risk my job, running around the city tracking these weapons down because I thought this was a joke?" he asked.

"You went looking for them?" Nyalla looked at him differently. Will felt his heart stop. Perhaps she had seen him in a new and dangerous light.

"I've been keeping my eyes on Police scanners, online reports. Some got into the hands of dealers, Mob types. But the majority of those blank guns were nowhere to be found. I think he kept them from release."

"Do you have any proof?" she asked.

"The serial numbers check out as normal in the directory. The ordinance shows them in stock, somewhere in the compound. And yet, no search results in the public database."

"You think he's really trying to make an army?"

"No one person needs that many guns, no matter how rich or how crazy," he said. After a bit of hesitation, she opened her mouth.

"A bounty hunter was just here, asking questions about you." He nodded. He must have known.

"I saw him. Thank you for doing what you did."

"Don't mention it. Was he tailing you?" she asked.

"He's been around some of my usual haunts, asking lots of

stupid questions. I don't think he's the only one who's been assigned to this missing weapons deal."

She raised her glass.

"Here's to never finding out about an army then?" Nyalla asked.

"Maybe for you. But this information has to get to the Police soon," said William. A look of worry was soon replaced by a jovial smile. This was all to be another wild goose chase.

"Good luck, Will."

"Here, here."

William raised his hand and brought up to her glass to mime a toast. She stared intently into the fire of the candles before finishing her drink.

CHAPTER FIFTEEN

He parked the car close to the church. The heater made it's loud, whirring noise. He watched from a block away. The car seemed to be in a good position; as good as you can get on a busy street. He noticed the fleeting amount of gas in his tank. Paavo turned off his engine and lowered his body to rest on the car door, his legs hung over the passenger seat. Better to save gas for the next day, he thought, as he found himself nodding off periodically. Dried blood began to stick to his skin through the shirt. His fingers teased the spot of black cloth now dark red which pulled the patch of skin along with it. Time could not pass fast enough.

Long found himself wishing he didn't call his wife. It was getting late. He wanted to check on her, like every night. The snow wasn't letting up just yet. He wanted to know if the basement was flooded, all that water would have to go somewhere. Kyoko was tired from a long day of cleaning the house. Long usually let her dominate the conversation, talking about whatever book she was reading. Tonight was different, she spoke with a lower voice, she was worried about him, and he didn't want to think about the shootout the day before.

"Do you feel any regrets?" she asked.

"Of course I do, my stomach turns every time I think about it."

"Why did you have to do that?"

"I had no choice. What do you think could have happened if I didn't do anything?" he asked. Kyoko would not let it go, he thought, every time this happens.

"What couldn't you let someone else help you? At least try to?"

"Because I didn't know if they could. What if they froze up?

What if they made a mistake? All that would be on me, to protect them, to save them, to take responsibility if they got killed," said Long.

"No one would judge you if something bad like that happened. I don't believe that. It hurts me to hear you say that. I above all others would never judge you," she said.

Long was silent, he could only listen to the engine noise of the running cars outside.

"I want you to get help. You need it."

Kyoko's last words echoed over the chatter of the radio, Long and his men were on their way to the church to make the arrest of the man impersonating Gordon Wen. All Long could think about were the words of his wife, and the young man he swore to look after.

Paavo shook his body, chilled to the bone in the back of the car. The heat had dissipated, and he was left with an old blanket to cover himself. He was a mess; clothes began to stink with sweat, and he scratched his sides and smelled his fingers to see how bad it was. The snow outside had stopped to a few flurries, the air grew colder and more bitter, Paavo shrugged it off by rubbing his chest, trying to keep the blood circulating, it created some warmth. The church down the street was desolate, empty. All visitors were long gone.

It was time for the priest to come out of hiding. Paavo was waiting all this time to confront him. He began to worry about Miss Aki and her daughter. Where could she be? It's been so long since the last one, he thought. Was I going about this the wrong way? Did I look for here in all the right places? Did I put all my effort into one place, not thinking of other theories? Paavo felt his heart grow heavy, his insecurity casting a dark shadow over his thoughts. He stepped out of his car and walked slowly towards the church. He turned the corner down the familiar alleyway towards the shelter. He would start there. He needed proof and needed to stay out of Long's way. Get what you need and leave. He will take care of the rest.

The alley was empty, Paavo quickly ran around the side, he noticed a busted window covered by some plastic; he looked around before ducking inside. The room was full of dirt and dust, the walls were old brick washed grey with patches of red that could be barely seen. Out into the hallway revealed a hole in the roof, the shelter was part of an abandoned building. Paavo moved silently through the shadows around the corners. It was filthy, he could not imagine people spending the night, or even trying to enjoy any food here. Paavo moved quickly through the area, he carefully stepped over broken glass, wood and bricks. A row of tables sat at the end of the room, a white cloth splashed with red was strewn over each. The stains had to come from the scraps of red meat on the ground. It looked as though there was a struggle. There were red handprints on the cloth and on the walls. Across the length of the wall was a quote, splattered across the brick.

"For anyone who is alone, without God and without a master, the weight of days is dreadful."

Paavo produced his camera and took a photo of the words. They carved a place into his mind, what could they mean? He put aside the camera and revealed the spray device and quickly spread the liquid across the table. If it was the same substance that covered the meat sold outside on the streets it would turn yellow. If it was blood, it would turn green, just like the photographs, he thought to himself.

Paavo watched as the red prints turned a mix of brilliant colors, all yellow and green. He furrowed his brow. Of course the meat had come from inside the shelter. This would have been the perfect place to craft the drugs and sell them to those folks nearby. The best customers were those with a little bit of money and weak souls. That explained why there was no one there, it was all a show for the cops. For someone like me, who wanted to take a look around, he thought. The dealers would bring them in, with the promise of whatever they wanted, what they needed, make a show for those wanting to see inside.

After we were gone, they would give them their drugs and kick them back out. They would wander the streets, back to whatever small homes they had, if they even had homes at all. Those poor people would always come back; they were given food just for showing up. Pretty soon they would have to pay for every piece, and then it would be too late to go back. Paavo sprayed small amounts on the floor, the yellow and green painted a trail throughout the rooms, he followed through the short hallways, they led into a back room, there were piles and piles of dirty clothes the furthest corner. The yellow trial began to fade to make way for deep waves of green on the floors, leading up to that corner. He moved his foot across the pile of clothes, there were shirts and pants, balled up and discarded, all wearing the mark of yellow and green.

The clothes were covered in it, it was a dark green now, Paavo came across a tiny shirt of white cotton with pictures of colored stars, stained with the darkest green. It had to belong to a little girl, the smallest piece of clothing. It was blood. Paavo clenched his fists when he heard a noise in the distance. He walked slowly around the corner, edging along with the wall; the noise was coming from the end of the room. There was a shuffling of noise, as if someone was searching for an item. There was grumbling, curses coming from the mouth of the man in the shadows. Paavo produced his gun, he took slow breaths. The man was coming out of the shadows. He wanted to see his face. Paavo stayed hidden for a few more minutes. His hands began to shake slightly. There was trepidation. The vibrations of his footsteps were felt. His heart rate began to increase, steadily at first and then became a heavy pound. Paavo tried hard not to lose control, a nervous energy overcame him and he barreled out of the room, his gun pointed out towards the figure.

"Stop!" He called out.

The man ceased moving, hands raised, his face was barely visible. It was the false priest, the man who had posed as Gordon Wen days ago. He spoke softly even in his current situation.

"What's happening? What is going on here?"

Paavo did not move, he began to breathe, he felt the heat of his heart, he felt the blood rise.

"What are you doing here, Father?" The man known as Gordon Wen seemed to recognize Paavo from before, he smiled as if relieved.

"Hello, my son. How can I help you?"

"Why are you here? Where are the people from the shelter?" asked Paavo.

"They all went home. We are closing the shelter for now. Let's get you home now," said Wen.

"There's blood everywhere."

"My son, you do not understand what is happening here."

"I understand that you were feeding something to those people, and now they're gone," said Paavo.

"Those people wanted to be saved; they wanted to be freed of all their transgressions."

"What did you feed them?" Paavo asked.

"They wanted to be saved."

"What can you save them from?! They're already homeless, no one gives a shit about them, and you want to give them drugs. You want to make a profit. You want to make money."

"Why do you speak such awful language?" the priest said as

he looked up to the star filled black sky.

"In the presence of the lord?"

"The lord isn't here right now. There's only you and I, and all this blood," said Paavo.

"You're wrong; the lord is all around us."

"He's wasting his time watching over a dying man and someone pretending to be a dead man, Father."

The priest became quiet, then he smiled.

"Who are you?" Paavo asked.

Wen was silent. He turned around slowly and walked back into the shadows.

"We are the messengers of God's word."

"Where is the little girl?" Paavo asked the darkness around him. There was no reply, only a metallic noise, the clicking of bullets locking into place. Paavo's eyes widened, he ran back inside the room, diving away from the storm of shots fired.

He felt his heart beating too fast. It hurt too much, too quickly, he thought. The priest spoke again between blasts of the machine gun.

"The girl you speak of is no longer with us. None of them are. They tasted of the forbidden fruit. They are beyond our reach. Their destiny lies forever with God."

Paavo felt beads of sweat pouring from his head, and quickly wiped from his brow. He looked out into the distance to see another room only about ten feet away, there was some cover to be used, a load bearing pillar, solid stone. He grabbed a brick and held it ready.

"I'm not a dealer of filth and disease, not like those men." Paavo raised his eyebrows at the mention of the men; the sound of his voice became louder. He was approaching.

"They paid their debts; their duties were handed down from the church, from me, handed down from the highest order," said Wen. Another hail of gunfire shattered the air. Bullets ricocheted off the walls and corners, closer to Paavo's head.

"This is only a sign of things to come, those who pay their dues, and bow before him, are forgiven, and they will be taken away from such a damned, disgusting place."

Another blast of bullets, he felt the heat and air produced by the gun, his arm twitched. The brick from Paavo's hand seemed to move by itself. It flew out from the darkness and hit the wall on the other side, Wen turned for a second. It was all Paavo needed to dive towards the pillar at the middle of the room. The priest turned his head back to see him. There was frantic shooting. Paavo dove for the ground, rolling head first behind the pillar. There was a small glimpse of Wen's eyes, ravenous, his face lit up by the weapon's fire.

Paavo hid behind the pillar for a few seconds, the man advanced towards him, firing wildly in his direction. He readied his gun again and waited, the gun created the shadow of the man. He was closing in. Paavo's heart stopped for a brief second. He fired off some shots while he ducked past the pillar and into the adjacent room. Paavo threw himself against the wall to avoid the bullets and began to cough. He felt the blood welling up inside his chest, the wound began to sting from sweat dripping down inside. Paavo moved his tongue inside his mouth to collect the blood, it filled his mouth quickly. The bullets stopped for a second, there was no hesitation, he threw his hand out to return fire, and he pulled the trigger.

The man ducked behind the pillar, the bullets from Paavo's gun bounced all around the room, he was not aiming to hit him. It created a second of space to make a move. Paavo readied himself, until he heard a clicking noise. He looked closer to see a hand grenade. The explosion was loud and deafening. The priest laughed loud and joyfully. There was nothing but smoke and dust, all was quiet. No movement, no breathing, nothing but silence and darkness.

The priest stepped out from his cover, gun quivering in hand. He felt something hard smash into his face; a piece of the wall, concrete broken off. He stumbled back to cradle his face. Paavo ran out from the corner and circled the priest, his gun still drawn. He moved awkwardly, his side dripping with blood, injured from dodging the majority of the blast; a piece of metal lodged in his frail body. He winced as he pulled it out. The pain was sharp; he kept the metal piece in his pocket, trying not to leave a trace of his presence. Paavo closed his eyes, feeling the effects of the blood loss. The priest looked up, his face cut and bruised. He was still smiling. He began to laugh at Paavo.

"You can be saved too, you know," said Wen.

"Drop the gun," Paavo coughed out his words.

"There is still a chance for you."

Paavo struggled to breathe between the blood and lack of air.

"There is no chance for me, Father. I'm already dead."

The priest waved his hand with an air of understanding and wisdom.

"You will be saved. All is not lost. Think of all these lost souls, think about the little girl that you tried to save."

Paavo was silent, his chest wheezed, trying to catch air.

"It's not your fault; it was their destiny, what they were meant to do. You don't have to save them. You can join them."

"Don't talk," Paavo said. He heard the distant sounds of sirens.

"Do not lose your salvation," said the priest.

Paavo's heart stopped. Wen reached in his coat. He held up

the pin, missing from the grenade. The priest raised his gun and he fired straight into the darkness above. Paavo was already gone, running towards the exit. The noise of gunfire quickly vanished into his heavy breathing. Everything else now silent except his heartbeat, Paavo ran hard towards an open window, it led out to the alley. He jumped forwards at the opening. For a brief moment in midair, he tasted the cool night. The silence was ripped apart by the explosion. It rocked the foundation of the building and he met the ground with hard impact. Paavo rolled to his side, clutching his ribs as fire and concrete exploded overhead.

Long was approaching the building with nervous energy. The car was sliding along the slick roads as were the other officers behind him. The explosion was intense. Long's car rumbled for a few seconds. He slammed on the brakes while the other cars turned and skidded out, struggling to avoid collision. Pillars of thick smoke covered the streets for blocks.

Lights turned on in adjacent apartments and houses. The Police split up into groups. Some stormed the remains of the building with guns drawn while others began keeping back those bystanders and passersby curious and frightened. The group of officers on the inside of the building began to choke on the air inside.

They yelled their threats into the shadows of the building's interior. Long stayed behind. He thought of the words he shared with Kyoko then he thought of Paavo and his heart began to beat heavy. Long ran around the back of the blast area. He stepped over piles of rubble and trash. After a few minutes with no sign of him, Long began to call out his name. He yelled out at first, and then looked around nervous, wanting not to be heard. He called out again, but much lower and tried to walk through the rubble relaxed, trying not to draw attention to himself. He was not supposed to be here, he thought, stupid kid, what's wrong with him?

Long began to feel guilty for letting Paavo come here alone. I should have been here with him, I don't even know what the hell happened here, what is going on? His mind was full of frantic thoughts. He continued to call out his name, the other officers inside searching the area. He finally came across Paavo's body; in the corner of the alley, nursing his wounds. The officers covered the remains of the building. Some rooms were intact. Others were destroyed by the severe impact. A few flurries of snow began to trickle down from the black sky as different groups of officers attacked different rooms, finding nothing but garbage and pieces of wood and stone. A pile of ashes covered the remains of the clothes found by Paavo. They were burned badly, yet pieces of clothing covered in blood were still intact.

Paavo was alive but shaking. Long picked him up. Paavo winced when he made contact with his ribs. Grimacing, Long quietly apologized and moved Paavo as fast as possible. There was a serious wound near Paavo's right side; a piece of shrapnel from the grenade had grazed him. No one had spotted them yet. Paavo was delirious. He mentioned the apartment. Long whispered to him.

"Shut up." Long opened his trunk and tossed him in.

"I can't have you bleeding all over my car. Damnit, you're not supposed to be here."

In the center of the room, one of the officers stopped and called for the others. The priest was there; a mere shadow of skin, blood and bones. Black ash encircled the body. The blast had thrown him back to the floor, his arms outstretched, welcoming, as if he was being carried. It was disturbing to see, the face burned into a hideous black smile. The officers were frozen staring at the remains of the priest. One of them made a motion towards the room hidden away in the far corner. As Long attempted to close the trunk, he heard some of the men calling his name. Paavo grabbed his hand, he struggled to speak.

"No hospital. Apartment."

"What?" Long looked up, hearing his name being called frantically.

"Take me there, when you're done."

"You're crazy, I'll be right back. You're going to the hospital."

"I can't go there. I need my medicine," said Paavo.

Men were approaching the car, Long lowered the trunk nervously.

"What medicine?" he asked.

"Sir! We found something, you need to take a look right now," one of the officers called out.

"Show me, quickly!"

The men led Long away from his car. They hurried through the debris on the street and into the remains of the building. Paavo tossed and turned on the inside of the trunk. As the smoke cleared, the building was fully revealed; torn apart by the blast, the collective detonation of at least ten grenades. It was black on the inside, burned from the fire and fury, a hollowed out shell. Long walked towards the bizarre shape in the center of the building. He stopped suddenly, taken aback by the figure with arms outstretched towards the night sky. Long was repulsed. One of the officers pulled him towards the hidden room. He walked in with eyes wide open not sure of what he would discover.

It was more blood, more clothes, more of what Paavo had found before the battle. There were streaks of red across the walls, still visible on the burned bricks. There was a terrible smell that moved through the room, a smell of flesh, dead and rotted out. A mix of men, young and old, struggled not to inhale, it made them sick. An officer pointed towards shapes hidden in the deep darkness, he spoke with a tremble.

"Holy shit. Look at that."

Long turned toward the corner and moved into the shadows, he reached down to see an abyss of blood. He took a step back and spoke with a haunted voice.

"My god. What were they doing here?"

Paavo's foot kicked open the trunk. He winced as he climbed out. Blood poured from his side. It was hard to move, too light-headed. No one had noticed him yet, but the car was still a distance away. He had to drive. Paavo moved slowly alongside the sidewalks and mixed in with the bystanders. He held himself straight to not appear hurt. Those paramedics might approach me, he thought. They had not noticed him. Suddenly they were called into the building by a frantic officer flagging them down. A few more blocks, he said to himself. The cold wind was even worse now as the sirens faded into the dark night. Paavo made it to the car. It barely started, and the engine had lost all its warmth kept up the hours before. He turned the car around completely. The pavement was filled with salt struggling to melt the built up snow. Paavo made the turn after a few excruciating minutes. He drove towards the apartment, it was late. The streets would be empty.

A few minutes later Long had stepped away from the scene to check on Paavo. He walked nervously towards the car, hoping he wasn't bleeding out into his trunk. He had to get him to a hospital. The old man kicked himself for leaving him behind to follow the officers. On his way to the car, the image of the body in the center of the room replayed in his mind over and over. The mouth was open, as if laughing, welcoming the blast, Long shook his head to lose the image. He opened his trunk to find it empty. Paavo had left spots of blood in the car. Long cursed and began searching for the wounded young man. He gave up when more officers came. Long decided to leave a message and get back to his work; there were families to be contacted, reports to be made.

It took Paavo an hour to reach the apartment. The drive was a nightmare. Before he reached the expressway, he felt his heart slow down. He checked the time; thirty minutes off schedule from the next shot. Pain was worse than the night before. His vision began to blur as he swerved from lane to lane. There was cold sweat building up on the back of his neck. Paavo was filled with nervous energy, yet his body was shutting down. He moved his hand off the wheel to roll down the window. The cold air hit his face and woke him up. Paavo picked up speed; he twitched his elbow, feeling the delay between nerve and muscle. He felt disconnected from his own body. His mind was awake while his body quickly fell into sleep.

He hated himself for letting this happen again. There was no preparation for this, no planning. If I'm going through with this, he thought, I have to bring it with me. Travel from place to place would be impossible. I'll have to sleep in the car. Paavo made mental notes swerving back and forth around the few cars still out that late. He tried to keep the car steady with one hand and cover his wound. The duffel bag still on the floor of the passenger side held supplies inside. The car moved back and forth from one edge of the lane to the other.

Paavo finally felt the wrapping inside. He pulled it out and put the roll between his knees. A long piece was yanked loose and ripped away from the rest of the roll. He tossed it away and began to unbutton his shirt. With as much precision as possible, he wrapped the tape around his ribs. It was horrible; no way to get it around proper, at least while driving. After a few minutes of almost crashing the car, Paavo had thoughts of giving up. The tape had a sticky coating which he put it firmly to the wound. He winced as it stuck to his side and went over the first layer with another. Each row of tape had a piece that rolled into bumps that travelled all the way down his right side. Good enough, he thought, still rolling down the highway.

The apartment was only a few minutes away. Paavo slapped himself to keep awake. He kept twitching the arm as the elbow's reaction became more delayed. He nodded off and opened his eyes to further down the street. The car was cold inside and he shivered uncontrollably. Paavo shook his head to stay alert. He pulled into the driveway. The tires screeched along the curb. The door opened and his limp body fell out, stumbling towards the stairs. Paavo hit his knees against the bottom step. There was no time to feel the pain. He climbed hand and knee over each step. The apartment door opened violently and Paavo crawled in. He slammed the door, locking it behind him.

He felt a sharp pain. All the effort to pull himself into the apartment had triggered an attack in his chest. He took slow deep breaths but couldn't fight it; holding his air, trying to stifle it but Paavo coughed hard, spitting up blood. His side began to ache; the bleeding and cut skin was being pulled by the tape coming loose from his body. Paavo pulled towards the bathroom, grabbing the kit and moving towards the center of the apartment. He had no energy left. The blood in his mouth left an iron aftertaste, his wound became live, and more red began to pour from his chest.

There was no time left, the shot was produced from the bag and the golden liquid was taken from the bottle, just like the night before. Paavo couldn't even remove his shirt. The shot went through the cloth and into the wound. It made a strange sound as he felt deep warmth enter his veins. It felt almost soothing. The warmth overcame Paavo as his head fell back and hit the wooden floor. He was finally alone, finally safe and asleep with the syringe still sticking out from his body.

Hours had passed when Long came to Paavo's apartment to check on him. There were a few knocks on the door as the old man stood around for a minute or two beneath the hallway lights of the apartment floor. There was a slight trail of blood going up the stairs, it was barely noticeable, Long saw it and became fearful. He climbed the stairs, clutching the revolver in his holster. Thoughts of him being attacked ran through his head. He reached the top floor, slowly inching his way towards Paavo's apartment. The floors were slick with ice, he slipped a few times, cursing aloud.

"Shit! Who cleans this shit up, man?!"

He began to bang on the door, he called out for Paavo. Fearing the worst, he kicked at the door, Long drew back in pain, the door was bolted up tight. Another two kicks and the door flew open. There was a body on the floor. Long closed the battered piece of wood behind him and moved towards Paavo. He was sprawled out, his mouth open and limbs outstretched. He saw the syringe lodged inside his heart. Long observed the wound, he was afraid to touch him. Paavo was deep in sleep, his body still bleeding out all over the place. He decided to stay and locked the door. Long slowly moved his hand toward the syringe and pulled it out quickly before placing it on the table. Long looked at Paavo's body and he thought of the priest in nearly the same position hours ago. Outside, a few snow flurries began to fall. It was just another storm on the horizon.

CHAPTER SIXTEEN

Miles away from the city of Perdition, an old woman looked quietly towards the torrent of snow and ice. She placed her hands on the glass. The cold feeling of the window made her jump. Though her eyes were open, she could see nothing but white. Chi Lien had been blind for many years. Every morning she found herself grabbing the same objects to gain her bearings. Her senses were dulled from age and time, but she had memories. She would hold these objects and paint a picture through their textures; this was her sight now and forever. The window revealed lonely walks through the snow mixed grass as a child. A sweet and delicate smile crept across her face remembering the crunching of snowy ground underneath her feet.

She knew today would be special. Paavo would soon call to speak with her on the telephone. A quick turn of a black knob created a spark of fire on the oven. She left the lights off this early morning. Without eyes, the lights were never on in her house, why waste electricity? Rushing water hit her ears as she filled the pot with cold water. It had been so long since they spoke last, she thought. Two small white bags were dropped into the heated water. She salivated at the smell of fresh tea as the steam began to rise from the pot.

Chi Lien drank the last of her cup of tea and waited for the phone to ring. It wasn't like Paavo to be late. After a moment, she paid no mind. Young men are always busy in the big city, always on the move. It was like that every month; her waiting by the phone, Paavo would call in to check on her. It was him who brought her to the village outside the concrete walls and overwhelming nature of Perdition. There were only a few modest homes then. The rain brought such deep colors of green, from what he described to her. In this place, her flowers could thrive. Chi Lien remembered them planting the first seeds years ago; he coughed every few minutes, it hurt to be moving around so much. She told him to sit down but he kept saying not to worry.

That was him; never complaining about the pain brought on by his condition. She knew that it took great strength to ignore those pains. Hours later, she found him nursing his wound in the bathroom. He laughed it off once again when she tried to scold him for risking his health. So full of pride, she thought, always grateful. She sat and waited, wondering what kind of adventures city life could bring.

Paavo's eyes opened sharply to the window open and a small trace of sunlight burning through the grey of the new snowstorm. He looked around fearful, his back strained as he sat up. There was an intense pain in his chest. Paavo stood slowly. He looked down at his wounds to realize the blood had begun to pour down his stomach. There was dressing where the shrapnel had hit him last night. He didn't remember doing that. He stumbled to the bathroom to the shelf across from the bathtub and reached for one of his black towels.

They hid the blood better than any color. Some days they were necessary, especially out in public if doing his laundry, as opposed to washing them by hand. He wiped the blood away and tossed the towel in the tub, Long spoke suddenly.

"What happened to you?" Paavo's head remained down and he stared at the black tile floor.

"Nothing worth mentioning."

"What is this?" Long said before he held up the syringe, stained with blood and small remains of the serum.

"I know it looks strange right now," said Paavo.

"What the hell is this thing? I thought you were dead, you took off from the scene, and you bailed out of my car."

"I needed to come back here. I thought you said I couldn't be seen." Paavo said.

"That's not the point! You almost died!" screamed Long.

"I'm not too far from that either way."

"Why didn't you go to the hospital? Why did you come back here for this?" Paavo was silent, Long spoke again.

"Why was this thing sticking out of your damned chest?"

"I needed it. I used to be fine without it, but I went to a doctor and he gave it to me."

"What's this doctor's name? No one needs to stick a six inch needle into their chest, I don't give a damn how sick they are!" Long shouted.

"The doctor's legit. He was going to keep me in the hospital overnight, I would still be there now probably if I didn't agree to start taking the shot."

"This is insane. Paavo, why would you agree to do this to yourself?"

"I don't know."

"You're dying. Is that right? Is that why you disappeared? Two years without a word?" asked Long.

"It's not like I haven't been taking care of myself. It's been getting worse. I went to the hospital to know how long I've got left."

"How much time have you got left?"

"You can't honestly think that someone can survive with a hole in their chest," said Paavo.

"How long?" asked Long.

"It doesn't matter."

"You're just a kid. It matters."

Paavo stared into the corner. There was a brief silence before he continued.

"I've been like this my whole life. I never told you because I knew how you would react."

"I would have helped you, I don't understand why you would hide something like this, the entire time I've known you, I tried to protect you," said Long.

"You did. That's the point; you've done a lot for me. This needed to be kept hidden. I couldn't do half the things you allowed me to do if you had known," said Paavo.

Long was shocked. There were so many questions, no idea where to begin, there were a few minutes of quiet hesitation between both men.

"Does it hurt?" asked Long.

"Constantly."

"Were you born like this? How does it work?" Paavo was quiet for a moment, he turned toward Long and approached with fingers spreading open the wound.

"The hole in my chest leads through parts of my heart, lungs and abdomen. It requires careful management of inhaling, exhaling, laughing and food intake. Strenuous activity cannot be allowed, running and playing as a child was practically nonexistent." Paavo demonstrated by coughing, which provided a stream of blood.

Long offered him a towel.

"How did you survive so long like this?"

"I learned how to control it. Some days are better than others," said Paavo.

"What do you control?"

"Length of breath, tightening of the muscles in my body allows me to move more freely than others with my condition."

"There are others with this?" Long asked. He could not believe it.

"I think I'm one of the few left. Everyone else died off somehow."

"I've never heard of this before, how is someone born like this? If you were like this as a baby, what stopped you from crying out and hurting yourself?"

"They gave us medicine to keep us calm and quiet," said Paavo.

"They drugged you? That is sick. How could this never have been reported or documented?"

"It was labeled as a medical anomaly. They blamed it on anything and everything; pollution in the cities, made it out to be a developmental disorder, caused by our surroundings," said Paavo.

"Ridiculous. I never heard of any kids who lived near the factory district being born with holes in their chest. What about this hospital now? Where is it?"

"Closed down, there were only a few doctors and nurses who took care of us. After a few years, they lost funding for the program, since there were only a small number of us. They figured it would be better to grant money to other things," said Paavo.

"Where are those doctors and nurses now? This is crazy. How could you not tell me about this? For all these years, you never confided in me about this?"

"It was something I had to handle on my own...and still do."

"That's why you've always been so quiet, so withdrawn." Long realized.

Paavo looked at him with a tired face.

"Let's not talk about this anymore," he said.

"Alright, we can talk about something else then. What

happened at that building last night?" asked Long.

Paavo remembered the face of the priest. He heard the gunfire once again and felt eyes of fire looking down upon him.

"He had a gun, and more."

"Why did a priest have a gun?!" asked Long.

"He was the leader of the operation. He knew we were coming. They made their money and tried to burn the evidence and move base."

"How the hell did you make it out of there alive?" asked Long.

"Just lucky."

"Did you use any bullets?"

"What?" Paavo was confused.

"Did you fire off any rounds back there?"

"I had to. He had a machine gun and grenades. That kind of thing needs a bit of an equalizer."

"Damnit, Paavo. They'll find those rounds; they can link you to the scene now," said Long.

"You want me to get rid of the gun?" asked Paavo.

"You're going to have to. They'll question you. It's been such a long time, and they'll probably think you're working for them. You want to be treated like a suspect?"

"No. I'll get rid of the gun for you," muttered Paavo.

"This is not how you want to restart your career."

"I think I'm doing pretty well so far, I haven't died yet. Close though."

"No shit, did you find what you were looking for?" asked Long.

Paavo looked down. He ignored the question.

"You should go. I have things to do." Long was surprised.

"What do you mean? What are you going to do?"

"I have to make some calls," said Paavo.

"What about the little girl, did you find her?"

"No, nothing at all."

"So, what are you going to do?" asked Long.

"Keep looking, no choice."

There was hesitation in Long's voice as he tried to continue.

"I have to get back to the station, there are reports to fill out, and I've been keeping them at bay for a few hours now. You should feel grateful for all this attention you're getting from me."

Paavo was silent. He was staring at the phone, thinking of Chi Lien.

"I'll leave you to your business. We'll talk later. Don't try and disappear on me now, damn it. Come to the house tonight, we'll have some beer and talk more," said Long.

The old man showed himself out the door. He felt strange leaving like that; so many more questions to ask. He tried not to feel betrayed. Paavo never lied to him; he only kept this bizarre condition hidden for years and years, never showing any signs of sickness.

He was always a pale, skinny kid, he thought, I never got the feeling that he was constantly near dying. Long walked down the steps with a feeling of sadness. He struggled down the concrete stairs, his warm feet now shocked with the cold wind and moisture from the fresh snow falling. More storms, he thought. The car barely started as he made his way towards the station. He thought of some ways to explain his absence. The storm grew in strength as he approached the city.

Nyalla dozed off for a brief moment at work, a vision of falling to the ground from insane heights. She looked to her right to see William missing again. The day was at a standstill. Another attack on the systems, computers were down on the first 100 floors. Bulletins ran across the television screens, telling everyone to stay in their seats, that the systems would be online in a matter of minutes. The message had been displayed for two hours. Other employees were walking around freely. She wanted to join them. Charles flagged her down as she got from her desk to stretch her legs out.

"Rice, how would you like to do me a favor?" he asked.

His smile ripped across his face, jagged teeth peered from his lips. He really made no attempt to put out a good outward appearance.

"Sure thing, what do you need?" Smiling, her voice rang loud with the false, upbeat attitude associated with the corporate world.

"I need you to take something upstairs to the man's office."

"No problem, which one?" she asked.

"The big office, on the top floor." That was the chairman's suite, the place that Hiraga had warned her not to go.

"Really?" Charles wiped the sweat from his brow with the sleeve of his jacket.

"Yes, the downtime in the system has slowed down our ability to send out messages. Normally, I would have emailed him, but we don't have that right now."

"You look tired," said Nyalla.

"There was a package that finally came in today. There was a lot of confusion with the Police, something about some criminals doing deals down at the docks. Some of them were on the ship when it came in. They were finally able to release it and I need you to go upstairs and drop off the paperwork."

She became nervous at the thought of meeting the man after talking with William the night before. What does he look like? How do I act?

"I'll take care of it," she said.

"That's why you're here, Rice. You're reliable."

He handed her the paperwork and stumbled off to catch his breath. She headed towards the elevator. She wondered how the elevators still worked if some of the electrical systems were down. Maybe they ran on a backup generator, or have an additional set up in case these things happen. The lift moved higher towards the top offices. She had never been past the 150th floor. This was the first time. She took a moment to straighten her dress, she checked for any food in her teeth. First impressions were more important than anything, in this city, anywhere you go.

"Executive suites."

The mechanized voice worded her destination in cold, separated language. She stepped out of the elevator and into a hallway of red carpets and gold lights. It was almost a different building altogether. A part of her felt like she was back in Parker's. The sliding glass door at the end of the hall allowed entry into the executive suite. She followed the path and placed her hand on the door, it was locked.

"Welcome, please enter."

Another voice came through an old loudspeaker as the door was unlocked and opened on its own. Nyalla entered more nervous than before. The floor was nearly abandoned. The same color schemes followed into the suite. She stood still for a moment once inside to look around. Far away figures stepped into focus and then away again. Maybe they were watching her. She moved ahead, past the ornate bookcases on each side towards the main office. There were several enormous televisions, broadcasting the news, weather and financial updates. Classical music played quietly in the background. Men in suits walked through. She tried to smile at them. They did not respond, she felt like an alien walking through those rooms. At the door of the main office, she knocked timidly. A man opened it, his appearance was striking. She was staring into the face and eyes of the chairman of the Kirilov Company.

"Please come in," he said.

Nyalla walked in with paperwork in hand, her head down towards her feet. His suit was a jet black with a striped red tie. The man's voice was deep, booming, she looked at him, finding her unimpressed with the picture painted by her co-worker.

"I'm without a secretary at the moment. Most of the time, there are groups of folks here, doing the work for me and for a few others." He noticed her moving tentatively.

"Your name?"

"Nyalla Rice. I work in Cataloging. Nice to finally meet you, Mister Caine."

"Call me Xander," he said. She nodded with a slight smile.

"How can I help you?" She caught herself and began to laugh.

"Charles asked me to bring this to you."

"What is it?" he asked.

"It's some paperwork to sign off for your delivery that was held up." Caine had taken the papers from her hand and began to read them. He grabbed them in such a way that his fingers slid across her own. She looked around the office, trying to avoid any flirtations with the man.

"How are you doing?" She did not want to engage in a conversation with him. Her eyes travelled around, searching for those occult items that William had mentioned, nothing yet. She began to feel a little uncomfortable in her skin.

"Are you familiar with the name of Kirilov?"

"No, I'm not," said Nyalla.

"He's a character from literature. He committed suicide based on what he calls logic. For life to be worth living, God must exist, and yet he is convinced that God cannot exist. His suicide is essentially a revolt against the idea that God does not exist."

"Do you believe that God exists?" she asked.

"Of course, I do. When I look at everything around me, I have no choice but to believe," said Caine.

"And what made you choose this name?"

"My grandfather was an elder of the city council. My history belongs in the origins of this city. Their beliefs were strong in the redemption of man. Making money in the modern age, one would say, works against a person's moral compass. But my faith is hand in hand with my passion; safety for our country and for ourselves."

"I've heard that you have a lot of artwork," she said. He smirked, looking down at the floor.

"I am a sort of collector."

"Art is a big passion of mine as well," said Nyalla. Caine took her by the arm.

"Come this way, I keep my collection behind closed doors." She followed him to a backroom. A pair of old wooden blocks covered an alcove in the wall. A lock and chain sat wrapped around the pieces.

"Please forgive the archaic appearance," said Caine. From his pocket, he produced a key and placed it into the lock. It opened, the chain dropped to the floor. He picked it up and placed it on the small table to the right of the opening in the wall.

"I'm planning to put in special doors, the crew I use is off working on a special project, when they are done with that, I'll have a proper entrance."

He pushed the blocks apart, revealing a dark hallway into the room behind the wall.

"For now, this will have to do." The room covered in oil paintings, perfect recreations of works from the time of the Renaissance.

"I love this period, because of the attention paid to realism, the reconstruction of the human body using only a brush and color. Think of all the things you may have created, nothing you or I will ever match the beauty of a person, reborn as art."

Nyalla looked around at the paintings. Each was framed in a border of shining gold. There was so much red inside the room; on the floors, the walls, in the paintings themselves. Crimson red was everywhere. It made it difficult to enjoy the works themselves. She moved away from her boss, moving from piece to piece, admiring each one.

"You look distracted. What is it?"

"Is red, your favorite color?" asked Nyalla.

"It is. It gives anything it touches vitality, impossible to deny. The color is a symbol for so many things. Life, creation, royalty."

"And blood?" Nyalla asked. She looked back at him to see his eyes, watching her. He spoke from a place of introspection.

"Yes, blood as well, death even."

He waited for a moment to ask his next question.

"Are you fascinated by death?" She did not wait to respond.

"Not as much as you, apparently." He laughed to himself.

"Fair enough."

Nyalla paused at two paintings in the back of the room.

"These look familiar to me," she said.

"One is a fresco, from Michelino. It was inspired by The Divine Comedy. It's a portrait of the poet, Dante, standing between the city of Florence and the entrance to Hell, with the spheres of Heaven all watching from above."

"It's amazing," she said.

"Have you read the poem?" he asked.

"I haven't."

"I'm sure you are close to the library from here. I recommend that you read it." The next piece was a charcoal sketch, Caine moved towards it.

"I made this one," he spoke with a distinction."

"It's very good," said Nyalla.

"I didn't ask if it was."

She tilted her head to the side, staring at the audacious smile across his face. He laughed again.

"But thank you, very much," said Caine. Nyalla looked at her watch, perhaps it was time to get going. Caine continued talking.

"This is a sketch of one of the illustrations from the poem. Here, Dante's guide Vergil keeps a group of demons at bay."

She looked around to see that the entire back wall was covered in similar sketches from the book. His skill with shading was incredible, she could not help but feel put off by the amount of drawings and their subject matter. A man with wings falling from a star covered night sky, groups of men in hoods walking in straight lines, dead bodies laid across the ground, tortured souls pleading for salvation. It was over the top, she began to feel overwhelmed by the atmosphere in the room.

"This is my favorite; one of my earliest sketches as a child, the story of Enoch."

Nyalla took a breath, staring into the darkness of the charcoal and ink. Heavenly bodies, falling to the earth, women crying on their knees spread across an endless white landscape. Caine began to speak in a deep voice.

"And behold...He cometh with ten thousands of His holy ones, to execute judgment upon all, And to destroy all the ungodly: And to convict all flesh of all the works of their ungodliness which they have ungodly committed, and of all the hard things which ungodly sinners have spoken against Him," he said.

The air was tight; her breath shortened, needed air. When moving backwards, she stumbled into a sculpture, the table rocked back and forth. She stopped it with her hands. The object was light but was long in length. Nyalla made a noise and stepped back, it was the skull of Baphomet.

"Ah! What do you think?" asked Caine. The skull of a goat made from hardened clay, it looked incredible, life-like. Two horns of acrylic, painted black stretched out from the head, at least three feet on each side.

"It's horrifying..." She did not hold back this time.

This is what William was talking about. The man was definitely an eccentric with a taste for beautiful art. The skull looked amazing, but she could not ignore its meaning. To the side of the skull, the sketch of a sword, the length of the wall, stood in silence over the symbol of evil.

"My family crest is nothing but weapons. A sword hanging over a shield, nailed together with beams, adorned with the image of the cross meant to protect the righteous from evil. It was said that my great grandfather was a soldier in the war. Family records were lost in a great fire that burned his home with his wife and children inside.

We never knew of his name."

Nyalla's mouth opened.

"My God..."

"Before he died in the last surge, he dreamed of my ancestor, it was said that he dipped a sword in the fire that burned his home. That night, he had a vision, similar to Moses and the burning bush...The flame of God. Those who witnessed his last stand against the soldiers took up the sword and placed it in an unmarked grave and called it the Nameless. In honor of those lost, forgotten in the fury of war."

Nyalla was speechless.

"We have an art project coming up in the next few days, at the Museum of Natural History, friends of mine are getting together for interpretations on several art pieces, a look at the various forms of religion throughout our cities' history. You are invited to come, if you like." She politely declined.

"That's very flattering, Mister Caine..."

"You can call me Xander, Miss Rice."

"Thank you, but I do have plans. I appreciate you letting me in here, it was great to finally meet you and enjoy your artwork. It was an honor."

"The honor was all mine, my dear."

"I should get going, work to do."

"Of course." She turned to leave the room.

"I'll see you again soon, yes?"

Nyalla turned back to him for a brief moment.

"Somewhere on the art circuit..." she said.

Back at the apartment, Paavo did not move. He was

preparing himself to speak with his grandmother, she would detect the sorrow in his voice, and he took in deep breaths to clear his head of previous events. He picked up the phone and waited before he dialed, he looked down towards the floor for a minute or so, Chi Lien was startled by the ringing of the phone, she picked it up after three rings.

"You are late." The brief silence was stopped by sweet laughter.

"Yes I am late, grandmother. My apologies."

"That's alright, my child, it is good to hear from you again." Chi Lien grabbed the pot on the oven and began to pour the remains into her cup, the steam rose out from the cup and flew up and into her face, it felt warm and tickled her face, Paavo moved his hand across his wound as he continued.

"Yes, it is. How have you been?"

"I'm well; the village is quiet and prospering. My flowers in the garden are surviving this drop in temperature for now."

"The snow is horrible in the city. It's hard to move down the street, let alone drive. I'm jealous of your peaceful surroundings." He said.

She began to add more sugar to the concoction inside her cup. She took small sips, adding smaller and smaller amounts, until it was just right.

"All the more reason for you to visit, then."

"Things are hectic now with my work, but whenever you want, I will be there." Chi Lien smiled as she spoke.

"Thank you. Will you visit me this evening?" "Of course."

Paavo thought about the investigation, and Miss Aki. He was not finished with the case, there was more to do, still so many questions to answer.

"We'll have some tea, and I'll make some food for us."

"Sounds good. I'll see you soon."

"Don't forget about your old grandmother."

Chi Lien hung up the phone and took a sip of her sugar sweet tea. She became excited once again, Paavo was on his way. After what felt like hours, Long arrived at the station, he wiped the snow from his coat and walked in sync with the squeaking of his boots against the tile floor. One of the officers was standing by waiting for him.

"Sir, we've been waiting for you."

"I know." Long waved his hand.

"There were some things I had to take care of, what's happening around here?"

"There's a bit of an uproar about the explosion last night, reporters have been all over us trying to find out details."

Long began to walk faster towards his desk, the officer followed. "Damned vampires, they'll get their answers," said Long.

"We've got a positive ID on the priest."

"The priest? I thought he was just some fool who dressed the part?"

"He wasn't. He was an actual ordained priest; went into exile years ago. The official reason says that he was chosen for a religious pilgrimage, but not one of his people knew where he was and why he came here."

"Especially under these circumstances. He stole another man's identity and sold drugs under the guise of trying to provide food for the homeless. Where was he from?" asked Long.

"From America."

"That explains a lot, that place is full of psychos. Give me his name," said Long.

"Officially, it's Lawrence Falcone."

Long stopped and looked at the officer. He had heard the name before, somewhere, he had come across it.

"Falcone? Are you sure about that?"

"Yes, sir. Why?"

"Then, this case got a whole lot more interesting." He headed for his office, and the young man followed.

"What is it?"

"Deep in our investigation on the Capotelli and Celino crime families, we made a chart of all connections, in terms of family, friends, and business partners," said Long.

He opened a drawer in his desk, revealing the chart.

"There isn't a Falcone crime family, neither are they involved with either family." The officer interrupted.

"You're right, we checked the systems. But, we came across something strange during the investigation."

"What's that?"

"Many of the men in each family were forced to take on another name. This was the doing of the Recluse, when he just got into power," said Long.

"Any of them named Falcone?"

"One of them. He was working for Jimmy at the time. They were close."

"So close that he still had to change his name?" asked the officer.

"He doesn't think like a normal person. To him, different names would throw off enemies trying to locate their wives and children for retaliation."

"Did they separate themselves from their own wife and kids?"

"Every single one of them," said Long. He followed the chart before opening his mouth.

"How young was the priest, given the blood you found?" he asked. The officer searched the folder.

"Late sixties, maybe? Why?"

"The man who changed his name to Falcone for the Recluse was originally a Celino. That makes the priest a relative of Vincent Celino."

"The one who got killed at the Outlook bank?" Long stood up.

He paced around the office.

"Why would Jimmy set up a bank job, hire a team to assist with the proceedings, then have them gun down the son of one of his closest confidants?" asked the officer.

"Your guess is as good as mine. It's possible that they had a falling out. Respect plays a big factor in his day to day. He's known for killing someone for even the slightest indiscretion, maybe even for a snide comment. The man is damn near insane."

"What are we going to do about this?"

"Finding a connection between the real priest and the Mob is first," said Long.

"There's a prepared statement written for you in your office, they want answers as to what the hell was going on last night."

"Really? That's great."

"I didn't mean to impose on you, sir."

"No, that's great, this will help us. What do they want to know about last night?" asked Long.

The young man stood at attention and spoke.

"They want to know who these people are. We already released a statement about the men we caught around the church were connected with the men from the hotel a few days ago. Their names were released to the public and everything. Earlier on, we were able to get our hands on a shipping manifest for the ship that came in from the docks," said the officer.

Long was handed an open folder.

"An official list of the contents on the boat?" he asked.

"Yeah, we went through each entry, tracked them down."

"What did you find?" asked Long.

"Along with the meat, there was a lot of red paint. It was shipped out to several stores and chains within the city, all checked and accounted for."

"Red paint, you say?"

"Some of it was used on the walls of the shelter. They found traces of it beneath the ash. The explosion had burned everything in sight," said the officer.

"Get those traces of paint to the rats. We need to study it. Any word about a package picked up from onboard the ship?" asked Long. The kid shook his head, not sure of what to make of it.

"There was a box that was picked up later on. It was left behind in the ship after the deal. There was a name. Jupiter, Daniel Jupiter. We'll get some guys on it to bring him in."

"I suppose now we have another dead end, don't we?" asked Long. The officer waved his hand.

"I wouldn't say that, we've got plenty of evidence to link both of these events together as one criminal conspiracy," he said.

"So, you think that they were working together?" asked Long.

"No, there's got to be smaller groups working underneath something bigger, something more organized."

"You're talking about a cartel." Long said as he moved past a woman working in reception, he stormed through desks and the greetings of fellow officers. The officer followed him directly into the office. Long grabbed his written statement and began to skim through.

"I don't like it."

"What's wrong with it?" the kid asked.

"We found out that dealers were using the church as a front for their operation, something must have gone down, they butchered everyone in there and the last one left must have fried himself, you saw it didn't you?"

"I did, sir, I was there. But there's something else we found."

"Besides all the other shit we found? What else?" asked Long.

"We found some bullet shells at the scene, some were from the weapon that belonged to the priest, and some were from another gun."

Long immediately thought of Paavo and kept a straight face.

"A gun from one of the other dealers?"

"Well, there were no other bodies close by, it might be another one of them who got away, and maybe he capped the priest before lighting the place up," said the officer.

"Where are the shells now?" asked the old man.

"At the lab, they took some ballistics, we'll have info on the gun pretty soon, fingerprints, registration, all that." Long became angry, but stayed silent, his face remained still.

"Good work on that, tell those bastards to come down for their statement. I'll leave what you wrote intact."

"Ok, thank you, sir." The officer stepped out of the room.

Long slammed his fist down on the table, he felt the bones in his hand shake, it hurt him. Paavo had fired off rounds there, and they picked them up. Pretty soon they'll have his information and he'll be brought in for questioning.

"Hopefully he got rid of that damn gun."

They would find him, they would question him and maybe the boy's got enough sense to talk through it.

"But maybe then I can bring him in to help in some cases. He needs the work, obviously, wasting away like that, needs something to occupy his time."

He could not see the cops solving a strange crime like this without his help.

"Sure he's rusty now, but in time, he will improve and he'll be better than before. Long stepped out of the officer towards the oncoming reporters, he would put out the word that one of the dealers escaped."

There would be an ongoing search for the man. He knew they would find Paavo today. They would question him, find nothing and so his movement back towards being detective would begin.

Paavo stepped out of his car once again and began the slow climb towards the small courtyard that led to the house of Chi Lien. The weather was fair; no cold, no snow, in what only felt like a few minutes ago, Paavo had to turn down the heat as he sped away from the cold heart of the city. Soon enough he was sweating and had to roll down the windows. The village seemed silent next to the bustling expressway he traveled down. The only sounds that remained were that of his engine, which reminded him to slow down immediately as the roads would soon turn from concrete to dirt. The quick change in road created a huge bump that shook the car and

Paavo.

He kept his hands on the steering wheel as the car threw up clouds of dust around him. He drove slow and quiet into the village, small houses passed by as he navigated the dirt roads, he observed the flowers all around him. They produced such a sweet smell. It almost made him smile.

Paavo inhaled the tranquility, the peaceful aroma and felt his heart relax and rest. He stopped his car a mile away from Chi Lien's house, Paavo opened his door and stepped out from the car. There was a trail of fog beginning to set in that surrounded the village. It further separated him from the city, now barely visible from this distance. As though it was trying to make me forget, he thought to himself. He moved towards the piece of grassland off from the main road. The piece of land did not go on forever, after a few paces he began to see the waters beneath the highlands the villagers occupied. Paavo soon found himself at the edge of a cliff. He looked down at crystal clear waters that washed up onto jagged rocks below. From his jacket pocket he produced his weapon, he was prepared to throw it off the edge, but something stopped him. He felt attached to the gun; it was given to him by Long years ago when he had begun working for the Police department. Paavo stopped with his arm outstretched, ready to drop the old heirloom into the water.

He stopped and looked at the gun and turned around slowly to make sure no one was watching him. No one anywhere, he thought, too quiet out here. He waited for a few minutes, it never left his hand. Paavo hesitated dropping the gun, it was the only one he had and didn't really have the money for a replacement. The gun fell out of his hand. He slipped it back inside the jacket pocket. He watched blades of grass fall silently down to the waters below. He owed it to Long to get rid of any evidence linking him to the battle last night.

No signs of Naoko, only blood from the same person found

at the crime scene. They went to school together. Maybe they were targeted by the same men, picked up at the same time, playing around innocently, naively, on the streets they've always known. Paavo turned back towards the car, put it in gear and slowly inched up the hill to the house of his grandmother, He extended his finger and the silence of the hill was filled with a press of the doorbell, only a few minutes passed before Chi Lien opened the door with a smile across her face.

Long finished his statement to the press, the flashing of the cameras died down as he moved away from the crowd of raised hands and questions. The reporters received the new information the public was clamoring for. They had a person to attach to the crimes committed. A pool of blood spilled out onto an empty street that had no leads, only the name of a little girl, her and another remain undiscovered, another innocent victimized and revealed to the public, hungry for knowledge and sensational news; Naoko Aki. Long spoke of the little girl he promised to help Paavo find, there were officers out looking for her for two days now. No traces of the girl, he thought, maybe this will raise awareness.

He thought of calling Paavo, the officer from before ran down the hallway with a name he dreaded hearing spoken, not right now, he thought. The young man had a smile on his face, he felt accomplished as he spoke.

"We got him; address, and phone number." Long's head rose up from his thoughts.

"Good work, let me know when you find him."

"Yes, sir."

He wanted to call Paavo, to warn him. Long knew where he was. He remembered how Paavo cherished his grandmother. He told him years ago to never interrupt their time with each other. As if her knowledge of the crime in the city would taint the old woman somehow. Long didn't blame him, she shouldn't have to know. His eyes followed the officer into the meeting room. He hoped that the kid would take care of business quickly, that they would find him by the end of the day, and any hopes for bringing back into the graces of the department would be long gone.

CHAPTER SEVENTEEN

Paavo held the door open for Chi Lien as she stepped out through the back door and into the garden behind the house. The old wood was painted white. Dark brown cracks stretched along its foundation. She kept her hand on the rail, still sturdy and solid despite the moist air. They walked through the gardens. Paavo admired the flowers with a near smile on his face. She had maintained them all throughout the wintertime, at least, what could be considered winter. There was never any snow here, only soft rain and the deep fog that covered the entire mass of land. It was almost hidden from the world, unlike the harsh atmosphere of Perdition. In the village, people moved slowly and cautious, relaxed and peaceful, completely content. Paavo was envious, but couldn't find himself living there. There was so much left for him to do, to experience before the inevitable death he was dreaded.

"So, what do you think?"

Chi Lien looked up at him with closed eyes and a broad smile.

"It's amazing, like walking inside a dream," said Paavo.

She bowed slightly to accept the compliment.

"I knew you would like it." The fog was beginning to settle in now. It crept over the far off hills. Paavo watched it rise and fall over the village. Chi Lien put her hands out as a cool wind filled the air.

"Once you're done with your work in the city, you can become a boring, settled down middle aged man. You can bring your wife and kids out here and enjoy life."

"I don't know about that, grandmother."

"What do you mean? You can't raise children in the city. You'll worry yourself sick. Such hard business to try and watch over your creations, surrounded by that craziness."

Paavo was silent, he thought of being married for a second, and then threw the notion away as fast as it came. His thoughts moved quickly through his mind, as did more cynical words.

"I imagine what my children would be like. Hopefully not like them." Chi Lien frowned. It pained her to hear him speak this way.

"Your parents did the best they could with so many things going against them. You were all lucky to have each other," she said.

"I can barely remember them, you would know more than I."

"Don't lie to yourself, you do remember, you just choose to forget." Paavo scowled at her, he knew she could feel the tension.

"Maybe," he said. She tried to reassure him.

"But that's okay. Sometimes you need to forget things to move on. Those things that have no place in your mind always dig a space in your heart, and it will be close to you, when you don't want them to, when you don't even realize, they are a part of you, it's up to you to own them."

Paavo placed his hand on his wound. He closed his eyes and pressed his hand inward. He felt the pain. It was another reminder. Chi Lien reached out towards him, Paavo turned towards her and saw her approaching. He moved to her and they embraced carefully as the fog encircled them. Chi Lien's eyes could not survey the moment, but his eyes were wide open, watching the space around them become a dream, away from reality for a brief second.

"I received a phone call, grandmother. The family is threatening to take you from me," said Paavo.

"So, that's what's bothering you."

"I don't want to lose you, as well."

"You will be fine without me, if there is nothing that can be done about them," she said.

"Don't say that. Do not let them take you away from me."

"If they are coming, then let them. I'm too tired to run from anyone. I will always belong here, because of you. When I am gone, you will return me to this place."

"We can't let them. It's only about the money for them," said Paavo.

"People will do what they do, their nature cannot be changed. You have to remain strong, stronger than them, to do what you must."

"I have so much anger. It's difficult to let it go."

"You must release it; drags you down eventually. What good would you be then?" she asked.

The flowers faded in and out through the oncoming grey, dashes of pinks and greens and purples. She was right, he thought, but he stayed silent. They were quiet for a few minutes after. They soon walked back into the kitchen and drank another pot of black tea. Paavo did not stay long. He said his goodbyes and promised to return in a few weeks, she thanked him for coming.

"You don't have to thank me, I owe it to you," he said.

Paavo walked alone back to his car and began the drive back into the city. He wanted to make it to the apartment, to tidy up, continue looking for the girl.

Long watched the news for the first time in weeks, the television was covered in dust, it sat on his desk, a brown wire trailed behind the old device, it ran off the side and to the floor, where it plugged into the wall. He finally picked up his cell phone, he pressed out Paavo's number. It rang a few times before he picked up.

"Yes?"

"They're coming. You should be getting home soon," said Long.

"Why would I do that? Maybe I should go on the lam, let them work for it."

"Don't be stupid, they'll find you, they have you're name and address."

"How do you know that? What if they found a phony address? A phony name?" asked Paavo. Long stopped for a moment.

"A phony name?"

"Wendell took care of me, and I always paid my bills in cash."

"But they got fingerprints on the bullets."

"Not mine," said Paavo. Long furrowed his brow.

"What the hell are you talking about?"

"That gun hasn't been used in three years, the last time it was loaded by me, I had gloves on." Long's face quickly turned from puzzled to pleased, and relieved.

"Really? Who taught you that trick?" The old man asked.

"I believe you did, sir."

"And what about the phony name and address?" Long couldn't help but laugh.

"An empty room in the building, down the hall from my office."

"Well done. But why the hell did you have me going like that this morning?" asked Long.

"I wasn't in the mood to argue with you." Long seemed impressed by this display, he had waited for the moment the kid would wake up with a steady mind once again, maybe now was that moment.

"I'm broke and I'm not giving this gun up. See you soon." Paavo hung up the phone.

"Yeah, see you..." Long said as he lowered his hands and walked towards the window, seeing the squad cars leave the building. He smiled wide as he watched them speed onward towards a dead end. Soon after they disappeared into the grey distance, he was contacted by the receptionist downstairs. He was needed immediately at the front desk. An old woman had just walked into the station, demanding to speak to someone in charge. Long decided to come down to meet her, he walked down towards the main floor to see a small woman shouting and pleading with the front desk, they placed their hands forward, trying to get her to calm down. Long approached and introduced himself, the old woman seemed scared and paranoid, her name was Lina Aki, Long's eyes widened, his heart dropped, according to the woman, her daughter had been missing for two weeks now.

Long walked the old woman to his office, he wanted to know about the situation, this was Paavo's client, it had to be, he thought. The name's match up, missing daughter, it all makes sense. She began to speak.

"I need to find the detective, I don't have a phone, and I don't know how to contact him. He said that he would find her, he promised me."

"I understand, of course, we've been looking for her as well."

"Now the people in my neighborhood, they ask me questions...Where is Naoko? When is she coming back? Why are there men on the news saying they found her blood at that place? What happened to the church?"

"Ma'am, the downtown area is full of a lot of bad people, some dealers took over the church and they were using the closed down shelter to sell drugs to people."

Miss Aki shook her head in disbelief.

"Why the shelter? They took care of people once, why would anyone let this happen?"

"We didn't know, the detective was helpful in finding this information out for us, had he not been here, we may have never found out"

"Shows how sloppy the Police are around here," she said.

"I have no excuses for the mistakes of my men. I'm sorry for that."

"Where is the detective? How can I find him?" she asked.

Long looked down at his cell phone, this was unexpected, he hoped that Paavo was out there now continuing the search.

"Let me contact him now, we'll find him so you can speak to him."

"Thank you." Miss Aki's face moved from angry to worried.

"Too long my daughter's been gone, she's not coming back..."

The office was empty when the Police arrived, the information from the analysis was written on a piece of crumpled paper. "Seiki Mitsuru". The fake name given for Paavo during his stay in Wendell's building. The place was near abandoned, with Paavo's office and equipment gone now, it was desolate. There was a knock that went unanswered, and then a kick that sent the door off its hinges and into the darkness of the room. Officers crept in slowly, with guns drawn.

"Mr. Mitsuru! This is the Police! You have to come with us." Silence followed the officer's words.

They looked around a few other rooms, no one in sight, nothing at all in these rooms. It took almost two hours. They gave up soon after. The men went back towards the stairwell through the hallway. Paavo watched the cops pull away from Wendell's old tenement building. He had dodged a bullet. Suddenly, the phone began to vibrate in his jacket pocket, he picked up to hear Long grumble. He cut him off.

"The cops are leaving, it worked, no worries about my footprints at your crime scene," he said.

"You have to come down here, Paavo."

"What do you need?"

"Your client is here, Miss Aki, is here, asking about you."

"What are you talking about?"

"She came down here, trying to find you."

"Where is she now?"

"She's still with me, I told her I would contact you and bring you in."

"Yeah, I'll be there."

Long raised his eyebrow.

"When?" he asked.

"Right now. I'm coming right now." Paavo assured him.

"Meet us across the street from the station, in the parking lot. Make sure no one sees you."

Paavo hung up the phone and started his car, the snow was beginning to harden on the roads, and the car struggled to move out and onto the street. After some more driving in horrible weather, he had arrived in the parking lot across the street from the station. Long met him first, he greeted him quietly before seeing her. She waited behind another car a feet away. A heavy weight fell upon his heart. Her face looked broken as she wept. Long stayed behind him as they approached.

Miss Aki moved towards him, slowly at first. She beat her

hands together, her sobs growing louder still. Paavo was silent; he felt such guilt and cursed himself, his inability to find the little girl he promised to do everything in his power to find. There were so many questions left to ask, there were no real answers about her disappearance. Her blood was found in the wreckage of the shelter, that doesn't mean that she was killed, doesn't mean it was her body amongst those found in the chamber. He thought of the fake priest, his heart became filled with a dark hatred, his sadness poured out from his pores.

"You said you would find her!" Miss Aki started to become hysterical.

Paavo was quiet, what could he do? He never gave up his search, Long had done his part in looking for the girl, they had done all they could do, right? What did he miss?

"She's gone! She will never come back to me!" Where did he go wrong? Miss Aki began to hyperventilate.

"She was just a child. How could they do this to her?! To me?! Why? Why couldn't you help me? Why couldn't you find her?"

Long placed his arms around the old woman, she tried to push him off, she struggled with him, but soon stopped to rest herself. His thoughts moved wildly, though still in sync with the sad movements of Miss Aki. Long's head moved down towards the ground, the snowfall continued to pour on the city street.

"You didn't find her! They found her blood! At the church where she used to go with her friends every Sunday! Now they say that drug dealers took over the building? Is that true?

"It's true..." Paavo spoke quietly.

"Why didn't you tell me these things? I have to know what happened! Now the only people who might know are dead!"

"Where is she? Where is my daughter? You promised me!"

She beat her hands on Paavo's chest, her fists made a small but sad sound. Her face held frustration and fear.

"You know I lost my home today, I lost my home! I tell them I have no money and they don't listen. They don't care!"

Her eyes stayed locked on Paavo, he couldn't even look into her eyes anymore. He only stared down at the ground, he watched the snow still endlessly falling.

"They don't care about nobody but themselves, just like you. You didn't care about my daughter, or you would have found her by now. I blame you for this."

The blows were slight, it didn't hurt him, but the sorrow was overwhelming. Long came around from Paavo's side and walked her back inside the station. Paavo stayed still for what felt like hours, he felt his heart become smaller and smaller, his chest tightened until he felt like falling to the ground. He stumbled to stay on his feet, the snow was cold on his feet, the moisture began to sink through the sneakers once again, his body shivered as he waited for Long to reappear. He thought of his grandmother, sleeping soundly in her bed, in the warm apartment, Miss Aki would have to find somewhere else to sleep, in the cold again tonight, all alone, he felt responsible for that.

The snowfall continued on as Paavo walked towards the car, he inhaled cold air and began to cough, he felt the familiar sharp pain once again. He didn't fight it. He shortened his breath and held it as the coughing came up through his mouth. A burning sensation ripped across his chest as he moved towards the open door. He stopped to slam his fist on the top of the car, he cleared his throat loudly. He felt the warmth enter his mouth and released a mix of phlegm and bright red blood into the greying snow. He waited for Long to look back and signal to him that things would be okay. He didn't get a signal. They both disappeared into the Police station. He waited in the car as a press of the button caused cold air to fill the vehicle. Paavo decided to wait for a phone call. He waited for over an hour, there was no contact, no phone call. The silence only deepened his depression, his thoughts took a desperate turn, would Long abandon him now that he failed to find the girl?

"Miss Aki would report me to the Police for letting her slip through, he has to ignore me for now, right? Who's to say the girl is really gone anyway? I can't just give up like this, not now. There has to be more to it than just those dealers, why was she playing around that area? Why didn't anyone want to talk about her? They just wrote her off as some kind of lost cause...What the hell is going on in this town where no one cares about a lost child? I have to know what happened."

Paavo decided to take a look around Miss Aki's apartment, he waited until after dark. Once again, he had found himself watching the sky for hours. The snow seemed to subside after the sun had died down, these days it was difficult to see the sun, the white skies above were indication enough. As the day moved forward, the white began to wither into a pale grey and then form a dark brown shade before turning to true darkness. The time had come for another shot to be taken, Paavo produced a syringe from his pocket, he remembered loading one before leaving for the day, in case something had come up and he would be away from the kit. He pulled the plastic coating off the top of the needle and tossed it away. The shirt would have to be open to accept the shot. He unbuttoned it slowly and wiped away the small rivulets of blood that dried on his chest. He inserted the needle into his chest, after only four times, Paavo had become used to the feeling. A strange warmth coursed through his veins, down into his fingers. He could feel the liquid travel through his entire body, it was almost intoxicating now. Paavo shut his eyes to let it filter through his system. He made a note of the time. He had only a set amount of time before his body would slow down and soon fall into a deep sleep.

The building was quiet and dilapidated; the landlord had just finished locking up and took off down the street. Paavo watched from his car as he passed. He discarded the needle and stepped out into the night, the wind remained strong as the snowfall began to die down. The streetlights above Paavo's head revealed each individual flake of snow as they fell behind the white and golden backdrops of light; he watched them as he walked across the street. Paavo was always fascinated by the falling snow, the way they descended past surrounding lights, and how they created their own small shadows. It seemed like a reflection of all lost souls falling from the heavens above. The warmth of the serum filled his body, for a few moments he could inhale normally. His mouth curved to the side to take in a small amount of the cold air, his throat began to itch as he fought off another cough. He held it in and moved his tongue inside his mouth to throw off the sensation. The door to the apartment was taped off. The locks were changed. Paavo flicked the handle and it would not move.

He looked around for another way in, a shock of wind caused him to flinch and hold his arms together. The black suit jacket failed to deflect the rough air. There were no other doors to get in the downstairs area but he remembered the window in the kitchen of the apartment had been busted out by some kids. All that lay between the outside and the apartment was a sheet of plastic. Paavo moved back down to the street and around the side of the building. He hoped that the sheet of cover remained, if only to allow him to break inside.

The side alleyway was dark and there was a foul smell coming from the cans of garbage. Paavo scratched at his nose to try and avoid the stench. The window was still there, the sheet of plastic nearly torn off the corners, the blasts of wind pushed it to the point of falling off. Paavo looked around slowly and lowered himself into the apartment and kept his hands in his pockets to avoid touching anything. There was trash everywhere and it looked as though the landlord was tearing the place apart. What could he have been looking for, he wondered to himself. Paavo moved through the rooms of the apartment, he began to think of Miss Aki; her fists beating on his chest, trying to inflict some kind of damage, make some kind of impact of something around her. We're both helpless, he said to himself, as helpless to find the girl as she was to blame me. He wanted to know why she was taken, and how, there was only this theory, the pool of blood, tainted with some kind of unknown drug, this connection with the shelter that closed down, taken over by some petty dealers and some crazed man who dressed and gave sermons as if he was an actual priest. There was no way he could make sense of it now, he had to focus, think straight, and get all the facts from Long and his people. Maybe they missed something. It wouldn't be the first time. There was still more to do.

Paavo opened the door in the back of the apartment with his foot as he stepped inside Naoko Aki's room one more time. He surveyed the room, quiet and still, almost as if it waited for her arrival. His eyes moved from the clothes on the bed to the drawings on the walls; doodles of animals with inverted colors and all sorts of characters with suns, stars and moons across a dark blue galaxy. He marveled at the girl's creativity. A sweet moment of admiration was interrupted by a noise. The creaking of wood hit Paavo's ears as he quickly looked up towards the door. He saw the closet opened farther than before, followed by the end of a small shadow fleeing the room. He followed silently, there was no other noise. Paavo stepped out from Naoko's room back into the kitchen and stayed in the dark of the corner. There was no one there. The figure had jumped out from the opening and out to the street. He waited to see if it was a trick and someone was waiting for him to reveal himself.

The apartment was empty; the feeling of still life was there, stronger than ever.

"Someone had to be here just now," he thought

"Am I being paranoid? Was someone watching me?"

His thoughts raced as he felt his heartbeat rise. Paavo resigned to leave now and head back to his own quarters. He stepped out of the opening and back into the alleyway. He put his hands back into his pockets and began to walk back towards the car. The alley was all but quiet except the brief gusts of wind, the snowfall had nearly stopped. Paavo moved quickly to his own rhythm, his own footsteps scraped across the pavement. He waited for another noise to signal the presence of another.

He walked a few more feet, almost to the end of the alley when he heard a slight scrape and stopped and turned around quickly to view the small child that had followed him. Paavo looked upon the face of Naoko Aki, dressed all in white, patches of dirt on her pale face. She looked both frightened and angry. Her black eyes were wide and pulsing as she stared through him. Paavo was still. He offered his hand to the girl, saying nothing. The girl stepped back a few steps. Paavo stayed where he was. He was not going to move towards her. She will run, he thought. Naoko Aki placed her hands behind her back as Paavo withdrew his outstretched hand. A slight snowfall surrounded them in the alleyway.

Another gust of wind blew past them. The girl felt for something behind her as Paavo was unsure of what to do. Naoko lowered her eyes as she pulled a large gun from her side. She looked up at Paavo and pointed it towards him. Paavo eyed the gun pointed at his chest. He took a step back, and made eye contact with the little girl.

He wasn't sure of how to feel. He didn't think of how she got hold of a gun, or how she was able to keep the weapon raised. She couldn't have been much older than Simona. He put his hands up, showing he was unarmed. The girl's face did not change; her eyes followed his as he moved slowly away. Naoko held the gun with an intensity that unsettled him. She knew what she was doing. Her intent became more and more clear. Paavo only took two steps back before she fired the first shot. The bullet entered his stomach. He didn't feel it at first. All became quiet, even the wind brushed silent yet cool air across his face and he felt the blood run from his wound, down his clothes and out onto the ground. He only saw the second shot. The next bullet dug a hole into the middle of his chest and Paavo felt his body collapse onto the ground. He was powerless. The smack of his head hitting the concrete unprotected sent a wave of vibration through his fingers. The warmth of the treatment began to exit his body.

Naoko Aki lowered the gun and turned around, she ran off into the darkness, Paavo curled his body into a ball as he watched the child disappear into the night, the snow continued to fall. He heard sirens off in the distance, Paavo felt himself leave his body. He felt nothing but the cold; no blood, no pain, not even fear. Only the cold that covered him, it wrapped around and held him still. The dark was so inviting to him, he could not help but fall into a deep sleep, into a deep and beautiful death. It felt like the village.

CHAPTER EIGHTEEN

"Wake up, we have so many things to do..."

The child awakens to their mother and father, scrambling through the papers and books thrown around the trashed apartment. He is afraid. Both parents ran through pages and pages of books, arguing, taking turns checking the windows. The child is motionless, it was time to leave again, he thought, the evil men were looking for us once more.

"Found it!"

The father shouts as he opens the book and finds an empty space where the last third of the pages should have been. He puts his hand in and pulls out a small bag, he throws it on the table. He and mother begin to rifle through. The child looks around the apartment. What was supposed to be his home; windows blacked out or covered in newspapers, the green shag rug in the middle of the room, wallpaper torn off on certain walls.

It's horrible, but the child is happy to be with his parents again, he remembers the days at the great big house. The old women stalking the halls, watching his every move. He hates that place, there were never any curtains, the sun was always shining inside every room, it always blinded him. Hurt his eyes. It's so rigid there. He could never touch anything but they gave him food, very few toys, and a piano to learn how to play. He never remembered the songs they taught him, throwing them away to create space for his own song. It didn't last long, only a few chords and a descending riff down the keys. He presented it to them once. They didn't like it, he hadn't written any music since then.

The child remembered the night when his mother came to him in a dream, told him things would soon be ok. He woke up to the backseat of a car. Father was driving, Mother sat in the front seat, she seemed to be coughing loudly, she only looked back a few times, smiling and patting him on the head. There was smoke in the car, it made him dizzy and he fell in and out of sleep until they had reached their new house.

Things were happy there. He went to school, played with the other children next door. School was almost like the big house he remembered. The teachers were very angry. But he found a way to get around them through his studies. He read constantly, books they told him were too hard for him to understand. Too adult, too mature, they said. He didn't care. His favorite was Jack Kerouac. "Desolation Angels". The title grabbed him, he looked up the words in the dictionary. He loved the word desolation, what it meant, just the way it sounded, it was cool. He could picture such creatures so vividly.

He imagined them as beautiful women, wide-eyed and glowing light from behind their shoulders. They would have black wings, he thought, tattered dresses and black feathered wings. The idea of wandering from place to place, creating art on such careless whims with good friends, it was something he wanted for himself. Not now, though, the child was told he was too young to venture out on his own. When his father took him to the park, he dreamed of the city. He dreamed of walking its streets, he wrote short poems of few words that he liked. He didn't care that his poems didn't rhyme. Even though the teacher had said that they're supposed to. He showed them to his friends, they said they didn't get it. He didn't show them anymore of his writings. They stayed buried underneath the books, and in his dreams along with his literary companions.

Before the end of the school year, he remembered a man in a suit coming to the house, he could hear yelling from his parents and the man in the suit. The parents dressed him up in fancy clothes and went with him to the great big house. The old women were there in the living room. Large columns of white and dark red carpet that made the floor look like it was made of blood. There were other people there, all wearing suits. His entire family sat in chairs all around them. They spoke for hours, talking quietly, then yelling, screaming and pointing fingers.

His father was the only white man in the family. The others, like the old women, like his mother, had yellow skin, black eyes, black hair. The child was told his family was Japanese, though he never knew where his father came from, he assumed it was America.

The child's mother and father stormed out of the house. Mother was standing in the doorway, her hand out towards the child. He wanted to run, but the man in the suit held him back, his hands on his shoulders. His father grabbed the mother and they drove away. He was back at the great big house again. It was painful for him there; the old women talked horribly of his parents. They spoke of purity, of spoiling the family, and creating this child with poisoned blood.

He didn't feel like he was poison, maybe they were just angry. Mother told him that everyone says things they don't mean. People hurt each other with words all the time, she said, that's why love exists, to cancel the words. Only what you feel is important. The child wanted back with his parents, after only a few weeks, they had come for him again, they looked different, he thought. They looked scared, their faces changed, they were ugly.

It was the middle of night, they told him they were going to the city. He was excited to go. Driving into the city was amazing. The lights and buildings were so beautiful, inspiring. They found a small apartment away from the lights, but they told him he could down there whenever he wanted to. They went every day onto the main streets of the city.

Mother and Father talked with everyone down there, laughing, eating, drinking. Most of the time he sat nearby, admiring the scene, the lights, the freedom. He loved it. He often dreamed of walking down those same streets with his desolation angels. He stayed in his room during the day, reading books and writing pages and pages of words. Fragments of stories and songs and ideas. At night he went with his parents to the main street. The child did not care about moving from place to place. He was happy to be there, underneath the river of lights, doing the things he wanted to do. But he always worried about his parents, they looked so tired, so afraid of whatever was coming after them, that's why they had to go someplace new.

The room was unrecognizable and covered in white, Paavo strained to open his eyes to a bright and blinding light. The hospital bed was stiff. He felt tightened muscles inside his back. He searched around for a few minutes, trying to gain his bearings. There was no one else there; the other beds empty, the television turned off. The windows were shut by heavy black curtains. A mobile table that held a tray of food, still unopened, covered in a thin plastic seal.

A large machine lay next to the bed, pumping air and liquid through several tubes that followed up from the floor and into his arm and mouth. Paavo pulled at the one inserted into his mouth. There was movement deep in his throat; it was more than a foot long after he removed it. Paavo choked and struggled to take in breath even after removing the tube, the traces of drool and phlegm were gone with a quick wipe of the heavy grey blanket. He placed his hand on his chest and felt an intense pain shoot through his body. A long tube of plastic ran over the side of the bed and was clamped directly into his wound.

There were deep red stains of dried blood on his chest. Paavo cringed as he tried to remove it. The pain was paralyzing. He tried to twist and turn to distract his senses. He rolled from side to side, trying to tighten the muscles in his arms and legs. It took a few moments for the pain to pass. It was excruciating. Paavo stared blankly into the ceiling above.

All was quiet for a long time as his eyes searched the area. Numbness from his left arm crept in slow. Paavo moved the blanket to reveal more tubes sticking from his veins; they ran down the length of the bed and onto the floor where they connected to the machine at his side. A small clicking noise made Paavo study the device. A familiar gold liquid filled one of the plastic cases sitting at the top of the machine. The case emptied it's content into the tubes, the liquid traveled quickly into his arm and he felt the warmth enter his body. It was the same as the shots he'd taken before; the same rush of energy and heat. He fell in and out of sleep. Paavo awoke to the noise of footsteps.

"Hello there, Paavo. It's good to see you again."

"Likewise, Doctor." Wiles held a clipboard covered in scribbled notes and words. He smiled slightly as he looked over his patient.

"You gave us quite a scare, you almost didn't make it here. Consider yourself lucky," said Wiles.

"Hard to feel any kind of luck when you've been shot."

"Perhaps, just so you know, there's an Inspector Long from the Police department here to see you when you're ready."

"How long have I been here?" asked Paavo.

"Three days. This is the first time I've seen your eyes open."

"I've been here three days?"

"The Police were unsure of who had attacked you, but we did recover the bullets from your body. They will find out, I imagine," said Wiles.

"Yeah..."

"The Inspector has been very anxious, he's asked a lot of questions and really wants to talk to you. I let him know you were in no condition to talk."

"I am now."

"I know, I know. Shortly..."

Wiles approached the bed. Paavo followed him with his eyes.

"How has the serum been treating you?"

"Detrimental to my work, but I've been able to handle the weather a little better," said Paavo.

"Progress of some kind?"

"Not exactly, it's been great working with you, Doctor, but I'm done with this serum."

"What do you mean?" asked Wiles.

"I mean that I can't continue my work this way, I sleep for nearly a day at a time, I lose daylight too quickly. My last job, I made so many mistakes."

"How so?"

"I missed certain important details. I took too much time going in and out of sleep, disorganized. I was sloppy, out of control. This treatment is taking too much out of me. I can't keep going this way," said Paavo.

"I do apologize about the effects of the medicine."

"Then you'll take me off it."

"Paavo, you can't be done with the serum, not just suddenly. It's doing something to your body; it's starting to change you."

"Why can't you take me off the treatment?" asked Paavo.

"The effects of the treatment have begun to change your blood flow, your body is starting to adapt to it. Weaning you off the medicine would only cause your condition to worsen. It may even deteriorate your body past its original state," said Wiles.

Paavo clenched his fists listening to the doctor's words. He was trapped into habit now, at the mercy of this drug.

"So, you're saying I can't stop taking it now. That it might kill me to quit the serum," said Paavo.

"There's enough in your system now, to see a change has begun inside your blood, a change that we have to study and document. It is essential to your continued survival."

"I don't have that much time left, how much of me do you really want? Should I donate my body to the hospital for study?" asked Paavo.

"That wouldn't be a bad idea, you know."

On the other side of the wall, Long stood against the plain, white walls. One hand was shoved deep into the pocket of his leather coat. His vision lost in the threads of black wool in his sweater. Ever since Paavo came back into his life, he had been wearing black more and more. He held his phone close to his ear, Masonori on the other side, tearing through the receiver.

"What the hell is going on? Is there something wrong with you? Not only did a building explode, taking out the main suspect, as well as damn near all the evidence we needed for the case, but you also failed to tell me that next to the priest's body, they found a machine gun. One that was missing an ID number and one that was unaccounted for during the heist of Kirilov weapons."

Long searched his mind, he did not see that in the report. Was it hidden from him? Was his mind playing tricks, concerned solely for the safety of Paavo?

"You also killed another man, right in the middle of a goddamn interrogation room."

"Things were under control before he snapped," said Long.

"I gave you one more chance to keep things like this under wraps, but no. It always has to be chaos with you. I'm assuming control of the station's operation from here. You report to me directly. All the evidence you have will be given to me. Whatever you have going on for the missing case will be handed over to me in 24 hours."

The old cop took a breath, trying to calm his nerves.

"Do you hear me, Derek? This shit is over, you report to me tomorrow morning. The sessions with Doc Sakura begin this week. No ducking this shit anymore, you need help. I am giving you the help, whether you want it or not. The load is on my back now, so relax and take some time off before you end killing someone else. Do you understand me?" asked Masonori.

"Yes."

Long looked to the outside window, the snow was endless.

Inside the room, Paavo and Wiles continued their argument.

"Are you serious? I came to you for a diagnosis, and you're taking over my life."

"I want to help you," said Wiles.

"I didn't ask you for a cure, just an answer."

"Just an answer? What about a longer life? Do you want to die?"

"Everybody dies." Paavo deadpanned.

"If you don't care, how can you expect anyone else to?"

"You can leave now, Doctor." Wiles placed his hand on Paavo's arm.

"We'll talk later," he said. Before leaving, he turned back around.

"So I don't forget, there is a letter for you. It's under the plate on the table to your left."

After Wiles left the room, the door shut behind him. Paavo rose up fast from his position and reached for the note, hidden underneath. It was a few words, written in red ink. It was from the woman, her voice broke through the dead air of the move, as if she was speaking to him directly. He read them slowly.

"Good fireworks. I'll keep him alive long enough for you to reach the end of the road."

A large print of two lips dotted the end of the sentence. Paavo jerked forward and kicked the mobile table in front of his bed. The plastic tray and utensils fell to the floor with a loud clang. The table itself crashed onto the hard tile floor. The anger he felt had surpassed the pain momentarily, Paavo inhaled once or twice before it began to set in. He felt the intense sting once again and held the tube inside his chest still as he lowered himself back into the middle of the bed, deciding to stare deep into the corner of the room. He did not notice Long as he stepped into the room quietly.

"How are you, young man?" Paavo turned towards him.

"I don't know," he said.

Long looked wary of all the machinery in and around him.

"What the hell are they doing to you?"

"He's turned me into his pet project. How did I get here?"

"Is this supposed to help you with your condition?" asked Long.

"Supposedly, we'll see how long it keeps me alive," said Paavo.

Long's face became worried.

"Is that how long you have?"

"It doesn't matter."

"Yes, it does. How long are you supposed to have?" Paavo stared towards the corner of the room.

"Nine months," he said.

"Jesus." Silence lingered between them.

"How did I get here?"

"People nearby heard gunshots and they called the Police. Our boys found you in a pool of blood outside Miss Aki's apartment. You were talking nonsense; something about flowers and fog," said Long.

"I was delirious, I thought I was going to die."

"Sorry to disappoint you. But I must ask, why the hell were you at that old woman's apartment sneaking around?" asked Long.

"I felt guilty. Wouldn't you?"

"Yes, I would."

"She had no money, they took her apartment. All she had left was her daughter, who I couldn't find. I have to keep trying," said Paavo.

"You can't, she's dead," said Long. Paavo looked up suddenly.

"What do you mean? You found her?"

"No. You did. Remember? The blood samples you took? You found her blood all over that place. We found the clothes, fingerprints, and she was one of the victims. The dealers that you helped to catch, they're going to be convicted. You did well."

"The girl is not dead, she can't be," said Paavo. Long moved towards the bed, his eyes traveled over the tubes sticking from his chest and arm.

"Listen, you couldn't find her, you tried, you came to me for help and we couldn't find her, she had been dead for a while. Don't blame yourself."

"I'm sure of it."

"What makes you think so?" asked Long. Paavo hesitated to speak, he remembered what he saw that night, Naoko Aki, with a gun drawn, her black eyes staring through him.

"What if I told you she was the one who shot me?" asked Paavo. Long stopped, his face turned from comforting to confusion.

"What are you talking about?"

"The daughter, she was there."

"That's impossible," said Long.

"She was the one who did it; she was in the apartment, watching me."

"No. That doesn't make any sense."

"She followed me outside, she actually pulled a gun, she

looked into my eyes, I can't describe to you what I saw, what I felt."

"Paavo, it couldn't have been her, we found body parts in the shelter. All that blood?"

"It was, I'm not insane."

"I believe you saw a little girl. But it wasn't her, she's dead."

"What do I do now, then?" asked Paavo.

"You get better. Damn near killed, again. That's twice now in two days. You're starting to develop dangerous habits."

"Perhaps."

Long continued to speak, he could not hear his words, his eyes only saw the alley from nights before. He walked over snow, crunching the fragments to concrete with his damp sneakers, trying to shake the feeling of being followed. Paavo tried to re-imagine the scene, the little girl with a gun in her hand. Naoko Aki's face stared deep as she approached with the pistol. The color of her eyes changed before him as her hair grew out and turned a shade of brown. Paavo looked around the alley, the snow and wind blurred his vision more and more. Naoko Aki's face has changed into one of some other child, lost and wandering the streets.

He was trying to convince himself, for Long's sake, for his own. The trigger was pulled, and the scene went silent. A flash of light forced him to blink his eyes. Paavo opened them again to see the face of his attacker. Naoko Aki, it was no use in trying to replay those moments. The girl was alive and her image was cemented into his mind. He fell to the ground, bleeding out into the concrete. She looked into his eyes, trying to watch the life leave his body.

"I'm taking the dossiers back from you, the case has been reassigned," said Long.

"What?"

"I shouldn't have asked you to help me. There's heavy fire

coming down on us for the explosion. I won't have you exposed to the public. You are risking your life, too much reckless abandon."

"Giving up comes easy to you, now?"

"Paavo, can I ask you a question?" The alley disappeared into the black curtains, replacing the surroundings with the pale hospital room.

"What is it?"

"Why did you leave for so long?"

"My own choice, I had to disappear," said Paavo.

"What made you want to vanish like that?"

"To be alone, I had to face my own death."

"Without telling anyone? Without telling me?" asked Long.

"No one else was going to help me. I had to keep moving forward. No one else cared."

"You poor kid." Long shook his head in disbelief, he looked down towards the ground, trying to picture this strong willed figure in his life so unable to let go.

"You still lay out those pictures all over your desk? Those files you used to make. People at the station thought you were crazy."

"A lot of people think that I'm crazy," said Paavo.

"You give them good reason."

"They told you to give up on me. More important things to take care of rather than a sick kid. Those missing people, they were the same as the girl, that's why I went back to the apartment."

"I never gave up on anyone, there was such a lack of evidence, no leads, no witnesses, no connections to anything going on in the city. Those people just vanished off the face of the earth. How can you solve something like that?" asked Long.

"How many of them were there? The number of people who disappeared, no one thought that odd or peculiar in the least?"

"I don't remember, that's not the point."

"How many of said people were reported missing, or vanished?" asked Paavo.

"I have to keep it quiet. There will not be panic in this city."

"How many of them were there?"

"For the last time Paavo, I don't remember, I swear. I tend to not obsess about these things."

"Over fifty."

The number hovered in the air, over them both. The old man finally broke, unable to avoid it any longer.

"I know. We were on the case together."

"Fifty people reported missing in Perdition in fifty days. Those were the words you told me before I stepped into the church," said Paavo.

"There were so many things happening at once, we couldn't keep track of them."

"No one said a word."

"People go missing, Paavo. Even if it was some kind of mass conspiracy, there was no indication, there was nothing to go on."

"You just weren't looking hard enough."

"My hands were tied! They still are if you haven't been paying attention. How much luck did you have in two years time?"

"I'm going to die, what do you expect me to do about it?"

"So that's why you came out hiding? You want to try and change the world?" asked Long.

"You called me and I showed up, remember?"

"That was one out of about a thousand calls, the one message I had left for you at the office. I didn't even know if that number still worked. The machine picked up, so I figured you would see it, sooner or later. I didn't know if you were alive or dead, but anytime something big came up, a case or a job opening, I made a call. The machine would pick up, and I would worry. That's why I look the way I do."

"All those people gone, the old woman's story reminded me of them, I had some jobs during that time. I barely left the apartment for anything besides food or books. I have no money, no other clothes. This is all I have to my name. My reputation as an investigator still matters to me even if people still think I'm crazy. But I have to do something good before I'm dead. Right?"

"Maybe you could just take care of yourself, enjoy whatever time you have left," said Long.

"There's no time left, sir. That's why I have to keep going."

"Don't be a fool. Masonori is in control of the case now. Who knows what I'll be doing."

"Did you hear anything about Lia Jones?" asked Paavo.

"No, nothing. Why?" Paavo thought about it for a moment.

"She broke into my apartment, wanting me to find the priest, find out why her brother had to die. If I refused, you and Kyoko would die," he said.

"What happened to her?"

"I agreed, not much of a choice. She disappeared right after that."

"The lead came up cold, too." Long said after a dead silence.

"What are you talking about?" asked Paavo.

"Daniel Jupiter doesn't exist. No matches in the database. No one in the city with that name."

They were interrupted by a knock at the door, Long turned away from Paavo for a slight second, he looked up from the corner of the room to turn towards the approaching noise.

Wiles stepped back into the room, his hands raised.

"Sorry to interrupt, gentlemen. But Paavo needs his rest, his wounds are not quite healed as of yet. Do you mind coming back later to check on him?"

"No, that's okay. We're done here," Long said as he turned back towards Paavo.

"Take care of yourself, I'll find you when it's time," he said. Paavo turned back towards the side of the bed. He was silent once again. Long suddenly went for the doctor.

"Listen, I don't know what the hell kind of operation you're running here. If I wanted to I could shut this whole thing down and move him to a proper hospital right now."

"What are you talking about?" asked Wiles. The doctor became defensive. Long continued.

"Don't pretend like you don't know what I'm talking about. This shit you're pouring into him, I don't like it. We don't know the effects of it long term, you don't know what it's doing. I've seen it first hand; it takes so much out of him."

"I can assure you that the serum is not detrimental to Paavo's well being. Besides, I doubt any other hospital would know what to do with someone like him," said Wiles.

Long moved towards the doctor, Wiles moved back nervously.

"What the hell do you mean by that?" asked Long. Paavo's face turned into a slight smirk seeing the doctor break a sweat.

"I'm saying that he is in good hands. The best hands possible!"

"He better be in the best hands, because he's family to me. I'm taking care of him, not you. Stay on your game, Doctor Wiles, is it? I might even get a second opinion about this serum, and about you as a matter of fact."

"Do as you like, officer. My work is legitimate, I have nothing to hide." Long backed away from the doctor, Wiles dusted himself off.

"Now, how can I put your mind at ease in this matter?"

"Just help the kid get better. Don't turn him into some kind of damned experiment," said Long.

"He will not be harmed."

"Good." Long stormed out of the room and slammed the door behind him. He walked away from the office smiling. He knew Paavo would appreciate that. Wiles wiped beads of sweat from his brow before speaking.

"You'll be released tomorrow morning, stay tonight and rest."

He left the room without making eye contact with Paavo. The door closed behind him and he was left with the silence of the room. The faint noise of wind crept out from the black curtains covering the windows. Paavo closed his eyes. He felt the serum, warming his blood. For a moment, he felt relaxed, at peace, until he looked down towards the wires and tubes forced into his body. He lowered himself carefully back down onto the bed and fell back into a deep sleep.

Kyoko opened her eyes. A cold sweat coated her neck. Stains of perspiration dotted her black nightgown. Another nightmare, the same as it was almost every night that her husband was not by her side by nightfall. She rose to her feet to grab her pink robe and head downstairs for a glass of water. As it was for Derek and his partner, it was the same way with her and her daughter, Simona. The young girl was beautiful. She had wanted to become a doctor. Thirteen years ago, a man swerved through oncoming traffic, finding his way to a busy downtown street. She was on her way back home when the car had made a hard right turn. She froze in place, no one rushed to help her once the vehicle made impact with her body. Those standing in the street were silent, caught in the moment just as the girl was. The driver fled the scene immediately.

When she and Derek received word, they heard that no one caught the license plates of the car. Those eyewitnesses were unreliable. Drunkards left the nearby bar barely able to stand. The man behind the wheel was in the same condition, and somehow no one reported a drunk driver. The tears came and went for months and months. Every anniversary of the day she was born was soon replaced with the day she died. Soon, they stopped altogether as time went on. Her memory faded into the darkness of their minds. It wasn't because they wanted to forget. The pain of remembering was too much for them.

Lights were off, Kyoko moved quietly through the dark kitchen. It was getting more difficult to sleep these days. The last two nights, there were knocks at the door at all hours. Her husband, wrapped up in his own cases, told her to relax. Some extra cruisers had circled the block a few more times, making sure everything looked normal. This did not make her feel safer. The water was cold to her lips. A bitter taste from the tap filled her mouth. The best photograph of Simona used to sit in the photo album next to her bed. it was of her at age eleven, a blue dress and matching shoes made her the belle of the ball at her elementary school dance. When she died, Derek took it with him to work. He told her that it sat inside the desk drawer of his office.

A sound startled her, the glass fell from her hand to the sink. Shards connected with the iron basin, sending pieces of glass everywhere. She cursed under her breath and moved quickly for the phone. The knocking was loud, angry. When she opened the door, no one was there. More games, she said, more taunting from kids on the street who need to be taught a lesson. She began to close the door when she saw the package on the ground. What was this? An envelope wrapped carefully with aged paper. There were lines of faded writing across the wrapped. The seal was broken. Kyoko lifted it off the ground and inserted her finger in to open it. The paper keeping it together, ripped from a bible. The passage was Genesis 6:1-4. It was from the bible in the living room. She ran back inside, leaving the door open. Tearing books down the shelf, she searched for the same book.

"It's not from the same...No one's been inside my house."

The words were repeated like a mantra. Books littered the wood floor. The bible was where it had always been. She turned to Genesis, the page missing. In its place, words in kanji, written with dark red lipstick. Kyoko felt a jolt of adrenaline shoot through her body.

"Watching?"

The bible was tossed against the wall. She looked down fearful as to what was inside the envelope. With shaking hands, she grabbed at the contents inside. The picture of Simona, her blue dress beautiful and bright, was staring back at her. The screams, she could not control. Who had gotten to his desk? Who had gotten into the house while she was asleep?

"Kyoko!"

The sound of her husband's voice was there, shocking her back into reality. The car, still running outside, was parked across the driveway. He had come home, just in time for the sight of his wife, lost in pure terror. The eyes were watching, all around them. She showed him the picture of Simona before falling into his arms, drained of her own energy. He cradled her for the first time in years. The sounds of Police sirens cut the tension of the storming skies. Cruisers filled the streets as Kyoko was brought outside to make a report. The picture and envelope were taken as evidence.

CHAPTER NINETEEN

The next morning was blurred as Paavo found himself in the front seat of a car speeding down the street. Long cursed loudly as he made his way through early traffic. He seemed a bit out of sorts. Paavo wiped his eyes. He kept them closed as he was unable to adjust to the light yet. Bright white and blue filled his eyelids as he caught a small glimpse of the outside world. It hurt, and he placed one hand over his eyes to remain in darkness.

"Where are we going?"

"I'm taking you home and I'm going back to work." Long spoke casually, it offset the erratic driving and sharp turns.

"How was the good doctor?" Paavo asked.

"I don't know. I didn't see him. The nurse made you a new case with some more medicine."

"Thoughtful."

"I must say, they treated you like you were made of glass in there. You must have something special that they want," said Long.

"My condition is said to be the modern medical discovery."

"He's going to hound you forever, you know. You're a special case. They take care of the special cases. You should feel proud." Long said.

He swerved around a pickup truck and turned the corner towards the highway.

"It doesn't matter how I feel about it."

"What does matter then?" asked Long.

"Getting back to work." Paavo lifted his hand to let his eyes settle into the light.

"Doing what exactly? Getting killed?"

"Yes," said Paavo.

"You're a fool, just lie in bed, and let yourself heal proper. I'll keep you updated."

"What are you going to do?"

"There's nothing to do. The blood we found belonged to a little girl, the same one you were looking for. We tracked the trail to the whereabouts of some drug dealers; they had prints and blood all over the place. Dealers stopped, murderer gone thanks to you. That would be a case closed."

The highway was near empty, a light snowfall began to appear from the blue covered sky. Paavo stared out into the distance.

"What about the drugs? Substances your people found in the food?"

"Strange, I know. We are trying to find traces of this DRI or designer drug, whatever you want to call it. Whoever has been handling it has been more than careful. Worse than the docks," said Long.

"The docks?"

"Before I saw you at the hospital, there was a shipment of drugs coming in, we had a guy on the inside and took part in that for one of the deals. Don't you remember?"

Paavo thought about it for a moment, he truly had forgotten.

"It turned into a complete joke, for the most part. We think the same deal that was going down there had something to do with whatever they tried to move out at the church. But nothing in what was recovered from the deal can be linked to what we found in the food. Not chemically or physically," said Long.

"What did you find there?"

"I don't remember all the details, there were some artifacts shipped from different countries, nothing that could be traced back to what was mixed into the food. But there were also regular products, some household chemicals for visual appeal. Plenty of red paint."

"You don't think maybe it was made overseas and brought into the country?" asked Paavo.

"Listen, I have people working on that, under the radar, I still have superiors to report to and explain the reasoning behind more dead bodies."

"Keep me posted on that."

With no cars or traffic in sight this morning, Long had reached the thin driveway of Paavo's apartment within thirty minutes. It was difficult for Paavo to breathe, he felt himself nodding off as he inhaled the hot air. He found himself falling in and out of sleep. He closed his eyes for a moment to find that so much time had passed. Long's hand pushed at his shoulders, waking him slowly. Paavo was weak from the treatment, he fumbled with the handle. It was difficult to exit the car, no real reaction in the muscles of his legs. He took a step out onto the ground only to fall into the pile of snow collected upon the curb.

Long rushed around to the other side to pull him out. Paavo began to shiver, his hands shaking from the shock of intense cold. Long looked down at him as he pulled him from the snow and helped him to his feet, he was drained of energy and could barely keep his eyes open. Paavo pulled up on the pockets and sleeves of the old man's trench coat to hold himself up. His arms shook, barely able to stand.

"Come on, let's get you inside," sighed Long.

The apartment looked the same as it did almost a week ago. Papers littered the floor. Candles were burned down to their ends. Long held him against the wall as he stretched his arm out to shut the door. A strong wind blew it open once again, flurries of snow passed Paavo's head and into the room. He cursed aloud before finally slamming the door shut tight. He helped him to the bedroom and let him fall to the mattress.

"You can undress yourself," said Long.

Paavo could barely move, he could only slide off his shoes and socks. A sweep of his arm caused them to fall to the floor. He wondered to himself how things would be if he had never left the apartment; relatively safe and unharmed, dying still, but unknowingly, blissfully, without any wounds to hide or guilt.

"I never should have left here," said Paavo.

"Well, you did, and you're here now, back in reality, back to real life." Long threw a long black blanket over him.

"So, make sure you stay in it. Don't wander off, don't disappear. Don't leave us again."

"What else can I do but stay here and die?" Long placed his case of serum on the side of the bed.

"You won't die. I know you won't," he said.

"What makes you think so?" asked Paavo.

"You live with the angel, in your heart, on your side. It walks with you, protects you."

"All this lost blood would disagree with you."

"You wouldn't have made it this far if they weren't," said Long. Wounded still, he turned away to rest, he moved his body to take some of the pressure off the wound in his chest. He faced away from Long. He buried his head into the pillow at his side.

"I don't know if I deserve your angel," said Paavo.

"You do. If you don't now, you will soon enough." Paavo held his hand up to salute him. Long returned the gesture.

"I'll be in touch, stay alive and well. Your car is outside, full tank."

"Thank you, sir." Paavo was soon left alone in the apartment as the door shut, sealing off the cold wind from the outside. The outstretched hand reached back to the inside pocket of his suit jacket to produce a set of small keys. He dropped them onto the floor, next to his shoes. He had taken the keys from his pocket when he had been helped from the snow. Predictable still, he thought to himself. Routine is a dangerous pattern. The keys would unlock the weapons cache in the downstairs locker of the Police department.

Long reached the station. The traffic began to build up halfway back into the city. The snowfall had become more violent as the sun rose over the city. A bright white blinded those on the streets. The light reflected off the snow to create an angelic shine that covered its surroundings. He brushed himself off as he walked towards the office. His right hand covered his eyes momentarily to allow himself time to adjust to the artificial light. The office was empty, no notes or papers about what needed to be done, Long took a breath of relief at the lack of busy work, he reached in his pockets to pull out his wallet and phone. He stopped for a second and looked through each pocket of his coat and pants, the keys were missing. Long lowered his head and moved around in a complete circle, a sigh of frustration was uttered. He had been re- assigned. Masonori had taken over the case. What happens when Paavo gets back to full health?

He reminded himself quickly that the kid knew what he was doing. He had to leave him alone to figure things out, to take care of himself. He sat back in his chair and hoped that he would not fall into darkness once again. An officer stepped into the room without saying a word, Long looked at him for a moment before turning away from the door. The young man stopped to look out the window. His hands were clenched tight behind his back. He was silent, after a few awkward minutes, the young man turned towards Long as if to speak. A stream of blood ran down the side of his face. Long finally looked to see no one was there.

"I know," he said.

The sunlight moved directions, it made the room brighter. It became more difficult to see outside. A quick motion of his hands caused the blinds to fall, and shrouded the room into a shade of grey. Long's eyes followed the streaks of light that danced along the wall for hours. The card sat on the desk with the name and phone number of a good therapist. Kyoko would want this, he said to himself. Signed by his superiors, he was to begin his sessions bright and early tomorrow morning. Long sat in silence and prayed for the young man lying wounded in a bed, hours away, to find what he was looking for, to take care of himself in the days ahead.

The drive to the village was a frantic one. Something in his stomach had stirred. Getting dressed to head into the city, the flashing light of the answering machine stopped him. During his time in the hospital, he had received a message from Chi Lien. There were men and women in suits, knocking on her door, asking to come in. Paavo felt his heart drop. With pain shooting through his hands and feet, he threw himself into the car and made his way there. It had to be Kazuhiko, with the other family members in tow. They were going to make good on their threat to take her from the village and place her in hospice care. The old woman was blind, but she did not need to be taken to some shit hospital. The family was out of money, and they were going to take it from her. It was just hers, set aside to keep the house going. It was separate from the money he had made, saved and deposited there for them both.

Kazuhiko was his second cousin, and a prince in the Chiharu bloodline. He was never able to handle the reputation behind his name and respect that it demanded. For all its bigotry and prejudice, the family name was written into the list of the elites long ago. The land that Perdition was built on was once owned and governed by a Diet. Decades ago, their system was two chambers that passed the laws controlling the freedoms of the people inside the city. It was dissolved for a democracy. The patriarch of the family was a man named Kenji, who was a member of the high chancellors of the Diet.

Jagged turns through the dirt from the off ramp threw Paavo back into his seat. He remembered life at the palace, the mansion where Kenji's wife and children lived. They never had to worry about making the rent, or spreading out the food so everyone ate. All they had ever known was luxury, relaxation and wealth. They had the freedom he had always wanted as a child and even now. Some of his first memories as a small boy were visions of bumping into the butler in the hallway. His nose turned up, eyes speaking nothing but a silent disdain even he could understand despite his age. Paavo's father was a white man. The family looked down on both parents, calling them foolish. They never let his parents forget the mistake they made in coming together. The mistake was creating a child, he was a half-breed, a nothing, an anomaly, something to be forgotten and left alone. Those words he heard everyday from complete strangers. They told him that they were family, that they were just angry and that they would take care of you if anything should happen.

The Diet chose the Prime Minister of the country for many years. As industry and technology increased and became more essential to the growth of the city, that form of government was put on the back burner for a republic that decided its leaders by voting themselves. The ones pulling the strings behind this move were those in organized crime feeding the chambers of the Diet. They stood to make more money and gain more control over the interests of the city. Kenji Chiharu was at the forefront of the move and with enough politics and financial investment, soon became the speaker of the House of Representatives.

The road to Chi Lien's house was covered in a damp fog. His mother's words clung to his side like a spear. The blind woman was the only one to support them. Love has no color and people are brought together for a specific reason, she told them. All the accusations of the young Paavo poisoning the bloodline were tossed away. With as much power as she had, she was only one against an entire family, spoiled beyond the point of redemption. In time, Chi Lien was forced to sit in the corner of the dining room and listen to her children destroy the good name, for what it was worth, with pathetic spectacles in the city streets. Kenji had worked himself to death for his children, and soon after the Diet was dissolved, his entire family followed.

At the height of their decadence, the mansion was filled with over 30 people, living off of the wealth of brand new corruption and control of the city's resources. Paavo's parents were not allowed inside. Their apartment was on the other side of town, falling apart at the seams. Pictures of the rooms he grew up in came only in dreams. This was all he had known as a child, was the struggle of those with nothing trying to get along living among those who were given too much. A black car parked outside of the small house stopped his heart. The front door was opened, shadows moved inside behind the faint kitchen light. Paavo quickly parked on the other side and got out to see Kazuhiko standing in the doorway, a crooked smile across his face.

"You shouldn't be here, cousin." Paavo's hands clenched into fists, they were shaking fervently.

"What the hell are you doing here? I told you to leave her alone."

"She is the key to our survival. Things have taken a turn in the household. We've had to make a lot of cutbacks the past few years."

"You are out of your damn mind. None of you living in that house even have a job. What makes you think you can come here and claim our grandmother's money?" asked Paavo. A voice echoed from the inside.

"It's not the money they are after, Mr. Harker. It's the well being of their oldest living family member, the matriarch of the

Chiharu name."

A man in a blue suit stepped out on the porch with him.

"Who are you supposed to be?" asked Paavo.

"His name is not important," Kazuhiko interrupted him.

"This is my attorney, along with a court order, requesting that grandmother be taken into our immediate care and custody."

"A court order?"

"I told you that I was serious, half breed. You've been keeping our mother away from us, living in this stinking village for years. It took us so long to find her," said Kaz.

"Your grandmother is eighty two years old and blind, Mr. Harker. She should not be living alone like this. As much as I want to commend you on helping her maintain her independence during this time, I cannot in good conscience let this continue. The risks are too great."

There were others inside the house. Paavo looked inside to see who was there. Nothing but shadows, unidentified faces staring out at him.

"And what happens to her assets?" he asked.

"They would be dissolved into the family members' accounts. After speaking with Mr. Chiharu here, it is obvious that your relationship is estranged. Your involvement with the family is practically non-existent."

"And it will stay that way," Kazuhiko added. Both men met eyes, and Paavo's fists began to shake violently.

"Sir, please do not attempt to stop what we are doing. The written order is legitimate. Any acts of violence or harassment against us would be considered a violation and you would be charged in a court of law."

"This is not happening," said Paavo. His hands would not

stop shaking, his heart raced.

"You got what you wanted. You got the fucking money..."

Paavo moved towards the steps, the attorney stepped in front of Kazuhiko. He did not stop moving. He pushed the attorney, who had to be at least a hundred pounds heavier than him, to the wall of the house. He had pinned him against the prince, both men trapped to the bricks and the edge of the staircase. They strained and struggled as he moved his head closer until he was nose to nose with the young heir of the family.

"You're a coward and have done nothing but slowly take everything away from me, piece by piece."

"Mr. Harker, let go of us."

"Until there is nothing left but a quiet shell, what you see in front of you now." His voice became louder.

"Paavo! Do not make us call the Police."

"You took my mother, my father, my life."

"Guards?" Kaz called out. The shadows from inside the house stepped out. More men in suits grabbed at his arms. He did not let go.

"Now you have grandmother and her money. What else could you want from me? From anyone?!"

Kazuhiko was whimpering like a child. The men took hold of him and yanked him off of them. Paavo lost balance and fell forward, the guards threw him off, and he fell off the steps to the ground. The impact was rough. His ribs felt the full force of the fall. Blood began to well up inside his wound. The attorney and the prince dusted themselves off. They stood tall once again, the guards stood with smirks on their faces, their fists clenched, waiting for him.

"You should leave now, Mr. Harker."

"So powerless, you should know that by now," said Kaz. Paavo got to his feet slowly, coughing up blood. He wiped the dirt from his hands. A single tear moved down the side of his face.

"Enjoy your fortune. Your time will come."

Paavo looked around slowly, the view of the village still beautiful, now tainted with the crime and darkness of the city. How long could he have run to keep it away from her? The men went back inside, to bring out Chi Lien. She moved her eyes in circles. Foreign figure around her, pulling her away from the comfort Paavo had created. He coughed roughly. She felt it as they escorted her to the car. There were no words. There was no time, only silence and words unspoken. From the inside of the house stepped a group of older women, they were in their late forties. Paavo stared at them, these women of the family.

They all wore black pant suits, with glittering golden jewelry. Necklaces and expensive clothing stuck out in the rural space of the village. Their hairstyles were all the same, as if they were meant to be the same person. Nothing about them gave the impression that they wanted to be there. No signs of wanting to help Chi Lien, it was all business to them. There were three of them, the same looks of hate from his childhood. He was locked in sight with the sisters of his late mother, Shien Chiharu. The visions of his father, Simon, locked in argument—came back again. They placed the old woman into the backseat of the car and got in. Kazuhiko was the last one into the vehicle. Paavo watched them get in, one by one, wanting them to die. The anger inside was out of control. This curse inherited by his parents, bestowed upon him. To be hated, and to be at fault every moment of your life. A family of wealth before him still, it had always been a cracked portrait of values and loyalty. His father came from nothing, as his mother was handed everything. They only turned their back the moment she wanted something for herself. What she wanted was him. They placed the young lovers into exile when she was already carrying him.

Chi Lien's stories painted a picture of magic, of romance. Nothing like that exists in this world, she said. Perhaps it did once, but not anymore. Now, he had nothing. Paavo was still, long after they had left. The walk back to the car was slow. There was no energy left in his body. Nothing remained but disdain and failure. What had he gained by stepping back out into this world? Another reminder of the way things were in this cursed city?

For a glimmer of hope, he had been given nothing in return but a deadline for his fleeting life, spit in his face and a bullet for his shortcomings. And now, she was gone, his anchor, his reason to continue. They had taken her far away from the peace of the garden and the madness of his city. His steps were loud and for the first time and his heart was calm. He was tired, empty and nothing else. The words of Lia did not leave his mind. She was watching and waiting for an answer, a reason for her brother's death.

Hours later, Paavo found himself walking quietly into the Police department. Officers walked through the hallways without paying any attention to him. Another stress filled morning would provide enough cover for him to gather whatever needed from the lockers and exit through the back door that led to the parking garage. The door led out into the second floor of the lot, only thirty feet where his car was parked. Paavo moved calmly through the hallway, he tried not to look lost to those eyeing him as he moved deeper into the station. Different men and women watched him move but they didn't stop him. He wondered if they recognized him from his time here. Paavo kept moving. He didn't walk straight for the weapons cache, but made several stops outside of nearby offices and backs of lines. He wanted to make it seem he was there for routine things, traffic school information and court dates, trivialities that stalked all people. Don't appear as if you don't know where you're going, he said to himself, make it seem as though you've done it a thousand times. The room was down towards the jail, two floors above the furnace of the building.

He was coming closer to the stairwell, the tiles and paint of the floors began to appear ripped up, chipped. They never fixed up this part of the building, Paavo realized, he remembered walking these same steps years ago under Long's tutelage. He stopped dead to see there were two officers standing close to the stairs. A quick look around showed no one else approaching. They would see him, tell him to head back the way he came and the trip would be for nothing. Paavo moved back towards the opposite end of the hallway and searched for a small place to hide. He felt foolish in doing so. The officers began to walk towards Paavo's direction and he saw them in sight. They faced each other, still not noticing the strange figure in black standing before them. Paavo quickly ducked back out of the hallway and pulled the fire alarm close by. The noise was loud and startling. Paavo pushed the lever of the back up to hide the false alarm he grabbed his chest as he felt his heart jump, a sharp pain shot through his body. Both of the officers were startled as well.

"Shit!"

"Come on, let's go."

They bolted towards the hallway, Paavo took a breath and suddenly threw himself in front of the men. They collided and Paavo acted as though he was hit by a truck. He fell back towards the floor. He kept silent but grabbed his knee. One of the officers looked down at Paavo in disgust before taking off as the other officer who ran into him stopped to help.

"Are you alright, sir?" he asked.

Paavo tried to get up but slinked back down to the floor.

"I'm fine, but my knee." The officer tried to help him up, the second man returned.

"We've got to go, they're trying to find out where the alarm was pulled."

"Let's get him out of here first."

"No. I'm alright, I just want to get to my car, is there another way out of here?" Paavo asked.

"Down the stairwell, there's a door that leads out to the garage. Are you sure you'll be ok?"

"Yeah, thank you," said Paavo.

The men ran down the hallway to meet up with the other officers. Paavo quickly got up and jumped down the stairs towards the weapons locker. He held his breath to avoid any pain. He was under the gun now to grab what he needed. He passed the door leading to the garage and looked up to memorize it. The sign above listed the door as number 2. Paavo reached the locker and pulled the keys from his pocket, the key for the door was covered in a blue covering, just like before. Paavo walked into the weapons cache, he was surrounded by guns and ammunition. He was never a collector of such things but he knew that he needed protection from any threat. The same applied for him still, Paavo put on a pair of black gloves and began searching through the cabinets for something easy to conceal but powerful. He had space for two guns in his holsters. a stock pistol was the first that caught his eye. Everyone in the department had one of these. Any bullets found the crime scene that belonged to him would be ruled out if he used the same guns as they did. Paavo loaded the gun and placed it in the holster. He pocketed four clips of bullets. Nearly 100 bullets, he counted to himself, enough for now.

Paavo turned towards the armor that decorated the walls around him. A series of black Kevlar vests caught his eye; it made him think of the wounds that traveled around his own body. He could afford to wear some protection, if not for parts of his working body, but for the hole in his chest. He removed his jacket and holster to put on the vest. No way to carry it out in his hand, everything he would take needed to be worn outside and not noticeable. He struggled to find one to fit his thin frame as he looked at his watch;

four minutes already, he had to hurry. The third vest fit him exactly and his jacket and holster were thrown back on. Paavo turned to leave when he found a Desert Eagle sitting on the top of the table, fully loaded. He placed it in the second holster, the gun was heavy. Its silver finish gleamed in his eyes as Paavo couldn't help but smile at his find.

With six minutes and counting, Paavo buttoned his jacket and filled the remaining space with clips for the Desert Eagle. He stepped out of the locker and locked the door, and carefully climbed the stairwell. The alarm had stopped and he could only imagine officers storming the hallways soon. He continued heading towards the garage. The guns and vest weighed him down as he moved but he made his way out into the parking lot. The gloves were removed and tossed into the passenger seat as he started the car and nervously left the station. The snow had subsided for the majority of the day, leaving only small flurries that decorated the streets and surrounding vehicles. It allowed for a quick and easy exit from the scene.

Paavo turned the corner and breathed a sigh of relief. Within minutes, officers stormed the staircase, searching for Paavo. Cameras had seen him up until the alarm, when they suddenly cut out due to electrical interference. Panic amongst people handcuffed caused a commotion as they began pushing and pulling each other. The men who ran into Paavo were called down to separate a fight that broke out between two men in the holding area. They wouldn't find the sensor he dropped behind the alarm lever. It was the only one he had and made to be smaller than a penny. There were no prints, no signs of forced entry and Paavo was free now to begin his research. There was something behind Long's theory of a connection between the dealers and the men he was investigating, some kind of link between what they brought to the city, and what was being dealt out to the streets.

Paavo stopped at a red light a few blocks away from the station. He pulled out his cell phone and began searching through the list of numbers. There were still some allies deep within the city, he thought to himself, not friends, but those who hold information. Paavo stopped at the discovery of one in particular. The light turned green and he dropped the phone to his side and continued to drive out of the city, back towards the apartment. The visions of scattered papers and burnt candles across his floor flooded his mind, letting go of those missing people, he still struggled with the idea. Long had told him to forget, just like he had before, all those years ago. What good are we if we do not carry on? How valid is our promise? Our word?

The cops are too busy, too distracted to focus on the most important things. The forgotten people of the city, not the wealthy chosen for success, they're the only ones who matter now; not the strong but the small, the beaten, the weak and the wounded. Those without choices, without freedom, who hold their heads down and do not speak of their own tragedies. He felt no anger towards Naoko Aki, whether it was her or some devil made dream as Long said.

Paavo had never believed in any sort of religion or God. As a child, it never occurred to him that faith would bring anything more than what he had already been given. An existence wrapped in such pain and questioning, what could a god do to make things any better? He asked himself year after year, no one ever had a straight answer. It came to a point where any faith or conviction belonged to himself, his own actions. Paavo had no masters, or gods, or any other figures to dictate or control him, he was free unto himself. He had to keep looking, no other choice.

Only death remained, lurking behind him in his shadows. In his flowing blood were constant reminders and teases of his true destiny. Paavo had to find those people to make himself worthy of this fleeting life. No assistance, no lessons to learn anymore, only these final days to drift and travel. He would dedicate them to the citizens of the city, lost and nameless, like him, stepping away from Long to carry out his own investigation, his own journey, prepared now more than ever.

CHAPTER TWENTY

Seven days had passed. A new morning brought more snow and storm to the battered city. Now was the test for those who lived inside the walls of Perdition, notorious for its near unbearable winters. Large maps and diagrams of the city flashed on the television, along with a crawl of words warning young children and the elderly to stay inside. A man in a stark blue suit appeared and said that the storm would continue on throughout the next two weeks. Nothing had changed in Paavo's absence. With time and new freedom on his hands, he was allowed to work on his own needs. The entire week had been spent asking questions, trying to find a clue of some kind. Fathers and mothers of those missing nearly attacked him upon his arrival. They had been led down paths of deception by the Police, and now by another group of investigators. The last thing they needed was another freak, their own words, poking around trying to get involved. One of the parents had spit in his face. He said goodbye while wiping the liquid from his face. With every waking moment, Paavo found himself becoming more and more alone in the world.

The clientele had disappeared. His mentor had seemed to fall into a trap of bureaucracy and saving face. There was nothing left but for him to find the girl, that was his job. The one good thing he could do before dying. Find the girl, he told himself, find out what the hell happened to those people in the shelter. The old cop's life had depended on it now. His debts had been paid off to Wendell. Grandmother knew he was still alive and somewhat well. Whatever traces of his own personal weaponry were replaced now with Police equipment. Long had told him to let go, promised to let him rest his injuries, that he would contact him when the time came to bring him back into the graces of the department. A secure job with benefits, perhaps, was waiting for him. A petty excuse for a profession in order to keep him quiet, but mainly to become a desk jockey and live a small and unimportant existence until his untimely death.

The apartment was full of noise as blood dripped from a high shelf in the living room. Paavo took long and deep breaths, pulling himself up and back down, over and over again. His thin arms rippled with muscles, slowly revealing themselves through the pale skin and outlines of bone. His thoughts traveled far distances along with the blaring music playing through the old radio. The scanner that he had left on the entire week gave reports of violence taking place in and around the area where the shelter exploded. Those lashing out were the ones buying from the dealers and were now acting out on their own. There had to be a connection with the substance and their behavior. It was frustrating that all these things were happening, and all Long could think about was an office job for him. Paavo humored his mentor about the offer, but he promised himself soon after that he would decline the job. Their conversation in the hospital reminded Paavo of days before his exile.

That day troubled him deeply. The families of over fifty men and women who disappeared the night before flooded the station with tears and anger. The cops were overwhelmed with the tasks handed to them. Long was no different, as strong a leader as he was, he was pulled in all directions by the state, his superiors and by the unions. He gave up on those families, something that Paavo would not do and he promised to take their cases all on. He was laughed at, especially when no leads had been found. Paavo walked the streets of the city in silent desperation, feeling he had failed those people. Days before he left, both he and the inspector would sit in silence, away from the Police. They would argue about the next step. He told Paavo not to let that failure destroy him. Despite all good words, he also stood by and watched those families spit on him for not finding their loved ones. He told me to let go, Paavo said to himself, I suppose I will. That was only the beginning of the exile. Soon he was lost in the mundane tasks of his day job. His quiet voice of reason was silenced by the policies of the station; more rules to follow, set in place by those in control. It was nothing new to him, but the time for staying in line had passed. He needed to step out from the normal with more focused thoughts and action. A day job would only distract from his purpose. He would never disrespect Long by taking a position under him and then going back on his word, so he chose to disappear.

The beaten and cracked phone sat on the table in the middle of the room. Four new messages displayed but were unopened. As promised, they were from Long, sent days ago. Paavo had spent the time cleaning the apartment, gathering equipment and packing the car. He had found some of his albums in the closet. The discs were covered in dust. The artwork was faded and scratched away. One was a pink blur of a young woman's face, her eyes closed and mouth open, surrounded by smoke and the circuitry of a guitar, barely recognizable. The word 'Loveless' was written along the spine of the case. Music had always fascinated him. He had been introduced to it at a young age. Memories passed of walking with his father along cold downtown streets, heading towards a show. There was a dull, faded noise coming from inside the bars. He watched the drunks dance and laugh slowly breathing in the cold air, trying to avoid coughing and bleeding out.

The album had been playing on repeat for hours since the early morning. Paavo pulled his body towards the top of the shelf and came back down. With each movement there was a pain in both his arms and his chest. The guitar lines were laced with delay and chorus that bounced back and forth between the walls as a trickle of blood continued to pour out from his wound. He felt his heart move back and forth as it pumped. The singer was female; her voice was blurred with noise and feedback. He couldn't make out the words, but the music was covered in her angelic moans. He felt the bass and drums deep in his chest. The band played in a dream like haze as he continued his exercise. The snow moved violently across the window. Outside the white lined shadow of the city loomed that painted a strange picture of serenity and anger.

Paavo dropped slowly to the floor. His arms quivered, tired and spent. A quick wipe of the space underneath his feet left the white towel a deep red. He tossed it into the small pile of clothes on the floor and moved towards the tub. He turned on the hot water, removed the rest of his clothes and stepped into the stream, wincing for a few moments before exhaling as he felt the burning move across his skin. Paavo closed his eyes and inhaled the warm air. The water washed over his frail body, his muscles tightened and then relaxed in the warmth. He turned to face the shower and let the water fall into the hole in his chest. The water welled up within his wound. Clouded and red, it spilled back out onto the ivory below him. A heat began to rise near his heart. He clenched his hands and gritted his teeth. Paavo waited for a few seconds before looking down to see his heart, quivering with every breath taken. The hardened blood washed away. He could take the heart out of his body if he chose to. There were times when he would stare it, struggling to move, wanting to take it in his hands and rip it out. His heart was a shade of purple which expanded and pumped an irregular beat. Fresh blood began to pour around the organ. He let out a grunt and turned his back to the water.

Paavo stepped out into the bedroom. All his clothes lay on the floor, still covered in dry blood and dirt were to be washed clean. He tossed them into the bathtub as the hot water was turned down to a stark cold. He gathered his soap and a small cup filled with blue fabric liquid. He soaked his clothes in the water and emptied the cup into the tub. After a few minutes of scrubbing furiously, he hung the shirts and pants up to dry. Paavo returned to the bedroom to the black collar shirt, pants and the case that held the syringe and a few unopened bottles of the serum. He checked his watch, only four hours since the last injection. There was enough time to step out. He made a note of the time. It would be another eight before he needed the shot.

Underneath the bottles of serum was a roll of gauze and

medical tape. Paavo wiped the small traces of blood from around his wound. He slowed his breathing down, ripped a square of gauze and placed it over his exposed heart. The medical tape was pasted on all four corners to hold still. He moved himself in different directions, trying to stretch out the carefully taped wrapping. Naoko Aki's case had been closed with the girl proclaimed dead and a majority of the dealers being jailed. Paavo wanted to know anything he could about this new drug that's been surfacing. There was a contact that used to provide information to the Police about the drug trade.

Than Kasagi, otherwise known as Angel, ran a club on the far end of downtown. A brash and outspoken mainstay of the party scene in the city, she was also a high priced contact for designer drugs. Angel was flamboyant and eccentric, yet she was the only person outside of Long as one of the few people Paavo could get along with somehow. One of the private dealers for the Mob owned the club before he was gunned down. Even in exile, Paavo kept tabs on her. Than took over and bought the building from the other dealers, turned it from a strip bar into a rave hall and has been going strong ever since.

The dealers would provide protection for his club in turn for details on what product was coming in. If there was anyone who would know about the deal made last week, it would be her. Paavo created a slight friendship with the man, solely for his connections within town. Than made her affection for Paavo clear from the very beginning. It didn't make him feel uncomfortable, but the feeling wasn't mutual. He had no desire for Angel, or any man for that matter. Paavo just went along with his taunts and teases with a strange look on his face.

Angel had to have some information that could help. Something had to be hidden within the drugs they found, or maybe hidden on the ship. Maybe there was a substance in the meat still unidentified. At some point, he would have to find out what was in the food, which meant contacting Long's forensic team. That would come in time; he wanted to avoid the risk of seeing him for now. He had already stolen from the station, going back there would be too much, too soon.

Paavo looked at himself in the mirror, if he was going to get back in Angel's good graces, he would have to play along. He ran his hand through his hair, it stuck up in all different directions. He put on his shirt with the Kevlar vest underneath. It was sturdy but light enough for Paavo to move around. He returned to the bedroom and grabbed an unopened syringe from the case. He made a small hole for the needle to peek out from the plastic and he plugged it into one the bottles of serum. Paavo filled the syringe, capped it and placed it in his right jacket pocket. He stepped out and into the storm. The snow was raging on without signs of slowing down unlike the previous days. The car started with the familiar rattle of clanging metal. It was a slow start moving through the snow as the plows had not begun moving through the parking lot. An old woman with a small, child sized plastic shovel struggled to move the snow away from her car. She lived two doors down from Paavo.

They met eyes while he was leaving the lot and she stared at him with a strange and indifferent look, it made him feel more uncomfortable than any flirtations Angel would throw his way. He looked ahead and continued the drive into the city. Halfway onto the expressway, Paavo realized that he forgot the album. He was sad for a few seconds and then turned on the radio. The stations in Perdition were nothing unique; the usual trivial talk of pop culture, ridiculous sound effects, several periods of commercials and foolish celebrity obsession filled his ears for about thirty seconds. He turned the knob to another station, two men arguing back and forth like children. He ignored it and turned to another station, a lone saxophone stretched its solitary note across long distances, and Paavo took a breath and settled into familiarity as he left the jazz station on for the remainder of the drive.

The car stopped three blocks away from the club. Familiar

dead leaves piled in the center of the courtyard. Paavo sat in a brooding silence as he watched the snow. The old one assembled the pieces on the board. He was quiet as well. Each flake of white landed onto blankets of ice and water that created a patchwork across the stone platform. Both players were solemn. The day was dark, with few signs of life amidst the city and its looming structures. Paavo wanted to ask why they were there on a day like today. He felt inclined to open his mouth about something besides the game on this day.

"Why are we here, still?" The old one continued to assemble pieces.

"Why not here?"

"I figured we would find another place to go," said Paavo.

"Do you not enjoy the view?"

"Three days in a row, even with this weather, is a little too much, wouldn't you agree?"

"Would you feel better if I told you that I had nowhere else to go?"

"Are you a homeless man?" asked Paavo.

"I rent the ground," said the old one.

"Why come here?"

"I come to this park to relax and play a game with whoever comes my way. You happened to arrive as I did. You are here by chance."

"Am I the first?" asked Paavo.

"This park was built decades ago. The courtyard is the only remaining piece of the original design. The stone stairs lead over a view of the city, that's what remains in the minds of forgotten folks like me." His hand stretched out towards the sky and the towering buildings. A white hand followed from the shadows of the coat.

Paavo's eyes widened. This was the first time that he had seen any part of him.

"Those who are not given the proper respect by the systems of government or state, or common courtesy on the street, will always hold onto the memories of the town as it was, before it outgrew them."

The hand was drawn back into the sleeve.

"And yes, you are the first one to ever sit and play a game with me."

There was a moment of silence. It could be taken as a thank you, or perhaps a moment of vulnerability between them.

"Do you need a place to stay?" Paavo asked.

"It seems you share the guilt of those who walk the streets with oblivious eyes. Are you going to let me stay with you? Eat your food and drink your water?"

"I would give you money for a hotel for a few days, if I had any," said Paavo.

The old one laughed.

"Fair enough."

"I know you have no desire for a handout. I've already been attacked by people wanting more than I could give," said Paavo.

"Desperation drives us to extreme lengths."

The game had begun with the first move of a piece. A pawn was moved two spaces up. Paavo thought for a moment before beginning his defense.

"You are desperate yourself."

"What makes you say that?" Paavo asked.

"Your eyes scream of deception. For all the right reasons of course, but a lie is still a lie, regardless."

"What would I have to lie about to you?" asked Paavo.

"You've been lying since we began this game."

"Do you mean this game?" the old one shook their head.

"We have played once, and you lost. The game is now to see how long it takes you to beat me," he said.

"I'm a little rusty, that's all," said Paavo.

"No, you're not. You're distracted. Something's wrong inside you."

"At least you didn't say I was stupid."

"You have your moments. But that is why you are here now, why you came back, because you want to win."

"What happens when I win?" asked Paavo.

"If you win, then you won't have to worry about how smart you are anymore. You can go back to worrying about your occupation." He was puzzled; the black knight in his hand hung over the board, dangling from his fingers.

"What about my occupation?" Paavo asked.

"It's false. You don't do data entry, do you?" asked the old one.

"Of course, I do."

"Then why is there an ad in the phonebook for a detective with the name Paavo Harker?"

The knight finally found its way to the center of the board.

"That's not me."

"I checked the book. I had enough time being a bum and all. You're the only one with that name. You're a detective."

"Okay, say that I am. What happens next?" asked Paavo.

The old one moved another piece. The white bishop found a

crucial point, which forked the knight. Paavo was forced to choose between losing the knight or a bishop of his own.

"Nothing happens next, I want to know who you are."

There was a click underneath the table. Paavo was propped forward, gun in hand, pointed at whatever was behind the old one's coat and blankets.

"I have no weapons; you need not worry."

Paavo nodded and holstered the gun.

"Is there anyone that you trust completely?" asked the old one.

The bishop had taken the knight. Paavo returned by taking the attacking piece. Even game, once again.

"No," he said.

"So imposing you were a moment ago. You've never killed anyone before, have you?"

"That's correct," said Paavo.

"You put on a good front, kid. You don't have to lie anymore, we're friends now."

"What makes you think that we are friends?" asked Paavo.

"From wanting to put me up for the night to pulling a gun? We've gone through so much together. The good times and the bad! Am I right?"

The wind was colder now than before. Paavo looked up to the sky. All dark blue with a mixture of white. Somewhere in that darkness was sunlight burning through as much as possible.

"Maybe you are." Inhaling the cold, he coughed into his hands. There was a sharp pain in his chest.

"Are you sick?" asked the old one.

"Something like that."

"What's wrong with you? You got sick trying to find that Aki girl weren't you?"

"How did you know about that?" Paavo asked.

"People throw away newspapers every day. They make great blankets, as well as good reading materials. You're the one the Police are looking for. That's why you were gone so long."

"I don't give a damn about the cops anymore, or people for that matter. If you aren't able to help them, they spit on you. It doesn't even matter that I tried, and damn near got killed trying to do so. Every time I step out into this weather, I could die." Paavo spat out.

"So, you want someone to thank you for your sacrifice?" asked the old one.

"Not anymore, they wouldn't give it out, even if it was deserved."

"You think you deserve thanks for what you are doing? Not finding the lost girl fast enough?"

"I don't know what I deserve," said Paavo. The old one moved another piece.

"Do you believe you deserve thanks?" Paavo looked back into the darkness and spoke.

"No."

"Then why expect the same kind of good in others?"

"I don't know, I thought there was some kind of justice in this city. No one cares about respect, about civility anymore. It makes me sick."

"People don't change with the times, kid. I have been around long enough to know. Hearts are dark, the city only magnifies it," said the old one.

"I don't deserve thanks, but no one is grateful for anything they have. They take it all for granted. What are possessions if not something to show off? What's the difference between confidence and ego?" Paavo asked.

"There is no difference, son. I gave up on thinking people had good in them a long time ago. You looked like you've been wronged too many times. Maybe you should do the same, before you end up like me."

"The ones I care about gave up on trying to change what's around them, or doing their part to stop the innocent from getting killed. A word like that doesn't even exist in these times. The father of a missing child spit in my face when we were unable to find him," said Paavo.

"No excuse for that, kid."

"How can I continue wanting to help you if you spit in my face? If you don't want my help, don't beg and plead, and cry for mine."

Paavo had been moving pieces frantically, lost in thought. He did not realize that he had trapped his own king behind a line of pawns. The old one waited for him to finish venting his frustrations before attacking.

"Checkmate," he said.

Paavo did not care that he lost again and simply got to his feet.

"This is my last case. I find out what happened to the little girl, and then I am retired from this shit for good."

"You're a good man. You don't deserve to be spit on. You do what you have to," said the old one.

"I spent two years trying to find them. No clues, no signs, nothing but angry eyes, condemning words, and blame."

"They're foolish to blame you for something out of your

control."

"Sad thing is, they won't even realize it. They're too stupid to recognize their own ignorance, even in the face of death," said Paavo.

"You sound like me, a long time ago. Why would you want to protect people like that? Because they've done nothing wrong in the eyes of the Police? Or the corrupt courts?"

"I don't want to protect them. We're all on our own, and we can choose to not give a damn about each other the same," said Paavo. He bowed his head in thanks.

"You're welcome. Continue on your refusal to take part in the journey, until next time," the old one said as they continued to set up his pieces for another game.

Long walked into the reception area, colors of bright red and brown attacked his eyes. A young lady was seated at the desk. She greeted him kindly. He had been there enough times to remember his name. The waiting room was quiet and unpleasant. Painted walls and curtains heavy with starch gave the office the style of an old mansion. The television displayed an old black and white cartoon with the sound off. No magazines of any kind, just a small row of chairs lined across the wall. He covered his eyes to escape the blinding sunlight of the outside until his name was called. Day seven of therapy, seven days without work and still no contact with Paavo. The wife was proud of him for doing this, but it made him feel ill. Long counted images of the dead men.

The cell phone in his hand began to vibrate. When opened, pictures of the house taken from a distance, flashed across the screen. The pictures zoomed in to reveal Kyoko though the window, staring into the snow, oblivious to who was watching her.

He saved the message, hands tightening with both fear and

seething anger. The bounty hunter stepped forward, her message clear. The words capped the photos, concise and haunting.

"We are still here."

Long exchanged nervous glances with the young receptionist. They smiled at each other briefly before the door opened and he entered the room. A subdued voice greeted him; the therapist, Sakura, was almost too polite.

"Hello, Derek. Come on in, have some coffee." Long stood quietly before speaking.

"No, I'm alright."

"Listen, I know you came here against your will, but talking to someone can only help."

Long took a breath in and sat down on the blood red couch. Sakura took a seat and produced a pair of eyeglasses, he folded his hand together.

"Let's begin with the visions today," said Doc. Long rolled his eyes.

"I'm not crazy, you know."

"Where do you think they come from?" Doc cut right to the chase.

"I see the faces of men I've killed, but they're all kids caught up in crime, no life outside of stealing, of drugs and murder," said Long.

"You try to envision their circumstances."

"These kids today are all the same, born into those kinds of situations, no real escape."

"But you couldn't possibly know their lives, the choices they made. Did you know them personally?" asked Doc.

"Not one."

"Then you don't know them. Anything that has happened to them to make them want to pick up a gun and choose to steal and murder is something we will never know. That is, in a sense, a romantic idea. That the youth of the city is being corrupted by some kind of unseen evil."

"Romantic?"

"You're an idealist, Long. You tend to place things under ideas of a grander scheme, a much bigger picture."

"The notion that young people aren't corrupted and led into gangs is a stretch, that's stupid. Of course they can, and they are. They're buying drugs and eating raw meat on the streets. You can't sway me. Those are the people that worry me, where is their guidance? Their help?"

"That may be something that drives these visions. You've harvested extreme guilt over what has happened in your career," said Doc.

"It is guilt, it has to be. No one should ever be killed for something they were forced into. Just like those boys at the hotel."

"That's why you are here, Derek. The shootout at the hotel, you rushed in on your own, leaving three officers outside. You killed four men, smashed another's face in."

"And you want me to not feel guilty about that?" asked Long.

"You were doing your job, in a sense, the problem lies in that you made yourself accountable for everything that took place. Not your team, which you left behind watching the building in case some of the men tried to flee the scene."

"They're dumb as hell and wouldn't have known how to handle it. They would have made mistakes, maybe even gotten themselves killed."

"It was a noble thing to do, but everyone in the Police department knows the risk of their career, it's something that they choose to do. Why do you burden only yourself with the consequences?" asked Doc.

"Would you prefer a crying mother over a haunted old man?" Long looked into Sakura's eyes for the first time.

"No one forced those boys in the hotel to put a gun in their hands and pull the trigger at you, and the little girl."

"It doesn't matter, someone has to suffer. Let it be me," said Long.

"You can't think about things this way."

"There's enough innocent blood because of me, no one else will go through that again."

"You've been coming here for a week. We still haven't gotten to the root of the problem," said Doc.

"That's all you talk about is the root of the problem. There is no root cause. Just death. Nothing but death all around me. It follows me. It's beginning to follow others that I care about," said Long, getting to his feet.

"That's why you're here. You have to bring this to light. Sit, please."

"I hear voices sometimes. They speak to me, I turn my head and there is no one there," Long admitted.

"Someone you know?"

"One of the cadets, Kino. Many years ago, he was killed during a raid. It was badly planned and turned into a hostage situation. The men we were after were pinned down behind a building. They had been firing wildly into the open air from the alleyway. Random people across the street were running out into the streets. Some were shot through their walls and open windows. It was chaos. I wasn't watching over him and he stepped into the line of fire."

"I'm sorry," said Doc.

"No need to apologize for his mistake, for my mistake."

"Is he the one that talks to you?"

"He asks me questions, as if he were standing there with me, looking down on another dead body, another pool of blood."

"Your previous case was very bizarre. I can only imagine the mental toll it's taking."

"Paavo is starting to see ghosts as well," said Long.

"Who is that? Is he your son?"

"No, he's just a kid. I used to take care of him a long time ago, kind of a victim of the streets in his own right."

"What does he do?" asked Doc.

"He's a detective, even though he's really young, he's really accomplished in terms of forensic study. He's the best in the city, very quiet and weird, to himself, you know."

"I'd like to meet him."

"You won't, so don't worry about it. He's been hiding for some time working on a big case." Long chose his words carefully, trying not to reveal too much about Paavo.

"We met up and compared notes on our own things, next thing I know he's shot up in the hospital. He told me that a little girl shot him, the same little girl that showed up dead at my crime scene." Sakura took down more words to his pad.

"I think he's inherited this problem of mine. I'm worried about him."

Sakura interrupted him.

"You said that he was a victim of the streets?"

"Yeah, he grew up without parents, just an old blind woman to look after him, as ironic as that sounds, he's always been alone," said Long.

"Do you think Paavo will turn into one of these lost causes you speak of? No choice but to turn to crime?" asked Doc.

"No, he knows how to take care of himself; he's survived this long without committing any crimes."

"That's good."

"He's safe, but I don't want him to be haunted by things he's done, like I am."

"Has he ever killed anyone?" asked Doc.

"I don't know," said Long.

"You trained him?"

The sunlight began to burn through the curtains. Long took a moment, then smiled and nodded in agreement.

"He's like a son to me." He lost himself inside images of Paavo playing with the same sword which sat behind the wall in his house. He remembered standing back, watching him, giving advice on his movements.

"I have so much respect for him."

Sakura took more notes.

"Why?" asked Doc.

"He's dying. He's still out there right now, fighting for people he has never even met, risking his life for complete strangers."

"What's wrong with him?"

"It's a heart condition. Really bizarre form of disease, it makes him damn near unable to go outside in weather like this," said Long.

"You admire his strength?"

"The fact that he does what he does, fighting off this sickness, trying to help people that don't even give a shit about him."

"Do people treat him badly?" asked Doc.

"The cops in my precinct started taunting him. He looked straight ahead, no emotion. I could never do what he does. The strength it takes to carry his body through all those situations is insane."

"Do you consider yourself weak?"

"My wife doesn't recognize me anymore," said Long.

"She does, but she wants you to recover. The goal of these sessions was to have you open up, let go of pent up feelings and thoughts, release them so you can get back to work and family."

"What do you want me to do?" Long asked.

"You're doing it now. Just talk and keep talking about all the things that haunt you. These visions that manifest are not permanent."

"I still don't know how to move forward."

"How you move forward is all up to you. This is your last day with me, Derek. This was a place for you to vent, the one thing that you talk about, more than anything else, is death. You are obsessed with it. A man of your stature, of your wisdom should think of training the young men of the city to take your place," said Doc.

"Retirement," muttered Long.

"You should think about yourself, Kyoko, your lives together."

"You can say what you want. She will feel at ease about me, but I know I am going to hell."

The room was silent as Sakura made notes on his pad of paper. Long moved towards the window and he opened the blinds to see the snow. Long had never doubted Paavo's words. The case was closed, but the young man's delirious words had troubled him. Part of him wondered if he had somehow passed on the cursed thoughts onto the kid.

Club Angelfire was closed though a group of people were standing outside with four hours to go. The neon sign draped across the side of the building. Paavo walked around the line and stared downwards to avoid their eyes. If he didn't know Angel personally, there would be no way for him to get into the place. He hoped that he would remember him; two years is a long time in the city. Paavo placed his hands in his jacket pockets. He kept his gun hidden as he stepped inside. The lobby lights were turned off, making it look closed down. The walls were painted different combinations of white, black and red. The large doors at the end of the hall were painted a dark purple.

Paavo waited in the corner of the lobby. Those out in the snow complained and pointed at him through the windows. Two guards in black stepped out from a side door at the end of the hall, followed by Angel himself. Paavo tried to get a good look at him and caught a small glimpse of his face. He made his move. The guards stopped him immediately. Both were gigantic men. Their frames eclipsed Angel all together.

"Hello? Asshole? We're closed." said the big man on the left.

"I'm looking for Angel, I'd like to speak with him. Or her." Paavo deadpanned.

"Are you on the list? You have to wait outside until doors are open."

"I'm not trying to get into the club. I'm an old friend."

"Who the hell are you?" asked the big man on the right.

"I see him behind you there. Maybe if he steps out so he could hear me a little better, he would know that this is Paavo."

A tall figure stepped out from the shadow of the guards. It

was him.

"Paavo Harker? What are you doing here?"

Angel's sense of fashion had evolved from outlandish to alien. He was wearing a thin black suit with silver inlays and a purple bowtie. A large pink feathered boa wrapped around his neck and a line of black makeup was painted over his eyes and from ear to ear. He wasn't wearing any shoes, Paavo looked down to see Halloween socks, complete with pumpkins, ghosts and black cats.

"Do you have a few minutes to discuss business?"

"That's all? After two years?"

"Can we talk? Yes or no?" asked Paavo, slowly being surrounded by the guards.

Angel was impressed and offended. She curved her body like a snake.

"Where did you learn how to talk like that? Of course I have time to talk business with you. But you have to ask me nicely...So?"

Paavo looked down. He knew it was only another game to play.

"Please..."

Angel smiled and moved through the guards. She put lips only inches away from his ear and whispered to him.

"Only because you said please."

She extended his tongue and licked the outline of Paavo's ear in a quick motion. Paavo tried to keep his face straight. Angel quickly turned around and threw her arms into the air, to make an announcement.

"Listen up! This lovely gentleman here is named Paavo. Learn his name, remember it well. He is always welcome here, in this club at any time for whatever he needs!"

Angel extended his hand to Paavo.

"This way, we'll talk your business in a more luxurious setting."

Paavo nodded and followed her. The guards let the others inside. Angel strutted to the purple doors and threw them open to reveal the main room. Multi colored strobe lights traveled to and from the outer reaches of the room, The bar at the end of the room was lit up with white lights put inside black painted glass. The bartender, a beautiful woman with jet black hair, was surrounded by dozens of bottles of alcohol. Each of the tables were dotted with ornate candles with melted down wax that coated most of the surface, each one was lit with it's own fire.

"We've done some redecorating; the best drinks, the best men and women available, and the best tech," said Angel.

The dance floor was filled up immediately. The floor was almost made entirely of lights, groups of squares sectioned off and separated, making hundreds of colored patterns.

"You know how well we move in the darkness, Paavo. So, in a way, you could say this design was inspired by your sensibilities. People moving and dancing in the shadows being unable to really see anything; very mysterious, very sexy."

Angel walked with Paavo to one of the tables at the far end of the room. Paavo turned and couldn't help but notice the group of both women and men standing off to the side were stark naked except for carefully placed pieces of tape. Angel pulled out a chair for him then went towards the bar. She returned with two colored drinks in hand and offered one filled with blue liquid to Paavo.

"Blueberry whiskey." she said as she placed a red straw into his crimson red martini glass, Paavo took a drink and grimaced at the amount of alcohol, still undiluted by the sweet blue drink.

"It's been a long time. Where have you been, kid?"

"I was dead for a while," said Paavo.

"That sounds awful."

"It is, but I wanted to ask you some questions."

"You want to know if I'm currently available and or lonely? The answer is yes."

"No," said Paavo.

"Business as usual. No fun at all, Paavo. How will I ever get you to break out of that shell?" asked Angel.

"Tell me what I want to know."

"If you ever decide to get into the whole dating thing, that is. Either way, in courting and questioning form, I'm all yours."

"I'm sure you still keep up on current events these days."

"I try my best. My time is both short and expensive," said Angel.

"There's word of some new members of your little club, some new blood that's been coming out, dealing in the streets."

Angel laughed suddenly then licked her bottom lip.

"Where did they come from?" asked Paavo.

"I wish I knew, but they've been the talk of the people in my little circle, as you say. It's not just a circle, Paavo, it's a family! An empire! The debutantes, the whores both wealthy and not so much have been asking about it non-stop. I don't know where they came from. So tell me, how did you find out about it this quick?"

Paavo opened the blinds to view the snow outside.

"I still have some connections with the Police department," he said.

"You're such a traitor."

"They were listening in on a deal being made down at the

docks. A shipment was brought in, supposedly drugs, actually household chemicals."

"Sounds like bad intel, the great detectives that they are. You help them too much. You're great at your job," said Angel.

"Thank you."

"Someone's got to give you credit, and they sure as hell didn't."

"The dealers slowly went crazy; started kidnapping people, killing them, selling raw meat to the homeless people by the church."

"I heard about that. It's tragic. That's why this club exists, to escape from such harsh realities and horrors," said Angel.

"There's something that points to this being more than just sick people selling rotted meat to the homeless lying around the city. Maybe an unknown substance in the bloodstream?" asked Paavo.

"I dropped out of high school, love. The science thing is your deal, isn't it?"

"Maybe they were selling whatever it is to people in the streets, which means that it's got to be spreading throughout the city."

"Very astute of you," said Angel. Paavo leaned forward.

"You're telling me you don't know anything? Where did these guys come from?"

"I can't tell you exactly, I honestly don't know. I heard some from Japan, some from America," said Angel.

"What about the dealers? Some of them are dead, some in jail, there's got to be more of them."

"You seem like you really want to find these guys. What would you like me to do?"

"Anything about them; names, locations," said Paavo.

"Are you in a hurry? You're fidgeting. Stick around, make yourself at home. I can be a great housewife. My place is right upstairs. I'll make some calls. We'll hook you up today, I promise. There's going to be some gentlemen coming down to visit in a few days. Business, as you put it."

"Are you still doing deals in the club?" Paavo asked.

"Yes, I'm still totally doing illegal drug deals in my place of business. Are you going to spank me? I provide them with a safe place to conduct themselves, for a sizable percentage for my loyal servants and myself."

Paavo took a small taste from his drink; the alcohol sat behind a wall of melted ice and food coloring. He swished the liquid around his mouth. The idea that Angel would drug him had never left his mind.

"Quite an arrangement you've got."

Angel leaned back and smiled.

"Thank you, a girl has got to take care of herself," she said. Paavo continued to the taste from the glass, Angel watched him.

"I need to show you how to drink one of these days. At the rate you're going, we'll be here all night. We move at a quick pace here."

"I suppose I should leave, no? In case some of your gentlemen enter," said Paavo.

"They won't be here this evening. You're safe to frolic." Around the club, the people on the dance floor were moving to the music at a blinding pace.

"This drug is hurting people, Angel. All of them went crazy and began to destroy whatever or whoever is around them."

"You really want to help those people out, don't you?" she

asked.

"What's there left to save out here?"

"You continue to impress me, Paavo. Anything that comes my way, you will know."

"Thanks, I'll take a rain check on the nightcap as well," said Paavo.

"Of course, but you don't know what you're missing. I'll show you the way out. I just hope you'll stay in contact this time? I worry about you; a cute boy playing the lonely outsider. I've never seen you even look at a woman. You make me want to cry, sometimes."

"It's been a long enough time apart from stranger minds," said Paavo.

"I'm glad you decided to visit. I've missed you."

Paavo nodded as house music began to play from the speakers. The sound men were setting up for a new DJ. Loud horns, bass and drums that filled the club. Angel began to dance. The lights started to move in sync with the music that flashed across the walls in splintered patterns as Angel jumped onto the table, kicking the drinks onto the floor, Paavo looked down to see the glass shatter and glide across the tiles. The time for regretting the decision to stay was past now. She was going to look into the substance for him, or at least provide some information about whoever was left in the city connected to the case.

Paavo's eyes moved around the room. A heartless move to make them wait so long. There's something about her he couldn't trust just yet. Even as she was dancing on the table in front of him, pulling on his hair. Paavo sat still. He looked up and their eyes met for a brief moment.

"I'm not going to dance," he deadpanned.

CHAPTER TWENTY ONE

A game of chess was needed. The old one's challenge was calling out to be taken. The trees and gardens were slowly being buried beneath white. There were no children. The cold was too intense. He held his breath and exhaled between nervous steps towards the courtyard. The view of the park was obscured by the reflection of sunlight from the piles of snow. Paavo had to hold his arm over his eyes to dull the pain in the back of his head from staring into the light. He tried to remember the path he had taken before. The stone steps remained the same. His feet followed until he reached the top. Sweat drenched his neck and hands. The courtyard was still visible, as if someone had swept the snow away. Stone benches and tables still lined in a row. Four piles of snow had been neatly pushed to separate corners of the area. At the end of the row sat the old one, covered in the same blanket and shawl. The board sat on the table, already in place. Pieces were scattered across the landscape. Paavo placed his hands back into his pockets and approached. The old one did not look up when he stepped towards the seat facing him.

"Are you ready to play, young man? I thought you would have forgotten about me."

"I need a worthy opponent."

Paavo had not played regularly in years. After losing so many games, it was obvious. Paavo sat down on the stone before them. It was cold and damp from melted snow. He winced as he moved around to find a comfortable spot. The old one's hands had already descended upon the pieces. They fell to the board, each one making a loud, cracking sound. He watched him re- arrange each piece into place. Paavo sat in silence and waited until it was time to begin.

The old one motioned for him to move first. Paavo tried to look into the shadows beneath the hood.

"You are black?"

They turned the board around so that the white pieces faced Paavo.

"It becomes me well," said the old one.

Paavo took a moment to study the pieces and their possible movements on the board. There was only one defense that he could remember from his early days of school. It was called the Sicilian Defense. It had been first studied in 1594 by Roman and Italian scholars as the easiest way to anticipate every attack while being wary of your opponent's strength. He replayed the old lessons in his mind before making his move. Pawn to c5. The white knight f3. Paavo moved his pawn to d6.

"What made you come back here?" asked the old one, intrigued.

"I wanted to test my wits."

"You thought that you could best me."

"Staying sharp," said Paavo.

The old one made a sudden move, trading queens right away. The game carried on for a good length of time. With both queens gone, there was no position of power. No dominant piece to dictate the pace of the game. It was all a matter of placement and attack on the board. He would have to find a way to move through his defenses to trap the king. Paavo took time in between moves to study the ground. He looked around, staring into the cracks between the stone. The rows of tables and benches had been battered with time. Some of them looked as if they were ready to crumble to nothing. Dead leaves, dirt and melted snow were tucked between each fissure. The old one was silent for most of the game. Paavo did not speak, focusing rather on the game itself. He needed to clear his head of the case, of Long's constant reaching out. The old one forked two pieces of his with a well placed knight.

"Are you always this afraid to talk?"

"Not afraid, I prefer to stay silent and watch," said Paavo. He moved his bishop several spaces back.

"The trees, the dying grass, the snow, the dead flowers, all of these things are alive and listening to us," the old one said as their knight took the pawn left behind.

"Let them listen to nothing," said Paavo. He kept his eyes on the pieces. He was trapped between both knights. He would end up having to sacrifice a piece to escape checkmate.

"Tell me, what are you thinking about? Perhaps I can help."

"I'm stuck on a puzzle," said Paavo.

"Tell me."

"For anyone who is alone, without God and without a master, the weight of days is dreadful."

"That's Camus; philosopher and author."

"I've never read him. What does it mean?" Paavo asked.

"He says that without a master, a man is left alone to his own devices. This creates fear, and dread for what his next move will be. Not just his next move, but what he will do from that day forward. From the day he revokes the need for a master to the days he carries himself on his own two feet, until his own death."

The old one moved their bishop to the middle of the board, trapping the king to the piece behind him. A rook stood in the way of escape, with nowhere to go for the piece, he had no choice but to accept defeat.

"Checkmate, son."

"Very well."

"That is something that we all have to do eventually, Paavo; shed the weight of expectation, of belief. Only then can we truly do what we are meant to do. Without fear or dread of the supposed next life, we are free to move as we may," said the old one.

Paavo nodded in agreement.

"Does that help you solve your puzzle?"

"Part of it."

Paavo rose to his feet. The old one had begun to assemble the pieces for another game. He did not want to play again. Unsure of what to do next, he simply bowed to the figure and turned towards the stairs leading back to the park.

"Will you come back?" the old one called out.

"Am I invited?" he asked.

"You will know where to find me."

Paavo began the descent back to the rest of the world.

Long took the scenic route back to work. His time in therapy was complete. Doc Sakura had let him get back to work on a provisional basis. They would be monitoring him. He would have to check into the station; find out what the hell they had planned for him.

The drive in was hell as usual. Familiar faces recognized him, they waved their hands, asked him where he'd been. Long was more than happy to pull out the court order to show off. Those who asked moved to the side with wide eyebrows. His desk was untouched. As he turned the knob, he realized that the door was locked. The blinds of his window were left open for a view of his office. Some of the cadets walked by, snickering at him. He did not respond and only looked down towards the folder of evidence sitting on top of the pile of papers.

"Did you forget what I told you?" It was Masonori. His voice came up from behind him.

"You have been relieved of your duties. I'm running this station's day to day now, as well as all cases."

"What does that mean for me, then?" asked Long.

"That means that this office is locked. You need to go home and spend time with your wife."

Long turned back around towards the chief.

"How can I when there is so much left to do?" asked Long. Masonori laughed but Long's expression was stone.

"You leave all this to me. I'll handle it. We will find those people, or at least figure out what the hell happened to them."

"Sir, that woman is after me, after Kyoko. There's been messages to my phone and envelopes left at our doorstep."

"We realize how serious the situation is with Lia Jones. That is why you need a break. An overdue, more than extended goddamn break. Sit at home and be with Kyoko."

"Do you have extra detail on the house?" asked Long.

"A couple more than the ones you set up yourself without clearing it with me. I know what you are trying to do. But be upfront. We will protect you, Derek."

Long looked to the floor.

"I feel so helpless."

"Take off, man; find your car, head home."

He handed Long a padlock.

"I made sure to lock up your belongings. Your files on the case are with me. Some of the boys like to play games with whoever leaves their locker unopened."

Long's stoic expression changed. A tinge of anger appeared.

"Just like the crazy bitch who is toying with my family?! How long is this going to last?"

A smirk stretched across the chief's face.

"As long as it takes for you to rest and rebuild yourself," he said.

The former Inspector took the lock and headed downstairs.

Nyalla had arrived slightly later than usual to work. The crowds were fierce. She fought through walls of people that seemed to do nothing but stand around and block fresh air from getting in. William was there; he sat somewhat drowsy and unaware of his surroundings. His clothes were tattered and wrinkled. She approached with a smile, her teeth shining white between the crimson red of her lips.

"Hey, Willie. Where were you yesterday?" Hiraga was near sleep. She called out to him, he finally responded.

"Yeah, I'm here." His manner changed once he caught a full glimpse of the beautiful woman in front of him.

"Rice, how are you? I was really busy yesterday. Crazy things going on these days."

She grabbed the ends of her blue dress and took a seat.

"Like what? More conspiracy theories?"

She knew that the type of people he hung around with, they were geeks and computer nerds. Good people, but a little off center. When he tried to court her, he invited her to join him on an evening with his friends. She remembered sitting there reading a book to the soundtrack of them arguing back and forth about the JFK assassination.

"You don't have to believe me. There will be proof soon enough," he said. She removed her denim jacket and scarf.

"You've spent enough time trying to convince me Caine is the devil."

"This is different though, something really bizarre is happening."

"Do tell," she said.

"Have you heard about people protesting the Police department? There are dozens of families popping up saying how their relatives had vanished and that the cops are paying them to keep quiet until they find out what happened to the missing people."

Nyalla laughed it off.

"Willie, that doesn't make any sense. Why would the cops pay them to keep them quiet? Their job is to find missing people."

Hiraga bent down and lowered his voice.

"You're right, so why are there over hundred people with signs posted out in front of the station right now?"

She looked at him strangely. Was he serious? The computer screen behind him changed with the press of a button. Angry faces with painted signs of black and red replaced the bland text of shipping data.

"There is something behind it. I think the cops may be involved with the abductions," he said.

"No missing people have been reported in the news, besides that girl."

"Those families, each one had a picture of their missing sibling, son or daughter. Now, news reports have come out, saying that their names and pictures aren't a part of the city's database. They were saying that those people didn't exist!"

"Police are denying the existence of actual people?" she asked.

"Not just one or two, forty nine! Does this not freak you out?"

Nyalla put up her hands.

"Yes, but what can we do about it?" Hiraga raised his finger and went to his desk.

"Do you remember where I live?"

"Yes, why?" she hesitated to ask.

"I have to get going. I know Charles wants to see me. If he wants me to get his work done, tell him where to drop it off."

"Where are you going?"

William got to his feet and put on his coat.

"See you around, Rice."

He turned the corner and made his way through the crowd for the elevator. She sat in silence, wondering what was happening inside his mind. His job was in jeopardy as it was, but he didn't even care. Where was he going? How did he get those pictures? The news had posted nothing about these protests. Did this come from his so-called friends? Thieves and hackers? She finally turned back to her desk and started her computer.

Besides the blazing eyes and gunfire of the priest, the words from the church were all Paavo could think about. They were painted in red letters across a stone wall. The apartment was filled with pictures taken from the church before the explosion. Paavo spent several waking nights searching for clues to the meaning behind the words.

He took on odd jobs for the money; housewives suspecting their husbands of cheating on them, nervous husbands checking on their footloose wives. Naoko Aki had damaged his reputation, whatever small niche of respect, now gone and replaced with even more strange looks and snickers from onlookers. He looked to the streets when he walked. In time, their insults changed into the bleating of sheep. There were days when he had shot back. They returned with more noise, that's all they ever do. They were nothing but sheep and never shut their mouth for a second. There was no time for air, only the constant chatter of bullshit tossed towards the same quiet kid he still was. Nothing had changed since those times.

Early morning light poked through black curtains covering the windows. There were noises coming from the machines sitting on the table, lights spinning wildly. Pieces of the paint chiseled off the wall were collected and now being analyzed. Paavo's eyes remained on the computer screen searching for reports about any vandalism containing Camus' words. Paavo was unfamiliar with his writing. The phrase had spoken to him. The paint used in the church was more than a few weeks old. There was more than one shade of red in its mixture. It's colors could still be purchased somewhere in town. He printed a list of places in town to go and inquire about Gordon Wen and the last places had visited before his end.

The church which housed Lia had closed down. No paint or graffiti of any kind found its way across the walls. She was in his dreams; seductive, violent and sick. His heart still ached with hatred as he dreamt of her fingers twisted into his open wound. The anger, the embarrassment and the pain tore him apart inside. He wanted to find her. But what then?

Angel had provided him with a connection to a list of less than reputable characters; it meant access to more information on what was taking place underneath the eyes of the law. He had asked around about the woman in red. Lia may have been only an alias, another proxy name. Her brother Clayton was caught dealing and put into community service as part of his probation. According to Angel, she ran a group called the Red Sun. It consisted of bounty hunters, hackers and assassins for hire. They were known for high profile kidnappings and ransoms. The hunters operated outside of the rules. Once a target was captured, they would demand twice the ransom or they would kill their prisoner. The Red Sun were notorious outlaws outside of Perdition. The cops had no clue who their leader was, but somehow they let one of the deadliest women in the world loose in the city.

The analysis from the machine had completed. No fingerprints, but something was strange about the sample. He took another look at the analysis. Unknown elements were in the mixture. Was there a malfunction in the machine? The device was designed to search for fingerprints in the substance. It was giving him an error.

The settings were correct, it was in the substance. Frustrated, he stood up and ripped the black curtain from the wall, bringing brilliant white light into the darkness of the room. Reviewing the settings, he recalibrated and ran the machine on each setting. Paavo sat with pencil and paper, taking notes, searching for an issue with the hardware of the machine. Error after error went off. He tossed his paper to the side and turned the dials with precision. After over an hour, the machine finally displayed its customary green light of completion. The mistake was not in the machine, but the liquid. It was not just paint, but a mixture of ammonia and blood. Human blood. Paavo recorded the results into his computer.

What the hell was going on down there? He was shocked. The dedication of the priest had truly known no bounds. As if the poisoning of those people weren't enough, he needed their blood to paint his message for the world to see. The ammonia was lighter than the other mixtures. The machine across the table was able to identify the source of the blood; Nobu Sadao, a man reported dead only a few days ago. He found the name within the city's obituaries in a matter of minutes. He was a city worker.

The last job noted was as night watchman at Nakagaki Towers for Allied Arrows. There was a chance that his body would be on ice, not yet submitted to the autopsy table. Paavo grabbed his phone and sent a message to Long's associate. He needed to look for a body before it was opened up and drained by the coroner. Word had gotten about Miss Aki and her missing child. Paavo was starting to lose his patience since the disappearance of his small reputation among the common people. Most office calls held not potential customers, but people with nothing but time on their hands. They called Paavo a bastard, a freak, someone who does nothing but dashes hopes and wastes the time of needy people. Prank calls had started. Kids giggling, followed by cursing until a dial tone. He never hung up on any of them. Part of him still felt guilty, that he needed to hear the insults. It was the only thing left that he could do after failing to find Naoko Aki, let alone save her from dealers working for a crazed priest. By the time he had found her, she had changed into something else. She was lost, without a mind just like the people in the hospital, and those on the street, even Clayton Jones. Something sinister stirred a madness that had taken them.

The punishment would do him good, he thought. Without warning, a rush of anger would fill his heart when the laughing had stopped. What the hell did they know? No one knew him. None of these little bastards know a thing about me. Why say anything? What good could they do given the same situation? It was all so absurd, the opinions of common people. He remembered the old woman, beating her hands onto his chest. She had spit into his eyes. Paavo let it run down his face, until it had fallen to the ground. How much hate was in it then? Would it bring back your daughter? The answer was no. Nothing you could do would change what happened. Paavo would find the young girl because she needed to be found. They were as helpless as the ones missing.

A wave of intense sadness hit him. Why do I hate them? He could not find another answer but the most obvious. They were careless, and they were lazy. It seemed that the love and virtues of the city were slipping away, replaced with foolish townsfolk from the dark ages, all burning torches and naysaying. The more he thought of Perdition, his mind drifted further away from the way he felt when stepping out on his own, trying to embrace that personal freedom away from his mentor. His thoughts fell deeper into a spiral of anger, and of regret for spending so much time on their petty paranoias and thankless actions. They were nothing but fools. A message was received from the lab. Results from the database had come up empty on the name provided. Paavo had asked him to keep things quiet for now. He took a moment to step away from the computer. The cell phone began to vibrate, showing a new message from Angel. When opened, Paavo learned that there was a man asking for him at the club. He wanted permission to give him this number. Paavo replied, agreeing to speak to the man.

"Do you know anyone at the coroner's office?"

"Why? Did you kill someone?" she asked.

"Sure. Do you have someone or not?"

"Yeah, he's an oddball, even for my standards. A beautiful creature obsessed with death," said Angel.

"Ask him to find Nobu Sadao."

He sent the information along. After a moment, he deleted the subsequent message from Angel, nothing but a smiling face. There were X's, O's and hearts. Within minutes the man called him. Paavo answered.

"Hello."

Music was loud and booming. Angelfire did not ever stop.

"This is Paavo? Okay, good. I am glad he got a hold of you, I need some help. You've got to help me, man."

The man spoke with rattled nerves. Perhaps too many drugs, as he seemed to over exhale after each word.

"And your name?"

"I work for a company called Allied Arrows."

"With all due respect, I don't work for people without knowing who they are," said Paavo.

"Look man, don't ask so many questions." He sounded

fearful.

"Angel can vouch for my loyalty to the club. Just for this call, I want to remain anonymous, or whatever."

Angel's voice interrupted in the background, barely audible over the drum and bass.

" He's legit, Paavo." It was enough for now.

"How can I be of service?"

"Allied Arrows is a major security company in the city. We do electric work all across town. The Outlook, any downtown nightclub, the Kirilov building, pretty high profile."

"Congratulations," said Paavo.

"We've been having a lot of problems keeping work, keeping clients. There's been a hacker who's been toying with the security systems."

"Security systems?" Paavo asked.

"We got a smaller operation to handle a lot of wiring. You know, security doors, climate control, etc."

"So your tech people have been overwhelmed?"

"It's really fucking us up. A lot of guys were let go," said the man.

"How do you know it's one person?"

"I don't know if it really is, but it needs to be stopped. Hopefully you can help us out with this, man. Please."

"Why would you ask me to do this?" asked Paavo.

"Well, to be honest, you weren't my first choice. I heard that you were kind of crazy. Your name is all over the papers, which is exactly why I wanted someone else more low key. Angel wanted me to call you. You were recommended by him. He says that you have..." Angel's voice cut him off.

"A distinct knowledge on hacking and tracing others in that profession as well as plenty of experience dealing with what one could consider the scum of the city."

Paavo replied without emotion.

"Flattering."

He could hear Angel screaming from a distance towards the phone.

"You're welcome!"

"I mean, it all depends, you know. All this shit with your name in the papers and the missing girl, might make things harder to do your job. But I can make it worth your while. We didn't find a bank account number with your name, though. If you want to help, how would you like to be paid?"

Paavo thought about it for a moment.

"There was an account number where you could place the money. I no longer have it." A silence poured out from the end of the phone.

"Not a problem, we can pay in cash," the man said finally. Furious clicking could be heard. A flash of faded red in the corner of his phone caught his eye.

"Let me know if this is enough, alright? I mean, I got more, but not that much more. Shit is hard nowadays."

Paavo got another text. He was offered two thousand dollars. He was not used to jobs like this.

It seemed people were now throwing money at him. How desperate could they be? He had decided to use the money from the bank job for his equipment and whatever needed to be fixed up. He stopped for a moment. A few days ago, his money would have gone directly to his grandmother. The latest savings in her account were almost made up entirely of his paychecks from the desk job at the

Police station and other odd jobs he picked up being a P.I.

"So, I hope that this is enough cause, I'm broke after this," the man was not so confident that Paavo would agree.

"Angel! You have to give me a dose after this, man. You owe me."

"Here's the deal...Take half of that money and keep it. Don't worry about offering me any more. I'm in," said Paavo.

Angel's client was overjoyed.

"This is good news, man. This is fucking great news. When can you begin?"

"Right now," said Paavo.

"You're my savior."

"No, I'm not. Have you got any other information for me?"

"Nothing. Thanks for all your help, Paavo. You're a good man. Don't worry about that old woman. And try not to vanish, alright?"

He froze for a moment, thinking of the old woman in question, her daughter wandering off into the snow.

"Will do." Paavo's voice trailed off. He moved towards the window and began to stare out into the light. The sun and snow were blinding. How long will this winter storm last? The phone rang again. Angel had called right back.

"You were great back there," she said.

"Thanks."

The club was dark. Angel slipped her feet in and out of velvet slippers. Her body propped up on the bar. The windows were barricaded to keep the sun out.

"Was he one of your customers?" asked Paavo.

"That and more, don't you begin to make judgments. I got

you some more work. And money, even!"

"How did he know about the old woman?" asked Paavo.

"No patient-doctor confidentiality with me. What can I say? Your skeletons are all laid out in the open when you go into business with me, love. It pays to be my friend."

"How do you know about the bounty hunter?" Paavo asked.

"Lia is more than a femme fatale, Paavo. She's a living legend in our circle. A nightmare for anyone within the crosshairs; like you. Care to explain how you ended up pissing her off as well as getting blown up?"

"Her brother was killed in the Police station. He went crazy during the interrogation. Shot dead right in front of her," said Paavo.

"The word is that the Red Sun are dead, and that they were killed by her, their own leader. Apparently, Jimmy the Recluse hired her to do it, using her estranged brother as bait. That's why she didn't know how he came to be an addict on the street. She was kept in the dark about this new drug and under the noose if she tried to step out on her own to find the truth."

Angel writhed on the bar.

"I love the sound of your voice, by the way. You and I had better start spending more time together now; one of the most dangerous bounty hunters alive wants you dead."

"I wasn't the one who shot him," said Paavo.

"Does it matter? Jesus, Paavo. How long have you been in hiding? Did you just wake up one day and decide to play the hero?"

"She was being strangled by her brother."

"Family is stronger than death," said Angel.

"Since when do you give a shit about what some old cop does?" Paavo asked.

"Cops never have to kill. They make the choice to kill someone, right or wrong. He's responsible for the deaths of more than a few of my friends. Someone like me doesn't make a lot of those."

Angel sighed a breath of air before sticking her chest out.

"But let's be honest, there will never be another like me."

"You're all guilty. Your friends weren't smart enough to place their mouths on the ass of the Mob's heavy hitters," said Paavo.

Angel agreed.

"Guilty or not, they didn't deserve to be gunned down."

"Those drugs made the guy insane. The people at the hospital began to lash out at the doctors. Something is connecting all of this together. She wants me to find out what, to avenge her brother."

"You're starting to lose it. This is too much for you. You need a drink. Derek Long has killed more people than any other cop on the damn force. Lia is a hunter. She does not play games with her prey. If she wants to kill you, she will. If she's lying in wait, it's not because she wants to. It's Jimmy keeping her on the short leash."

Tension began to build. Paavo could feel it in his blood.

"People in our line of work are walking the streets in fear. Who knows what she's really capable of? You had better be ready for a damn war. Jimmy made her kill her own team just to tie up loose ends and prove her dedication to find her brother," said Angel.

"I'll keep that in mind."

"You better. Don't make me worry more than I already do." Angel began to pace through the darkness of the club. She was careful not to step on the bodies of several dancers who had passed out in the midst of the fury of the night before.

"This is not like you, Paavo. You're supposed to be on top of these things. You're supposed to be on the cutting edge. You barely have a working cell phone."

"I get by with what I need," said Paavo.

"If you say so. Come on down when you get a chance, the club is just shutting down."

He looked at the clock.

"It's seven in the morning."

"Like I said, we are closing down. You can enter through the back door. No one will stop you this time, they know who you are."

Paavo hung up but heard her voice one more time.

"Be careful not to step on anyone."

CHAPTER TWENTY TWO

Recent police reports included several written statements from Allied Arrows workers. There were similarities in every account. All electricity was drained from the building in a matter of seconds. Lights would flicker off and on, creating a spectacle to those outside. There were eyewitness statements calling it beautiful. The doors would lock and unlock at random intervals, leaving those inside trapped in a game of cat and mouse. When they were done, everything would shut back down.

One of the workers had left their home number for the Police to call. Paavo decided to pick up the phone and ask her some questions. The woman was named Mary Akai. Her manner was easy to deal with; polite but uneasy to disclose information about the case. She had been an employee for the Outlook. The place had been attacked by both Jimmy the Recluse and Seven. She had asked him if he was the same detective from before. Paavo said no, but inquired about who approached her. She described him as fat with little to no hair and a strong lisp when he spoke. Fat man had stopped by unexpectedly to ask questions about the incident. Apparently looking for the same hacker, one by the name of "Snow".

His name was Smalls. The cops were on Snow's trail as well, he said. There was never enough evidence to find where he was. Another ghost in the storm, escaping at the right time. She searched her office for his business card as Paavo spent a moment searching for any leads on him using the database. He jotted the number down in his notepad and thanked her for her time. The inside man from the coroner's office sent him a message, wanting to arrange a meeting. Paavo replied wanting to know where and when. The city morgue was good enough. The man introduced himself as Mikio. If he got there before noon, he could sneak him in to take a look at the body before his shift ended. The drive into the city was uneventful. Nothing but radio chatter and reckless passing of cars.

A folded paper was placed underneath the gun in the glove box. It contained the findings from the blood analysis. Finding a place to park in the city was becoming more and more of an impossible task. On sheer luck, he was able to position himself close to the right building. He tried to dart through the spaces between thoughtless zombies behind the wheel, beeping their horns and shouting obscenities. Paavo held his breath as he stepped out of the vehicle and began to walk across the street and towards the coroner's office. Mikio sent him directions once in the building. He studied the steps through the cracked glass of the cell phone. Straight in, hard left, he had to follow a curving hallway and a flight of stairs down to a right turn. Paavo moved quickly and quietly. No one bothered him until the stairwell. The I.D card worked with no issues. Once down to the stairs, he received another message saying that the body was finished with its autopsy.

Now was the time to slip in and discuss his findings. He would have to move fast. Paavo moved through the drab green halls in haste. He tripped over his own feet and steadied himself on the wall. The slip was sudden and he found himself sucking in too much air, agitating the wound. He began to cough violently, rivulets of blood now running now his chest. Paavo punched the wall in anger, the endorphins shot through his veins, numbing the pain flowing through his body. There was a slight reprieve, and then he quickly grasped his hand.

He looked around to see if anyone had seen him do that. Regretting the punch came later on as he walked into the morgue. The room was wrapped in jade paint along the bottom half of the walls. A bright fluorescent spotlight hovered over the body. His eyes moved through the area to see gleaming metal tools, bowls of blood and a man covered in white scrubs, stained in a deep red. The body was ripped open, organs and pieces of flesh sitting to the side. Mikio greeted him with a handshake and a smile.

"You're Paavo, yes?" Without realizing, he extended his

hand that made contact with the wall, bleeding slightly.

"I am..." He stopped for a moment.

"Holy shit, are you okay?" asked Mikio. The grip of the handshake went from strong to timid in a second.

"Quiet type, eh? That's fine. Try not to bleed anywhere. I could lose my job."

He was rambling, unsure of how to break the ice with a man holding out a hand covered in blood.

"Show me what you've got. I will not keep you," said Paavo. Mikio chuckled nervously. Paavo looked pale, sickly. He began to feel ill due to the loss of blood. Sweat began to bead upon his forehead as he took in deep breaths to avoid passing out. Both men approached the body.

"Here he is. Nobu Sadao. Approximately five foot eleven. One hundred ninety five pounds."

"This can't be him," said Paavo.

"Why not?"

"The guy I'm looking for was just reported dead, this body has been decaying for at least a couple of weeks."

Mikio was quiet.

"Where is the body I'm looking for?" Paavo was becoming irritated; he did not want to be wasting his time with some punk cleaning up bodies for Angel, let alone the Mob.

"I'm telling you that this is the right one."

"How is that possible?" Paavo asked.

"This is how they brought him in. Relatively untouched."

"Anything else unusual about him?"

"Reported dead less than 48 hours ago. Angel gave us a call and told us you were looking for a body. We ran his blood earlier," said Mikio.

"You guys take care of the casualties back here?"

"Pretty much."

"So you go ahead and take out the bullets and patch up the bodies before the real hospitals get their hands on them?" asked Paavo.

"Yeah, this one was put on the backburner for a day. We've been kind of backed up lately."

Paavo looked at him strangely before focusing back on the body.

"Do you have his personal effects?"

"Yeah, right over here, behind the counter," said Mikio.

He moved towards the table and looked over the side to see a cell phone, a watch and a package. That was it, what was left behind on the ship. The name was an alias. This was Daniel Jupiter.

Paavo opened the case to reveal a small key with a sheet of paper. Scribbled on the paper were a date, time and place.

"I'm taking these," he said.

The cell phone was empty, no contacts. There was only one number in the call list, along with a picture in the memory. Another glimpse of the mountains outside of the city looked back at time, a piece of obscure art. This time a circle of figures in white hoods stood over some kind of drawing. He quickly pocketed the items.

"There's some kind of deficiency in his blood; going through the process of rigor mortis, much faster than usual," said Mikio.

"Have you already gone through the contents of the stomach?"

"We found some rotted meat. Very bizarre." Paavo put on a spare glove and prodded the organ, protruding from the open carcass.

"There was a red substance we found in the stomach lining. It was really weird; something I've never seen before."

"How?" Paavo asked.

"It melted the inside of his body. Kind of like a piece of wood being a catalyst for a fire to grow. Once the red stuff hit his system, his body just seemed to speed up rapidly, and then just shut down. The deterioration process accelerated almost double the time it takes for a body to decompose."

"How can you tell?"

"Here, watch this."

Mikio inserted a syringe into the stomach of Daniel Jupiter. Paavo watched him take a small amount of the red liquid and drop it into a plate containing gelatin. Both men stood silent for a few minutes waiting for it to react. Nothing happened.

"What are we waiting for?" Paavo asked.

"This doesn't make any sense." Mikio looked at the liquid sitting idle within the plate.

"The gelatin from the first sample was liquefied. This is just floating there, aimlessly."

"There was another sample?"

"Yeah, someone from the hospital. They were picked up during that raid a week ago," said Mikio as he looked to the liquid in the container.

"One of those people outside the shelter?" asked Paavo.

"They went ape shit, crazy. Then they collapsed in the middle of the room and spewed red out onto the floor, like a huge pool of blood."

"Can I take a dish or two for myself?"

"Sure, take them all. I don't get paid for this type of thing." Paavo grabbed several of the dishes and sealed them.

"Are you able to take out the red stuff and analyze it?"

"I figured we would show you what we found first." He produced the flask from his pocket and poured a small amount inside. Mikio began to smell the mixture inside the dish; he began to flinch in reaction to it.

"This smells really good," said Mikio.

"What did you say?"

"The red liquid, it smells like candy."

Paavo looked at him with disgust.

"Just find out what the damn thing is made of. I have to go."

Once away from Mikio, Paavo patched himself up in the front seat of the car. Pressure alone would not stop the flow. The gauze had been sitting on the floor of the passenger side. It was damp on one side, patches of dirt from the careless placement of shoes. He wrapped the tape around his shoulder, covering his heart. Phone calls to Detective Smalls went unanswered. He decided to pay him a visit in person. He worked out of a sweatbox office in the downtown district.

Paavo fell into a trance after an hour of driving. Seeing through the windshield was difficult. Fog coated the windows as heated air inside met the wind below zero outside. Was the man working for Angel in some way? Perhaps he was an assistant, given the task to leave behind cryptic messages after his work is completed. Once in reach of the man's apartment, he parked the car and made his way towards the building. The office was locked tight, windows were blacked out. Paavo stepped around the side, looking for a way in.

The morning air was raw. Thick smoke had begun to descend upon the city from the brisk rain clouds colliding with the warmth of the open sun. His figure moved through the fog like a wandering shadow. When checking the front door, he realized that it was left open. Paavo drew his gun as he walked up the stairs. Each step creaked his old age, alerting the unknown of his presence. The hallway leading up the office was in terrible shape. Patches of mold and rusted nails dotted the wood. There were spaces alongside each wall with water damage, perhaps a leaking pipe from upstairs.

The office door sat at the top of the stairwell. It was covered in screws and nails, which had been driven in from inside the room. The man had spent some time trying to keep something or someone from getting in. The sharp edges jutted from almost every inch of space surrounding the door as well. It resembled a death trap, waiting for someone to stumble across and impale themselves in its many, awaiting hands. The glass of the window was cracked. Paavo used a well placed kick to break through and reach over the nails to unlock the door. He stepped into the room. There was a feeling of haunting here. No signs of life. There were no pictures that covered the walls. It was a mirror image of his old room.

The detective was gone. His desk was littered with pictures, just like his. Old cups, still filled with coffee made weeks ago, sat upon letters and words that looked like they were written by a madman. He lifted one of the cups to see a conversation. It was via instant message, printed out on yellow paper. The edges were frayed from the heavy tossing and turning. Smalls was obsessed with finding the hacker. Other photos revealed the inside of the buildings that Snow had defaced. Was Smalls following the eyewitnesses? Why go missing unless he stepped over the line? Paavo held papers in hand with parts highlighted and underlined. Deep circles of ink cut off paragraphs of writing, impossible to translate. The faded colors traveled along all sides of the room. Smalls was tucked away from the rest of the world. Paavo wondered if he had ever crossed paths with the man at one time. The pace of the city was out of control. You lose memories here, Angel would say. This is the city you come to forget who you are, let go of your morals and your hang ups. So many get lost in the shuffle, this detective agency sat between the busy section of downtown. Smalls was just another one lost in the cracks, falling through the movements of big business and the evolution from a bustling city to a nameless metropolis. Words could be deciphered between the blotches and lines. The phrases were bizarre, worse than the one at the shelter. Find the daughter. The words were repeated everywhere. Until he came across something he has seen before. La Récolte.

The phrase was repeated over and over throughout the pages, along with others. Fructus autumni. Messis fortis. What the hell did they mean? He took pictures of everything. The camera shutter fired loud blasts of noise. Paavo's body tensed up. The silence of the room made him nervous. He was waiting for someone to pop out from a hidden area in the floor, brandishing a knife aimed towards his damaged heart. What the hell did this have to do with Snow?

Perdition had a massive library in the downtown area. He decided that now would be the time to take a look at their collection of Camus' works. The main hall was empty. Paavo listened to the echo of his steps as he made his way through the library. He had not been through these halls in some time. Memories of walking with his father moved with each swipe of his arm, knocking dust away from the card catalog. His black jacket now covered in shades of brown on his left side. An anthology of Camus essays sat buried behind newer editions of fiction.

Hours were spent going through each volume, searching for the names scrawled in red along the walls of the abandoned office. Back at the apartment, he searched through some hacker circles, looking for a way to pick up on the trail where Smalls had left off. He started with the places he used to frequent himself, trying to find anyone with a name related to the writings of Camus. Paavo invented a guise to find his way through the series of vague answers and subtle clues. He used the name Mersault. No one picked up on the reference, or gave him the information we wanted. None of them would give up Snow. The other hackers had said nothing about the Police, or Smalls. By midnight, he was done, until he received a cryptic hint to his destination.

"Snow makes you prove yourself to gain his trust."

It was an anonymous message. Paavo was unable to trace the source. He decided to play along.

"What do I have to do?" Paavo asked.

"It's all in the details. Snow loves to play games with your head."

"I don't play a lot of games in my line of work."

"Then why are you here? All we do is play games. Others have tried to meet the best and failed. Anyone may be worthy of passing."

"Passing what? A test?" asked Paavo.

"Pay attention, connect the dots. Once you get the stone up the mountain. Everything becomes clear to you," they said.

He would have to find him alone. The office was the key to finding Snow. Paavo went back to study the pictures, look for clues. The conversations between Smalls and some of these followers of Snow yielded the same results. He threatened them with violence. They did not give in at all. It came across as childish. How could Smalls hurt them from a computer screen? These people were skilled at manipulation. Watching them was how he learned the system and ways to bend it to your will. The Police database was his playground for years.

Paavo stalked every single room of the office. On the inside of Smalls' desk drawer, he found a strange message followed by a web address;

"Every story is a myth. Nothing is what it seems."

The letters were carved into the wood using a blade. The address sent him to a black screen, asking for a login. Paavo had hit a wall, the same way that Smalls had. Back at the apartment, he paced in furious circles. His bare feet slapped against the hardwood floors. His clothes were laid out in the bathtub, shirt soaking wet, scrubbed clean of blood. He stopped and turned to the anthology of Camus. Myths, he said to himself. What had he written as a myth? The pages of the index revealed a single title; "The Myth of Sisyphus". Paavo opened to it and began to read. A man, doomed to push a rock up a mountain in the underworld, only to have it fall to the bottom once he had made it to the top. There were enough connections to make him wonder if minutiae is what drove Smalls into exile.

Jupiter was the one who had stolen the daughter of Esopus. Smalls' warnings called out for someone to find her. Who was the daughter? Could it be Naoko Aki?

Perhaps she represented Mercury, who brought Sisyphus back to the underworld, snatching him away from the joys of earth. The black screen accepted Naoko and dropped Paavo into a blood red MS-DOS directory. Did Snow know her location? Maybe it was not about the girl at all. Maybe this was all just another game to play with another detective on his trail. The keystroke commands led him to open a table of contents, asking for another login, which only accepted ones or zeroes; binary code. Five digits in the correct sequence would allow login. He entered a line of ones and pressed enter. Only three of the five numbers were correct. He replaced one at random with a zero, to see how far off he was from guessing correctly. 10110 was the answer, he was let into another drive, another table of contents and commands that mirrored the menus of the Police database. He searched through each, revealing nothing but the same quotes and lines scrawled across Smalls' office. Paavo selected one labeled 'truth' that asked for a port key. Paavo had no clue what to do next. He pressed enter to see another line of scrambled binary code rush across the screen. It was too fast. A time limit appeared on the right, thirty seconds remaining. Paavo pressed enter again to see the code rush by, followed by three blank spaces. He quickly tried combinations of one and zero. No luck. The counter continued, he pressed enter again and watched the code. There was a number buried inside; the number four. It was in a different spot each time. Ten seconds left. He pressed enter three more times, watching the sample code rush across and searched for an anomaly in the line. No four that time, but a nine. Five seconds remaining. He typed 409. Rejected. 419. Code accepted. A voice recording began to play. It was the voice of a woman. Was it Snow?

"Sisyphus, still pushing the stone to the top of the mountain only to watch it fall."

The message wiped itself from the screen. Paavo found himself staring at darkness once again. Another puzzle appeared with another time limit and a tries remaining counter. Paavo wiped sweat from his brow and studied the puzzle. Nine panels, each representing a piece of a character of Kanji. He moved through each panel, reviewing the options. There were seven different options. He was unable to guess which ones they were, a phrase in green appeared beneath the puzzle, asking a question.

"Why her?"

Paavo looked at the question. He remembered from the myth that she was stolen because of Sisyphus himself, that he had stolen the secrets of the underworld and forced her father to provide water in exchange for her location. He emptied his mind of everything but the characters for these words. Paavo drew out the characters for these words in kanji. The timer was ticking away. Nothing matched. He randomly clicked through the other options, but he was almost out of time. What would happen if the timer ran out? Would he be reset to the beginning of the puzzle?

Perhaps another story to find and decipher. There was no

time for mistakes. The timer was coming closer to its end. He closed his eyes, then it clicked; knowledge. This was the reason for punishment in the case of Sisyphus. Ten seconds remaining on the clock. Paavo clicked furiously, three on the left, two on the right, five on the top left, six on the top right, two in the middle, three on the lower left, two on the lower right.

With three seconds remaining, he had selected the final panel to complete the character for knowledge. The screen cleared itself once again. Paavo took a breath. He would not be stopped. The computer returned to the home screen. A message appeared on screen against the familiar darkness. Something was different now, the sender was Egina. Paavo looked to the myth for the connection; the daughter of Esopus.

"From the dark unknown, another curious mind approaches." Paavo checked the keyboard. It was back in his control.

"Is this another game?" He asked.

"Not a game, friend. A test of your mind, to see if you are worthy."

"I take it that others had not come this far."

"They wanted to solve the puzzle, but in turn became a part of it. The same can happen to you."

"I'm here to find the answers to questions," said Paavo.

"And the answers you shall receive, if you possess a strong mind."

"Are you controlling my terminal by remote?" he asked.

"We are showing you the path to follow, if you seek answers." The computer's mapping program appeared as an address appeared in the search bar.

"Is this where I can find Snow?" he asked.

"This is where you can find me."

The terminal had highlighted a club not too far from Angelfire. The evening brought with it calm from the earlier storms and snowfall. Streetlights coated the world around him in shades of ember. Paavo found himself staring into his shadow as he walked towards the building. The music from Angelfire was intense. It could be heard from blocks away. Nightfall covered the skies as streetlights began to flicker on.

The 119th floor of the Kirilov building was almost deserted. Nyalla sat alone underneath a lamplight, finishing the remaining workload from William's assigned clients. He had left behind some serious assignments, leaving again today surely meant his job would not be here for him tomorrow morning. The funds transfers were huge, more than anything she dealt with on a daily basis; these were hundreds of thousands of dollars that needed to be moved from place to place, orders that were placed over a month ago were not entered into the system. She tried to clean up the mess as best as she could but some of it was unavoidable. Willie wasn't a creep. He was a good guy. She was watching his back for all the times he had covered for her, which was almost never the more that she thought about it. Charles stepped out from his office and noticed that she had not left. He walked up to the light with tired eyes. Nyalla waved at him.

"Almost done," she said.

"You know, your friend is going to be walked out tomorrow."

"Don't worry. His work is all caught up."

"The funny part is that he left in the middle of the day and you didn't even tell me," said Charles. She looked up at him.

"He said he had a family emergency. I told him I would cover for him until he returned."

"So, you not only lied to me, but you broke company rules in handling another employee's clients? You're not allowed to see their information, it's a violation of the policies put in place to keep this place running," he said.

It was a mistake to say that. Too much work, things had gotten carried away, she tried to cover.

"I didn't lie to you. I thought I was helping," she said.

"Well, you can help take his shit and put it in a box, and drop it off to him. He's not getting back into this building. I suggest you clean his desk out for him if you want to be let back in come tomorrow morning."

After a moment, she nodded.

"No problem."

Hiraga's desk was cleaned out in half an hour. She was able to put his posters and figures into one box and made her out of the building. The janitors watched her nervously as she stepped out into the quiet hallway and waited for the elevator. The eatery on the bottom floor was dark and abandoned. The receptionist's desk was empty. Only two low bulbs placed behind hardened glass lit the area. It was a dull glow of red and brown as she made her way through. It was another few minutes to head outside and towards the train station. The directions to his apartment were easy to follow.

The building was on the lower east side, not the best place for a woman to spend a snowy evening walking around. Shadows from the buildings above were large and loomed heavy over the white sidewalks. Her footsteps were loud, crunching the snow beneath her feet. The elevator took its time coming down from the top. The lobby was a mess, garbage cans were turned over and their contents seemed to be spread around the place to fool anyone from thinking that it was inhabited by actual humans. With a bang, the lift had made its way to the bottom. The doors opened up with jagged movements. She stepped inside and pressed the button for the 7th floor. The bulb was bare and burned bright, giving off a mist as it waved back and forth with the motion of the elevator. The lift stopped and she jerked forward. With the same movements, the doors opened and got stuck halfway, leaving her to push through with the box full of his belongings. How am I going to break it to him that he got fired today? She asked herself. The hallway held no light besides the open elevator to see the path ahead. The entire floor was covered in dirt.

She wondered if anyone else lived here. The paper showed the way. 7th floor, room 723, right side door, end of the hall. She looked up to the door in question and saw shadows ahead. Nyalla froze. Her heartbeat grew louder with each stifled breath. There were men in black entering Willie's apartment. She looked around for a place to hide. No time to run back to the elevator. There was no one downstairs to call the police. She was trapped. Before the last block of rooms, a hallway led to the right, then out to a fire escape. She took it, hoping that the men would leave through the other side. She heard a struggle. She kept her hand over her mouth. Were they after Willie?

Maybe it was someone else's room. Her eyes slowly turned the corner. There were men in black coats. They carried a body out of the room and down the staircase opposite the corner. Were they carrying William out? How did no one else hear these noises? She waited for a minute or two before frantically knocking on the other doors in the area. Her calls out for help went unreturned. No one answered. She looked down at the bottoms of each door, no lights. Had no one else lived up here with him?

Nyalla stopped at the sight of the open door, leading inside William's apartment. A fear set in which caused her to break a sweat. What the hell was going on? She moved carefully into the darkness ahead. Anxiety took over her body. The shadow came closer until it swallowed her whole. Inside the dark room, she struggled for a light switch. When flipped, she found herself in a destroyed kitchen that held a pool of blood as large as the table turned over to its side.

The blood was fresh. The smell made her sick. Sweat rushed down her neck and down the small of her back. A severe chill ran through her body. Was this Willie's? Who were those men? What is going on here? Too many questions to ask. She quickly realized that her fingerprints were all over the room. She looked around for a phone. Would it be better to dial from the room? Downstairs? Her movements were frantic, stopping instead to find a towel to wipe her prints from the light switch and wall. The desk sat in front of the bed, facing the window. Moonlight peered through the black clouds in the dead of night. There was no cell phone. There were notes covered in dirty fingerprints. The computer itself was coated in dust. Something looked out of place in the pile of papers on top of the keyboard. A black case sat wrapped in a piece of paper, the word "Open" scrawled across it.

The inside of the folder piece revealed an intricate pentagram, hand drawn with a shading pencil. It was beautiful, unsettling. The case itself was unlocked. She opened its doors to a blank data disc. What was on it? She pocketed the disc and its wrapping. The apartment was swept for any remaining prints. With the cloth over her hands, she turned the switch off. Nyalla was alone, bathed in black once again.

Her apartment felt more exposed than the elevator, and the car. The disc went to the top shelf in her room. The mattress was cool and inviting. She collapsed, breathless. Her dreams were dark and violent. Hours later, she woke in a cold sweat and dialed the Police to report the incident.

Miss Aki's apartment was still sealed off with orange tape. Long turned off the car and stepped out into the snow. New boards of wood were nailed into the windows where Paavo must have been before. The scene seemed out of place with it's surroundings. A white light shined bright down the opposite end of the alley with pieces of snow flying out like feathers from that made it look almost angelic. He turned his head back around to the dark city street.

Long picked the lock and stepped in the front door. He chose not to kick in the boards. He knew that there couldn't be any trace of entry in the building. Long avoided rips and tears in the tape as he made his way into the apartment. Things looked the same as before, the same dishes left in the sink when Miss Aki was taken from the building. His eyes moved towards Naoko Aki's room. Here was where he found the girl, according to Paavo, she had been watching him and when he turned around, she ran out into the alley and disappeared.

The door of the room was closed, just as it was that night. He opened it to reveal the little girl's room, empty and pitch black inside. Long turned on a small flashlight and looked over the area. He was unsure what to expect, was he waiting for Naoko to appear and shoot him? It was foolish to come here. The little girl was dead; whatever was left her was found at that damned shelter. Long became filled with sadness at the idea of Paavo having hallucinations becoming more and more an undeniable truth. The kid was going crazy. Long turned around to face the darkness and stopped to see a gun, lying on the bed.

Paavo studied the place from afar, unsure where to go. He looked to the right to see a fire escape in the alleyway. The rungs were rusted metal. Paavo stepped with care. Each exhale brought a plume of smoke from his lungs. The rooftop was smothered in snow. A large board of neon light displayed 'Angelfire' in bright shocks. Paavo moved towards the middle of the sign with his gun ready.

"Impressive." Paavo heard a voice and turned around to see a woman.

"Are you Snow?" he asked. She was wearing a pullover and jeans; all dark hair and dark eyes. She was taking the cold a lot better than him. Snow nodded her head.

"The one and only," she said. The Desert Eagle was loaded, ready to leave the holster.

"Rest easy. This is a neutral space. After what you did earlier today, I had to see you face to face."

Paavo didn't move.

"What did I do exactly?" he asked.

"You passed the test. The clues were there, lying in wait. It led you to this place, it led you to me."

"Is that why Smalls disappeared?"

"We didn't kill him. But you stopped the ones who did."

"I'm not going to vanish into thin air. Whatever obstacles you have in place don't matter to me. A man paid me to find you, to stop the attacks on those buildings," Paavo said.

"You can trust me, please."

"It's getting harder to trust at all these days." She was an older woman. Late thirties. Her clothes were old and worn. Faded black leggings underneath the jeans with small rips and tears that revealed open skin. A tattered black sweater carried stretched sleeves to cover her extremities from the cold. She had no shoes on. Barefoot in the dead of winter? She didn't fit a profile of any kind.

"I know. Believe me when I say that they weren't attacks, but signals. I used to work there. I know the system, it was easy to break in and make the lights dance. I wanted to make it beautiful, like a ballet in the snow."

She watched the flashing lights of the neon sign.

"Signals?" Paavo asked.

"I was calling out for help; for someone to answer the call, another to rise from the ashes of this fallen city to the cause."

"Are you expecting me to bring you in?" She nodded, smiling.

"At some point, yes."

"Well, I won't," he said. Snow was taken aback. The look on her face told that she already knew why but wanted him to say it for himself.

"Why?" she asked.

"I need to know the connection between you and Daniel Jupiter. The name was a fake. If the clues were laid out for me, then you are saying that I was meant to find his body. Why me?"

"I'd have thought you had figured that out by now."

"What do you mean?" asked Paavo.

"You were the one I needed to find. You can help us, Sisyphus."

"That's not my name," he said. Snow turned back towards him. The neon signs flashing on in blinding colors. The cold was beginning to get to him.

"You're right, Paavo Harker."

"And yours?" he asked.

"Shiori."

"Much nicer than mine."

Paavo took a bow.

"A gentleman as well. You seem more and more unreal. You didn't come from a place like this. Maybe you came from a dream," said Shiori.

"Who are your people?" he asked.

"We are faceless. We have day jobs, deal with parking tickets, mandatory overtime, traffic laws, jury duty. We are city workers, lawyers, Police, and street trash, just the same."

"What are you talking about?" asked Paavo.

"I'm talking about a group of women and men, a community gathering of those who want to take the city back from corrupt officials. For every turn in the balance of power, the Underground is watching. We have been watching you as well, Paavo. The struggle you undertake is massive. That is why you are Sisyphus."

"That's not my name," Paavo said.

"But it is. You were hired to find me just as I had to find you."

"Why did you have to find me? Because of the priest? What do you know about him?"

"I know pieces of the puzzle, not a complete picture. Who he was working for," said Shiori.

"There are others higher up?" Paavo asked.

"People with more resources, more power, and perhaps many more guns that play a part with what we are both investigating."

Paavo looked away from her.

"Who are they?" he asked.

"I have no clue," she said.

"Tell me why you were tracking the priest."

"To find those same missing people you are searching for." Shiori moved closer to him. Paavo went for the Desert Eagle.

"Please, listen. There is no need to fire your weapon."

"Tell me what is going on."

"You're always followed in this city, it is better to be tracked by us. We're not killers," said Shiori.

"I'm already in another's crosshairs." Paavo sighed.

"The bounty hunter is reckless, crazed with vengeance." A vision of Lia forced its way in again, almost on command. Her dark eyes melded with those of the priest's. Shiori became somber at the mention of Lia.

"The woman has already marked us, by taking two of our own." Paavo's eyes widened. He thought of Seven. Was he a member of this underground group?

"He was a thief. I thought you said that you don't cause harm."

"Any gathering will have its wayward sons. Better sons always bore worse ones," said Shiori.

"Why the myth of Sisyphus?" he asked.

"It was my husband's favorite story. A puzzle is designed to do two things; answer a question, and lead someone to the truth."

"What truth?" asked Paavo.

"The names were the key to make you realize our connection."

"What the hell are you talking about?"

"The puzzle you solved to gain entry to the server served a dual purpose," said Shiori.

"Besides getting inside my computer?"

"One that allowed me entry into specific Police files, not accessible from the main database."

Paavo looked towards the ground. He wondered how she could have broken into his system. It made him doubt his own skills.

"Hidden files?" he asked.

"Even away from your old encrypted shortcuts. They've not only buried the missing from the minds and questions of the people, but their families have been taken into protective custody."

His eyes widened.

"They were paid to keep quiet from the major media outlets. The idea being that if the mass abductions of random people became public knowledge, panic would spread," she said.

"Who is trying to wipe the memory of the city?" asked Paavo.

"I can help as much as I can, but we need you." Paavo thought of Long, asking him to help on the case. The words he used, keep it private, away from the media. Why?

"No records of people missing in large numbers two years ago or now but there are traces of an incident many years ago. It's happening again, perhaps it's bigger than we both realize," said Shiori.

Long had said that the people within the dossiers were reported missing in line, one per day the exact same way. The wind began to rise in intensity. Fresh white spread across the open air, flying from higher rooftops like a desert wind. Paavo took off his jacket and offered it to the woman. She accepted and let him drape it over her shoulders.

"Nobu Sadao was a friend of my husband; another gone missing," said Shiori. She turned away from Paavo. He followed her.

"Your husband, too?" he asked.

"I needed to find someone who I could trust to help me find him. There is so much at risk in what we do. You passed the test. You can help me find my husband. He's like you; someone who fought back death, put it in chains."

She pointed to her heart. The other hand went towards Paavo's chest.

"You have done more for me than anyone else these days."

"How?" asked Paavo.

"By being who you are; caring about the people who were forgotten and lost this citywide cover up."

"You don't know anything about me."

"I know that you are a good man," she said. He turned away from her.

"I don't care about saving the city. I just want to know what happened to them," said Paavo.

"And despite that, you have my trust and my loyalty."

Paavo was uneasy. He bowed his head to her.

"Thank you. But I'm not a good man. I don't exist. I'm a shadow."

"You're still fighting back death. Aren't you? I can see it in your eyes; trying so hard to stay alive while the underworld is calling, scratching at your heels to bring you back, chasing you down?" Shiori asked.

Across the way, from a distant building, a figure in white stood on the adjacent roof. A hood covered their face.

"Something is chasing me, the inevitable," said Paavo.

"You're still here. That must mean something, doesn't it?"

"What good is it if no one wants to let you help them? Those families didn't want my help. They spit in my face."

She kept her eyes to the sky.

"Grief makes us do terrible things. We are capable of anything when we suffer," said Shiori.

Back towards the tower, the figure was no longer there.

"If you hate them, then why help them?" she asked. Paavo

struggled for an answer. He inhaled through his nose. The cold was taking effect. His chest burned.

"I don't have a choice. Before I die, something has to change."

"You have the power to make a change. You must help me. My husband is a courier. We both were. I'm retired now. He goes by a code name. It's a way for him to do the work without being traced."

"What did you carry?" he asked.

"Knowledge. Information. We fight for people who hate us as well. We carry on with no support for the cause. We deal in information that will someday save our city."

"What cause?" Paavo asked.

"Stopping the groups vying for control of our city. Everyone has felt them in some capacity, through the laws that govern us; tyrants and thieves. There was a time when the city had a name, when there weren't homeless walking the streets and asking for change. It was a real city, before the crime, before the Mob created a dynasty. Three of the richest families born in the country, all involved with organized religion, politics, finance, law."

Paavo looked to the city's skyline; all black in the distance, streaks of brown over the beams of light burning high into the dark. The city still pulsed with energy despite the storms. It was alive and breathing. When he was young, it was easy for him to grasp the idea of corruption. His body was born the same way, broken and hanging by threads. He remembered walking the streets and creating a world he could escape to.

Like his parents, so many had come here for new beginnings, crammed together in small apartments and housing projects. He left it behind two years ago. It was when he went into exile, away from the systems pushed upon him. He knew what was to come and he had turned away from it.

The city was once great. What could it be now but a sea of lost souls? Money became the root of their existence. Those souls began pushing and shoving toward unreached dreams. They talked fast and littered the veins of the city with garbage; the slow destruction of a beautiful creature.

"This is the reason for the Underground," she said.

"What kind of work do you do now?" asked Paavo.

"I live with my husband away from the struggle. Something has happened to him. He is my life. Without him, I will die."

"What are you? Freedom fighters?" Paavo asked.

"No way of living inside these concrete boundaries can be considered free. Our lives used to be simple. Ever since he came across this briefcase, we've been hounded and chased like dogs."

"What's in the briefcase?"

"I don't give a shit. I want him home safe," said Shiori.

"And what name does he go by?"

"Mirror."

Paavo reached out to her and cradled his hands over hers.

"What is La Récolte?" he asked.

The woman smiled at the mention of those words.

"Do you know what it means?"

Shiori said nothing at first.

"Others who have gone missing seemed to know. First the machinist, and so did the detective before me."

"Lyoto. I knew him...La Récolte means the harvest," she said.

"Why take these people? You say that this has happened

before, but why take random people? Was the machinist a hacker as well?"

"He was a comrade. He was family. Not everyone in the Underground needs to risk their lives. Some just have to believe in what we believe."

Paavo kept quiet. He was tired of any talk of faith, of believing in something. What was left in this city to have faith in?

"How do we proceed?" he finally asked.

"We find a motive behind the abductions," said Shiori.

"Do you think that many people could be connected?"

"Mirror may have the answers. Maybe the case will, too."

"If I choose to help you," Paavo said. Shiori closed her eyes to the snow, awaiting his decision. Paavo moved in close to block the wind from shadowing his words.

"Thank you. I will do what I can to find your husband." She bowed to him, as he did before.

"I'm grateful to have met you, Sisyphus."

"My name is Paavo."

The wind kicked up as they said their goodbyes for now. He watched as the woman moved away towards the edge of the building. Another assignment, but he was getting closer finding answers. Why were these people abducted? Why the pools of blood? The rumors of a new drug....had it already hit the streets?

How could he trust Long now that the case had been practically buried beneath more secrets? Paavo stood alone on the rooftop, letting the wind and snow shake and collide with his broken body. Mirror had been carrying a briefcase containing more secrets. If it meant finding the girl, he would find him.

Suddenly, a shot rang out from an unknown place. Paavo fell to the ground. He reached for his gun and looked around in desperation. Where did it come from? The distance was clouded with white. He was blinded and saw nothing but parts of buildings and lights. Paavo stood up and rushed to the edge. He looked over the street; Angelfire was alive with music and noise. The blood in his veins froze. What about Shiori?

Across the rooftop, a trail of blood could be seen from the distance. The neon lights shined on, revealing the mortal wound. Shiori had crawled on her hands and knees to the fire escape. Paavo ran to her, forgetting his own body's weakness. He coughed violently as he hit the ground next to her prone body. Shiori was face down. He flipped her over carefully to assess the damage.

"Shiori, are you alright?"

The wound was deep. A bullet had passed through her body completely. There was too much blood. He removed his jacket and began to apply pressure.

"Speak to me...Say something!"

Her eyes were moving from side to side, barely open. She was dying. What the hell had happened? Paavo looked around, where had it come from?

"Hang on...I'm going to get help."

The gauze was in the glove box, blocks away. He thought of bringing her down to the street and carrying her to the car. The hospital was not far from here. He felt a hand reach on his arm, pulling at his shirt. He pressed down harder on the jacket. The blood was flowing down to the ground, it mixed with the snow. Paavo was running out of time.

"I have to get you out of here. You can't die like this."

She waved her hand. Rivulets of blood ran down.

"Find my husband."

A hand came up from her side to caress his face. It left

behind a trail of blood that ran down to the ground. Shiori smiled before her eyes settled and her mouth left wide open. A final breath of air left her body. He watched the woman pass away.

Finally, a scream of anger shot from the damaged lungs in Paavo's chest. He looked out into the distance again, more figures in white standing across rooftops further away. Was he seeing things? Were they really there? No, he said to himself, nothing there. There was no one watching him, he waited for the mirage to appear once more. They did not. There were no figures in white. A dead woman lay before him. He looked to the sky in anger. Words came from his lips, cursing the sky, baying for the blood of those responsible. He looked down toward this fallen woman. What did she do to deserve this?

The cold was getting to him. He felt his hands begin to shake. What was happening? His body was reacting to something, was it the weather? Was it the shock of watching another person die? Paavo looked down to see his hands shaking furiously.

Soon, his whole body felt frozen in place, he fell to his side, writhing. There was no pain, but an intense ache inside his chest. His limbs were twitching. He moved in desperation, checking his body. Was there a second shot? There was no blood besides what was on his hands. Paavo stared fearfully at the body of Shiori, was he about to join her?

The Crimson must be taking effect, he thought to himself. Out of control of his own arms and legs, he looked down to see his body flail wildly, as though it were being possessed. How long had it been since his last shot? Paavo struggled to move to his side, then to his stomach. Rolling across the roof to place his full weight onto his hands, he pressed down on each, feeling the blood rush out of his hands. He began to move his fingers and slipped them inside his jacket pocket.

Paavo felt for the syringe and pulled it out. His grip could not keep the shot in hand and it fell into the snow. The shake was violent. He screamed for the syringe to stay in between his fingers. Using his teeth to pull open the needle, he plunged it deep into his heart and pressed down on the plunger. The warmth flowed through his body like a river. The shakes stopped almost instantly. Paavo dropped to the ground again in fatigue, gasping for air, next to the fallen body of Shiori.

How close was he to becoming like her?

www.ingramcontent.com/pod-product-compliance
Lightning Source LLC
Chambersburg PA
CBHW070614260626
47161CB00007B/2431